Inviolable

JayJay D. Segbefia

All characters in this publication
are fictitious and any resemblance
to real persons, living or dead,
is purely coincidental.

Copyright © 2024 JayJay D. Segbefia
All rights reserved.
ISBN: 9798711156208
Cover design: DezignSpace
https://jaysegbefia.com

For Nana Akosua Ansaa
Daughter. Happiness. Sunshine

To Emmy,
Who taught me loyalty, faith, and how to love unconditionally.

"Who is to say what is only a Story,
And what is truth disguised as a Story?"

- Belgarath the Sorcerer to Garion
in David Edding's *Pawn of Prophecy*.

CHAPTER 1
Jubilee House
Accra, Ghana
Thursday, 7th March, 10 A. M.

CHIEF SUPERINTENDENT H. AMADU, Commander of the VIP Protection Unit of the Ghana Police Service was an unhappy man. The platoon in charge of parade security had been military led, yet it was his unit that had attracted the government's flak for what the press had termed the 6th of March Attempted Coup. The paratroopers had started the whole confusing shindig, but the military had stuck to their script that it was the paratroopers that had prevented endangerment to the President by camouflaging him in what they had called a smokescreen.

Smokescreen, his left butt.

While true that two shots had been heard, it hadn't been because someone had fired them. The Army had claimed credit for that too, saying they had fired the warning shots to prevent the attackers from carrying out their mission unchallenged.

Everyone was accounted for as far as his unit was concerned, and after reviewing footage from the parade throughout the night, he'd had no choice than to declare it as smoke theatrics gone bad. The government had chosen to call the episode an attack. Even if it was, he wasn't sure the President had been the target of it, or the brunt of what the opposition had called an expensive joke.

No one could tell for sure. Which is why he had been ordered by the IGP to present to the Jubilee House to answer directly to the President.

What was there to answer to? The whole damn thing was on TV. Smoke had covered everywhere, and shots had been heard when the Air Force had sent in winged men to the parade. Nothing could have been simpler than that.

Of course, it had ushered in the chaos that had truncated the 6th of March Independence Day celebrations at the Black Star Square, but like his grandpa of blessed memory liked to say, all's well that didn't end too badly.

The meeting occurred in the President's office. Amadu had been there before, so he paid little attention to the zeitgeist of the presidential palace. Around the President's official desk in the corner of the immaculate office, sat nineteen men: The Cabinet of the Ghanaian

Republic, plus senior Intelligence, Police and Military Officers.

"Alright, Gentlemen," President Offei boomed, signaling that the meeting could start. He usually would have commenced with a prayer, but God apparently had to wait while he got to the bottom of a seeming embarrassment. The press had not been kind in their descriptions of how he'd shivered under the onslaught of a coup-making army of smoke and firecrackers, and everyone knew President Offei was quick to an insult.

"Has anyone come up with *better* intelligence for yesterday's debacle?" he asked of his assembled Cabinet. His question, while simple, had an ominous undertone. President Offei had a no-bullshit reputation among his appointees. By stressing the word, he was signaling that he had already sifted through the reports making the rounds from the intelligence agencies and concluded they were a load of horse poop of the diarrhoea variety. He would drill into anyone who repeated the same tosh. Thus were the most meticulously prepared notes quashed before they were out of their folders.

"We honestly don't know, sir," Amadu said on silent cue from his IGP. In matters of national security, the Police held preeminence over other agencies, and it was best to get it all out before the political butt-kissers got the President riled up. As one of the president's brows shot up, he hastily added, "I mean, we know what happened; we just don't know why."

Noting his plain, dependable face, President Offei's eyes slightly softened when he said to him, "Humour me, Chief Superintendent. Tell me *your* version of yesterday."

Amadu chose his next words carefully.

"As far as we can tell, the confusion started during the Paratroopers' event."

The defense minister rose to interrupt, then obviously thought better of it and sat down.

Amadu shrugged.

"Until the affair involving smoke, things happened as we all knew they would. The seven troopers free-fell in formation and played it by the book until they activated their signal flares. While we haven't accounted yet for the unusually heavy smoke from the flares, things would still have been fine but for the smoking canisters released from under the presidential dais. Forensics are still examining them, but we don't know who put them there, and even worse, why?"

"Did you question the paratroopers?"

"We would have, but the military aren't letting us," Amadu said with a sidelong look at the Chief of Air Staff.

"I'll deal with them soon enough," the President promised with a frosty look at the defense minister. "If I'd gotten shot, would it have made sense why?"

"It wouldn't have," Amadu answered truthfully. "While true that all that smoke would have prevented National Security operatives from shooting at anyone for fear of hitting you, if any assailant had planned to kill you, the smokescreen doesn't make sense. A bullet to the head would have been much simpler. That's how I'd have done it, at least," he shrugged.

"The plausible scenarios are two: kidnapping and diversion. If kidnapping was the objective, it would have been impossible. No one could have seen through all that smoke to kidnap you or the Vice President. How would they have gotten you out of the smoke into the open and away from the Square? Your security detail had you literally covered on the ground. Putting it all together, you are alive. As is the Vice President. In fact, no one got hurt except from some of the contingents' stampeding, and all these have the makings of a diversion. Only, we do not know what it was a diversion from. No one in the government has been reported missing to date, and nothing appears stolen. The gunshots and screams we heard were cinematic. Whoever it was that shouted *protect the President* absolutely wanted all attention on you. And there is no doubt that was what happened. We just don't know why, your Excellency," he finished.

"When you say the screams were cinematic, what do you mean?" The Vice President, a soft-spoken academic, asked Amadu.

"They were playbacks of a recording, your Excellency," he replied. "We found a thumb drive in the central console. The technicians don't know how it got there. Until someone is found dead, or something of immense national value is discovered missing, we don't know what all this was about, sir."

President Offei decided he liked the policeman while looking him up and down and doing the same to his testimony. It all seemed to add up, and he knew his Cabinet and intelligence officers were as much in the dark as was Amadu.

"So, what do you propose we do now, Chief Superintendent?"

Amadu shrugged in perplexity, scratched at his bald head nervously and responded, "I guess we have to wait to see, your Excellency."

"Isn't there anything we can do to confirm that it was all some kind of a mistake?" the President asked his Cabinet with ice in his eyes.

The National Security Minister raised a hand apologetically and said, "My team and I are also sifting through the footages. We will report back whatever else we find, but I believe the Chief Superintendent has covered everything important."

Then his phone rang.

The President scowled.

He picked up the call.

The President's scowl got darker and the looks of surprise around the room widened. Phones weren't allowed inside the Jubilee House, to speak less of the President's office. Before the President could issue a blistering ultimatum, the National Security Minister dropped his phone on the table as if it was a snake and turned to the President.

"Eight judges of the Supreme Court have been unaccounted for since yesterday!"

In those short moments following the announcement, the room began to spin for everyone around the table.

"Why would anyone want eight Supreme Court judges?" the President asked incredulously, the first to find his voice.

"With respect, your Excellency, and with your indulgence," Amadu asked with his mind in gear, "may I please present the six-minute video we have compiled of the incident? I believe, with this new information, more light might be shed on the episode, and if we all watch together, some of you may see things that my team and I may have missed."

"Six minutes?" the Vice President asked in surprise. "The attack lasted all day as far as I am concerned. What can we glean in six minutes?"

"My apologies, sir, but the whole smoke episode lasted six minutes, twenty-eight seconds. Also, even before we do, I would like to respectfully request the presence of a CTU Commander," Amadu pleaded.

Impatiently, the President ordered in his deep baritone, "Show the video!" Then he turned to the IGP and ordered, "Get the Commander also!"

His ADC walked in with an urgent look and a Jubilee House speakerphone clutched to his chest. He announced breathlessly, "There is a person – a woman – who is demanding to speak to you immediately, sir, or she says she will kill the Chief Justice."

"*A woman*?" a chorus of more than nineteen voices sounded.

"Connect her now!" President Offei ordered. Unlike his Cabinet, he didn't give a pig's gluteus maximus about the kidnapper's sex.

CHAPTER 2
Black Star Square
Accra, Ghana
Wednesday, 6th March at 9 A.M.

KIDNAPPING JUDGES AT the Supreme Court would have amounted to suicide. Five Squads, each commanded by battle-hardened Staff Sergeants answer to a Lieutenant who commands the inner platoon of the complex. Four other Lieutenants command the outer platoons, all of whom answer to the implacable Major Hanson of the 44th Company, 9th Battalion of Infantry of the Ghana Army.

Asabea had warned that this was not to be a suicide mission. Instead, it had been resolved to stage the kidnapping at the Black Star Square on Independence Day in the presence of three battalions of marching forces and service contingents, 30-thousand spectators, two-hundred and seventy-five Members of Ghana's Parliament, sixteen Justices of Ghana's Supreme Court and a phalanx of members of the Diplomatic Corps. Of course, the irony was not lost on Asabea, but the Square was a safer bet compared to kidnapping them at their homes, also, and it offered a bigger media mileage if they pulled it off.

"Aisha," Asabea had said to the first member of her team – her Justice Team – "You and Efe will ride as police adjutants to an all-female motorbike contingent that will usher the President into the Square. Afterwards you will secure the exit and keep it unobstructed when the twins and I come racing through. If all goes according to plan, our exit won't require the use of arms."

This was in August of the previous year. Between then and 6th March, they had perfected the plan to a tee, all the time as part of the parade contingents' routine rehearsals for the annual 6th of March Independence Day parade of the Ghanaian Republic. Asabea seemed to have cultivated limitless connections across every aspect of Ghanaian power. Through those connections, she got State Protocol to agree to an all-female motorbike police escort contingent, touting female equality and diversity in a hitherto all-male contingent..

Asabea had said, "During Independence parades, none of the marching contingents carry ammunitions. No civilian president is comfortable facing three battalions of live musketry. The job of security falls to the National Security Agency which, on 6th March, will comprise twenty armed platoons from the three branches of the Armed Forces and the Ghana Police Service. Their coigns of vantage at the Square will be known to us; I will train you to secern their insignia from the contingents. But," she stressed and turned to Dede with a smile, "I know that armed men will be the least of your concerns. I am aware of your overwhelming acrophobia. Unfortunately, I have to plant you in a chopper with six other airmen to wing your way down to the parade. You will train for three months as a skydiver in the Rub al Khali while I convince Ghana's Air Force that a paratroop and skydiving unit is good for a sixty-fifth parade to excite a crowd of Independence Day celebrants.

"The jump from the chopper will itself be routine at 10-thousand feet. The Air Force's chopper will be visibly distressed because it is used to flying no more than 7-thousand feet, but you need not worry about it, Dede. You will wear different jumpsuits to reflect Ghana's national colours, and all seven of you will deploy in rapid free-falling succession and gain the expected 300kph in thirty seconds.

"That will be your signal, Bubuné. You will sit next to the first lady in the uniform and badge of an usher and escort the President and Vice President away from the canopied dais to the open, ostensibly to enable them to see the paratroopers' stunts better. Dede's signal flares will fill the air a hundred feet above the President and his deputy with red, yellow, green and black smoke that will envelope the two gentlemen in an extremely short time. More smoke will bellow from under the presidential dais.

"For a hundred metres in all directions from the two presidents, not a thing will be seen. Our whole plan is to deceive everyone into thinking the President's life is being targeted, but the smoke will prevent an all-out shootout for fear the NSA might hit the President. With everyone confused and looking for the smoke to clear, Oye and Nhyira, and I will drive three SUVs to the judicial dais and use the chaos as a cover to evacuate seven of the judges. The Chief Justice must at all costs be part of the seven. The kidnapping cannot exceed sixty seconds, and we must be prepared to hurry the robed adjudicators along as much as we can.

"We will pick up Dede at the exit, and then Aisha and Efe can escort us to the mountains. We should be well out of range before it dawns on the government that the air display gone bad concealed judicial abductions."

The SUV convoy wound its way eastward from Accra. Limited traffic due to the holiday enabled them to cross the regional border without incident. They arrived at the destination in an hour at furious speed, further aided by Aisha's and Efe's sirens.

The twins quickly ushered the judges out onto a concrete courtyard and hurried them into the main building, a complex of storeyed apartments surrounded by thick fence walls and electric wires. During the quick dash through the corridors, the Chief Justice had asked Oye where they were, and she'd replied, "Your Lordship, it is best you don't even know where we are. One can't reveal what one does not know."

No one had spoken after that and, one by one, the justices were ushered into palatial living quarters and asked to be comfortable. Each quarter housed a living room, a bedroom and en suite facilities. There was a small library near the living rooms that was decorated from floor to roof in more law books than they had ever seen. But that was not the only thing. The clothing laid out for the Chief Justice on the bed were his judicial robes, shirts, trousers and casuals with tags that were his exact size. He turned from contemplating the bedroom to the small balcony. That was when he saw that he was in what could pass as a fortress, with nothing in his view but forested mountains and a perimeter fence that looked exactly like a castle's walls.

He looked at his watch. It was a half-hour to noon. Now that he thought of it, he had no memory of how they'd arrived here. He clearly remembered being whisked out of the dangerous events at the Black Star Square, but the MPs had ordered him and his colleagues to stay down to avoid getting shot by whoever the terrorists were. He'd stayed down below window level and prayed the hardest in his life. But he felt hungry now and walked to the door to see if anyone could tell him anything about lunch. The door was locked, and a blue light indicated that this was an electronically operated door. He didn't remember being given a key. He looked around the living room and found a telephone by one of three sofas in the white-painted room. He picked up the handset and heard numbers dialing automatically.

A female voice said, "How may I assist you, Mr. Chief Justice?"

"Uhm —" he started, taken aback momentarily.

"Is there a plan for lunch or something," he asked.

"Yes, sir," the voice said. "Lunch will be ready at noon. Your door will open then, and you will be escorted to the dining room."

The line died before he could ask more questions.

He turned around to survey his room once more. It could be the effect of witnessing the attack at the parade grounds, and maybe the excitement of escaping with his life from a deadly situation, but he had a foreboding sense about this place and about the clothing that were his size. How could these military police know he would be needing to be rescued in time to acquire his size in clothing? He had always been laughed at as a person who lived on the verge of paranoia, and maybe this was one of his episodes, but still, a door he could not open from the inside, a phone call that died on him, an answer that was denied, and no other communication with the outside of this fortress – he had checked and there was no television, radio or internet in any of the rooms – all gave him his uneasy sense. He needed to find his mobile phone and call Ellen, his secretary, to find out what had happened after they'd left.

His phone was not in his pocket.

Strange.

He remembered pocketing it as soon as he rose on the request of the MP and made his mad dash for the open door of the V8, amid the awful shooting and screaming.

He checked his watch again.

Only a few minutes until lunch.

Oh, he would have his answers, he resolved, or he wasn't Chief Justice of the Republic of Ghana. These men couldn't keep him in the dark no matter who was trying to hurt the government.

Men?

He doubled back.

He had seen no men at all in this whole undertaking; only women.

He frowned, as he tended to do when he was thinking. Every one of their rescuers was a woman. He remembered noticing that fact when he'd looked at the motorbike riders too on their way into the building from the courtyard.

An all-women rescue team.

He checked his watch again.

CHAPTER 3
Jubilee House
Thursday, 7th March, Noon.

I AM PRESIDENT Kwame Amponsah Offei," the President identified himself as soon as the speakerphone was attached to the routine paraphernalia in his office for a call this important. "State your name and your business."

"Hello Mr. President," the female said in cultured, Ghanaian English. Neither friendly nor hostile. Businesslike.

The voice continued, "You must be aware by now that I have some important people of yours in my custody. Not to worry, no harm will come to them at all – especially if you're a good sport and do as I say. In fact, we could have concluded these negotiations yesterday, but no one picks up your listed lines. You may want to investigate that.

"Anyhow, my name is Akua Sakyibea Asabea, and my team and I abducted eight of your supreme court justices yesterday at about –" the voice paused, as if confirming the time. "– 10:05 in the morning. I must apologize but the original plan was to abduct seven. Unfortunately, the last one got into the car before we could stop her, and seeing as how we didn't have much time on our hands, we carried her along as extra insurance. I hope the remaining judges you have stuffed the Supreme Court with can dispense with justice until I return these to you. I am sure they won't be missed, considering how excruciatingly slow justice in our apology of a republic gets dispensed anyway."

The President blinked for a full minute before asking, "What do you want, Akua Sakyibea Asabea?"

"I want justice," was the instant response.

When it became obvious that *that* was all the caller was going to say, President Offei asked, "How do you propose we give you the justice you want?" he said more calmly than he felt. "Why should I even trust that you have the judges? Kidnapping government officials is a treasonous offense."

"Actually, Mr. President, kidnapping and abducting anyone in Ghana is only a second-degree felony, not treasonous. Secondly, take a closer look at all the footages of Independence Day. Focus on the six and a half minutes surrounding the business of the smokes. You should see your judges getting into our cars willingly," she told him.

The President nibbled his lips.

"When you say you want justice, what do you mean?"

The caller said, "We are going to have a trial, Mr. President. In three days, I will call you with the details of how we will conduct that trial. This call is to assure you that your judges are alive and well. I had to steal your deputy Attorney-General and one of your public prosecutors, unfortunately. I am both plaintiff and executioner, and the guilty defendant is also here with me. At some point, we will have to negotiate to pick up his lawyer or I'll come and grab him too from your office."

There was a pause, and then she concluded, "I assure you, Mr. President, at the conclusion of this trial, justice will be served. Let us speak again with clearer minds on Sunday."

The termination tone was the assurance that the caller was no longer on the line; that, and the horrible invectives the ADC hurled at the console.

"What's the matter?" the President demanded irritably.

"VPN," he replied apologetically. "We couldn't trace the call."

"Did you really think she was going to expose herself?" a new voice asked incredulously from the tail end of the conference table.

"Who the hell are you?" the President asked the speaker.

"Uhm –" Amadu hastily rose to introduce his colleague, "This is Chief Superintendent Atukwei, Commander of the Police Counterterror Unit, your Excellency. He arrived during the call."

The President mumbled something under his breath and asked, "Can we confirm the whereabouts of the deputy Attorney-General?"

"I have, your Excellency," the Attorney-General replied. "He too has not been seen since yesterday. His wife thought he was here at the Jubilee House."

"What did she mean about grabbing someone's lawyer from my office? Does anyone *know* this woman?" he asked in perplexity.

His abstruseness was shared all-round the table. If all were honest, no one knew what to think about the surprising developments.

"Perhaps the answers we seek will be found in the six-and-a-half minutes' footage the woman referred to," Chief Superintendent of Police S. Atukwei said diffidently from his side of the room. "I am told the military refused to surrender their footages so I can't speak to what we may find in *theirs*," he finished with a disgusted look.

Before the Army Chief could respond, the President said to him with laser-focused eyes, "Is it just me, or is there a trace of butt hole in your general disposition I am smelling, Chief Superintendent?"

Atukwei, looking offended, seemed about to respond but looked at Amadu instead and said frowardly, "You had to invite me here, didn't you?"

Smiling apologetically, especially when he saw the President's eyes flare, the IGP said, "Please forgive us, Mr. President, but CS Atukwei is uncomfortable with formal meetings, and his words tend to sound a trifle more offensive than he intends them. We've all gotten used to him, as I know you will eventually; but he is the best counter strategy officer we have. That's why he heads the CTU."

The President looked unconvinced but let it pass.

"Shall we examine the footages then, your Excellency?" Amadu asked respectfully. "CS Atukwei will lead because he first propounded the diversion theory."

The President nodded his permission, and Atukwei walked to the bank of computers and screens along the left wall of the meeting room. He plugged in a hard disk drive and played the video.

"Here is suspect number 1," he said, pointing to one of the paratroopers while the video was playing. The trooper was obviously female. "She had two canisters, and while the other six were spraying the national colours in a pattern, she directed all of hers toward the President and Vice President below."

While his audience took a closer look at the screen, he zoomed in to the two presidents just before the smoke hid them from the cameras and pointed at another woman – the escort. "She is the second suspect. She looked at her watch and activated her timer. She set it to six minutes, the exact time the caller-woman identified."

"The woman said six and a half minutes," the Attorney-General reminded him.

"The half is the time the paratrooper sprayed her canisters," Atukwei said gruffly, evidently angry at being interrupted. He rolled his eyes and turned his face to the screen.

The President had an unamused expression on his face but said nothing more.

"Suspect number 2 walked away from the smoke towards the judicial dais just when these three luxury SUVs arrived. She is the one who first talked the judges into leaving their dais. Notice that they rise and walk before the vehicles arrive and the two fake military police appear. Number Two's role was to lead both presidents to the smoke, and thereafter, to lead the judges away from it and into the vehicles. Numbers 3 and 4 are identical twins."

This time, even the President strained for a closer look.

"Suspect number five is the driver of the first vehicle in the exiting convoy," Atukwei continued. "Of all the seven, she is the one the cameras didn't catch. All the others were visible and identifiable."

The screens showed the vehicles racing out of the Square. Just at the entrance, two motorbikes barred traffic from the roundabout until the SUVs gained the highway, and then turned around, two women in face shields in pursuit of the convoy.

"Suspects six and seven," Atukwei announced. "We don't know how they infiltrated the escort contingent, but it doesn't matter now," he finished and turned to the President.

With ill-concealed irritation, the President asked, "It doesn't matter that a police contingent was infiltrated by kidnappers?"

Atukwei shrugged. "They infiltrated the elite Paratroopers and State Protocol, Mr. President. Either they are magicians, or they have unlimited access to government power and patronage. Let's not get hung up on the trivial, sir – with all due respect."

The Vice President's eyes widened. "You suspect insider assistance?"

"I suspect nothing – your Excellency," Atukwei checked his snideness at the last instant. "Like the lady said, she is seeking justice. Until the trial, there's only one thing we can do."

"Which is?" the President asked. His tone tolerated no more snideness and even Atukwei could tell.

"We need to find the lawyer in your office who helped the guilty defendant she alluded to in her call, and send him over," he declared matter-of-factly. "The sooner we do that the faster we can get the trial underway, and the faster we can retrieve the justices."

His brashness notwithstanding, the nonchalant way he spoke about the matter was rubbing off everyone the wrong way. They stared at him for a while, but it was hard to say what they all wanted to in the President's presence.

Sensing their hostility, Amadu cleared his throat and said, "What I believe Atukwei is trying to say is –"

"–We all heard him," the President barked, cutting him off. Then he turned to the IGP and asked, "How is this upstart a senior officer?"

"I am the best," Atukwei said, shrugging before the IGP could speak.

If it wasn't for the gravity of the abduction situation, the look the President directed at Atukwei would have ended in his firing. But Atukwei wasn't finished.

"In fact, the little I heard of the woman's words tells me she already has the person in her custody, Mr. President. No one puts on a condom unless they were ready to mate. If she told you she was going to negotiate for the person, she meant to apologize for taking a member of your direct staff away. There's nothing we can do but wait.

"Now, and unless your Cabinet and these fine people know the judges' location, I suggest we end this meeting and reconvene on Sunday at noon."

He picked up his drive from the console and proceeded right out the door.

Amadu got up from his chair, unsure whether to go after his nonconforming colleague or let the President order his guards to bring him back to answer for his insouciance. The President appeared unsure himself.

Eventually, he turned to his Minister for National Security and asked, "Do you agree with his assessment?"

The Minister stood up and said, "We will find out from your direct staff any that are lawyers who have been involved as defense attorneys in any case where an aggrieved plaintiff would resort to such means. While at it, we will circulate the photos of the suspects and see what we find."

"Discreetly?" The Air Force Chief asked.

"Absolutely," the President demanded. "Say nothing to the press. The last thing we need is a press circus."

"Do we really have to wait for Sunday or there's something we can do to track the judges down?" the Vice President asked the IGP.

"We've got the CID working on it from the Black Star Square, and I'll let you know as soon as they have any leads."

"So, nothing at all?" President Offei asked unhappily.

"We just got to know about the abductions, your Excellency," Amadu came in at that point obscurely. "That means working all over again from the start with the new information and seeing where it will lead. It's a waiting game now, sir."

"And they are all women!" the Chief of Naval Staff spoke for the first time in incredulity.

Amadu shrugged.

CHAPTER 4
Ground Zero
Thursday, 7th March; 3 P.M.

DUNCAN KING HADN'T bathed in days, as far as time went in an underground cell, and he felt like screaming his lungs out. Just who the heck did they think they were messing with? He was the don, the king of the microphone. A true fashionista and wearer of single-use haute couture. The master communicator, the evergreen, smooth, urbane icon. The distinguished one, with supernatural lyrical, verbal and stage presence; a true god emcee. And they had the nerve, the testicular temerity, the cauldron-sized gonads, the camel-toed pudendum to array him in prison garb and shackle him to a wall!

He didn't even know who *they* were, but for a whole week he had been offered nothing but stale bread and *brukina*; stuff he wouldn't feed his dogs. Worst, the upstarts never changed the bread; only the *brukina*, until he started eating the bread to ensure fresh daily supply. No, he hadn't been broken; he was merely surviving until the time he could rip their throats out for treating *him* as a common criminal. How *dare* they?

Duncan had been sitting at the Republic Bar & Grill minding his own business in Osu when she'd sat across from him uninvited. She'd sipped *his* cocktail suggestively, twiddled his cigar and winked at him, and had then headed for the private lounge.

Of course, he'd followed her. A quote he'd read somewhere came to mind.

"I can resist all things, except temptation."

Duncan remembered little else after that. He'd regained consciousness in this prison cell. Groggy, thirsty and completely bereft of any chance to assuage his concupiscence, he'd seen no one, and not for lack of screaming and yelling. As far as he could tell, he was in a storeroom with a make-shift bed and a bare-boned mattress. The grille where the door should have been, was as tall as the wall, and was operated electronically in the morning when it slid up to allow a robotic arm to bring in his food, which he could only reach with his free foot. One meal a day was the meagre fare, that and his diabetic medication. How they knew he was on medication was a surprise, but he couldn't imagine what he had done to be treated this way. Yes, he had his fair share of haters – which celebrity didn't, considering his royal *swagness* and all; but to abduct and incarcerate falsely? Gosh, how he would make them pay!

Suddenly the grating rose mechanically, letting in bright light into his dank cell. Then the single foot shackle unclasped his leg. He blinked at the shackle, and then shielded his eyes. No one entered the room for a full minute. He rose shakily from his cot, still covering his eyes, and walked to the open entrance.

His was the last cell. The corridor proceeded to his right along a bend. It led to a bathroom. He hadn't had a bowel movement for a week! He wasted no time purging himself. The water was quite warm too, and there was soap, a sponge and a small towel. He must have been in the shower for an hour before he noticed he wasn't alone. He toweled quickly and got out of the shower glass to find a man also toweling from a shower.

They both looked at each other.

"Duncan King?" the man exclaimed.

"What are you doing here?" Duncan asked in shock.

Ansah Premo was a longtime friend. He was also his lawyer and had gotten him off in not a few binds, without most of them even making it to court.

"I have no idea," Premo answered. "I left the Jubilee House on Wednesday evening after an exhaustingly long day with the Independence Day celebrations and entered my car. When I checked the rearview mirror, someone sat in the back. Before I could find out who it was, a needle plunged into my neck, and next I knew, I'm in this cell with nothing but bread and *brukina* for company."

Then he turned to look at his friend properly and said, "What are *you* doing here?"

At this point, all the days of being in the dark and fearing for his life overwhelmed Duncan and he broke down in tears. Unsure what to say, all his friend could do was pat his back reassuringly. When the crisis passed, Duncan sniffed and said, "I think I may have been here for a week or two. It's hard to tell time in the dark. What day is today?"

"Thursday, March 7."

"Then it's been ten days," he did the math. "I arrived in Ghana on February 26 and visited the Grill. Someone did to me there what they probably did to you. I regained consciousness in my cell."

He deliberately left out the part about a sexy-hot young woman. During their last case, Premo had warned he would not represent him in any more matters involving his *sexpisodes*, as he had then called the many sexual assault and harassment claims against him. They had parted as friends, but the warning had remained, made the more impermeable

JAYJAY D. SEGBEFIA

because Premo was now legal counsel to the President.

"This is really discombobulating," Premo said, chewing on his lower lip in thought.

"I could really do without your verbosity right now, Premo," Duncan said, half irritably. "Why have we been abducted? What have we done? This doesn't make sense at all."

"Where are our clothes?" Premo asked suddenly.

Duncan looked around for his prison dress and found them no more on the toilet door.

"Did they make you wear the blue dress favourited by Ghanaian prisoners?" he asked Premo.

"Dear God, no!" Premo said in disgust. "I had my own clothes, but someone's taken them. Maybe while we were both in the shower."

"How did you come into the shower?" Duncan asked thoughtfully.

"I woke up in a cell of sorts when it was opened. I saw the food but didn't touch it. Because the bars remained up, I walked and followed a corridor that led here. I figured whoever did this needed me to take a bath, so I did. Then I heard your shower and wondered."

"That's what happened to me too, except I haven't been here a night, and they took my original clothes away, a whole set piece by Ozwald Boateng, the British designer!"

Ansah Premo almost rolled his eyes. They found some cabinets at the entrance to the bathroom and opened them. Two sets of clothing were in there comprising suits, shirts, trousers and neckties.

"They look about our sizes," Duncan King said with his practiced fashion eyes. They donned them and examined each other.

"Not bad actually," Premo said, looking his friend over.

"Could be worse, I guess," Duncan King said with obvious distaste. He only hoped no one important would see him in this low-cost frippery.

Ansah Premo looked at him and said, "Your concern for fashion, even in prison, does become your vanity, my friend. Let's get out of here and see if we can confront our kidnappers or find an escape. The Jubilee House must be worried about me right now."

A woman wearing dark leather clothing was standing in the corridor when the two men left the bathroom. She had two pistols holstered on either thigh, and one of her hands patted the grip of one of the side arms when she ordered them to follow her.

Obediently, they followed her through a grating that seemed to separate the cells from the other side of the building. She led them up a flight of stairs, and Duncan King found himself ogling her butt in her tight-fitting leather trousers as she flitted up the stairs. He stopped when Premo directed one of his stern looks at him.

They were ushered into a room structured like an amphitheatre. There was the floor itself, with circular benches and tables, and then about four or five courses of stepped benches and tables. At the top of the three walkways out of the floor to the upper seating were witness boxes of sorts, each with a microphone. Ansah Premo stopped short when he saw the justices of the Supreme Court. He turned to look at their escort with widened eyes as the realization hit him.

"Move!" the young woman said quietly, and then they were shoved right onto the ramp leading to the floor, where the judges were milling around with the deputy Attorney-General and a State Prosecutor. They all turned when the deputy Attorney-General recognized Ansah Premo. It took Premo's introduction for the judges to recognize Duncan King.

"Welcome, everyone," a female voice announced sonorously in a microphone. They turned to look at Asabea, who stood in one of the elevated witness boxes. At the upper levels of the room, six other women walked the perimeter.

"Who the hell are you?" the Chief Justice demanded. He had expected to meet his captors for he had decided, when lunch and his meals were delivered by some robotic arm, and he hadn't been able to speak with his colleagues, that he was being held against his will. But the phone in his room stopped dialing whoever it was that he had first spoken to.

"My name is Akua Sakyibea Asabea," she responded in a calm voice.

Ansah Premo frowned. He had heard that name before. He looked up again at the beautiful woman but couldn't place the face. He looked at Duncan King. He too seemed a bit startled but couldn't place her either.

"Why have you kidnapped us?" the Chief Justice demanded again.

"To correct an injustice and turn back a pervadingly false sense of entitlement."

Ansah Premo's jaws dropped.

As did Duncan King's.

They *knew* her. It had been, what, ten years? Premo's eyes locked with Asabea's and he said, "You shouldn't really do this." To which Asabea replied with a smile, "Oh, but I must."

"Justice isn't served by kidnapping eight Supreme Court justices and three government officials," he pleaded. "Stop this right now before someone gets hurt."

The judges looked from Premo to Asabea, and then from her to him. Obviously, this was a conflict with deep history, and they were caught in the middle of it.

But Asabea wasn't there to banter. She locked her eyes on Duncan King as she said for the benefit of the judges, "Exactly ten years ago, your Lordships, I was 19. And this man," she pointed to Duncan, "raped me. Twice. I was a virgin."

She paused. A decade had passed, and it was still hard for her to speak about it. She steeled herself and continued, "I have abducted all of you in order to render the justice that was denied a decade ago. From 10 a.m. on Monday, we will hold a trial that will be telecast live across the country and on the Internet, and seven of your Lordships will examine all the evidence and return a verdict. I am the plaintiff, and I will be represented by counsel, and that man is the defendant, and he will be represented by his counsel of record."

She let it sink in for a minute.

"Your Lordships will be the jury."

"I am sorry to burst your bubble, but abducting judges does not a court make," Ansah Premo stepped forward at that point. "Any decisions would be tantamount to judgment under duress and unenforceable later. You have committed second-degree felonies. You cannot hope to turn that around into a kangaroo trial."

"Mr. Premo, you will have opportunity to present all these points after we file our processes with the Court's registry, and you have your chance to rebut. Their Lordships can and will waive the conditions for judgment under duress, and the trial will proceed accordingly. As to enforcement of the verdict, I will be the executioner thereof."

"Exactly what kind of verdict do you expect?" Duncan King finally found his voice.

"Exactly the kind you deserve, Mr. King," Asabea shot back.

"And if the verdict does not go as you wish?" the Chief Justice asked warily.

"The verdict will be fair," Asabea said confidently. "And it will be just, your Lordship. For now, we will show you what will be the Court's registry. The first application before your Lordships will be the matter of whether the rape should have been prosecuted or not, hence the presence of the State Prosecutor who, at the time, refused to act appropriately despite the evidence. I expect Mr. Premo to raise his objections to the validity of this court at that point, then we may proceed."

"And if we refuse to sit as a Court?" the Chief Justice asked again.

"I was hoping it wouldn't come to that, your Lordship, but take a look at these," she pointed to a screen against a plain wall of the room. The large screen emitted photos of various houses. "These are live footages actually," she explained, and cameras zoomed in to all the judges' houses.

"Each house has enough remotely detonable devices to cause them to implode, and I'd really hate to hurt your families."

"Surely, you jest," the State Prosecutor scoffed.

Wordlessly, Asabea activated another screen on another wall which showed a TV station playing the usual cacophony of Ghanaian music. Then she manipulated the cameras showing the State Prosecutor's house and asked, "It's 4:30 p.m. now, sir. Who would be home at this time?"

Thinking she was going to send in people to kidnap anyone that could be home, Kwasi Apaloo, the State Prosecutor said, "I have no one at home at this time."

"Fair enough," Asabea said and activated an app on her phone. It took a minute, but the sound of the implosion was unmissable, and in a short while, dust and smoke covered the cameras' lenses.

"I hope you have home insurance, Mr. Apaloo," Asabea told him in a strange voice. Apaloo was aghast for a minute, but his scornful leer returned.

"I am not a kid, Miss," he said haughtily. "AI simulations do not faze me."

"You know what they say," Asabea said sadly. "Wait for it."

In ten minutes, the screen of the TV changed from a musical video to their newsroom, and the newscaster announced in breaking news that a loud explosion had occurred at a home in Cantonments, and it was feared that leaked liquefied petroleum gas from the occupant's kitchen had caused it. An eyewitness had sent in a phone camera recording of the incident, and it *was* Apaloo's home.

Apaloo turned, ashen-faced and rushed like a bull towards Asabea. Within ten feet of her, one of the armed women fired once. Apaloo fell to the floor, alive but screaming.

The sound of the gun going off in the closed room had the abductees scrambling to the floor and under the benches. When the silence returned, a team of nurses rushed in with a gurney and took the injured prosecutor out to a clinic inside the mansion.

The Chief Justice rose with the others from under a bench and asked in a quivering but angry voice, "You plan to hold the murder of our families over our heads to your verdict?"

"No, your Lordship," Asabea responded calmly. "I plan to hold the threat over your heads to a *trial*. The verdict you will return will be a just verdict regardless. One will have nothing to do with the other."

The judges stared at her.

"But how can you decouple a verdict from a trial under duress?" Premo asked incredulously. "You might as well kill us all," he screamed angrily.

"*I* won't do that, but the judges will," Asabea told him. "The verdict they will return will be a just verdict or there will be unpleasant consequences."

With that threat hanging in the air, the abductees didn't know what else to ask.

"Is he going to die?" Duncan asked Asabea.

"Efe did not shoot to kill," she responded. "But if the bullet touched a nerve in his legs or splintered the wrong bone, he may need a wheelchair for life."

Then she reassured them, "Our nurses will take good care of him."

"Why are you doing this?" Duncan asked her. The bastard really did look afraid.

"After what you did to me, you have the balls to ask?" she replied dangerously. "Justice will be served here, Duncan King," she told him. "And when it's all done, no one will do to a woman in Ghana what you did to me and several others and get away with it. I pledge it to you."

Then she turned to everyone else and said, "You all retire to your rooms now. This will be the courtroom and the adjoining office, the registry. We have set up the computers for you in your libraries. The relevant laws, case files and so forth have been downloaded for you. You can send emails, but they will be screened by our servers. You will have no access to phones whatsoever, but that is not to worry. On Monday we'll go live with the trial so your families will know you are alright."

She paused for questions, but there were too many to ask.

Not for the fearless Chief Justice though.

"How do you plan to get away with this?" he asked, looking at footage coming in on the news and fire trucks moving in to the State Prosecutor's house.

"Who said anything about getting away, your Lordship?" she responded respectfully. "Your responsibility is to assess and rule on the evidence. You leave the rest to me, sir."

When no more questions were forthcoming, she dismissed them, and they were led back to their quarters. Ansah Premo and Duncan King were no longer led to their cells but to a section that had a two-bedroom apartment so they could work together.

"Why put us in cells when you could have made us comfortable in the first place?" Premo asked their escort.

"We hadn't decided at the time whether to treat you as animals or as men," was the calm reply. "Just remember Samuel Butler."

Thinking he was a person in a similar position, Duncan asked fearfully, "What happened to him?"

"He said, 'Man is the only animal that can remain on friendly terms with the victims he intends to eat until he eats them,'" Efe said, before locking them in with her electronic key.

CHAPTER 5
Jubilee House
Sunday, 10th March; 10 A.M.

THE DAYS AFTER the call with Asabea had been frantically chewed up by the Ghanaian government chasing leads that led nowhere, breaking into a mansion in East Legon that only housed a pimp, tracking down all presidential staffers, biting nails and drinking more caffeine than they did in a year. The only bright spots of information came from the much-disliked commander of the CTU who had designed collaborative protocols with the VIP Protection Unit to avoid the tail-chasing inefficiencies of the other agencies. His unit had even taken on Military Intelligence and prevailed, with the reluctant support of the President. Currently, he was bringing the President and his Cabinet up to speed while they awaited the call of the woman who had identified herself as Akua Sakyibea Asabea.

"We were able to pull up some information, first about the leader of the septet, and then about how they pulled off their stunt," Chief Superintendent Atukwei was saying. "Ms. Sakyibea was the valedictorian at KNUST Law seven years ago, and further graduated on top of her class at the Ghana Law School three years ago. Until the abduction operation, she ran the all-female law firm, Asabea, Plange & Afanu. Incidentally, all the partners are her partners-in-crime on the abduction."

A picture of the seven popped up on the screen of his presentation and were arranged side by side with the photos they could generate from the videos of the Independence Day incidences and from social media.

"Asabea reached out in July last year and set in motion the discussions that convinced the Air Force to include paratrooping as part of their display at this year's parade, and the Police Service to have a first all-female police motorbike escort for the President. Once she secured her two leading women, Dede Afanu and Bubuné Gado, into these two key positions, the rest were a piece of cake."

"Fascinating," the Vice President said. "How did they capture Apaloo, Ansah Premo and Umaru Tanko?" he asked, referring to the State Prosecutor, the Counsel to the President and the deputy Attorney-General.

"We don't know yet," Atukwei told him. "We found their cars at their offices, so we presume they were all abducted at work. Premo's car is still at the Jubilee House car park. That is the one that has us all scratching our heads – how they were able to remove him from his car and take him out of the car park without either security or the cameras detecting that something was wrong," Atukwei finished and abruptly sat down.

The Cabinet was still to get used to his quirkiness, but the President had ordered that they accommodate him, so folks kept their irritation to themselves.

"The key to understanding everything is the allusive defendant," Chief Superintendent Amadu came in at that point. "Atukwei and I, after learning that Ansah Premo was missing, decided to work as far back as we could on some of his cases involving women before he entered government. All his clients were male. Then, in the middle of the night, Atukwei called and had us work on the female plaintiffs in the cases he worked on."

"And that's when you found Akua Sakyibea?" the President asked with interest.

Amadu nodded. "It was a highly visible case. It dominated Facebook and Twitter for weeks. Does any of you know an entertainment kingpin called Duncan King?" he asked.

"He is an egoistic, chauvinist, son-of-a-bitch!" the Minister for Arts and Culture, a woman, said with disgust. "We all heard about the case but don't know why the State did not prosecute the buffoon," she finished angrily.

"Is this something you would know about, Patricia?" the President asked the Attorney-General.

"It was one of the closed dockets presented to us by the former administration," the A-G replied. "Umaru reviewed it once, but we felt it would amount to a perception of a witch-hunt if we reopened the case, so we let sleeping dogs lie."

"What did the docket say?"

"That the victim was no longer forthcoming with information. A nolle prosequi was entered when the State Prosecutor had all he needed to secure a conviction, and since Section 54 of our Criminal Procedure granted him that power unbridled by judicial review, the court was forced to grant it," Atukwei shot up vehemently in response to the President's question. He was furious.

"So, the case died as abruptly as it erupted," Amadu continued. He did not want another awkward situation between the President and Atukwei. "No one knows why the victim, after doing everything right from the time she was assaulted, refused to press charges. She checked into a hospital immediately after the rape and provided irrefutable evidence that aided in the prosecutorial charges. Most lawyers agreed the case was slam dunk for the prosecution. Next thing we knew, Apaloo was in court on the nolle, and that was it."

"It didn't end on social media, though," Atukwei said, a bit more composed now. "Last night, our analysis of comments on news portals and blogs that covered the incident indicated that Ghanaians were evenly divided between support for the teenage-raping scum and support for the victim. But she was so vilified and humiliated that she closed her Facebook account, only returning briefly for three hours some six weeks later when a writer penned the most damning article about Duncan King's alleged guilt in the whole saga and reopened the case in the court of public opinion."

Amadu continued, "If Ansah Premo was abducted by Ms. Sakyibea, then we believe that Duncan King is in her custody too, which explains her demand for trial and justice and answers the "why" question for the abductions on Independence Day."

"Alright," the President said when the two were done. "At least we can rest knowing why it happened. What's going to happen next? Is she going to harm the abductees because she has a vendetta against our justice system? Or her plan is to find a legal reason to harm Duncan King?"

"She is likely to reenact the trial," Atukwei said, referring to some notes he had made. "She has the State Prosecutor who failed to proceed to full trial, the defendant himself – we are sure – and the defendant's counsel. None of the judges were involved in the case in any way so they are innocent but – in her mind – necessary collateral since reopening the case and the subject of judicial review in a nolle prosequi are a Supreme Court matter."

"On Friday, Apaloo's house was razed down by fire but eyewitness accounts indicate the house kind of imploded, like when someone uses dynamites in a controlled setting," Amadu chipped in.

"There was a drone taking in the destruction and was gone when Fire and Rescue got there. I think she has played one card to convince the abductees that their lives won't matter the birth certificates they are written on unless they either rerun the trial or give her a verdict to punish Duncan King," Atukwei added. "I also suspect she will demand a televised trial. Everything points in the direction of a very public hostage-trial situation."

"Isn't that too far-fetched a scenario?" the Chief of Army Intelligence wondered at that point. "Won't a public affair make it easier for us to find them and free her hostages?"

"They don't need state-run TV cameras. This isn't 1982," Atukwei looked at the intelligence chief with a frown when he said it. "She has YouTube, Facebook, Twitter, Instagram, TikTok and so many other tools that she probably has more intelligence about this than our Chiefs of Intelligence. Let's think completely outside the box on this – and that includes you too, Mr. President," he warned. "You and the Cabinet may have to tone down with her to prevent any casualties."

"You sound like you're on her side," the President told him bluntly.

"We don't believe her actions are designed only for her case," the IGP came in to help his men at this point. "We believe she is attacking, first, the sense of entitlement to a woman's body that some men possess in Ghana, and second, the impunity with which powerful men sexually abuse women. Each of these is a national cancer, and if these are her targets, she seems prepared to make that point no matter the cost."

"And we can do a simple survey," Atukwei cut in. He looked around counting and said, "There are eighteen men here. Show by hand any of you who can swear by a traditional deity that you have not once in your life forced yourself on a woman. It may not have been brutal rape, but who here has not forced himself at least once on a manifestly unwilling woman?"

Only the IGP and the Vice President's hands went up.

Atukwei said, "84-percent of our society's men sometimes force themselves on women. I'd say only a nuclear bomb can uproot that sense of entitlement. Even here at national leadership, only 3 of us are completely innocent under voodoo oath. So, we now know why Ms. Asabea is angry."

That was quite a sobering thought for President Offei's Cabinet and, bereft of ideas, they had little else to do but wait for the young woman's call.

CHAPTER 6
Jubilee House
Sunday, 10th March, Noon.

THE CALL, WHEN it came, took everyone by surprise. The phone did ring as expected, of course, but as soon as the call was picked, all the TV screens in the Cabinet Room came alive like a video call.

"Good afternoon, Mr. President," the Chief Justice said, and his face shortly filled the screens.

"Good afternoon, your Lordship," a startled President Offei responded. "And it's actually quite good to see you in good health and vitality."

The Chief Justice smiled. "Quite the cliché if ever there was one, Mr. President."

"I agree," the President said ruefully. "Where are your abductors?"

The Chief Justice looked around. "They were here a while ago hacking into the Jubilee House TV and computer systems, they'd said. Did it work?" he asked curiously.

"Seems so," the President replied, scowling at his head of cyber security who shrugged helplessly. "You are all over our TV and computer screens."

"Interesting," the CJ said. "They might connect all the other justices shortly then. Asabea was kind of hoping *we* would handle the conversation today, but I have no idea why," he shook his head.

Just then the other justices came online in the Cabinet Room. The grid of their eight faces made for a nice appearance on the screens when a chorus of hellos sounded through the Cabinet Room's sound systems.

"It's obvious none of you have been harmed," the President said happily. Then it hit him. "Can you all see us too?" he asked incredulously.

"I think the young women hacked you both ways," the CJ told him. "We can see all of you in the War Room," he chuckled. The War Room was the unofficial name for the Cabinet Room, used only in times of serious national discussions. Otherwise, Cabinet meetings were held in the President's Conference Room.

"I also assume you don't know where you are," the President asked, half-hopefully.

"We have no idea!" One of the Justices – Justice Esi Arhin – bemoaned. "Are you aware your counsel and deputy A-G are here too?"

"Yes, I am. We've done nothing all weekend but try to account for all of you. I am glad that no harm has come to you, though."

"Except Apaloo, but he is out of surgery now," the CJ told him. Seeing the confusion on the President's face, he said, "He was shot trying to grab Asabea when his house got blown to smithereens."

President Offei looked sharply at Atukwei and Amadu and said, "That confirms what we were told this morning, then. So, we have a duress situation?"

"She wants us to waive it," the CJ said. "She says she is only holding the threat of violence over us to force a trial but has no intention of forcing a verdict. I say if it's a trial she wants, let's give her one. It's not like National Security can find us anytime soon. Why not give her a trial while you do your best?"

"Aren't you sounding more relaxed about this than the situation warrants, your Lordship?"

Chief Justice Adofiem shrugged. "I'm not afraid of her, but your other appointees feel differently."

"Damn right we do," one of the justices declaimed vehemently. "How can we trust that she won't kill us all after an unfavourable verdict?"

Asabea, together with the deputy Attorney-General, then popped up on the screens alongside the judges and said, "Glad that you all have been reacquainted. Can we get down to business now, please?"

"You heard all our conversation?" President Offei asked her warily.

"Yes, your Excellency," she replied. "Our location is no Court, but it can be if the justices so decide."

"And the grounding of that in law would be what exactly?" the President asked skeptically.

"That would be Section 2, Subsection 5 of the Courts Act. The portion reads that the determination of any question before the Supreme Court shall be in accordance with the opinion of the majority of the members hearing the case. If the majority decide that this court as I have constituted it can hear the applications for which I have abducted them, then the decisions of the court would be as binding as if they were made in the forum of the Supreme Court building."

"You can plead no such rights because you're a criminal who has abducted eight judges and four others and is threatening them to arrive at a judgment," the Attorney-General rebutted angrily.

"I hold no violent intentions toward the verdict of the justices, for I have determined that their verdicts will be just. In the event I go back on my word, you may set it aside as having been secured under fraud as espoused by Section 83," Asabea argued.

"What will setting it aside mean?" deputy A-G Umaru Tanko asked on the screens. "If your response to any verdict is to blow us up, will setting it aside put our bodies and spirits together? If you shoot the judges because of the verdict, how will agreeing to this trial under duress remedy that? You are asking us to play this game of yours with a gentle smile and a gun, and you expect us to act like we only see the smile."

"*You* pushed the smile away and necessitated the use of the gun, Mr. deputy A-G," Asabea retorted. "If your office had done its job, all this would have been unnecessary, but you didn't. And now here we are. If death was what I wanted I wouldn't be here striking a conversation with you. You will play in this sandbox of your making and, to the extent and the extent only of the agreement to a trial, you will have your life in exchange."

President Offei came in at that point. "I will not give any semblance of legality to your criminal actions by agreeing to any trial while you have the judges under your false imprisonment," he charged. "The best I can do, in exchange for your surrender and for the release of all your hostages, is to waive prosecution until your desire to find a decade old justice is satiated. You have made your point, Ms. Asabea. It's time to end this before I bring the full might of Ghana's security forces to bear on finding you and putting you six feet under the ground."

Asabea stared at him for a few seconds. Then she pulled out her phone and keyed in a few commands.

The sound could not have been thunder for it was a sunny Ghanaian day. But it reverberated throughout the Cabinet Room, and all the room's UPS devices kicked in due to the resultant power outage. Presidential Guards rushed in, ostensibly to protect the President. The East Gate of the Jubilee House swung on its hinges in the wind from the explosion that took down one of its pillars. Soldiers were already moving into position to counter the perceived threat, but nothing came in through the gate.

It took a while to calm things down, and when that happened, President Offei looked with resolute anger at Asabea.

"You will pay for this, young lady!"

"I don't think you are in a position to issue threats, Mr. President," was the calm response. "But if what I have just done hasn't taught you a vital lesson, then you can be sure more examples will follow until you understand the gravity of my position. You see, for every empty threat you make, my Girls and I have a dozen responses of which you know nothing. In fact, the next attack could be on the Cabinet Room itself," she argued ominously. "Would you like to put that to test, Mr. President?" she asked, brandishing her mobile phone.

For one tense moment, no one moved on either side. The President glowered; his face set in a way that his Cabinet had never seen before. The struggle within him was as real as an arm-wrestling match as his eyes bore deep into Asabea's on the screen.

Eventually, his shoulders slumped and the contest ended.

But not entirely. Looking at the judges he said, "Mr. Chief Justice, it really is your decision. If you refuse to consider her requests, even under the threats she is imposing, this episode will be over, and no matter what happens, we will find you and find her."

"How typical of a Ghanaian politician," Asabea said with a shake of her head. "You disappoint me, Mr. President. The decision *is* yours. On public policy grounds and on the safety of the judges, you can ask that they do whatever is necessary to save themselves until you find a way to rescue them. You can buy time, Mr. President, by agreeing to my demands and asking them to do the same. After all, there is no immediate threat to the government and people of Ghana. It's not like we have nuclear codes," she finished.

"There is just one problem, Ms. Asabea." This was from Atukwei, to everyone's astonishment. "If we remove all eight justices on grounds of infirmity of mind and body because they are abductees, where would that leave us?" he asked her. "You have staked all your actions on the appearance of a fair trial. You will bomb the Jubilee House, abduct more judges and cause as much mayhem as you can, but what you will not do is to showcase a false trial. A fake trial will shoot all your hard work to nothing," he said seriously. "So, where does that leave us all?"

Nervously, the Cabinet Room watched Asabea fiddle with her phone. And the nervous seconds ticked to an unbearable silence.

"You are right, Chief Superintendent," Asabea conceded. "I want a trial, and I have proven the lengths I will go to get one. You want your judges back. What are you willing to do to that end? I give you my word that no judge will get hurt."

"That's it? Just your word?" the President asked snidely.

"Don't push me, Mr. President", Asabea told him pointedly. "Other than routine discipline, like in Mr. Apaloo's case, or to quell an insurrection among our abductees or, if somehow you find our location and attack and we respond with violence, no one will be harmed. I promise you."

And then, addressing Atukwei she said, "In good faith, Chief

Superintendent, I will return one of the justices to a place and time of your choosing since I only need seven justices. Let it not be said that I gave you nothing in return when you asked," she told him respectfully.

Atukwei inclined his head gratefully.

"Which of the justices are you returning, please?" Amadu asked.

"I'll leave it to their Lordships to decide," Asabea replied, "but it cannot be the Chief Justice."

"Shit!" the President swore under his breath.

"I'll leave them to decide but let all understand that this is in exchange for a trial that in future cannot claim diminished capacity, duress and any such excuses. The deputy A-G is welcome to raise these arguments at trial, but the decisions of the court will not be gainsaid afterwards. Those are the terms of the release. Do you concur, Mr. President? I have given my word. It's time you gave yours," Asabea declared.

Conferring briefly with the Vice President and his Cabinet, President Offei agreed to the terms on the condition that nothing prevented or purported to prevent his government from attempting to find the abductors no matter the progress of the trial and freeing the hostages.

Asabea smiled at that and told him she'd be surprised if he didn't try to find them. The justices also selected the youngest among them for release on Monday, after which all documents and applications would need to be filed by Tuesday. The Court would sit every day from Thursday because these were not normal times, and the CJ hoped to end the nightmare as soon as possible.

CHAPTER 7
Ground Zero
Monday, 11th March; 3 A.M.

THE GIRLS MET in Asabea's room on time and group-hugged for a minute. The operation had had so many moving parts that they hadn't had time to take it all in and celebrate. And today was no different. They had one more group of parts to slap in place before they could settle down to bring the Girls' Justice down on Duncan King, whom they could see tossing and turning on his bed on the bank of screens monitoring every part of the Fortress.

"Have you texted him yet?" Efe asked Asabea, who looked back at her deputy with a smile. They were getting dressed for this morning's stint, and Asabea was filling the chambers of her pistol with ammunition.

"It was tough, but I have," she replied.

"What did he say?" all six girls asked her at once and laughed.

"He said, 'Took you long enough, didn't it?'"

"He's agreed?" Dede asked, surprised.

"Eight o'clock," Asabea told them.

Bubuné looked at her watch and said, "That's good. I really hope he comes around voluntarily."

"I hope so too," Asabea said in a strange voice. She cleared her throat and asked her girls, "All set?"

"All set!" They responded and proceeded out of the room.

The nurses met them in one of the corridors and wheeled a gurney into a waiting ambulance on the other side of the mansion. They strapped the patient into place and disappeared inside the building. Six of the girls boarded the vehicle and drove out the massive gates onto the little mountain road with Aisha in the driver's seat, followed by Asabea in a Land Cruiser. When they hit the highway after half an hour, they turned on the siren and raced towards Accra.

They arrived at the policeman's neighbourhood in Dansoman at 4 a.m., turned the siren off and drove silently to the house they wanted. They parked right in front of his driveway, switched from the ambulance to the SUV and left the engine and air conditioning running in the ambulance. By half past four, they'd arrived at the warehouse in Adabraka.

The twins were the first to get out of the car. They jimmied the fat padlocks of the aluminum doors open and called to the others.

The warehouse had three months' supply of food, water, and drinks neatly stacked in boxes and bottles in two mini trucks. In a corner of the warehouse, another stack of boxes sat waiting. Asabea and Efe wasted no time in moving those quickly into the SUV's large boot with Aisha's help while Bubuné and Dede played sentry.

They left the warehouse at a quarter to five and split with the twins, who headed back towards the mountains in the mini trucks. By the time the sun rose at 6 a.m., Oye and Nhyira, with Bubuné and Aisha, would have already left the highway and hit the dirt road to the Fortress.

Asabea now had Dede and Efe with her on the fast drive to the Kaneshie Estates. The first call was to a small house on Feo Eyeo Street, and the second was to another small house at Dan's Bar in North Kaneshie. The third house at Ringway was heavily gated at the front, but a mosquito-infested drain was all that stood between Asabea and Efe at the back. Dede dropped them near the drain and drove towards the front of the house a block away.

They scaled the wall and opened the back door quietly. It led to a kitchen. Three steps out of the kitchen they froze. Someone was using the adjourning bathroom. The corridor light was off, but the bathroom light identified their query. Asabea fired her Taser and the man slumped to the floor. They disengaged, picked him up and quietly opened the front door. They came around the front gate holding the semi-conscious man between them and fired at the only guard. They fled the neighbourhood as quietly as they had entered and headed out towards the University of Ghana where they left Asabea by the first house on Vice Chancellor's Crescent and wished her well.

Then Dede and Efe drove off with a clerk, a court reporter and a prosecution witness immobilized in the back seats.

Asabea checked her watch. It was 6 a.m. She was two hours early. She scaled the short white fence, walked across the manicured lawn in leather trousers and jacket and picked the lock of the door, being careful not to make a sound. She located the bedroom once inside and found the door locked. She was even more careful with it than with the front door and opened it so slightly until her eyes grew accustomed to the darker room.

He was asleep. Even in the dark room, she could make out the orderliness, the implacable OCD that she had found the most annoying about him. She pulled a small stool from near the side drawer of the bed and watched his gentle breathing. It had been eight years or so. She missed him so much the tears welled up in her eyes, which is why she hadn't noticed he'd woken up until he turned on the bedside lamp. They locked eyes; she with tears glistening in hers and him, with sleep in his.

Wordlessly, she took off her jacket, raised the sheets and threw herself – boots and all – next to him. He held her gently to him, at first tentatively, and then tightly when he felt the sob escape her.

For how long they stayed that way, Asabea did not know or care. He had always been perfect. Eight long years since she threw him out of her life, and not a word or look of approbation at her sudden reappearance.

Asabea and Owuraku had known each other since kindergarten. They had held hands to cross the street to school way back then and had refused to be separated during senior high school. Although he'd gotten admitted to Presec, Legon and she'd gained admission to Aburi Girls, they'd harassed their parents, demanding to both be allowed either in Presec together or in Aburi Girls together. In frustration, their parents had sent them to Achimota School, and their friendship and love had grown with each passing year.

It was Asabea who'd first proposed. It was from all that peer pressure. Third year was ending, and though they lived in the same neighbourhood, Asabea felt if she didn't let her true feelings for him show, she might lose him to the more desperate girls seeking to nail down whoever they could after three years of playing hard to get. No one wanted to get to the university with a 3-0 love score. Without much luck in senior high, the odds of better luck in the university were always slim. Unless one was fine jumping from one caricature to another.

She'd proposed at the school canteen with one cube of choco-milo and one wrapped Chupa Chups lollipop.

He hadn't laughed, to his amazing credit. Of course, she would have made him pay, but he hadn't laughed. He'd accepted her simple display of affection, held her hands and had taken her on a walk under the tree-lined avenues of Achimota School.

He'd laid down the rules: No sex, no cheating, no cry-baby drama, and no break-up. Those were his conditions, and if she accepted, he'd be hers to infinity and Buzz Lightyear. She'd kissed him right there, and when his face had registered shock and consternation, considering that getting caught would have led to a public disciplinary action, she'd kissed him again. They'd both been sixteen then, and he'd enforced the rules to the letter since.

He had wanted to be a molecular scientist and she, a fashion designer. He'd gained admission to the Kwame Nkrumah University of Science and Technology a year in advance while she'd examined her options with three schools of fashion. She'd eventually chosen Law School and enrolled shortly before she'd turned 19, but she'd never missed a fashion show and took short courses so she could make her own dresses.

He'd come down to Accra for her 19th birthday a week before she was sexually assaulted. He was the only one she'd called that afternoon. He'd wasted no time at all. He'd ordered her not to so much as wipe herself and had taken her to the Pinecone Medical Centre, and right from there to the Airport Police Station where, armed with the medical report, he'd raised such hell the Police had arrested Duncan King the self-same day. And every day thereafter he'd been there, missing school for a month until therapy had ended. He'd vowed he'd kill the son of a bitch, and not a day had passed that Asabea had not feared that he would.

She couldn't bear to live with the fact that he'd remained a virgin while she'd lost hers so brutally. He was clean and she was not. He was pure and she'd been violated. He deserved a virgin, for that had been their vow until marriage; she no longer deserved him.

So, she'd broken up with him two years after, and had cut off all connections. It had been painful for him and worse for her but before she'd blocked his number, email and messaging apps, he'd gotten a message through:

> *Shadows are falling and I'm running out of breath.*
> *Keep me in your heart for a while.*
> *If I let you leave it doesn't mean I love you any less*
> *Keep me in your heart for a while.*
> *Because I'll wait. For ten years at least.*

Three years had passed before she'd realised that most of it were words out of a song. And she'd never forgotten it. She could never sleep without that song and when, without a word, Owuraku had stretched his hand to play the self-same song while he held her, as if reading her thoughts, Asabea broke into such tears it was all Owuraku could do to hold her tight to his chest and keep her heart from breaking.

Again.

He fixed breakfast at 8. It had taken a whole hour for her crying to stop, and another in a hot shower for the tears to spend. It was during the meal that she realised he hadn't spoken a word at all since she'd stolen into his home. She really hadn't let him, to be honest, with all her crying, and now, sitting across from him in a small dining room, she took in his fierce, professorial face; his comfort with silence, and the gravity developed from years of experiences she hadn't been a part of. She had a million questions to ask him; a million stories to hear from him. She had nothing to share with him, for nothing had consumed her more than her vengeance. Her therapist had said that this was ten years of her life she was never going to get back but she hadn't cared.

Duncan King had taken her life. She had died that afternoon.

Shaking herself from her mournful thoughts she looked up at him and said a bit hesitantly, "If I asked you to, would you come with me so I may pursue justice delayed?"

He got up to do the dishes, wiped his hands on a towel, kept everything in its place and turned calmly to her.

"Is there danger involved?" he asked in a deeper voice than she remembered.

"Yes."

"How long would it take?"

"Probably forever. We may never come back."

"Would we be together?"

"We would be inseparable."

"Does it involve a certain Duncan King?"

"Yes."

Owuraku made one call on his mobile phone. Then he walked to the door and pushed it open. He looked back at Asabea still sitting in her dining room chair and said to her, "What are you waiting for?"

CHAPTER 8
Cabinet Room
Monday, 11th March; 9 A.M.

I FOUND HER inside the ambulance right in front of my gate," Amadu was telling the President. "I don't know how they knew my house. I woke up in the morning and the lights were flashing at my gate. The engine was on so I thought the driver was on board, but he wasn't. I checked only to find that the judge was asleep on the stretcher inside the ambulance. She had no memory of how she got there, so I called the IGP and reported it."

"Didn't Asabea promise she was going to meet you in a place and time of your choosing?" President Offei asked.

"We never got around to deciding that before Sunday's call ended," Atukwei chipped in from his corner around the table. He got up suddenly and proceeded to the screens. "But we may have caught a break to finding out where the judges are."

"Was the ambulance tracker active?" the health minister, a member of the Cabinet asked.

"It wasn't," Amadu responded. "These girls are no fools. They deactivated it."

"After Amadu reported the ambulance we made searches on all regional borderline cameras, especially the ones stationed near tolls and found that this ambulance crossed the Ayi Mensah cameras at 03.47 this dawn," Atukwei explained. He manipulated some images onto the screens and said, "There were two women in the front who fit Aisha Yeldidong's and Dede Afanu's descriptions."

"That means they are still in the capital if they left the ambulance behind?" Vice President Domwine asked.

"Their leader was driving an SUV right behind them," Atukwei told him, pointing to Asabea in a leather jacket right behind the ambulance on the camera's video frame.

"Entering the city from Ayi Mensah tells us their base of operations could be in the Eastern Region. Right now, our suspicion is centered around the Aburi Mountains, obviously because it is easier to run in and out of Accra using those mountains as a base, but that is still a large area to find a staging ground."

"Do you think the disappearance of a Supreme Court clerk and Court reporter are their doing?" the Vice President asked Atukwei.

Atukwei manipulated more images onto the screens again and said,

"Asabea's SUV was photographed exiting Accra at 06.37 at the same Ayi Mensah post. She was not on board this time. Dede Afanu and Efe Plange were in the front, and we found two people slumped in the back and a third person in the third row. The two at the back could be the court employees but the third person was Lawrence King, cousin to Duncan King and a possible witness to the sexual assault."

"Alleged sexual assault," the A-G corrected.

Atukwei glared at her. "Larry King was present in the Gold Coast Hotel suite when the sexual *assault* occurred." He threw a challenging look at the Attorney-General, but she did not pick up the challenge. "During the prelims of the trial, he begged to be excluded entirely from testifying. This is why we believe he is a person of interest to the septet."

Then he turned to the Vice President, "Based on the evidence therefore, if any of the girls remained, it would be Asabea because she was not in the vehicle when it returned back to the Eastern region, but without a car we can identify, it may be difficult to find her in Accra."

"We do know, however," Amadu interjected, "that the Land Cruiser made a brief visit to the University of Ghana."

He too displayed a series of images on the screens.

"Asabea drove herself, Dede and Efe with three other passengers into the campus," he announced, pointing to the image from the campus cameras, "but at the Ayi Mensah booth, she was not with her girls. The time frame between the shot at Legon and the shot at Ayi Mensah is eighteen minutes. Whatever it was they did on campus did not take long, and the only way a stop makes sense is if they dropped Asabea off on campus."

"Is it eighteen minutes from Legon to Ayi Mensah?" the A-G asked.

"At that time of day, yes," Amadu responded.

"Wait a minute," the tourism and arts minister said suddenly. "I believe there was talk ten years ago about a boyfriend that was a scientist, wasn't there?"

"Owuraku Ampem Darko," Atukwei said. "A molecular biologist; KNUST trained. This is Legon."

"Yes, but wasn't he appointed Associate Professor of Molecular Biology two or so years ago?" The education minister objected.

"He was, actually," Amadu said, looking up from his mobile phone. "I just googled his name and Legon's website says he was appointed three – you think she went in to see him?" Amadu said with his eyes wide open.

Atukwei was already on his way out the door, with the Chief of Military Intelligence right behind him.

"We may have caught a break," the IGP said to the President in self-congratulation.

"Maybe," Amadu said, rushing out to catch up to Atukwei. "You all stay and consider what we should do if we catch her. How would it affect the hostage situation? Would it put the judges in potentially more danger? Please ponder over all that and let us know before we grab her," he shouted from the door and started running after Atukwei.

"What is there to ponder over?" the Attorney-General asked in confusion. "We cut the head off the snake, we are done, right?"

"What he means is that it may be more complicated to arrest her than not to," the President said, scratching thoughtfully at his short white beard. "Catching her could mean the end. It could also usher in the beginning of terror. Leaderless and probably afraid, the other girls might become more dangerous," he said unhappily.

"So, we are screwed if we catch her, and we are screwed if we don't?" the Vice President asked.

"Let them catch her first, and then we can decide in which direction we are screwed," the President said darkly.

Amadu and Atukwei were in the same police cruiser hightailing it to the University of Ghana campus in Legon with the Military Police in tow. Amadu was on the phone with the IGP who had men reaching out to the university authorities to track down the Associate Professor.

"The Registrar called a second ago to say that Dr. Ampem Darko phoned his secretary five minutes ago to say he was taking his accumulated leave starting this morning, and to file the necessary paperwork," the IGP told him breathlessly. "He is no longer answering his phone."

"Copy that," Amadu responded. "Which is his bungalow?"

"Number 12. Vice Chancellor's Crescent."

"We'll be there in a minute. Can you ask the university to lock all exits and stop vehicles from leaving campus until we get there, sir?"

"Right away then," the IGP agreed.

When they arrived at the Okponglo entry to the campus, there was already traffic several hundred metres long on the exit side.

"Have your men search the vehicles," Atukwei ordered the head of campus security at the entry post when he got out of his car, almost

INVIOLABLE 38

knocking a motor rider and his passenger off their bike with his door. "And repeat that order to the other two exits. We are looking for Professor Ampem Darko. He will be travelling with a 29-year-old woman."

"Yes, sir!"

They arrived at the bungalow and fanned out with the soldiers. They had the house surrounded in seconds. They didn't even need to kick the door in. It was unlocked. The two Chief Superintendents took in the room and its orderliness in one look and raced outside to the garage. There was no car inside. Amadu reached out to the university Registrar.

"What car does Dr. Darko drive?"

Atukwei watched Amadu's face shift colour from determination to consternation in response to the Registrar's answer.

"Dr. Darko does not drive a car. He rides a motorbike," he said to Atukwei.

"The – the bike I almost knocked over at the Okponglo entrance?" he replied with wide eyes.

"Let's go!" Amadu ordered the men under his command. They arrived back at the entry post raucously and asked the head guard, "Remember that motorbike we almost ran over?"

"Yes, sir," the guard said. "But we don't know which way he turned at the Okponglo traffic light."

Amadu was on the phone with the Registrar again. He cut the call and issued an APB for the motorbike and its registration number. He then reached out directly to the Ayi Mensah police and ordered a roadblock to the mountains for three hours. Atukwei was cursing horribly in his native Ga when he got off the phone.

"What's wrong?"

"They already crossed the Ayi Mensah toll!"

"How do you know?"

Atukwei showed Amadu his phone's screen.

"The same motorbike crossed the cameras ten seconds ago."

CHAPTER 9
Ground Zero
Monday, 11th March, Noon.

THEY WERE GATHERED in Asabea's office again and were fussing over Owuraku, who didn't look perturbed about being the centre of attention. He seemed more interested in how they had pulled off an abduction of supreme court judges at a national parade. Asabea's office overlooked the enormous gates of the mansion, so he stood inside the office with his eyes alternating between taking in the beauty of the scenery and watching the judges and state officials interact with each other in the central dining room on the screens. He darkened when he saw Duncan King sitting in a corner with his lawyer on one of the screens and asked, "What's the ultimate plan for that horny toad?"

"Depends on the verdict," Dede told him. She had taken a personal liking to him; she was the first to hug him when he and Asabea had ridden into the courtyard.

"You are sticking to that line?" he asked her with a querulous look.

"It's the official line," she shrugged and hugged him again.

The other girls turned to Dede, and Aisha asked her, "What's with all the plenty hugging?"

Dede shrugged and said, "One hug for every year this bitch here left you heartbroken," she said playfully at Asabea and hugged him again.

"So let me get this straight," Owuraku asked them, standing by one of the glass windows. "You plan to have a trial and seek the Supreme Court's ruling that Asabea's assault should have been prosecuted by the State, even without a willing witness; that the State had enough evidence, no matter the preferences of the victim, to seek a conviction?"

"Essentially, yes," Bubuné told him.

"I know you have many questions," Asabea told him gently, and then patted a sofa in the middle of the room. "Please sit and let's fill you in."

And so they did.

When they were done, he asked Asabea, "Why now?"

The question hung in the air for quite a bit. Eventually, it was Nhyira who answered, "I know the only story you know is Asabea's, Owuraku, but the reason it's us seven doling out the long overdue justice is that we are all his victims."

Owuraku's eyes widened.

"Yes, we all are," Oye also told him. "Even us twins – he harassed me first and then did the same to Nhyira a year later. Both of us were

INVIOLABLE 40

Miss Ghana pageant contestants. Every one of us here is a victim. That's what unites us; the idea that we, his victims, are about to pile on some real justice for years of unchecked entitlement to the vaginas of beauty queens, helpless girls and fashion idol-wannabes. Asabea's case is the face of a thousand complaints and represents women without number. Each victim of his has contributed cash and kind to this cause of justice, and when we are done, Duncan King will suffer death by a thousand cuts when we call out the roll of each assault, each rape, and each defilement."

Owuraku could not even blink when she was done. The passion, the pain and the resolve were so strong that he had nothing to say. And here he was thinking nothing could have been more painful than living through Asabea's trauma.

"Do you think our cause is just?" Efe asked him gently.

"I have no thoughts either way concerning the methods," he told her truthfully. "I just want to see that bastard hurt. If this is what will make it happen, it's fine by me. That beast should never walk again."

"The only thing," he added pensively, "is that I think you might need more help with holding this fort when the government comes knocking."

"They don't know where we are," Aisha told him. "We've been very careful."

"I don't doubt you for a second," he assured her, "but I think you need to understand that this is an election year. This is not a year a government would like to look weak, and while your stunt has not been leaked to the media, it's a matter of time," he further argued.

"Actually, the trial will be in the media," Bubuné told him.

"I beg your pardon?"

"We've hacked the Facebook and YouTube accounts of all the major news outlets. It will all be internet-based, and we'll drive traffic to our website, HangDuncanKingdotcom," Nhyira told him.

"And if National Security comes calling?"

"We have enough drones to hold the fort," Asabea told him.

"For how long?"

"A month, if necessary."

"That's not long enough. What if they bring tanks and artillery?"

"We can hold them," Efe said.

"Not for a month, you won't," Owuraku said calmly. "I know President Offei. He won't send in the Police."

Then he turned to Asabea, "Remember the Police Officer who

almost hit us with his car door when we were leaving campus?"

Asabea nodded.

"He was asking about me at the security post," he told her.

"Is that why you tore through Madina like a mad man?"

"Yes," he told her. "He was asking about me and a twenty-nine-year-old woman. Just a few minutes earlier at my bungalow and we would have been surrounded. How did he know about me? How did they know you would come to me? We need to be prepared, but it isn't being prepared to defend this place I am worried about. We need to prepare to leave on short notice."

"We're prepared to die, Owuraku," Asabea said to him in a voice inundated with conviction, speaking on behalf of all of them. "We are prepared to lay down our lives to see justice done."

Owuraku paused for a minute before boring into her with his eyes, "I have already died once, for you."

He let it sink in.

"I'm not doing that again. We can do both – carry out justice *and* live. When the government appears at those gates – and I notice there's only that one dirt road to and from here – we will need to break out of here where they will not suspect, or in a way they will not be able to follow."

"What are you saying, Owuraku?" Oye asked him. "Behind the mansion is a two-hundred-foot cliff, and beyond that is an impregnable jungle all the way to Adawso. Nothing and no one can come at us from behind."

"Then that's where we should plan our escape," Owuraku told them. "I have listened to all your plans, and everything sounds airtight except the exit plan. And you don't have a good one because you believed you were not going to survive this. The food, water, nurses and medication – all of them are symptoms of a suicidal plan. You may plan to end it all here; but I will not. If you really need me here, you all better include that exit strategy."

"We understand that Owuraku," Asabea came in at that point. "That's why you are going to be part of the trial – a hostage, brought here against your will to deliver a testimony that is crucial to the success of our legal strategy. When this is over, you and the judges will walk, but we will defend this place with all we've got."

Breathing in heavily to keep his beating heart in check, Owuraku turned on Asabea, pointing one determined finger, "You promised me we'd be together. Your words were 'we'd be inseparable'. And now you're talking to me about *walking*?"

Under the intensity of his gaze, Asabea felt herself wilting. The tears came unbidden again, but he was not done yet. "You all have done a great job so far because you kept single focus. Unrestrained and unconcerned even about dying, you have cooked up a solid way to hold Duncan King and the nation accountable. Keep your focus on that. Let me focus on the ways to keep you safe when the entire Army comes knocking. Let me work on getting you all to safety, for the sake of those like me who have done nothing but bleed for you, for your pain and for your selfishness. You think your life is yours and yours alone, but even in holding rapists to account, you have hurt people, and that hurt is a transfer of your pain to others, leading to an eternal perpetuation of that man's evil."

Then, looking at them in turns, he said, "Those are my terms." Pointing to Asabea, he added, "She broke my first terms by kicking me out of her life. But these ones cannot be broken. Either you let me prepare us for an exit, or best open the gates now and let me ride."

It took some back and forth between the girls to resolve this. They did not speak, but the looks they exchanged, faces they made, imperceptible shrugs, winks and frowns seemed to communicate their decisions on Owuraku's outbursts.

Eventually, Efe asked Owuraku, "What do you have in mind?"

"Do you have a map?" he asked them.

Aisha produced one from a nearby drawer.

"Where are we, please?" Owuraku asked.

Bubuné came to him and pointed to their mansion. It wasn't a mansion at the time of the cartography, but Owuraku saw the flat top of their plateau and nodded.

"Is this the cliff you spoke about?" he asked Oye.

She nodded.

He took a string from Asabea, made some calculations on the map, took some measurements and turned the map around a few times.

"One of my former students runs a wilderness rescue company," he told them. "Some Danish people went hiking in the Afadjato highlands and got lost. One of them broke her leg and fell into a cave. They tracked them in those mountains – and these mountains here have nothing on those – and brought them back, all alive. You say no one can come at you from behind. This guy can. And it's 18-kilometres from Adawso through the mountains to get here. If we let him cut a trail to the base of our cliff, he can set us up for an emergency abseil and evacuation. If the Army comes to the gates, we can beat a hasty retreat and disappear before they have an idea where we've disappeared to."

"Do you trust this fellow?" Asabea asked warily.

"I doubt trust has anything to do with it," Owuraku answered. "Let's bring him in just for a few hours and let him look over the edge. The next time you'll see him will be when we need him."

"No one who has ever been here has been allowed back yet," Dede complained. "He may betray us."

"We took the eighth judge back," Aisha reminded her. "We can bring this fellow in and when he leaves, he won't know where we are."

"That's not possible with Kwaku Opare Addo," Owuraku told them. "Even blindfolded, he can find his way back here by the sound of birds alone. We just must trust him. In less than two weeks he will cut that trail and say hello to us from the window. Are any of the hostages close to seeing the cliff?"

"None at all. They see the walls, the forest and the mountains in the distance but not the cliff. That is exclusively ours," Nhyira told him.

"Let's get him moving then. It will cost us, but he is the best shot we've got."

The septet had a lengthy debate, but Owuraku was unyielding, and eventually, they agreed with his plan. Only then did he seem to relax. They noticed and rushed in to give him one of their group hugs.

"If word of all this hugging got out, it would ruin your reputation, you know?" he told them sourly.

They only giggled at him.

"How would we call Opare?" he asked in the middle of the hug. "I didn't bring my phone."

"We wouldn't have let you," Dede told him. "We have secured lines you can call him on. Do you know his number offhand?"

"I don't but I can find it online. Is your internet secured as well?"

"It is," Asabea told him.

He broke away and arranged the visit in a minute. The Rescuer would be present in three days, at least.

"So, what happens next?" he asked them.

"We have filed our motions with the Court," Asabea explained. "The defendants will do the same – the deputy A-G and the State Prosecutor. We expect that Duncan King's lawyer will file to be a permissive joinder, but the issue before the Court on Thursday will be whether the Court agrees with us that, giving the facts of our case in particular, the prosecution should not have entered a nolle prosequi."

"I didn't think nolle prosequis were subject to judicial review,"

Owuraku asked with a frown.

"We'll see what the judges say when we make our case," Asabea said with a sly smile.

"Alright," Owuraku surrendered. "Can someone show me to my room? I feel I have about exhausted myself out today."

"You'll stay with me," Asabea said, quicker than she'd intended to.

"Please," she begged, noticing at the end that she'd made her plea sound rather like an order.

Owuraku looked at her gently. Before he could speak, she ran into his arms and said to him, "We have a lot to catch up on. Please stay."

"And not just with her," Dede said in a strange voice. "We all want to know how you survived knowing she'd left and wasn't coming back."

"Who said I survived?" he asked her, not unkindly.

"Then why are you here?" Bubuné asked him slyly.

He looked at Asabea and said simply, "I don't know why."

CHAPTER 10
Jubilee House
Thursday, 14th March; 9 A.M.

PRESIDENT KWAME AMPONSAH Offei was in a foul mood, and he blistered the walls of the Cabinet Room with epithets so vulgar the women in his Cabinet covered their ears on occasion to avoid blushing violently. No one had seen him this pissed off before. The offending party was the television set on the wall of a corner of the room. News of the abductions was running wild in the media and the conspiracies about his ineptitude since the judges were kidnapped a week ago was so offensive it was all he could do not to instruct the NCA to shut down all television and radio stations until the crisis passed.

"Who leaked the information to the media?" he asked his Cabinet and the high-ranking officers who ran Ghana's Armed and Police forces.

Before anyone could speak, the news cut away to a clip of Asabea. The president grabbed the remote control himself and increased the volume.

"Fellow Ghanaians," she was saying. "I have come into your homes this morning to announce that I have seven of your Supreme Court justices in my custody on a matter of some urgency."

"Can you all believe this?" President Offei shouted in surprise.

"A decade ago, I was brutally raped by Duncan King, a man you all know in the entertainment and fashion arena," Asabea continued. "I was too traumatized to present in Court to hold him to account, and the Republic, which owed a duty to me and to all Ghanaians to effect justice turned a blind eye. Last week I abducted eight of your highest judges, one of whom has been freed. I will keep the seven so the trial that I never had can be conducted until a just verdict is returned. Only then will I release the judges.

"The President is aware of what I have done, and why. He knows that the justices will come to no harm during the trial. The judges have agreed to oversee the trial as well and they all are in good health," Asabea announced. "Every day, from 10 a.m. until noon, the trial and issues for which I seek justice will be telecast live on television and on the internet."

"Over my dead body," President Offei swore, looking in the direction of his communications minister, who had power to shut down TV, radio and internet access, but Asabea wasn't finished.

"Feel free to let your voices count on our hashtag *HangDuncanKing* YouTube channels and on the channels of all major news media in case

INVIOLABLE   46

the government shuts down the telecasts. Today's will start in an hour, and when all of this is over, you will understand why we have had to resort to these drastic measures in pursuit of justice. Thank you all very much, and God bless our homeland Ghana!"

"Unbelievable!"

"This is outrageous!"

"The whore!"

The last denunciation came from the National Security Minister whose outfit had been beating about every town on the Aburi mountains in hopes of locating the judges. President Offei himself seemed to have lost his voice. He still stood in front of the TV with a dark scowl and seemed oblivious to the reactions of his Cabinet. But when Chief Superintendents Amadu and Atukwei walked through the doors of the room, the President shook himself out of his rage and turned to them before they could sit.

"Have you both heard the news?" he asked darkly.

"On the way here, sir," Amadu replied respectfully. "It's all over the radio."

"What do you two suggest we do about that?"

Atukwei shrugged in response and said, "I did think the lack of publicity was a bit weird in the beginning. Their abductions would make no sense without some public display."

"You approve running their criminal enterprise on TV?" the President quizzed with both eyebrows raised.

"Mr. President," Amadu tried to explain. "We would have been extremely worried if the girls hadn't used mass media to emphasize their agenda. Addressing the public gallery in their show means they do not intend to hurt the judges. Killing innocent justices of the Supreme Court will make them unpopular and make it harder for them to escape when this is over. Calling the media translates to carrying out their plans with some public support. That's a good thing."

"But how can anyone support *this* criminality?" the Vice President asked, aghast at the notion of public support.

"I just checked out their website," Amadu told him. "Three million visitors and counting in just three minutes."

"That doesn't mean people approve," the President said. "It only means people are curious."

"What do you plan to do about it, sir?" Atukwei asked as politely as he could.

"We need to shut it all down!" the President declared.

"You mean to shut down the telecasts and their internet channels?" Amadu asked carefully.

"Exactly that!" President Offei said. "We do not need to give them any public platforms for this else it will consume Ghanaians and detract from our agenda to break the eight."

Atukwei and Amadu blinked. Only the politicians in the room seemed to understand what he was talking about. When he didn't explain, Amadu said, "We need not shut them down, your Excellency. They could give us some clues, or the broadcast could reveal a frame of mind we could use to hit back at them. So long as we can see them, we will be fine, but if they go dark, we too will be in the dark. How will we know what their reaction to an unfavourable verdict will be if we don't have eyes on them, sir?" Amadu finished with more assertiveness than he'd intended.

"If you and your superiors in the Police Service and the Armed Forces had done your jobs like you were supposed to, we wouldn't even be having this conversation," President Offei fired back heatedly. "It's been a week and we are no closer to finding these criminals than we were on Independence Day. And now, without any clues to help you, you are proposing that we allow them to put our shame on public display so that we lose the elections in December? Do you have any idea how weak I would look if we let them run this circus in the media? I do not need this at all right now. We will shut the broadcasts down and order YouTube to pull down their channel. That will at least send them the message that they are not the only ones with cards up their sleeves."

"And their website?" Atukwei asked with a hint of his usual sarcasm.

"We have hackers working to take it down as we speak," the National Security Minister told him.

"Your hackers will fail," Atukwei told him, and then turned to the President, "as must your desire to shut down their broadcasts."

President Offei's face registered his anger at that, but Atukwei wasn't finished.

"So far, any communication between us and the hostages has happened under the Girls' auspices. Any proposal that reduces that privilege is dangerous and ill-advised. If they discover we are pulling the plug on their live trial and decide to pull an Apaloo on us, the media will have a field day. We haven't even gotten to the bottom of how they bombed the southern gate of this Jubilee House. Best not to piss them off at all, sir," Atukwei warned.

The President was quiet for a minute. As was his Cabinet. Then he asked them, "How many of you agree with these two?"

The IGP, all the Armed Forces Chiefs and National Security professionals raised their hands, a clear minority.

Turning to his Minister for Communications, President Offei ordered, "Terminate the spectrum of any television or radio station that carries the trial live. And shut down YouTube and any other social media platform that runs their campaign. We must not be seen to be condoning their cause with inactivity."

Then he said to his Minister for National Security, "Kobby, you and your men have 72 hours – and no more – to find my Justices alive and return them to me. If not, I expect your resignations on my desk before the expiration of three days. Do I make myself clear?"

"Y-yes sir," The National Security Minster stammered, quite taken aback.

"Enlist the support of foreign operatives if you must, but I want this thing shut down as fast as possible – and bring those Girls to me, dead or alive!"

"Yes sir!" he concurred.

"This meeting is adjourned, and if I turn on the TV in half an hour to see kidnappers being extolled on the screens, you will know that I am President of Ghana," he declaimed finally and dismissed his Cabinet.

On their way out the door, the IGP said to his two senior officers along the marbled corridors to the exit, "Set up a parallel unit to the Cabinet," he ordered with a sidelong look at anyone that might be eavesdropping. "If we let the politicians run this show, bodies will start turning up. I want the unit set up at HQ with TV screens and surveillance patchworks on the double. We need to be up and running before the Girls realise they won't be live and decide to show us some firepower."

Both men nodded and hurried along after a look at their watches.

The time read 09:22.

The reaction to news of the government's orders to broadcasters to shut down the transmissions was swift and condemnatory. Twitter got lit with an angry Ghanaian population criticizing the government directives and calling for the President's resignation, not only for failing to find the judges but also for thinking about shutting down broadcast of the all-important trial of a rapist scum. While the population was split on Duncan King's guilt, with every prior rapist rooting for the embattled celebrity, the greater majority believed that the Girls had a just cause, and to leave the matter of the morality of their actions for the future, so long as no one got hurt. The hashtag *HangDuncanKing* reached ten million retweets in five minutes and made life uncomfortable for the Communications Ministry.

Atukwei and Amadu were following all these developments from the CTU Conference Room at Police Headquarters in Accra. In a mere matter of minutes, they had redrawn the conference room to as close to the Cabinet Room as they could. Amadu had no idea what the IGP needed a parallel war room for, but his tone had tolerated no objections, so they had worked their butts off with Estate and IT to make it happen. Seven minutes to the time of the first telecast they had it all ready, and that's when the IGP walked in. With him were the six highest ranking officers of the Ghana Police Service. They were followed by a harried man with bushy hair neither of them had ever met. The man pulled a heavy cart behind him and surveyed the new room.

"Adequate," he sniffed.

The IGP then turned to point to the stranger, "Everyone meet Dr. Moses Obuobi. He is a psychologist and criminologist from the University of Ghana. He will be assisting us in the investigations."

Amadu looked skeptically at the man in faded corduroy trousers, a checkered shirt and a tie that had irrevocably lost its colour. He didn't remember when he had last seen anyone wear corduroy.

"How will he be assisting us?" Atukwei spoke what everyone else was thinking.

"I can get into their heads," the man answered casually in a stuttering voice before the IGP could respond. "And let you know what they are thinking before they think – you know, that sort of thing – and help you grab them before the President's 72-hour deadline."

"And what are they thinking right now?" Amadu asked before Atukwei could get in a shot.

"They are thinking of not letting Duncan King off the hook no matter the verdict. That man is as good as dead," Obuobi said matter-of-factly.

"You know this *how*?" the IGP asked, startled.

The man shrugged. "I don't sense that the justices are in any danger, or that anyone else is, but I'll bet my last trousers on the sense that Duncan King isn't walking out of this alive. If we all focus on *that* one fact, we might solve this problem faster than you can imagine." He paused briefly, then added thoughtfully, "He and his lawyer, but the sense of hostility isn't ominously towards the lawyer but the rapist."

"Alleged rapist," one of the Commissioners of Police reminded him after quite the pause.

"Of course," the man agreed, but his tone was profoundly skeptical.

Amadu looked at the academic again, taking in his badly kept afro, his wire-rimmed glasses and darting neck. The weirdo didn't seem the least self-conscious, and his years of police experience did not register any bullshit in the man's demeanour. Atukwei, when they exchanged glances, looked just as baffled.

"The 72-hours was not addressed to us," Atukwei told the man, referring to his earlier mention of the deadline the President had issued.

"Then we best get started if you plan to catch them in 48," the man said to him.

He then pulled his cart right into the middle of the room, folded his shirt sleeve and said, "Let's get cranking. Get the Attorney-General on the line!"

"What?!" A dozen voices asked at the same time.

"The Girls control everything," he complained with his shoulders in the air and his open palm facing upward. "We don't even know where they are. We need to take back a little bit of control, and for that to happen, I need the Attorney-General," he demanded insistently.

"You are getting ahead of yourself, aren't you, Dr. Obuobi?" Amadu told him pointedly. "I don't know who you think you are, but we have no way of contacting the Girls; they are the ones who contact us, and they won't even be calling *us* –"

"– That's exactly why I need the Attorney-General," Obuobi interjected. "And please call me Moses. Obuobi is my father's name."

Amadu just stared at him.

"We need to find a way for the Girls to call the President before the proceedings begin. The pretext for that call will be to replace the deputy Attorney-General with the A-G herself who alone must, under these circumstances, have the constitutional obligation to argue the Republic's position before the Court."

"Where did you find this chump?" Atukwei asked the IGP disapprovingly.

"You forget yourself," the IGP retorted threateningly. And then, turning to Amadu, he ordered, "Call the War Room and repeat Dr. Obuobi-Please-Call-Me-Moses's demands." Then he grabbed a chair around the glass desk and waited before the surprise left his officers' faces.

With a shrug, Amadu made the call on the central speakerphone. It took a full two minutes before they reached the President, who had remained in the War Room with the Vice President, the Communications Minister and the Attorney-General. He almost hung up the phone when Amadu repeated Obuobi's request. Only the voice of the IGP gave him pause.

"First off, who is Obuobi?" the President asked the IGP after his frantic shout to not end the call had been heeded.

The IGP made a sign for the weird man to speak.

"I am a double PhD criminologist and psychologist with the University of Ghana, Mr. President. The US Embassy reached out and asked me to help on the request of your Communications Minister, sir, and –"

"– The University of Ghana can hardly count as outside help, now, can it?" the President said irritably. "Why do you think it is smart to send my A-G into this madness when the deputy A-G has already been kidnapped? You have five seconds to make sense!"

Obuobi seemed unfazed when he responded, "The request for your Attorney-General to be allowed to represent the government in this trial cannot be refused because the Republic has a right, even in this charade of a trial, to put its best foot forward. The Girls will see no harm in the request, and they *will* grant it."

President Offei's customary glower was in place, sensed in his voice over the speakerphone when he asked, "They will grant it to what end?"

"It will give us the opportunity of a foot in their door – or their window, depending on the nomenclature you are comfortable with. So far, *they* call the shots. You can't even speak to them unless they call you. With this plan, we can take back a little bit of control that could aid in triangulating their location and rescuing the Justices."

The President said, "If you know that we have no way of contacting them, how do you suggest we get their attention enough to invite them to kidnap my Attorney-General?"

"By shutting down all their channels on the hour and forcing them to call you with ultimatums towards restoring the telecasts."

"Dr. Obuobi," the President demanded acidly, "What in the hell do you think we've been up to all this while?"

"If that was your plan all along, then the blackout must happen on the hour," Obuobi explained calmly. "Once the shutdown goes into effect, I expect their first reaction to be a call to you with one threat or the other. That's when you can respond with the demand to have your

A-G as Counsel for the Republic in exchange for restoring the broadcasts. It's not an unreasonable request, and one that can easily be granted if we insist the A-G will be representing the government on videoconferencing."

"To what end exactly?" the Vice President's voice came through the phone at that point. "Why does it make sense to you to introduce the Attorney-General to this sham of a trial when we plan to shut down the broadcasts with prejudice?"

But President Offei had already had it with Obuobi's talking round in circles. He gave one disgusted grunt and, cursing, terminated the call.

CHAPTER 11
Ground Zero
Thursday, 14th March; 9.59 A.M.

THE COURT WAS seated for opening arguments ten minutes to the hour. Today was more about constitutional arguments than about him, yet Duncan King felt the same debilitating fear he'd felt when the Police had knocked on his door at the Gold Coast Hotel suite ten years ago with the firm invitation to the Airport Police Station on charges of sexual assault and rape. The way his heart had thundered in his chest, he'd felt he might suffer a heart attack. And now, with the countdown timer moving inexorably to the top of the hour, he felt those heart-stopping constrictions again.

There was a bank of about twenty TV sets along the walls of the amphitheatre, and each was tuned into a different channel in Ghana's capital. Several laptop screens were lined up on desks at the base of the judges' bench, and seated at their consoles were an all-female team of technicians, one for each of the seven justices. They were disgorging innumerable lines of code towards running the same countdown timer on various internet sites and channels. These faced the bench, and only the newly abducted Court Reporter faced the gallery. He could count at least twenty-five cameras being operated from upstairs in a glassed Press Box. Apparently, no resources had been spared towards his public disgrace.

He was seated a row behind his lawyer, the State Prosecutor and the deputy Attorney-General on the left side of the small amphitheatre with his cousin, Larry King, who had also been abducted by the bitches.

The balls on these girls; the *sheer balls* on them to think to get away with all these!

The seats were comfortable, and in no way like the hard benches he had sat on ten years ago in the Accra High Court. He hadn't been on much talking terms with Larry since then. He'd expected his cousin to have unflinchingly corroborated his side of the story when the issue first came up but the *wormsie* had wanted no part of it. His lawyer had told him then that Larry's neutrality was better than turning prosecution witness, but what good was a neutral to him when his life and freedom was at stake? He had felt deeply betrayed and hadn't spoken to him much since then.

Now, it seemed the bitch was determined to reunite him with everyone in his past, but the joke was on her. Larry wasn't going to snitch

INVIOLABLE 54

any more now than he could have snitched a decade ago because Larry knew nothing and couldn't say crap.

He straightened his sterling-colored tie and assumed his god-Emcee pose. One blogger had called him a fashion toady for dressing in multicoloured hues to the opening of the trial ten years ago but he, the fashion god, was not in the habit of explaining his wardrobe to a frumpy and tawdry press. That attempt at trial had gone nowhere.

And neither would this.

There were some annoyances to this whole boloney that he couldn't shake off as easily though, try as he could. Even before the Chief Justice had banged his gavel, comments running under the live feed of the countdown on social media were calling him all kinds of predatory vermin. He'd no idea where all this would lead to in the end, but if the bitch wanted a piece of him, let her do her worst. He was the King, the god Emcee. He would take the limelight and the shine that came with it. This was his arena, his turf.

Camera. Lights. Mic. And action. That was all about him.

But none of all his narcissism prevented the fear from wicking up from the pit of his stomach to his throat when the Chief Justice banged the gavel at 10.

Why the heck was he banging a gavel for? It's not like this was any formal Court that required proper court formalities, was it? But it wasn't so much the formalities that bothered him. The sound of the gavel had upset something in his loins so badly that it was all he could do to halt the warm drop of liquid in his drawers. He could tell that it wasn't enough to be visible from where he sat next to his cousin, but the fact that the sound had brought a urinary incontinence to his sphincter, however briefly, was more than he could bear to think about.

A blip caught his eye like a flash. It was just at the time when the Chief Justice was about to give his opening speech for the trial. Startled, he looked at the TV screens and saw that all of them had turned blank. It couldn't be a power trip because the lights and air conditioning were still on.

"What's going on?" he heard the Chief Justice ask the bitch and her Girls on the right of the room where she sat with her lawyer, another one of the abducting bitches whose name he did not readily recall, and some academic of some repute, according to his lawyer Ansah Premo. The bitch seemed unsure of herself for once, and that pleased him incalculably.

A technician entered and whispered something to her. She looked up at the Chief Justice and said, "We apologise, Your Lordship, but it seems the government has shut down all the TV stations running our telecast, and has taken down YouTube, Facebook and Twitter where we have been running the live feeds."

Way to go, Mr. Government, Duncan King thought.

"It's the government's prerogative, isn't it?" the Chief Justice demanded, seemingly unconcerned since he had already elicited the pledge from the abductors that close-up shots of their faces will never be beamed to the watching public. "How does it affect our proceedings?"

"The proceedings will continue, Your Lordships," Efe came in at that point as Counsel to Asabea, "but we request a fifteen-minute break to confer on the way forward since the public is as essential to our pursuit of justice as this Court."

"The Republic objects, my Lords," the deputy Attorney-General butted in, rising from his seat before the Chief Justice could respond to Efe. "If plaintiff could not anticipate that government reaction would be appropriate and ill-disposed towards her, then she has no business wasting our time and the time of Your Lordships in this sham of her orchestration. While I understand her craving for time to lick her wounds, this Court owes her no quarters in that regard. Let the constitutional arguments proceed, and, in the unlikely event she prevails, then may she seek repose in the break this Court may grant when it rises to ponder and rule over the issues."

Several of the TV screens came alive just then. During his protestation, the technicians had called into the War Room of President Offei. The look he directed at Asabea on the screen was one of self-congratulation.

Looking apologetically at the Chief Justice, Asabea said to the President over the video call, "I see you have been busy, Mr. President."

"You left me no choice, Miss," President Offei replied smugly.

"In spite of all the evidence suggesting a counter approach to your current course, you seem willing to test my resolve, Your Excellency," Asabea said gravely.

"You must think I'm afraid of you, Miss Asabea," the President said to her haughtily, and then he suddenly mellowed, "But I must sadly think about the lives of the judges and people you have abducted."

Asabea and Efe blinked.

The President continued, "While I have faith in my deputy Attorney-General to represent the Republic, even in this criminal enterprise, I feel this country will best be represented by the Attorney-General herself. That is the only condition I will impose to restore your telecasts and lift the ban on YouTube, Facebook and Twitter."

Asabea exchanged a startled look with Efe, who did the same with the rest of the Girls toting weapons in the upper gallery.

"You are offering to restore all channels in exchange for your Attorney-General to represent you in this trial?" Efe asked warily.

"I believe that is what I said," the President said.

Asabea stared pensively for a while and then asked, "Why do you think we will end the Court's proceedings to come and find your Attorney-General – including the risk that this might be a trap – and return her here to represent you when there are things we can do from here to force you to restore all channels?" she asked the President.

"Things like what?" the President asked.

Asabea shrugged, "I could blow up your house, for example," she said matter-of-factly. "Or the Airport."

"All of which would be bloody, mess up your reputation and put your current public support in jeopardy," the President pointed out. "And you won't even have to bleed for my Attorney-General in case of a trap. She will argue remotely if you connect with my comms-systems. No one needs get hurt, and this is a simple request."

"A simple request that could enable your experts to hack into our systems and triangulate our location," Owuraku pointed out from his seat by Asabea, to everyone's surprise. "I apologise, Mr. President, but we aren't that stupid."

President Offei was taken aback momentarily, but he shrugged it off and said, "Mr. Umaru Tanko is not authorised to represent the Government of Ghana in this trial. The Attorney-General is, and you cannot force Tanko to speak when I haven't authorized him to. So, whatever your fears are, either you patch my office through to yours so your trial can resume, or we can keep threatening each other."

Chief Superintendent Atukwei was not one to give credit even when credit was due, but when the networks were shut down on the hour, even he couldn't help but stare in admiration at the weird man sitting with his multicoloured socks flashing on his skinny feet atop the glass conference table at Police Headquarters.

"Twitter, Facebook and YouTube have all been shut down too," he heard his colleague Amadu tell the IGP in surprise. "How did the government pull that off?"

"By shutting down the internet itself," Obuobi told them, pulling his feet from off the table and setting a few other implements by the first group of electronic gizmos that cluttered his side of the table.

"Someone, please call the Attorney-General now."

"Call her yourself," the IGP told him and handed over a mobile device and a number he had scribbled on a piece of paper.

"Good idea, actually," Obuobi wasted no time at all, connected the mobile device to his computer and dialed. The President was on the line, to his surprise.

"Very good thinking, whoever you are," President Offei congratulated him. "Those criminals have asked for fifteen minutes to mull our request over. Now, shouldn't you be here in the War Room?"

"That is not the plan, your Excellency," he replied and proceeded to tell him what he was thinking.

"Are you sure?" Attorney-General Patricia Quayson asked over the phone.

"Those girls have already hacked into your War Room and have eyes in there. If we turn up, they will know what we are up to," Obuobi explained over the phone with exaggerated patience. "All I need is one uninterrupted hour," he finished confidently.

"What if it doesn't work?" the Vice President demanded.

Obuobi shrugged.

"It will or it won't. I don't think we have time to get into the varying dimensionality of quantum probabilities right now."

The Septet and Owuraku were up in the Press Box overlooking the amphitheatre. With them was a young woman showing a complicated patchwork of computer networks on a screen. Below them, the Justices, the deputy Attorney-General and the President's Counsel were in conversation that carried up silently into the Box. But that was not the focus of anyone in the Box.

"Why did we need to come up here?" Owuraku began as soon as everyone arrived. "Surely, you anticipated that the government would shut down the internet, didn't you?"

"We did," Asabea told him calmly and looked at her watch. "The internet will be restored in five minutes, and there's nothing the government can do from then on to shut it down again."

"How so?"

INVIOLABLE   58

"It's harder to explain," the woman with the screen told him, "but by shutting down the internet, the government has actually handed over control of the internet to us."

Owuraku gave the woman an amused look.

"I am familiar with neural network theory, my dear," he said, "but I believe you when you say it's complicated." Then, turning to Asabea he asked, "So, if you'll take control of the government's power to shut down our public trial, why are we here?"

"We are here to discuss whether to grant the government's request to replace the deputy A-G with his boss," Efe said to him.

"What about my concern that doing so will give them a foothold into your network?" Owuraku asked them.

"Do you think that is possible, Regina?" Aisha asked the woman with the screen, smiling tightly.

She turned her screen to them and said, "I completed a sweep of all available nodes in the War Room's networks half-a-minute ago," Regina replied confidently, showing them a green indicator on her screen. "They have nothing inside that room that could back-hack us."

"What about from external sources?" Owuraku asked her skeptically.

"Anything that can hurt us would have to come from within the War Room itself," Regina told him.

Owuraku chewed thoughtfully on his lower lip for a second and then asked, "Can you do the sweep again? Can you categorize every single device sitting on their network and let us know what each one is doing exactly?"

"There's no need for that, Regina," Asabea said and then turned to Owuraku. "I understand your concerns, but I have no fears in that regard. Regina and her team are good at this. My concern is whether we should let the A-G represent the State on the trial instead of her deputy."

"That's exactly the reason I do not think it's wise to let her in," Owuraku told her, not unkindly. "The deputy A-G is the best government lawyer there is. Heck, he is even more competent than his boss. Pull out every case the government has been litigating in court over the past four years. Every one of them has Tanko all over it. Suddenly, and especially in a trial that it fears seven of its highest judges might die, Mrs. Quayson is the government's best foot forward? I'm not buying that hokum."

Nhyira asked him with a lot of curiosity, "What are you saying?"

Turning to her, he said, "I suspect that the government has found a way to hack into your systems independently of the War Room, and this request is the conduit through which that can be done. It's the only way this request makes sense."

"And I am telling you the government cannot do that," Asabea said to him with a slight hint of frustration. "It is impossible to hack us from outside their War Room. Let's not waste time on that and focus rather on the government's request."

Owuraku frowned slightly and tried another way. "If you ask me," he said, feigning diffidence at that point, "everyone you need is here for the trial. Isn't it because you believed Tanko was a better fit for this that you had him, and not the substantial A-G, abducted?"

Bubuné said thoughtfully, "It was more a matter of convenience than competence. We determined it was easier abducting Tanko, a deputy Minister, than it was grabbing Patricia."

"Besides, Patricia is a woman," Oye told him, "We didn't want to inconvenience women in this affair more than we needed to."

"Which is all really beside the point, Owuraku," Asabea said firmly. "We have the deputy Attorney-General here to represent the government in a trial we have orchestrated. Howbeit reluctantly, the government says if we want the trial, it must choose who should represent it. Shouldn't we agree? That way, the government itself will be giving legitimacy to our cause, wouldn't it?"

"I don't think you need government legitimacy. Besides, the same government that is asking to be represented by the Attorney General herself will show us no mercy if they found us. They are not giving anything away unless they are getting something in return."

Asabea rolled her eyes up at that.

Owuraku stared at her in surprise. "Did you just roll your eyes at me?" he asked incredulously.

Asabea and the girls were taken aback by the intensity of his inquiry, and Asabea made a show of her guilt at that during the uncomfortable silence that ensued, but the harm had already been done. Owuraku shook his head and walked out of the Box.

"That was totally uncalled for," Efe said censurably to Asabea.

"I'm sorry but I got a little tired of the back and forth," Asabea said ruefully.

"Aren't you going to get him back?" Dede asked her.

"Internet is back, and in our control!" Regina announced just then.

Asabea beamed happily and asked her team, "What's our decision?"

"I'm inclined to agree with Owuraku," Dede announced, and then she turned apologetically to Regina. "It's not that I don't believe you'll keep our network safe, but I wonder what the real motive is for the government's desire to replace the more competent Umaru Tanko. It may not be to back-hack us, but what if it's for a more sinister reason we haven't thought about? I generally feel we should refuse the government, especially now that control of the internet is irrevocably in our hands."

"Anyone else feels that way?" Asabea asked all round.

"I don't care either way," Aisha said with a shrug. "So long as we remain un-hackable."

Her sentiments were shared all round, so Asabea said, "Alright then. It is my determination that we allow the government this one request. I believe that doing so allows the watching public to see that we are serious about enacting a fair and equitable trial."

"What are we going to do about Owuraku though?" Dede asked again. "He seemed pretty upset."

"I'll talk to him," Asabea promised and led the way out of the Box.

CHAPTER 12
Ground Zero
Thursday, 14th March; 10.22 A.M.

THE COURT RECONVENED at the sound of a bell in the amphitheatre. President Offei had taken exceptional offense at learning that his government was not the one that had reversed the internet shut down. The transmissions were back online at 10:12 on the internet and via the airwaves. After that loss of control, his threats to his Communications Minister, and through him to the Director of the National Communications Authority, no longer mattered. The ISPs could not undo the hack without shutting down their operations in their entirety, and doing so meant that not even the President could make a phone call. The President had ordered a complete shutdown initially, but his Minister for National Security had insisted that would jeopardize much more than the government could chew, and the idea was quickly stymied.

The Girls had the government by the balls.

Literally.

Only Obuobi and his team of counter terror officers seemed unfazed by the development, so it was a furious Cabinet that watched the proceedings on TV and online. The Attorney-General was connected on the video call as was agreed.

In the amphitheatre, Asabea sat in the Plaintiff's section with Efe. Every now and then she would look up at Owuraku who sat quietly in the gallery with the rest of the armed Girls. The Chief Justice had prohibited the carrying of guns near the proscenium where he and the six justices sat behind their long, coffee-coloured bench. After she'd left the Press Box, she and the Girls had found Owuraku by the water dispenser in the tiled walkway connecting the Box to the gallery. There had been no pretense in the confident way she'd walked towards him. She'd stopped in front of him and looked into his eyes, surprised by the steel she'd seen in them.

"I am sorry, Kuuku," she'd said simply, using the endearing form of his name only she could call him by. "That was completely inappropriate and disrespectful of me, what I did back there."

"Yes, it was," he'd agreed gravely. "What was your decision?"

Looking even more miserable, she'd said, "We decided to allow the A-G to replace her deputy."

Owuraku had looked then at Efe and said, "I don't know much law, but the flaw I see in that decision, Counsel, is that the A-G now has the right to demand a continuance."

"We have already asked the Justices to suspend much of the High Court Civil Procedure Rules, as amended, since allowing the usual eight and fourteen days for the back and forth between filing of writs and statements, as well as the corresponding responses, would prolong this trial more than is needed," Efe had replied.

"She would need at least 48 hours," Owuraku had told her, and had then turned to Asabea. "If she asks for it, it will make the bench a bit uncomfortable not to grant it. Abducted or not, the court cannot force a newly appearing defense to argue its case one minute after it got the case."

Asabea had chewed on her lower lip in response. Efe hadn't looked too sure, herself.

"I think one way to go around this is to allow both Patricia and Umaru Tanko to represent the government in the interim," he had proffered thoughtfully. "That way, the continuance can be waived, and the deputy A-G will be permitted to continue with the understanding that he would bring his boss up to speed. Of course, allowing this collaboration between two A-Gs makes it more and more ridiculous to have agreed to Patricia; we all know that Umaru is the competent one here. I do not want to gainsay your decision, ladies, but I will hate to be the one to tell you that I told you so."

"We understand how you feel, Kuuku, but rest assured that we are in no danger of getting hacked," Asabea had tried to reassure him.

He'd looked unconvinced but had let the matter drop. And then he'd told them he'd feel much better watching proceedings from the gallery. That had profoundly disturbed something in Asabea, but Owuraku had already walked away towards the gallery.

She'd only been able to exchange a worried glance with her team until they'd heard the bell ring in the amphitheatre.

The Attorney-General wasted no time as soon as the Court granted her leave to directly represent the government, to verbally move the motion for an immediate continuance in accordance with the country's High Court Civil Procedure Rules. But it wasn't Efe that rose to challenge her. The Chief Justice was in no mood for games.

"Counsel," he boomed, "if the Executive Arm caused your personal appearance for dilatory purposes, let me nip that in the bud right now," he said sternly. "The pleadings before us cut to the chase, and the demands of Rule 7A of Order 32 as inserted in Constitutional Instrument 87, as well as Rule 2, Subsection C of Order 34 have already been met. Hasn't it occurred to you that we could very well have had this trial start three days ago if not for adherence to the rules? This is the reason we viewed your entrance with suspicion, although we do not impugn your right to do so. Your deputy is here. It is our ruling that you and he collaborate on representing the government in this action. Do I make myself clear?"

Taken aback momentarily, Attorney-General Patricia Quayson replied on the screen, "As it pleases the Court, my Lords, but the Republic would like to register its objection to the constitution of this Court."

"How so?" the Chief Justice asked.

"The Republic avers that this Court, as constituted, is improper and constitutionally unfit to consider the issues for which Plaintiff has caused the actions to be instigated. All decisions will become a nullity in the end."

"Many things might become a nullity in the end, Counsel," Justice Vincent Kotei, the third in seniority at the Court piped in. "We could all be dead in the end, blown to bit and pieces like the State Prosecutor's house. Or the Executive Arm could track Plaintiff down and serve her brute justice, or have every decision reviewed by a panel of nine. However, this is the sandbox we all find ourselves in, Counsel. Let's move along already."

Efe smiled slightly at that, rose and said, "Plaintiff has no objections to your rulings on both objections, my Lords," she finished respectfully. "We are most grateful."

"Alright then. Is Counsel for Plaintiff ready to proceed?" the Chief Justice asked.

"We are, my Lords."

"And the Republic?" he asked, glancing once at the Attorney-General and then looking pointedly at the deputy A-G.

After a brief ocular consultation between the deputy A-G and his boss on the screen, Umaru Tanko responded, "the Republic stands at the ready, my Lords."

"And the Second Defendant?"

Ansah Premo addressed the Court at that point.

"My Lords, we stand at the ready also. I would however request of the Court to bring the first Defendant, and by that, I mean the Attorney-General, up to speed on the motions accepted at our pretrial conferences, as well as bring the watching public up to speed concerning the second Defendant's joinder."

"Thank you, Counsel," the Chief Justice said and turned to the cameras. "At our Case Management Conferences under Order 2, Subsection B of C.I 87, this Court by a 6:1 decision granted leave, upon right application for the joinder of Mr. Duncan King, acting by counsel, Ansah Premo to the suit, as second Defendant. The general rule, of course, has been that the Court may add all persons whose presence before the Court is necessary in order to enable it effectually and completely adjudicate upon and settle all questions involved in the cause or matter before it. The purpose of this joinder is to enable all matters in controversy as outlined by both the Plaintiff's pleadings and the Defendants' responses, to be completely and effectually determined once and for all; and it was the majority's decision that Mr. Duncan King rightfully fit the description of an appropriate joinder."

There had been quite the debate during the pretrial conferences. Duncan King had vehemently opposed joining the action as a defendant. His lawyer had insisted that all his client had wanted to do was enjoy his holidays at a beach in Accra sipping on the nearest available pair of breasts. That wasn't what Ansah Premo had said, of course – he'd mentioned cocktails – but that was what Duncan King had thought he should have said. He had not consented to being kidnapped; how could he then be forced into a legal proceeding? But the Judges had ruled that in his absence, the court could not accord complete relief between the existing parties; nor could they overlook his interests regarding the action since he was so situated that disposing of the action in his absence may, as a practical matter impair or impede his ability to protect that interest.

Turning to Efe, the Chief Justice ordered, "Let's hear it from the Plaintiff."

Efe bowed formerly and addressed the Bench.

"My Lords," she began, "I seek the leave of this Court to invite the first and second Defendants to stipulate to the following facts."

As the memories rushed back, as they inevitably did every time the events of a decade ago came up for discussion, Asabea locked her eyes on to Owuraku's eyes for the entire duration of Efe's telling. That was probably the reason she didn't break down nervously this time. And kind Kuuku, although obviously unhappy with her earlier episode nevertheless made his gaze available to her across the amphitheater's space. He knew he was the strength she needed.

It was ten years ago and three months to the day. Saturday, December

27. No way she was going to forget that date. She and Abena Asaa, her cousin, had decided to participate in the Accra Fashion Week organized in part by one of Abena's friends. While the guests had yet to arrive, the three of them had decided to stroll around the hotel hosting the event – the glamorous Gold Coast Hotel. They'd run into Duncan King right at the porte-cochère who had flagrantly sized them both up, whistled and said, "What *glamazons* you tall girls are!"

Together, an insistent Duncan King had had them return to the lobby, and he had introduced her and Abena to his cousin Larry King and Billy Blanks, another organizer of the fashion show, as his new friends. He'd sworn there and then to both Larry and Billy that he would make the two beauties the faces of the Ghana Tourism Campaign.

Duncan King had been the star of the show. Upon his declaration, a celebrity blogger had appeared from seemingly nowhere and had taken photos of her and Abena with King. It wasn't long until all five of them – Asabea, Duncan King, Larry King, Abena and Billy – had taken the elevator to a suite on one of the hotel's floors. Three men and two teenagers.

This had been the reason both had refused the drinks Duncan King had offered in the plush, mahogany-coloured living room of the suite. Duncan had left for the bathroom and had returned shortly after to ask Asabea to assist him make-up for his presentation at the show. Asabea had seen no harm at all in the request and had followed him into the bathroom. As soon as she'd entered, Duncan King had locked the door behind him, pulled her by the hand, held her close and pawed at her. Alarmed, she'd pulled away, but the horny bastard would have none of that. He'd gotten aggressive, turned her forcefully around and bent her over the wash sink. Then he'd attempted to penetrate her from behind, pushing her skirt and panties aside.

She'd resisted some more at that point until he'd grabbed and twisted her arm behind her to keep her hands from blocking his manhood. She'd screamed out in pain and had begged him to stop. She'd even let him know she was a virgin and she'd done nothing of the sort before, but that had seemed to have inflamed the son-of-a-bitch some more.

Unable to stop him without breaking her own arm, she'd tried another tack. She'd asked him if he had a condom, and he'd replied in the negative. Then she'd pleaded that he found one, in the hope that doing so might free her so she could escape from the bathroom, but Duncan King would not budge. He'd forced her legs apart and had brought his weight crashing on her lower back. Then he'd taken advantage of her scream and temporal paralysis from the pain to force her panties down. And then he had penetrated her roughly from behind.

She'd bled like a stuck pig through the ordeal, and blood had stained the tiled floor of the bathroom. After he was done with her, gratifying himself twice, he'd offered her toilet paper to stanch the bleeding. It had not worked and soon, the tissue paper had turned crimson. He'd then suggested she sat on the toilet bowl for a while and allow the blood to flow. He'd given her more tissue when the blood had refused to stop after a couple of minutes while he'd washed blood off his own penis, promising to buy her an emergency contraceptive pill so she wouldn't have to saddle him with his bastard later on.

Someone had knocked on the bathroom door just then. Duncan King had responded in a way as not to arouse suspicion and had urgently asked her to clean up. She'd flushed all the blood and stained toilet paper after that, washed her face and left the bathroom with him. She had cried uncontrollably in the living room as soon as she'd set eyes on Abena and narrated the entire incidence to her right there in front of Larry King and Billy Blanks. Duncan King had disappeared into the bedroom as soon as she'd let out the first uncontrollable sob on her cousin's shoulder.

Abena had wasted no time. She'd called Owuraku because Asabea could do nothing then but cry, and Owuraku had set in motion the string of right decisions that had gotten the Airport Police Station, the constabulary responsible for the jurisdiction of the Gold Coast Hotel area convinced beyond all doubt that Duncan King was a teenage raping son-of-a-bitch.

He'd lied to the Police, of course. He'd claimed that the sex was consensual, but the medical report had spoken otherwise. The report had been unequivocal when it had declared that "the victim was not previously sexually active, and there were abrasions on both labia minora and majora, hyperemic redness at the external urethral opening and the posterior part of the vaginal opening, with hymen torn at multiple places plus pinpoint bleeding areas and the presence of spermatozoa."

The last word brought Asabea back into the amphitheatre. As she blinked Owuraku back into sharp focus, her heart soared. She had not wept during Efe's recounting, and that had been the one thing they all had feared would happen during the trial. She still held Owuraku's gaze; his eyes had not once left her face during the painful flashbacks.

"My Lords," Efe was saying, "these were the facts presented at trial, and bail was denied the second Defendant twice until two weeks later, when the Human Rights Court admitted him to bail on humanitarian grounds, citing ill-health. Not long after, the State Prosecutor entered a nolle prosequi. Due to the physical and psychological trauma associated with the alleged sexual assault, the victim was not in the right frame of mind to appear before the court, the Prosecution said.

"If Defendants would stipulate to these as the facts that were the bases of the Republic's Bill of Indictment, then we are happy to proceed, My Lords."

There was some silence after that. There was no denying the anger on the faces of the three female justices on the bench, however hard they tried to school their facial expressions, and one could tell by how they kept glancing in Duncan King's direction.

"My Lords," Umaru Tanko, his voice seemingly subdued after Efe's masterful telling of the facts, took the floor while consulting with a sheaf of papers on his table. "If we add that the Attorney General believed that it was not in the best interest of the victim and the prosecution to present her before the court at that point in time, and that the Republic reserved the right to reopen prosecution in the future, then the Republic will stipulate."

"Very well," the Chief Justice acknowledged.

"My Lords," Ansah Premo spoke up, rising. "Plaintiff failed to include that the complainant in the Bill of Indictment wrote a two-page letter indicating her disinterest in the case and demanding to withdraw. We would like for that to be added before we can agree to stipulate."

Efe rose to counter. "My Lords, no such letter was available in the dossier at the Attorney-General's Department, or in the State's filing at the High Court's registry. Even worse, my Lords, no such letter was filed by Counsel for the second Defendant at the Court's registry either. That letter rightly becomes controverting evidence."

The Chief Justice looked to the deputy Attorney-General.

"This is the first we are hearing of a two-page letter, my Lords," Umaru Tanko informed the Court. "We must agree with Plaintiff's position to exclude."

"Why do you want to now introduce an item that was not available at the termination of the trial, Mr. Premo?" the Chief Justice asked.

Ansah Premo consulted briefly with Duncan King and said, "My apologies, my Lords, but I was under the impression and believed same to be true that the alleged victim's letter of withdrawal was the basis of the nolle prosequi. If the first Defendant avers that they have sighted no such letter, then we are happy to stipulate. It will not hurt our defense to stipulate now and introduce evidence that strengthens my client's support for the nolle prosequi in stipulation or, even better, a complete acquittal in the future," he finished haughtily.

"Duly noted," the Chief Justice declared. He consulted with his colleagues for a full five minutes, scribbling judiciously on a legal pad.

"The joint memorandum of issues filed by all parties are adopted by this Court for determination as follows," he said finally. "First, whether the State had all the evidence it needed to secure a conviction, and for which its exercise of the power to enter a nolle prosequi was arbitrary; and second, in the event of the first issue being granted, whether this Court should proceed to quash the nolle prosequi on that determination and order a trial."

After careful consideration of their statement of claims to ensure that the issues as determined now for deliberation did not detract from the core points of their writ, Efe rose up and said, "Plaintiff concurs with the Court, my Lords. We are grateful."

"First Defendant concurs with the Court, my Lords."

"Second Defendant concurs, my Lords."

"Very well then," the Chief Justice declaimed. "Based on this memorandum, plaintiff has 24 hours to submit their memoranda to these issues, and defendants have 48 hours to submit theirs in opposition. We will have a third day for verification of documents, and the Court will reconvene on Tuesday, March 19 at ten o'clock in the forenoon to hear oral arguments. We are adjourned."

Major Philip Hanson was out the door before the Humvee stopped fully. He took the six flights of stairs to what he had heard was the parallel War Room set up by the Police Counterterror Unit, while his aides tried to keep up. In the courtyard half his platoon were at various levels of disembarkation from their trucks.

The Police Headquarters had seen little renovation since he was last here. The whole complex on Ring Road East was the centre of corruption, superseded only by the Seat of Government. The last perception of corruption index suggested that the Ghana Police Service processed one million, two hundred and forty-eight thousand, one hundred-and-sixty-dollars' worth of bribes a year.

There was nothing in the Service's outward infrastructure to show for it.

He knocked once and entered. He saluted smartly when he saw the IGP at the tail end of the glass table.

"Good afternoon, Sir!"

"Carry on, Major," the IGP replied gravely. "What brings you by?"

"I am informed that the best way I can get my judges back is to align with you, sir," he announced respectfully.

"Who told you that?" the IGP and the two Chief Superintendents intoned at the same time.

"If you two don't mind," the IGP said irritably to them and then turned on the Major. "How did you know about this Room?"

"The Chief of Army Intelligence, sir," Hanson stated matter-of-factly as he marched nearer the glass table to where Obuobi was intently poring over lines of code on a computer. "He said if any of our agencies were going to find my judges, it would be you, and to put all of the Army's resources at your disposal towards that end."

Right then the speakerphone rang.

Obuobi reached out a hand in irritation and answered.

It was the President.

"Yes?" he demanded over the speakerphone. "Any luck?"

"P-p-plenty luck," Obuobi answered quickly and pressed the call termination button.

"What the frack?" The IGP demanded, surprised that he would cut the call on the Commander in Chief.

"I need a fifteen-minute cellular black-out to triangulate," he explained and switched and activated the flight mode button on the speakerphone. "Kindly do the same for your phones," he further ordered without looking away from his screens.

"What about the President?" the IGP demanded, his face turning red.

"Let him wait."

"Let him *wait*?" the IGP was *this* close to exploding.

Major Hanson had however moved in to undo the disrespect to the President. He stretched out his hand towards the speakerphone when Obuobi, his fingers maintaining a frenetic pace on his equipment said, "Turn the phone back on and you'll never find your judges in time!"

The Major's hand froze. He looked inquiringly at the IGP who shrugged helplessly, himself unsure what to do. The President would have a fit if he eventually got through, but Obuobi kept working on his equipment. All kinds of light flashed on the screens as lines and lines of code interacted with each other. Despite the air conditioning, sweat broke out on his brow and his concentration was impeccable hacking into the Septet's seemingly hackproof network. He kept glancing at the clock in the middle of the glass conference table, and the more the

INVIOLABLE

seconds ticked, the more frenzied his typing became until his fingers became a blur on his keyboard.

"Done!" he exclaimed with a few seconds to spare to the quarter-hour. "You can call the President now."

"And tell him what exactly?" the IGP asked sourly.

"That we have a window into their network."

"So, we know where they are?" Amadu asked the weird man skeptically.

"We will know exactly where they are if anyone within a hundred metres of them makes a call on a cellular phone or uses an unencrypted line or approaches that window with a car's GPS or any other device's GPS."

"That could take weeks," Major Hanson told him unhappily.

"Or seconds, if one of them slips up," Obuobi said to him.

Having turned off airplane mode, the speakerphone immediately rang.

The IGP pushed his chair forward and shoved the device towards Obuobi. "You'd better take it," he calmly informed the academic.

Obuobi winced when the president issued a blisteringly vile epithet when he answered. The tirade lasted a full five minutes and concatenated largely into the many kinds of unpleasantness he'd have his security forces visit on him if he laid eyes on him or anything to do with his existential essence. And the more he tried to calm the president down, the more the president threatened and cursed, further invoking colourful language if what Obuobi had to say about not picking his call smacked of legerdemain.

Eventually, Obuobi got his chance to explain.

"The Girls have the most secure network I have ever seen, and that comes as no surprise. They would absolutely have detected us if we had tried getting in from your War Room."

"*The* War Room," a voice interjected through the speakerphone.

Obuobi had a quizzical look at that but ignored the interruption at the IGP's silent urging. "But I got us to the door and only need one of them to let us in."

"What do you mean, you got us to the door?" the Communications Minister, a contentious woman with an irritating voice asked.

"I only had a fifteen-minute window to triangulate and geolocate the source of their network activities and request that a satellite be positioned at the downwind target of the last trace element. This is a bit like a hound following the scent cone that spreads from a search target, but rather than use a neural network, I used satellite which, while detectable by their network, behaves chimerically and can be overlooked by an inattentive administrator. It however requires more patience on our side because it zones in only when we are let in by accident."

President Offei asked his Cabinet sourly after Obuobi was done. "Can anyone translate what he said into English?"

"Essentially, he's found a way to find them if they make a mistake," Major Hanson offered.

"Who is that?" the President demanded.

"I am Major Philip Hanson, Sir," he replied apologetically. "I'm the OIC of Security within the judiciary, sir, and personally responsible for the justices of the Supreme Court."

President Offei asked unkindly, "Not your best work, was it, Major?"

Major Hanson replied respectfully but firmly, "They were not abducted at the Supreme Court, Your Excellency. My platoon has no jurisdiction over the Black Star Square."

President Offei grumbled some things under his breath and asked eventually, "So that weirdo has found a way to find them. How long until he *actually* finds them?"

"It could be seconds, minutes, hours, days, weeks or months," Obuobi said with a shrug. "Best stand at the ready," he advised. "When the locator beeps, things would have to move at full throttle."

While unhappy that the judges could not be immediately located, President Offei's government took consolation in Obuobi's assurances.

This drama needed to end quickly.

Political tenures were at stake.

CHAPTER 13
Ground Zero
Tuesday, 19th March; 7 A.M.

BEFORE MOVING TO permanently settle at Odumase and Somanya, the ancient Krobos lived in the beautiful outcrops called Klowem, located just near the Akuse junction on the Akosombo Road. Every avid hiker, mountaineer or trekker worth his rank under the professional association of outdoor adventure operatives knew the Klowem outcrops. The moderately challenging, 10km-diameter wilderness had steep trails, grassy passes, rocky valleys and half-wild cattle to provide the background to wonderful adventures, and the occasional cow chase.

Kwaku Opare Addo discovered Klowem while searching for abseilable cliffs in the area. In the first iteration of his search, he and his team were assisted by Kloma Gbi, leaders of Krobo Youth in the traditional area. These youth wanted nothing more than to see all Krobos united for development. And the sacred Klowem was a visible symbol of that sought-after development. His adventure team would move off from that first search to organize over a hundred adventures to the site.

Just last week, at a meeting with the relevant chiefs of the area, he and his adventure company were slapped with a yard of calico, a couple of rams and the bones of a dead five-year old antelope, plus five thousand Cedis in fines, for making money running adventures on the hills behind the backs of the traditional authority. They had claimed the chiefs had needed to perform some gods-pacification rites before allowing adventurers to explore the hills. At any point, they claimed, the gods could have been offended and visited calamity on him, his customers, and potentially on the whole of Krobodom.

What the chiefs didn't know was that the Yilo House, the twin paramountcy of the Krobo, had stationed a usually half-drunk farmer on the other side of the hills, and the dude was extorting 10 Cedis – 30 Cedis if one was White – from anyone that would hike the hills.

Opare refused to visit the palace while the fines hung over his head and that of his company, but he continued to hike the hills all the same, not unaware of the potential conflict that could erupt should he run into any Krobos but using his superior knowledge of the hills to outwit any searchers. Eventually, the palace found out from Facebook that he was happily exploring the hills still. The chief himself called to offer a way out. Five thousand became 500 Cedis, and he could forget the rams, the calico and the osteology of the five-year-old Bovidae.

This morning, he'd driven by the palace in his moderately old Land Cruiser and handed over the cash, and then had decided to take another hike through the hills. October of last year had been the Ngmayem Festival, and every true Krobo had come to hike Klowem to pay homage to the ancestors. From his perch atop the highest outcrop, his practiced eye surveyed all the plastic littering every trail, rock, leaf and shrub. The greenery of Klowem had been violated by the indigenes, and empty water sachets, empty gin tots, and ice cream wrappers desecrated the outcrop.

When the chief answered his phone call, he said to him, "Your gods must be crazy if they found my adventures offensive but found no offense with the plastic littering and the other environmental violations of your people."

"I beg your pardon?" the chief asked haughtily.

"Your gods must be insane if they could threaten to punish me, who only leave boot prints, but do not punish you who have left these desecrations," he repeated, unperturbed that insulting a chief could bring back worse fines than five thousand Cedis.

Opare knew, as he descended the hills towards where his truck was parked, that it wasn't any love of the environment – or of any gods – that inspired the demand for money to explore what was really nothing more than an open wilderness. He did not begrudge any local authority or traditional ruler who monetized natural or environmental resources, especially of the sustainable variety. But he took exception to the extortion that was the stock-in-trade of almost all traditional authority in Ghana when an idea presented itself. No thought was given to business plans, or environmental impact assessments. Immediately, their default position was to slap fees in the names of gods as devoid of powers as his breath was devoid of the foul miasma of alcohol. Of course, the money and the drinks or rams ended up lining their pockets and cooking pots. Not a single indigene benefitted from such extortion.

As it would later turn out, the Klowem Hills was Government of Ghana property: there was an abundance of rocks for quarrying purposes. There were more than twenty active quarries in the area. And there were no angry gods either; just relics of ancient idolatry employing the fear of implausible spiritual consequences to keep chieftaincy elites in power.

Opare opened his Cruiser electronically and stowed his hiking gear in the boot of the truck. He took a quick towel bath and exchanged his sweaty hiking shirt for a cleaner one and swapped his long hiking boots for a shorter one.

The instruction from his professor friend at the University of Ghana was that he presented alone at the Aburi Botanical Gardens for discussions towards the signing of an extraction contract. The money was good, his professor had said, which was weird. In his experience, in a casualty evacuation or extraction, the goal was to rescue, resuscitate and preserve. Of course, he'd send an invoice afterwards, but money was hardly the prior motivation.

By the time the call had ended, he'd gotten the impression there was more to it, but he hadn't fathomed what. He wasn't one to read anything as depressing as Ghanaian news or watch local television or listen to the radio. He never knew what was going on in Ghana, but who could blame him? The politicians were all mostly idiots, and the news was always about politics. He knew the government had run the economy down borrowing and wasting it on nothing important to the Ghanaian people, but he didn't care. He lived in the jungle, and that was all he asked of his country – to leave him the hell alone in the jungle.

He drove out of Klowem and headed straight for the Akwapim Mountains. Professor Ampem Darko had asked him to arrive at the gardens at 8:30 in the morning. The face of his GPS watch said 7:30. He depressed his accelerator and strapped on his seatbelt.

He had never been late for an appointment before.

And he never will.

Oye and Nhyira, the twins, watched the Land Cruiser enter the Aburi Botanical Gardens from the East Gate with Dede in the driver's seat. They jumped out of their SUV as soon as Opare parked in the predestined spot and trained their guns on him from the driver's and passenger's side simultaneously. To his credit, and to their surprise, Opare maintained a calm, almost bemused posture. Both of his hands stayed on the steering cooperatively, unmoving as both women opened both doors, did a visual sweep of his person and of the interior, and ordered him out quietly. They took his keys from the ignition, locked the truck and asked him to head to their Landcruiser.

Opare moved along meekly. This wasn't his first time getting mugged, kidnapped or threatened under guns. And, as the few times before, the opportunity would come when his captors would learn that no one messed with an Outdoor Master-Guide.

To be honest though, he'd never been kidnapped by women before.

Perhaps that was why his heart was barely racing.

He wasn't chauvinist.

Maybe his heart was, but he wasn't.

They took off his blindfolds in what he could best describe as a large living room. Sunshine filtered through the interstices of the skylighted roof. When his eyes grew accustomed to the light, he found it was a plush living area with three aquaria, and more screens than he thought could be found in a TV showroom. And the screens seemed to connect to cameras showing all the rooms, courtyards and people in an enormous estate. But none of that interested him. He took in the coterie of eight people standing around him in the room and zoned in on the one he knew.

"Was all this necessary, Prof?" he asked of Owuraku Ampem Darko.

Before Owuraku could respond, Nhyira turned him around in the middle of the room to face her. Her question took him by surprise.

"Who are you?"

"What?"

He wasn't alone. The others seemed as equally surprised.

"What Nhyira means to say," Oye cut in at that point, "Is that we don't understand why you are so blasé about your abduction. You're too calm, too collected, too cooperative for our liking."

Opare blinked.

"I can raise hell if you want," was his calm response. "But really, was all this necessary?" he demanded again of Owuraku.

"They wanted to take precautions," Owuraku told him ruefully.

"Precautions against what exactly?" he asked him as if they were the only ones in the room. "And who are 'they'?"

"These ladies have abducted seven of this country's Supreme Court judges," Owuraku said by explanation, rightly assuming Opare had not heard about the abductions. "I suggested to them that they might need an escape plan, and that you're the only one I know who can extract prime targets from extreme locations and perhaps situations."

"Do you really mean to tell us that you've not heard about the abductions?" Aisha asked Opare dubiously. "I find that extremely hard to believe."

"Probably the same way I find it hard to believe that – what? – seven women have abducted seven justices of Ghana's Supreme Court," he shot back indifferently. "But that is still a lame excuse for getting me here by these methods. You could have asked me nicely. Whose silly idea was this, by the way?" he asked firmly in Owuraku's direction.

"Look at me!" Asabea ordered suddenly.

Opare turned his face and locked eyes with her.

She had a strange resolve in hers. As if she was trying to decipher if he was simply full of it, or whether he was genuinely insouciant about being captured, in which case he'd either be law enforcement or every bit the competent rescuer Owuraku had made him out to be.

Opare looked back at her stolidly, and in that studly gaze, Asabea understood one thing clearly: Opare had never known fear his entire life. Even kidnapped and outnumbered, there was no mistaking his prodigious intellect and strength.

She averted her eyes demurely and looked at Nhyira.

"We can trust him," she said simply.

Not all the girls shared in Asabea's epiphany, least of all Nhyira, but they let it drop.

Owuraku, after asking everyone to sit, and apologising profusely to Opare about the handling, proceeded to explain to him all that had gone on since Independence Day. Opare sat quietly through the telling; only his eyebrows shot up questioningly at some points of the narration, but he did not once interrupt.

When Owuraku was done, Opare said artlessly, "You're essentially asking me to be an accomplice to treason."

Owuraku smiled. "Essentially, yes."

"Probably why you tried to bait me with the mention of money."

"Probably."

Opare looked at the Septet in turns and said, "You seem to have a sizeable army. Why do you need me?"

"We need to be able to flee if the situation calls for it," Owuraku explained. "Each one of these ladies is ready to die for what we have done, but I for one like living. That's why I need your services."

"If I refuse?"

Owuraku shrugged. "We'll let you return as you were."

"Even though I could bring the entire Ghana Army here by noon?" he asked distrustfully, looking at Nhyira and pointedly glancing at her side arms.

"You were blindfolded," Nhyira reminded him. "You saw nothing of the way here."

"That I was," he agreed calmly, rising to grab himself a chilled orange juice from a pitcher he saw standing by what was clearly an uncleared breakfast table. After a couple of sips, he returned to his seat with the glass and looked at Nhyira again with the air of one who had all the time in the world.

"You took a right turn after you abducted me from the Aburi Gardens. Four alternating lefts and rights occurred therefrom at an average speed of fifty kilometres per hour. All other turns were fluid, indicating mountain descents, and there were 12 minutes of gravel."

The Girls just stared at him.

"If you'd like, you could blindfold me again, and I will give you the directions right back to my truck at the Gardens. What I'm trying to say, and Professor Darko knows this, is that I can get back to this exact location if I were released. Now that you know this, do you stand by your word that you'd let me go without harm?"

"Can he really do that?" Aisha asked Owuraku in a half-whisper.

Owuraku nodded. "I told you about this when I first suggested him."

"What do you think?" Aisha asked Asabea who seemed deep in thought.

"Why are you telling us this if you believe it might get you hurt?" she asked Opare. "You certainly know we don't want our hideout known. By saying that you can find us later, doesn't that put you in a dangerous position? Your smart-ass posture could be symptomatic of a fatal turn of mind."

Opare shrugged. "That's my exact point. At least one person in this room knows of my abilities. What that means is I really don't have a choice that does not come with potentially unpleasant consequences, and I'd much rather deal with it upfront than have you discover that later to my detriment."

"First, what's your decision?" Asabea asked. "Do you want to help us out of here if things go south? You answer that first, and then we can decide what to do afterwards."

"My company cannot be involved in any criminal enterprise," he told her calmly. "I'd get my licence revoked and probably get prosecuted as well. I'm not sure it's worth the trouble."

"I'll pay you a hundred thousand dollars for your troubles," Asabea told him, watching his face intently.

"One Million," he countered.

"You want us to pay your company one million dollars?" Dede came in at that point in surprise.

Opare shrugged. "My business is worth twenty million dollars," he replied, as if that was all the explanation he needed to give.

"What if it's not your company we want to hire, but you?" Owuraku asked him.

"That will cost you half a million."

"Cedis or dollars?" Nhyira asked him.

"We are global citizens," he chastised her. "Let's not degrade this conversation with Cedis."

Asabea asked, chewing on a lower lip, "If we agree to your terms, what will you need?"

"Full payment within three business days," was the instant reply. "Do you have a map somewhere? I had many in my truck, but your friends here didn't give me the time of day," he said with a curious glance at Oye and Nhyira.

The twins both scowled at him.

Owuraku handed over some maps to him. Wordlessly, he pored over the contours and asked for a pencil. Aisha gave him one as they stood around watching what he would do. He gulped down the last of his orange juice and set the glass aside on the light grey rug covering this portion of the tiled floor. Then he knelt and examined the map in detail.

"The Army will not expect you to escape by the impassable face of this cliff, so that is how we must get off this plateau."

Asabea exchanged startled glances with Oye & Nhyira and saw the knowing wink from Owuraku.

"Even if they brought in gunships, the thick vegetative cover might inure to our advantage. If they saw through the plan and covered the Adawso forest with Infantry, there are ways my team and I can show them that the Achiase Jungle Warfare School is a children's playground compared to real world jungle survival. If we create a network of camouflaged camps, we could hole up for a month until they tire, but I don't do well hiding in rabbit holes so my plan will be to get us out into the open as quickly as possible and keep one step ahead of them, as well as ahead of anyone else that will be looking for us. If we break through these mountains and connect through Assessewa and the Akatin side of Lake Volta, I can get you onto one of our islands in three days where no one would look to find you."

"Except you and your team," Nhyira said to him.

"Except me and my team," he repeated noncommittally.

"What if we aren't on the plateau you pointed to?" Bubuné demanded. "You were blindfolded coming in, so you saw nothing."

Opare gave her a withering look and turned to Owuraku. "If a tolerance for conversational tedium is part of this operation, I'm afraid

I'll have to charge double."

Bubuné was crushed.

"I don't like you," Nhyira just had to let it out now.

Opare bowed mockingly to her and then turned to Asabea.

"Are we aligned? You won't see me again until you walk up to that cliff and say 'Abracadabra'. We'll start work getting things moving once the funds hit."

He found an unused napkin and borrowed a pen from Owuraku. He scribbled his personal account details on the piece of tissue and handed it over to Asabea. Then he gave the room a once-over and settled on Nhyira before asking in an oracular tone, "Who is taking me back to my vehicle?"

Nhyira's face darkened when she turned to Asabea for confirmation.

"We might just kill him," Oye warned, half under her breath.

"What was that all about?" Efe asked Asabea when Dede and the twins had disappeared down the stairs with Opare. With no more than ten minutes to spare to the top of the hour, they had started towards the amphitheatre. Efe was dressed for the bar, but Asabea wore a green-coloured suit, a white shirt and matching skirt. She looked every bit a woman in her matching green pumps. "You seemed under some kind of spell with the man."

"I have never met a man this much devoid of bullshit," she admitted thoughtfully, looked at her watch and then turned to Owuraku. "You say you know him how?"

"He rescued some research team I was supervising a couple of years ago from the Atiwa forest when they came under the attack of a *galamsey* group," Owuraku responded. He sported a grey suit and a tieless lemon-coloured shirt the same shade as Asabea's.

"Were you personally on that team?" Aisha demanded.

"No, I wasn't.".

"But you sounded like you knew him personally and could vouch for him on a personal level," Efe reminded him plaintively.

"Well, you know him on a personal level now, and clearly, enough to contract him to save our butts when the time comes."

"This whole episode with Kwaku Opare was bizarre," Bubuné said with a frown. "We were not in charge of the narrative at any moment, and that disturbs me."

"We have to trust him," Owuraku told her gently.

"I know," Bubuné conceded. "I just don't like it."

Asabea turned abruptly to Owuraku, "He reminded me so much of you. I am learning to cede control to people that seem better at some things than I am. I hope I don't get disappointed."

"You won't be disappointed," he replied simply.

CHAPTER 14
Ground Zero
Tuesday, 19th March; 10 A.M.

AS THE JUSTICES filed into the amphitheatre, the Court reporter ordered all with business with the Court to rise. After the judges were seated, Duncan King looked at the plaintiffs' side of the room and locked eyes with Dr. Ampem Darko for the first time since this nightmare began. He remembered him as the man – the boy at that time – at whose actual instigation the police had hauled him out of the Gold Coast Hotel that fateful afternoon. Ampem Darko had been so angry at the police station it was all the Constables had done to stop him from attacking him. Looking into the professor's eyes right now, he could tell that a decade had not erased that anger. A cold fury burnt in those eyes, and the cool way the professor returned his gaze spoke volumes about what unspeakable retribution he would visit on him if he had an opportunity and a half.

Throughout the weekend he had been poring over legal strategy with Ansah Premo, his lawyer. He and Larry King had gotten into an argument over that strategy. His cousin kept insisting that in this rape saga, he saw no evil, did no evil and spoke no evil, and he wanted no part of this evil. Ansah Premo had indicated that no witness was going to be called at this stage, and that the arguments that would play out in Court would be constitutional. That had not placated Duncan King in any way, and he had a lot to say about Larry's unfounded quibbling, but he had let it pass.

For the moment.

The gavel was hammered and that brief incontinence in his groin returned. He glared balefully at the Chief Justice for doing that to him again, but the old goat was already speaking, all dressed up in his black robe and vintage horsehair wig. The original purpose of the wig was to provide a sense of formality and seriousness to proceedings in court and was seen to remove any bias or influence that might be brought about by a judge's personal appearance, as every judge would look the same in their wig. While Duncan King did not much care for judges and their outdated traditions, he took interest in the fact that these old toads at least had good taste to import them from London, where the tradition of wearing wigs in the legal profession originated. The wigs there were made by skilled craftsmen who used traditional techniques to construct them using horsehair, which was then woven into the fine mesh that became the wig.

Looking at the Chief Justice now, Duncan King was sure that all the wigs procured by the Judicial Service met the exacting standards required by the legal profession for horsehair coiffure, but to bring a gavel to this imposture of a trial was uncalled for. He'd rise and object if he wasn't afraid his groin, after the initial scare, might do him more *shege*.

"Are plaintiffs ready to proceed to oral arguments?" the Chief Justice asked Efe.

"Plaintiffs are ready, Your Lordship," Efe responded sonorously.

"Defendants?" he asked, looking in turns at the deputy A-G in the defence side of the room, and at Patricia Quayson on the screens, as well as to Ansah Premo.

"We are ready, my Lords," Umaru Tanko responded for the government.

"As are we, my Lords," Ansah Premo announced from the same side as the government.

"Alright then," Chief Justice Raymond Adofiem announced. "As a reminder to the watching public, this Court is in session to resolve the dispute that First Defendant, the Attorney-General, had all the evidence it needed to secure a conviction in the Republic v. Duncan King, and for which its exercise of nolle prosequi was arbitrary; and second, in the event of the first relief being granted, whether this Court should proceed to quash the nolle prosequi on that determination and order a trial."

The Chief Justice then looked to Efe and said, "Plaintiffs have the floor."

Efe rose from her seat to the lectern that was an extension of the furniture at the plaintiff's section and laid out her carefully arranged notes. Then she looked first to the bench, then to the defendants, and then finally to the cameras that were positioned in such a way that looking into them was the same as looking at the judges.

The Girls knew that there were two courts involved in this trial. This court was as important as the other court – the court of public opinion – for it was that other court that would mete out the justice that Duncan King deserved.

"My Lords, and the Honourable Court," Efe began, looking in every way the competent litigant she was in her black gown and white shirt, and the indispensable off-white horsetail wig that completed her outfit. She knew the Court. And Ghana's Supreme Court was not the most stodgy and sclerotic of courts within the Commonwealth, even after the unprecedented court-packing actions of President Offei.

"We are the first to admit that the use of nolle prosequi by prosecutors is generally a matter of prosecutorial discretion, and prosecutors are given broad discretion by law in deciding whether to pursue charges against a defendant. This court has time and again recognized that discretion as a constitutional and legal power belonging solely to the Attorney-General under the 1992 Constitution and under common law, and enabled it as necessary to ensure that innocent people were not prosecuted and convicted, that scarce judicial resources were not misappropriated in pursuit of cases with little prospects of success, and necessary to safeguard the public interest and ensure that justice was not only done, but seen to be done. A lot of nolle prosequi cases have allowed prosecutors to focus their resources on cases that have a greater chance of success, while also protecting the rights of the accused and preventing wrongful convictions. We agree with the court on all those rulings, especially when it allowed an accused to move on with their life and avoid the emotional and financial cost of defending themselves in cases that were lacking in prosecutorial evidence.

"My Lords, we however bring to your notice a peculiar exercise of judicial wisdom in all rulings involving the matter of nolle prosequi. This court and the lower courts, even while seemingly concurring with the Attorney-General on the nonjusticiable arguments of nolle prosequi, have emphasized that the decision must be made in the interest of justice and based on sound legal principles. Each of your rulings have demanded that the prosecutor must exercise the power with caution and ensure that it does not result in a miscarriage of justice. This court has on three occasions warned that nolle prosequi cannot be used in a manner that is arbitrary, discriminatory, or contrary to the interests of justice, in which case the use of the power can be ruled as an abuse of that discretion.

"My Lords, in one instance in 2012 this court was circumspect that allowing a prosecutor to discontinue a criminal case at will undermines the rule of law by giving the impression that some individuals were above the law. The court held that while the power of nolle prosequi might not be subject to judicial review, that power was nonetheless subject to the rule of law, and that the prosecutor could not abuse the power to shield offenders from justice. In the peculiar case of the Republic v. Duncan King, my Lords, we contend that the Attorney-General through the State Prosecutor abused that power to shield the defendant, Mr. Duncan King from justice. The prosecution well-nigh admitted this when, seeing the frown on the trial judge's face during the application, quickly assured her that the prosecution reserved the right to try the defendant again later. The Attorney-General herself issued a press statement in response to the public outcry, clarifying that the accused had not been let off the hook. She cited the mental state of plaintiff at the time, as well as the unwillingness of family and plaintiff's witnesses to testify on behalf of plaintiff."

Efe paused to flip over some of her sheets.

"It's been ten years, my Lords," she told the empanelled justices. "If the first defendant truly meant what they said, ten years is a heck of a long time to not have brought Duncan King to justice. While true that plaintiff was not in a good emotional state to present in court, the first defendant was armed with her affidavit, armed with a doctor's report, and armed with powers to subpoena plaintiff's named cousin, second defendant's named cousin, and Owuraku Ampem Darko, all crucial witnesses to the alleged crime. We vehemently contend that first defendant egregiously employed their powers of nolle prosequi to enable every caveat this court has imposed on that power. And for ten years, the second defendant has lived, walked, talked and allegedly raped with the impunity of a person that believed they were above the law. The consequences of that impunity, my Lords, is what you see today. All seven of us women who took up arms and orchestrated this session of justice did so because of our unhappiness with first defendant's conduct. All of you venerable judges would today have been happily at home with your families but for the Attorney-General's abuse of power. And this is a far less consequence than could have been meted out if we had not set out to make this trial as bloodless as possible, my Lords. There's therefore no telling what anyone in this country could do when they felt that justice had been denied them.

"In summary therefore," Efe concluded, "we contend that while the power of nolle prosequi can be a useful tool for prosecutors to discontinue cases that are not in the public interest, in the Republic v. Duncan King, there was a clear public interest that was violated by the Attorney-General, and that abuse undermined the rule of law, violated even the second defendant's right to a fair trial, and created a perception of injustice, reasons for which the exercise of that power needs to be rendered null and void, so we may try the second defendant and give plaintiffs the justice that has been denied for a decade. And this is because the legal adage is true in every form that justice delayed is justice denied.

"Thank you, my Lords," she finished.

Larry King had been watching the judges during all Efe Plange's opening arguments. He, like his cousin, was a media and entertainment practitioner, but unlike his cousin and *his* friends in the industry, Larry was not infected with the hubris that so often clung like bacteria to his peers. He was also a talk show host about current affairs, so he knew what to watch out for when talking to people in power to see in what direction their minds laid.

Three of the four male judges were largely unreadable, but there were three female justices on the bench who hung on every word of the lawyer for Asabea, the type of attention to a speaker that you knew meant they believed her every word. All the legal opinions they had researched over the past three days were in favour of the court throwing out the Girls' case, but what no one seemed to talk about was that the judges *knew* they were prisoners. Self-preservation was more important than judicial integrity, and the Girls had guns. He was not fooled at all by the fact of the Girls' friendliness and prima facie trustworthiness; he was informed and obsessed only by the fact of their abductions, and that meant that all the laws of jurisprudence were suspended.

Which was why he hadn't wanted any part in all of this.

But even he had to admit that ten years was too long a time to bring closure to this matter. If he knew it was going to come down to guns, he'd swear he would have seen a resolution to this a decade ago.

Because right now, Efe had four judges and a half eating out of her legal palm, and Larry had never been wrong about reading in which direction people's mind laid.

His thoughts were interrupted by deputy Attorney-General Umaru Tanko.

"My Lords," Tanko was saying to the judges, also walking to his lectern and arranging a fat book of legal arguments on it.

"The power of nolle prosequi is a settled matter in both constitutional and common law. The 1992 Constitution of Ghana provides for the independence of the Attorney General and Minister of Justice, which includes the power to discontinue a criminal prosecution at any stage. Article 88-3 of the Constitution states that, and I quote, the Attorney-General shall have the power, exercisable at his discretion, to institute and conduct criminal proceedings in any court, end of quote. This provision clearly confers on the Attorney General the power to decide when to commence, pursue or discontinue criminal proceedings, and that point has been made ad infinitum in our written pleadings before your Lordships.

"This same power is also recognized under common law, and in the case of the Republic v. Ayikwei, 2015, which held that the power of nolle prosequi was an essential attribute of the Attorney-General's office.

"My Lords, there is no concrete statute of limitations on crime in Ghana. Plaintiff avers that a decade is too long a time between when the trial was suspended by nolle prosequi and now, but plaintiff made no reference to any law that enjoins the Republic to return an accused to trial within ten years after a nolle prosequi application has been granted; none whatsoever.

"Therefore, based on constitutional jurisprudence, the precedencies of this court's past rulings on the matter, and common law, the Republic asks the court to deny the current application," Tanko finished summarily and returned to his seat.

Asabea and Efe exchanged startled glances. The judges seemed surprised by the brevity of the government's opening arguments too, and the one whose ox was most gored by it was Duncan King.

"That's all the government is saying?" he whispered angrily to his lawyer. "Just three sentences?"

"Relax," Ansah Premo whispered back. "The government doesn't want to give this sham of a trial any more credence than it needs to. All this will be overturned eventually, but for the sake of maintaining appearances and keeping us all alive, let's play our part, but briefly."

Then he started to get up, but King dragged him back to his seat by his robe and said sternly to him, "I don't give a rat's fart about what yours and the government's strategy is. This trial is on national TV. I have a reputation to protect as the god Emcee. You'd better do a better job than that deputy A-G or else hell will break lose, you understand me?"

Ansah Premo looked nervously at the bench and the room. Everyone was looking at him and his client. Therefore, everyone needed to understand that he, as Counsel to the President, was no one's pushover. So, he raised a stern finger of his own to Duncan King's face and said cooly under his breath, "Take your hands off me this instant, or you'll have to find yourself a new lawyer."

King let go of Ansah Premo's arm as if it was a snake, surprised at the residual threat in the lawyer's demeanour.

Ansah Premo rose to his lectern, brushed a few creases off his gown as if nothing had happened, and addressed the court.

"My Lords," he began, referring to notes he too had made on a legal pad. "It is generally required by law that an alleged victim of rape or sexual assault testify in court. A state prosecutor is responsible for presenting evidence to prove the charges against the accused, and the victim's testimony is often a crucial part of that evidence. When an alleged victim is unable, for whatever reasons, to testify, it puts a prosecutor – any prosecutor – in an untenable position.

"We agree, as plaintiff outlined in her written arguments, that there are some situations in which a victim may be excused from testifying. For example, if the victim is a child or is otherwise unable to testify due to a physical or mental condition, the court may allow the prosecutor to present the victim's testimony in the form of a written statement or video recording. In some cases, the court has allowed prosecutors armed with affidavits and doctors' testimonies to try sexual assault cases, but we all know how those cases ended. In fact, my Lords, there isn't a single sexual assault case in this Republic that has been successful without the victim's testimony. That testimony is often the crucial piece of prosecutory evidence that proves that the sexual activity was non-consensual. And in a country like ours where all alleged rapists scream consent, the victim's testimony is often the best way to establish guilt beyond reasonable doubt.

"Then, my Lords, there is the right under Ghanaian law to confront one's accuser, an important part of the accused person's right to a fair trial. This right is enshrined in the Constitution and is also recognized in international human rights law. My client, the second defendant had the right to be present in court and to cross-examine any witnesses who testify against him. This includes the right to ask the witness questions about their testimony, their credibility, and any potential biases or motives they may have. The purpose of this right is to allow the accused person to challenge the evidence presented against them and to test the credibility of the witness. To do this to nothing more than an affidavit and a doctor's testimony, my Lords, would have amounted to failure of prosecution, and that gave the prosecutors no other choice than to file a nolle prosequi. If there's therefore any one to blame for a decade of so-called injustice, then it is the plaintiff. She refused to present in court to substantiate her allegations and have refused to do so for ten years. And now she is here, threatening all of us with guns towards a self-imposed quest for justice whose denial is all her doing and no one else's.

"And that, my Lords, is why her prayer to this court must be denied in its entirety."

When Ansah Premo sat down, Duncan King clasped his hand gratefully and sat more erect, looking at the cameras directly and confidently. He even locked eyes once more with Professor Darko, but this time, his eyes tried to mirror the loathing he saw in the other man's eyes. He smiled briefly when the Prof looked away to look at the Asabea woman.

"Yeah, you do that," he thought to himself. "Look at a woman, because you are no match for this man that I am."

Chief Justice Adofiem looked at one of the dozen or so digital clocks blinking around the TV screens and noted that they still had some time before a lunch break, so he asked, "Does the plaintiff want to exercise the right of reply?"

"We do, my Lords," Efe said confidently from beside Asabea, rising again and walking purposely towards her lectern. The purpose of the plaintiff's right of reply was to ensure that the parties had an equal opportunity to present their case and arguments to the court. It was an important part of the adversarial system of justice, which was based on the idea that the best way to arrive at the truth was through the vigorous advocacy of opposing sides.

"My Lords, as officers and members of this court and of the judiciary, we all know that a nolle prosequi is a decision that affects the outcome of a case, and therefore has significant impact on the judicial process. If the decision is not subject to judicial review, it means that the prosecutor has the power to override the decision of the court, which violates the principle of separation of powers. In any case, in the case of Amidu v. Attorney General, 2013, this court held that the Attorney General's power to discontinue a case through nolle prosequi is subject to the supervisory jurisdiction of the courts. The Court stated that the power of nolle prosequi is not absolute and warned that it be exercised in a manner consistent with the Constitution.

"Then also, my Lords, if the decision to nolle prosequi is not subject to judicial review, it increases the risk of abuse of power by the prosecutor. The prosecutor may drop charges against a defendant for political or personal reasons, even if there is sufficient evidence to proceed with the case. This undermines the integrity of the justice system and creates a culture of impunity that we contend have been created by the refusal of the State to try Duncan King –"

"My Lords," Ansah Premo shot up to his feet just then. "We object to counsel's unsubstantiated insinuations. It's one thing to play to the gallery and another to defame my client."

"My Lords," Efe rebutted, "We have provided sworn affidavits in support of our allegations that the refusal of the State to hold Duncan King criminally accountable has resulted in the sexual assaults of thirteen more young women since plaintiff was raped –"

"– And again, My Lords, the incendiary defamation continues, and right under the noses of your Lordships too, my Lords." Premo responded angrily. "No court has found my client guilty of rape. This has gone on long enough."

"Then why did Counsel for the second defendant not respond to those claims of further sexual aggression in our written submissions, my Lords? We have provided scores of pages and affidavits documenting the predatory and aggressive sexual assault behaviour of the second defendant since the nolle prosequi. There isn't one text of rebuttal in their written or in their oral arguments that seek to deny those allegations, but we have provided all the needed bases for the alleged infractions."

"We refuse to get too drawn into arguments that give any semblance of credibility to this sham of a trial, my Lords –"

"– Let me stop you right there, Mr. Premo," Justice Esi Arhin butted in at that point. "And this goes to the Attorney-General too," she warned. "If your strategy is not to commit fully to this court because you believe it is a sham because of potential duress, I must assure you that you might be in for a surprise. This court is as duly constituted as if we were sitting in the Supreme Court building of the Republic until nine, and not seven justices of the apex court sit to overrule our judgements. I find your positions with respect to adequate representation as anaemic of practicality as I find some of your arguments. And plaintiff's counsel did present evidence that I am surprised you have not rebutted to in your written submissions. If you truly believe that this court can be overturned, then continue this course and it may well serve you. But if you're wrong, consider the consequences carefully for you and your client and act accordingly."

Ansah Premo blinked.

As did the deputy Attorney-General.

"Surely, my Lords," Premo pleaded when he regained his composure. "You don't really mean to say you're *considering* granting plaintiff's reliefs, do you?"

"Your job," Chief Justice Adofiem reminded him, taking over from Justice Arhin, "is to give us reasons not to consider plaintiff's pleadings, and so far, you haven't given us any," he finished bluntly.

"In any case," Justice Vincent Kotei added, "Plaintiff's counsel had the floor. Let her finish."

Efe spared one glance at Ansah Premo before she said to the judges, "We are most grateful, my Lords." Then she quickly scanned her notes and continued, "Not only did the exercise of the right to nolle prosequi hurt my client but it denied the second defendant the opportunity to challenge the decision and seek justice for himself as well. Duncan King might have had strong evidence in his favour when he claimed in his defence that what we complained of as rape was consensual, but he had no recourse to challenge the decision and attempt to clear his name. So, our asking for the nolle prosequi to be nullified also serves the interest of the defendant. He himself will agree that there are places and jobs he has not been allowed to visit or engage in because of the non-conclusion of this case. Just last month, he threatened to sue the Chief Executive of the Agyapa Broadcasting Company when the company refused his proposal to host a show because of the Republic vs. Duncan King. Even he stands to benefit from the granting of our pleadings.

"The argument that counsel for the second defendant makes about his client's right to confront his accuser in person is ridiculous when considered in the light of a murder case, for instance. My Lords, the true victims of murder cases are dead people, yet trials are conducted, and guilty defendants are jailed for their demise based on available evidence adduced by investigative agencies and corroborating witnesses. The argument that cases cannot be satisfactorily prosecuted for lack of a victim is laughable. Cases are won on the preponderance of evidence, and not on the preponderance of victims, and defendant's arguments speak even more to their connivance to see Duncan King walk free, and not on any true and proper consideration of law and criminal justice.

"Thank you, my Lords," Efe concluded her right of reply.

Chief Justice Adofiem then looked to the deputy Attorney-General and said, "Does the Republic want to exercise its right of rebuttal?"

"The Republic does not, my Lords," Umaru Tanko responded promptly with no more than one cursory look at his boss on the screen.

"Fair enough," the Chief Justice affirmed, and asked Ansah Premoh, "What about second defendant?"

"Second defendant will pass on the right to rebuttal as well, my Lords."

CHAPTER 15
Ghana Police HQ
Tuesday, 19th March, Noon.

DR. MOSES OBUOBI'S pen lay askew in his mouth. His butt tethered precariously on the edge, but while he remained in no danger of falling more than two feet to the floor from his chair, his inability to keep still concerned Amadu on occasion. There was no denying the geek's excitement, and his sharp eyes betrayed his sense of satisfaction as his computers – twelve of them lined up along the walls of the parallel War Room – beeped away the location of the judges.

Amadu and Atukwei had done their homework. And that work was what had fed into their newfound respect and admiration for the geeky academic who, until a few minutes ago, had multicoloured socked feet on top of the glass conference table.

Dr. Obuobi was the current chair of DefCon, the shortened name for Defence Readiness Condition, a series of annual hacker conventions held in Las Vegas in the United States.

DefCon was one of the world's largest and most notable hacker conventions, attracting thousands of participants from around the globe, including computer security professionals, hackers, government officials, and researchers. The event provided a platform for the exchange of knowledge and ideas related to computer security, hacking techniques, and the latest advancements in technology, featuring a variety of activities, including presentations, workshops, hacking contests, and discussions on topics such as network security, cryptography, privacy, and social engineering. The programme was known for its informal atmosphere, which encouraged open communication and interaction among participants. It aimed to promote education, awareness, and understanding of computer security issues, as well as to foster collaboration between individuals from different backgrounds and skill levels.

DefCon and its participants adhered to a strict code of ethics, promoting responsible and legal hacking practices, emphasizing that the purpose of the conference was to improve security and not to engage in illegal activities.

Dr. Obuobi was its current chair. And in the several hours since he'd informed the president that he had a window of discovery where the girls were concerned, he had done nothing but chew on his lips, suck on lollipops, write lines upon lines of code and seem unperturbed that his goal of a cellular ping on his radar might remain a chimera. He got off his seat at present and began to quickly type lines of code on his laptop in response to the clearly satisfactory beeps from his computer. He wore a wide grin as he typed and even the sulky Atukwei took freudenfreude in Obuobi's success. One of the screens lit up with a Google Earth rendition of satellite imagery and Obuobi let out what Amadu thought was a cackle; that sound witches made over a boiling pot of evil magic.

"Call the President," he ordered the IGP suddenly.

"Call him yourself," the IGP shot back, with a hint of tolerant irritation.

Inoffensively, Obuobi redialled on the speakerphone and waited for the president to answer. When he did, he said, "I have trilaterated their location now and will send coordinates in a minute, sir."

"You have what?"

Remembering who he was speaking with, Obuobi said, "You remember what I said earlier about the window of opportunity and trace source elements?"

"Yes," the President replied. His tone indicated he did not remember.

"So, I have done three things: I measured the time it took for the trace signals to travel from the last point to three nearby satellites. Since trace signals travel at the speed of light, I estimated the distance to each satellite by multiplying the travel time by the speed of light. Then I performed mathematical trilateration calculations to estimate their location based on their distance measurements, specifically to determine the latitude, longitude, and altitude of the signal's last position. I had to seek some help from some satellite geometry, and information from other sensors like accelerometers and barometers to compensate for factors like signal blockage or multipath interference. The long and short of all this is that I know where your judges are, confirmed by a hiking GPS device user called Jungle Boy Chupa Chups, who happened by those trace elements just when I was finishing the trilateration. I have sent the coordinates to the IGP this moment," Obuobi explained and sent the coordinates by SMS to the IGP's mobile phone.

From the War Room, President Offei blinked several times in his effort to process what Obuobi had said. When it all finally hit him, he ordered the IGP, "Get those coordinates here now!"

"I have just forwarded it to the CDS," Inspector General of Police Selasi Ocran informed the President.

"*Forwarded* it?" President Offei demanded dangerously, "Get your ass over here. And come with everyone that is inside that silly imitation of my War Room. In the meantime," he ordered the Chief of Defence Staff who sat to the President's left, "Switch your CTU's alert level to DefCon 3. We strike tonight!"

"DefCon 3?" Atukwei asked the IGP disbelievingly when the call was over. "And how did he know about this room?"

The IGP shrugged. "Politicians are ever dramatic, and the Chief of Army Intelligence must have told him," he said with distaste and rose from his seat.

The term "DefCon", the same name Obuobi's hacker conference adopted as a playful reference to global military systems, referred to the defence readiness condition of the Ghana Armed Forces. It was a numerical scale used to indicate the level of readiness and alertness of the country's military forces, particularly in response to potential threats or attacks.

The DefCon system consisted of five levels, numbered from five being the lowest state of readiness to one being the highest state of readiness. Each level represented a specific condition with corresponding actions and response procedures for military forces. The DefCon level was determined by the Minister for Defence in consultation with military commanders and intelligence agencies.

The exact details and protocols associated with each DefCon level were classified, but their purpose was to ensure the military was prepared to respond swiftly and appropriately to various levels of threats or conflicts. Categorizing the response to the Girls as DefCon 3 was like blasting at a housefly with a bazooka, which was why Atukwei was puzzled. Even the misbegotten trans-Volta Togoland secession shenanigans were classified as DefCon 5.

Within fifteen minutes, the parallel War Room was empty as each of the officers there, including Obuobi were harried into military trucks and police vans for the short trip from the Police Headquarters to the Jubilee House.

When they were ushered into the War Room, everyone that mattered in the country was there, and the room had been rearranged to accommodate military drawn models of the plateau where Obuobi believed the judges were being held. Not much mention had been made of the televised trial due to the excitement of Obuobi's discovery. President Offei did however remark sourly in passing when the IGP and his band arrived, that he took exception to his government being pilloried in the media about the seemingly inadequate defence his Attorneys-General were mounting in the trial.

"Ladies and Gentlemen," he boomed when everyone had settled into their seats. His orotund voice lent an air of gravitas to the situation. "After days and days of hard work, we have finally found the location of the judges, and an operation will be conducted tonight to bring them home and end this nonsense once and for all. This National Security Council meeting is convened to agree on how to conduct the operation. I will now defer to the Chief of Defence Staff to run us through what the military plans to do."

"The military?" Atukwei whispered unhappily in protest to Amadu, but the IGP shushed them before someone else could hear them.

Brigadier-General Nsonwah, taking over from the President, laid out an elaborate plan that involved storming the Fortress, for that was what the mansion the Girls were holding the judges was called. This came to light when they tracked down the properties on the coordinates Obuobi was able to hack.

A Nigerian oil baron had bought the land a decade ago and built what he designed as a fortress on it. There was no record of the property ever changing hands but that was of no consequence. Situated on a plateau the size of two football fields between the mountain towns of Aburi and Adawso, the Fortress was impregnable except for a narrow defile, barely large enough to accommodate an SUV, that the baron claimed could be defended against a platoon if needed. Army Intelligence had pulled every satellite image they could find, and from all indications, the girls were trapped.

"Unless they fly," the CDS joked when the Vice President commented on the fact that there seemed nowhere else, other than the pass, for the girls to go if the Army went knocking. The CDS explained that he had formed a crack platoon of soldiers from the 66th Artillery Regiment that was stationed in the Volta Regional capital, even though the judges' location was in the Eastern Region.

"You do realise that this is a hostage situation, don't you?" Obuobi asked the question that Amadu and Atukwei had been bursting at the seams to ask.

"Yes, we do," was the surprisingly light response from the CDS.

"So why are you sending in artillery?" he demanded. "I was under the impression that a counterterror police unit was on standby. If you deploy this plan of yours, not even the judges will come out alive."

The CDS shrugged. "We need to communicate to the Girls that we aren't there to play. They'll either must surrender or face our wrath."

"What wrath?" Atukwei had had it at that point. "There are about fifteen civilian hostages in there, General. If you go in there brandishing artillery, you'll have them all killed. Which is why I question the wisdom of sending in the military to begin with."

"Are you questioning my wisdom?" President Offei demanded dangerously.

"I am not questioning *your* wisdom, sir," Atukwei said, hoping he sounded a bit more respectful than he felt. "I am denying the existence of it in this plan to send in artillery when they have seven supreme court justices as hostages. Even the plan to strike at night is problematic. If anyone came to my door at night demanding the release of anyone in my household, I'd be sending bullets in response."

President Offei looked like he was about to explode at the dissentient police officer but directed his question to the IGP instead. "Does the Police Service share in this moron's prognosis?"

The IGP seemed both unsure and uncomfortable with the question. But the look the President sustained seemed to suggest an answer needed to be given or else.

"We don't believe sending in the Army is the answer," he said meekly. "As Dr. Obuobi first opined, this is a hostage situation requiring civilian Police, and not Army brutalities. This isn't a war, sir. I don't believe that much violence is called for at this stage."

"They blew up my East Gate, blew up my prosecutor's house and shot him. That doesn't sound like war to you, Selasi?" the President demanded, seeming to froth at the mouth in anger.

And then, turning to the commander of his Secret Service detail the President ordered, "Remove all Police personnel from this meeting immediately!"

It was when they were being driven out of the Jubilee House gates that the shock wore off Amadu's face. It had taken the Secret Service all of five seconds to hustle them out of the War Room, and perhaps less than that to see them out of the premises. Amadu feared what the IGP would do to them both as they were being driven by Constables back to the Police Headquarters. Not even Dr. Obuobi had been spared the indignity of the sack, but the president was all too happy for Major Hanson to stay even though, by all descriptions, he too was of the "Police" camp.

"What do we do?" he asked a fuming Atukwei in the seat to his left in the Police cruiser.

"We wait for them to crash and burn and call us back," was the surly response.

"I mean about the IGP," Amadu explained. "The look he directed at us at the gate could kill."

Atukwei seemed thoughtful for a bit before he responded, "Frankly, I am surprised the President didn't fire us outright. The way he was carrying on, he seemed like he wanted to."

"Yeah," Amadu thought so too.

They didn't speak again until they arrived back at the parallel War Room. As they mounted the stairs, they bumped into Major Hanson breathily taking the stairs a couple at a time behind them.

"What are you doing here?" Amadu demanded in surprise.

"I was thrown out too for suggesting you 'morons' could be right," he replied with a tight wink, and then held the doors open for them at the landing to the room. When they entered, the IGP sat with Dr. Obuobi at the end of the glass table, his face unreadable. Obuobi had turned on all his screens and was typing away furiously on his computer. They all grabbed chairs and sat down. The silence after that could have woken the dead, except for Obuobi's typing.

Eventually, the IGP said, "Pull in all CTU personnel and get them sequestered in the premises. I want all eight hundred of them here at the ready. Get them the protective gear they'll need, but do not overarm them. Just a couple of clips should be enough, but I want them here now. No one is leaving until this crisis and the next blows over, do you both understand me?"

Atukwei looked as baffled as Amadu. Seeing their confusion, the IGP asked, "Gentlemen, success for the next few days depend on a certain amount of speed. Move your butts! Get the men here as ordered and get your butts back here. No one is sleeping a wink until I say so, you feel me?"

They did not feel him, but that did not mean they could not carry out orders. Within an hour, eight hundred and seventeen officers and men were armed as instructed and ready, and the parade grounds at Headquarters were filled with Police trucks and armoured personnel carriers. Believing that the CTU was going to have overseen the operation to get back the judges, the IGP had had them training day and night, and had had their deployment orders issued as soon as Obuobi hacked the very first set of coordinates.

All bristling with adrenaline and excitement, Amadu and Atukwei were about to return to the parallel War Room from the parade grounds when their attention was diverted to three military trucks entering the grounds. Three score pairs of government boots jumped out of the trucks, and their commanding lieutenant had them all lined up, what the military often referred to as 'dressed up', in perfect order. She then smartly paid her compliments to Major Hanson who, in the excitement of the platoon's arrival, had walked down unnoticed to where the two Chief Superintendents stood.

"What is this?" Amadu demanded.

"This is my contribution to the CTU effort," he said respectfully.

"And the IGP knows about this?"

"It was his idea, actually."

"Let's go talk to him then," Atukwei grumbled. "We have done what he wants. He needs to explain what he has in mind."

The IGP was ending a call when the three officers accompanied by the platoon lieutenant entered the room.

"I'll have you all know that the President has decided to move the military in against the Fortress at midnight," he told them as they sat. "I expect we might be called on to clean up their mess by morning."

"I don't follow, sir," Major Hanson said, blinking. "What mess?"

"The flaw in using military assets for this operation is that soldiers don't make good negotiators," Obuobi answered cooly with his socked feet back up on the table. "I wouldn't mind soldiers going in after the judges had been released, but to send them in to secure the judges is to guarantee that more and more, the girls will use them as hostages if they weren't planning to do so in the beginning."

"I believe they were planning to use them as hostages regardless of any time frame," the Major countered. "I don't foresee my judges coming out of that house without a fight."

"And that's where you and your generals and the President are wrong," the IGP answered bluntly. "Everything points to the release of the justices right after their ruling on the substantive matter. Nothing shows that the girls will harm the justices in any way. The only reason President Offei is attacking is political. He simply does not want to look weak. He doesn't care about the girls, the issues for which they have resorted to these means, or even about the judges; he only cares about how chivalrous his government will look storming into the Fortress,

Rambo-style, and looking like some modern-day hero. The polls are not on his side for this year's election, hence the stunt he wants to pull."

"So, if you've known about his plans all this while, why did you have us looking like we were the only ones seeing flaws in his use of the Armed Forces?" Atukwei asked like he was owed a debt.

"Mentioning those flaws is what got us all removed from the National Security Council, didn't it?" the IGP asked Atukwei wisely. "And that was not the only flaw. I don't think the President and the CDS are prepared for the violence going unannounced to the Fortress will generate. In none of their planning did I detect a preparation for what they would do if the Girls fought back."

"Perhaps their response to that is the use of artillery?" Major Hanson asked, ever the soldier.

"Ground artillery in front of a narrow pass," the IGP reminded him. "Not exactly the makings of modern warfare, is it? Our intelligence indicates the Girls have armed drones."

Major Hanson chewed thoughtfully on a lower lip but could not come up with any other defence for his people.

"The sense I get is that the Army will throw in all they've got with the hope that the Girls won't actually hurt the judges while they are breaking down the Fortress gates," the IGP continued. "If the girls respond in kind, the Army will be exposed. I expect the casualties to be high. By morning, we'll have dead soldiers to collect from the gates, and perhaps less friendlier lines of communication with the Girls."

"Do you expect the President to call you afterwards?" the lieutenant asked.

Major Hanson immediately introduced her as Lieutenant Matilda Brooks of the Ghana Army and as his deputy commanding officer for the platoon assigned to protect the Supreme Court.

Although a democratic country, there wasn't any facet of the interior security of Ghana that did not involve the country's military. The politicization of the Police Service had seen to a culture where only soldiers could be trusted.

Or feared.

Which was probably why President Offei felt more inclined to deploy soldiers against the Girls rather than the Police. The current IGP had been working hard to change that culture but to no avail. Not a single Minister of State felt safe outside of their homes unless they had a soldier in their security detail, and this included the Attorney-General, whose job it was more to keep soldiers away from civil discourse by law than anyone else's, given Ghana's history with military coups and unrests and constitutional upheavals. And that was why the Ghana Army was responsible for the security of the Supreme Court instead of the Ghana Police. Of course, the half-witted politicians did not care that by demanding military protection in civil matters, they were perpetuating a belief that only by soldiers could true law and order be established in Ghana. And the madness had been extended even to the greatest Chief under the traditional rulership system – the Asantehene – who was usually surrounded by soldiers for his own security.

"I doubt the President would call us afterwards," Amadu said in response to Lieutenant Brook's question while examining the map where the Fortress stood. "But it's the CTU's duty to end this drama whether invited or not."

Then he turned to Obuobi and said, "Are we sure that no one and nothing can come to the Fortress from behind? If they run out of ammunitions and protection, they would have painted themselves into a bit of a corner, wouldn't they?"

"You would need grappling hooks, abseil and climbing gear, and ropes at least two hundred metres long to assail them from around their back, and expert skills to avoid detection," Obuobi told him without needing to consult the map. "Only one person in all of this country can do that, and that guy hates politicians so much he'd probably rather help the Girls if you asked him."

"We have special forces personnel who could do that," Major Hanson told him.

"And avoid detection in the process?" Obuobi asked him with a derisive laugh. "They'd probably drop grenades on you before you were halfway up the cliff."

Amadu was not convinced. "I'm not exactly looking at it from an attack point of view. If they cannot escape because of a treacherous cliff, they have backed themselves into a corner."

Atukwei scanned the map shrewdly at that and said, "Then they don't mean to escape," he said with meaning. "They plan to fight till the end."

"That's suicidal," Obuobi said with surprise, raising his feet from off the table and going about looking for something in his case of gizmos. "I don't get the sense that that's how they plan this to end, but it sure sounds suicidal looking at it that way," he said, suddenly sounding desperate.

"Of course, we know they cannot outlast our Armed Forces in a real fight, so we need to understand exactly what their exit strategy is," he finished, pulling out a sheaf of topographic maps. He searched methodically in the legend and then quickly pirouetted towards a quadrant.

"What are you looking for?" Major Hanson asked the weird man.

"If they cannot outlast our Army but have seemingly painted themselves into a corner," he explained, almost to himself as he kept scanning that section, "then what we think is a corner is an illusion."

"The cliff is an illusion?" Atukwei asked skeptically. "It says right there on the satellite images that the cliff is real."

"Maybe," Obuobi said half-attentively. "But the defile to the Fortress is only thirty feet wide and supported by hanging rocks. If they detonate anything close to a dynamite, those rocks will fall and make the Fortress as unreachable as the moon."

"And with it, any group of soldiers foolish enough to be standing there at that time," Major Hanson finished for him with his eyes wide open. Reaching for his mobile phone, he said, "I need to call the Chief of Army Intelligence."

"And tell him what exactly?" the IGP demanded. "If he says anything like this to the President, he too will have to move his soldiers here like you have. President Offei only sees in political spectrum."

"But we can't just sit still when we know any assault on the Fortress will end in disaster for our troops," the Major complained.

"Who is leading the operation?" Amadu asked the Major while consulting with another map of the Aburi area.

"I'm told Colonel Nartey of the 1st Infantry Battalion."

"He's a practical man," the IGP said approvingly. "On the ground he'll use his head. But that's not what I'm worried about. His head won't matter if the President insists on a certain course of action. All we can do is wait."

"Without a warning at least?" Major Hanson said plaintively.

"If you want to call him, you may do so," the IGP said disinterestedly. "Just remember that I don't have space here to host the 1st Battalion."

Major Hanson blinked.

"What's the latest on the girls, though?" Amadu asked Atukwei. "Last I heard, the government had refused to mount an acceptable defence."

"The judges say they will rule at 4 p.m.," Atukwei said and checked his watch. "That's only an hour and a half away."

"Do you still believe the girls will let my justices go after their ruling?" Major Hanson asked Obuobi, who was tuning his TV set to catch the latest on the trial. He, too, had forgotten to follow up in the excitement of the President's order to turn up at the Jubilee House.

"They will have no reason to keep them," he told the Major with his feet back up on the conference room table. "Unless they wanted the ruling of the justices reviewed, but I don't get that sense at all. In any case, a positive ruling would mean a high court trial, and a supreme court justice cannot sit on a high court, only an appellate one. My money is on the scenario where they release all seven justices and abduct a high court judge to try the case."

"Isn't there anything we could do at all?" Lieutenant Brooks asked the IGP respectfully. "The thought that soldiers could be heading for the slaughter tonight makes me uncomfortable."

"We are doing all we can," the IGP told her, leaning a bit more comfortably in his leather-backed swivel chair.

"Which is?" she asked, puzzled.

"We are waiting," was the unhelpful response.

CHAPTER 16
Ground Zero
Tuesday, 19th March; 3 P.M.

CHIEF JUSTICE RAYMOND Adofiem rubbed at his temple to try to keep not only the migraine away but the irritability as well. He had inherited that trait from his father, and it never took much to make him waspish. But current training on inclusive work ethics and sensitivity classes and all the gender equality whatchamacallits had taught him to keep his emotions from blowing up to the surface no matter the provocation. But by all the seven known gods of Sikaman, he had had it with the back and forth among his judges. They had been talking non-stop for well over two hours now, and the chatter was what was giving him this sub episode of psychotic rage.

They had retired for lunch at noon, and immediately after had convened in his library to ponder over and rule on the matters before them. That had not been difficult for the facts at law were clear and unambiguous. But Justice Beatrice Afolabi was trying to get dissenting justices to change their minds and concur with her. And she kept going on about not wanting to die and that any ruling that pissed off the Girls could spell disaster for all of them.

"Why don't we just give the Girls what they want?" she was saying fearfully. "You all saw what they did to Apaloo's house. And I heard they even blew up a portion of the Jubilee House and pumped so many drugs into Justice Kwesi Boateng when they returned him that his own dog couldn't recognise him."

"It's not about giving them what they want," Justice Kwabena Wale shot back. "It's about what we understand the law to be. And even under the threat of death, justice must be delivered fearlessly. And so far, I don't believe justice is served by granting their plea. That they hold us hostage and threaten to kill us if they do not get what they believe is justice is not a reason to rule the other way. Judges have died for less in this country. If the girls are going to kill us, let us go down in a blaze of glory where the law is placed right where it should be without fear or coerced favour."

"But granting their plea is the rightful place of the law," Justice Vincent Kotei reminded Justice Wale. "The case the Girls have made would have called forth the same ruling whether I was in the Supreme Court building or on the toilet. The evidence of predatory behaviour since the nols pros speaks to the error and corruption of administrative justice by the granting of same," he said, using the short legal form of nolle prosequi. "The affidavits corroborate scores of infractions. To deny them a trial when we know the egregious derivatives anterior is no justice at all."

"If they believed their cause was just, why resort to such means?" Justice Lydia Agana asked Justice Kotei in a piping voice. "They had no right cause, which is why they resorted to guns. And having done so, it won't matter what legally sound principles we argue in favour of one or the other ruling; we are all going to die. The question for me is whether I die painfully or painlessly, and for me, agreeing to their motion is the fastest way to get out of here alive, and that's why I will grant their motion. Don't talk to me about derivatives and anterior."

"But is the fear of death going to be your legal argument in support of their pleadings?" Justice Wale demanded of Justice Agana. "That hardly sounds like a good pillar to hang a ruling on, does it?"

"Neither does it sound logical to put our lives needlessly on the line just because some in our judicial history have died for their rulings. Remember that those judges never had the opportunity to rule on the matter of the law *after* their abductions, but we do. And the opportunity after the fact is ours to save our own lives. You think if the martyrs, God rest their good souls, had opportunity to recant, they would not have taken it? You only live once o," Justice Agana wailed.

And so it went for a full half hour more until, unable to contain himself any longer, the Chief Justice banged his gavel on his own colleagues. It did get their attention, but before they could protest that judicial rules forbade him from doing so, he told them in his deep, clear voice, "There are only two issues before us, and two alone."

He looked at his justices to be sure he had all their attention, and he did. His demeanour tolerated no other asides, and their demeanours indicated they understood. So, he went on, "One: did the Attorney-General, by all the evidence presented to the court by plaintiff, as well as by her own responses to the evidence, have all the evidence she needed to secure a conviction in the Republic v. Duncan King, and for which its exercise of nolle prosequi was arbitrary? Is the answer to that question yes, or no? Show by hand all who say yes."

Hands went up.

Chief Justice Adofiem took note of the number and asked, "May I record any hands that did not raise as 'no'?"

There were no objections.

"Very well," he proceeded. "Now to the second question: Should the

Court quash the nolle prosequi on that determination and order a trial? Yes, or no?"

He read the room again and took judicious notice of each hand. And then he said, "Let's return to the litigants, issue the rulings that correspond with our decisions and go home. In the comfort of our homes, or chambers, we can then provide the detailed reasons for our decisions, as is our right and authority. Are we all in agreement?"

All six justices nodded their concurrence.

"Good," the Chief Justice said in obvious relief. "And you all wonder why it was me that was made the Chief Justice," he said with a half-jocular expression on his face. "All the jibber-jabber was unnecessary."

In Ghana, as in many other legal systems, judges had the authority to issue rulings or judgments before providing detailed reasons for their decisions. There were several reasons why the practice occurred. Issuing a preliminary ruling, for example, allowed the court to provide immediate guidance or resolution to the parties involved in a case. This was particularly useful in situations where time was of the essence, and here, Chief Justice Adofiem did not want to prolong the duress of his judges any more than he needed to, and with their lives on the proverbial line, there was an urgent need for a decision. By issuing a preliminary ruling, the court could address the pressing matter of their freedom without further delay and issue their reasoning later. Of course, while preliminary rulings provided an immediate decision, parties were still entitled to receive the detailed reasons for the ruling at a later stage because the reasons for decisions were crucial for transparency, accountability, and the possibility of appealing or challenging the decision through the appellate process, as they provided a comprehensive explanation of the legal principles and analysis applied by the court.

The justices then sent word through the telephone that they had reached a decision, and needed the court readied to sit at 4 p.m. on the dot. The woman on the line thanked them and promptly hang up to inform the Girls.

Asabea received word from Regina that the Chief Justice had called. The court would reconvene in forty minutes, she said. She looked at her watch just when the twins were entering their living room on the upper floor of the Fortress and announced to them that judgement would be delivered in the amphitheater at 4.

Oye and Nyhira looked like twin thunderclaps when they sat down.

"What's wrong with you both?" Aisha asked. "You look pissed off about something."

"We are a bit unsettled about your Opare," Nhyira accused Owuraku.

"Why? What happened?"

"Oye blindfolded him and asked that he directs us back to where we picked him up, seeing how he was running his mouth in here when we were talking to him earlier," Nhyira told them.

"He was correct the whole time back?" Efe asked in surprise.

"You bet your butt, he was," Oye supplied angrily.

"Then he told you the truth," Owuraku reminded the twins. "Why are you upset then?"

"A man that can read directions backwards when blindfolded both ways is a dangerous man," Nhyira told him. "I would feel a lot better if we prepared to be attacked tonight."

Owuraku looked at the twins thoughtfully for a while, unsure exactly how to respond to their misguided concerns. Eventually he said, "Kwaku Opare Addo is a professional, an expert at what he does. I understand if that makes you uncomfortable, but even he would not apologize about being the best. But I don't think it's fair to begrudge him for being that good. Whatever happens with the government, Opare will be no party to it, and when you pay him, he'll be at the foot of that cliff when needed."

"Explain to me why Opare worries you," Asabea asked her twins.

"I don't really know," Nhyira admitted ruefully.

"There's just this thing about him that is unsettling," Oye finished for her twin. "Like he knows and plans to do more than he lets on. I don't think he even flinched when we pointed our weapons at him. We didn't feel safe the entire time we were with him, and we were the ones with the guns."

Dede turned then to Owuraku and said, "Is there anything else you haven't told us about this guy?"

Owuraku shrugged helplessly and laughed. "I don't know what else to tell you," he said finally. "Any fears you have should be pointed in any direction other than in Opare's, I assure you, and that's all I can say to you on the matter."

Asabea was thoughtful for a minute, but she couldn't come up with anything else to say. She looked carefully at the twins. Their feelings had not once been wrong about anything, and if she had not had that epiphany herself, she would have taken wild precautions. It was an unsettling feeling, to be honest, and she closed her eyes and ran her hands through her hair for a second to stop the confusion.

When she opened her eyes, her girls were looking at her with worried expressions.

"Are you OK?" Aisha, the most sensitive of them all asked her.

"I think I am," she confessed, only not as self-assured. "It could be because of the anticipated judgment. I feel like there is so much that hinges on their judgment, and that's perhaps what is making me nervous."

Efe walked up to her and held her tightly for a minute.

"Everything will be just fine," she reassured her. "If they rule in our favour, everything will be as planned. If they don't – well, we'll see what we'll do."

"Wait a minute," Owuraku asked intensely. "We only have plans for if they rule in our favour, but have none for if they don't?"

"Essentially, yes," Bubuné told him in a quiet voice. "Whatever they rule, we must release the Justices tonight. We couldn't agree on what to do with Duncan King if they ruled against us, only what we would do if they ruled for us, and that remains the only flaw in our otherwise perfect plan."

"We could always shoot him," Owuraku said with meaning.

Asabea smiled and went over to hug him. And then everything felt alright again.

"Let's go hear what our judges have to say," she said. Holding Owuraku's hand, she walked confidently towards the stairs that led to the amphitheater.

President Offei sat pensively in the War Room after the meeting of his National Security Council. Presently, only members of his Cabinet remained to watch the justices rule on the television, and later to follow the action of his military in taking back his judges. The Army had decided on the simplest of approaches: shock and awe. No way he was going to look weak before a bunch of girls in an election year.

Having decided to act, the rudiments of the trial no longer interested him. He was going to have the courts overturn the whole damn sham anyway, which was why he had instructed his Attorney-General to give as little credence as possible to the proceedings with any serious legal representation of the government. The girls thought they were in charge. They were about to discover that they had been on a leash all this while, and he was the one holding the other end. He would yank them out of their skins so hard the history books would remember him for centuries to come.

Chief Justice Adofiem's clear voice interrupted the President's musings over the TV.

"In the matter of Akua Sakyibea Asabea vs. Attorney-General and Another, we all find as follows, with Wale, JSC solely dissenting that the Attorney-General had all the evidence she needed to more than likely secure a conviction in the Republic vs. Duncan King, and that the Attorney-General's exercise of the power of nolle prosequi in this instance was arbitrary and particularly injurious to the public interest. Consequently, this Court quashes the granting of nolle prosequi by the lower court in the instant case and orders that the criminal trial of the second defendant begin as soon as possible."

President Offei, his face looking like a thunderclap, told his Cabinet when they all turned to him after the reading of the ruling, "It changes nothing."

"Except that a 6-1 ruling will be impossible to overturn later," Patricia, the Attorney-General seemed crestfallen.

"We don't have to worry about the ruling," President Offei, himself a former Attorney-General, told Patricia. "We will have the whole trial itself overturned, and then we will see what happens to their ruling," he finished with meaning.

The Communications Minister then asked the National Security Coordinator, "What are the girls going to do next now that the ruling has gone in their favour?"

"Chief Superintendent Atukwei of the CTU believed that they would release the justices immediately after a favourable verdict and probably abduct a high court judge to run the trial," the coordinator replied, gauging the president's face to see if the mention of any of the detested police personnel was a red line. Seeing no animosity, he continued, "Based on that assessment, we have men assigned to each high court judge for their protection."

"What need would they have for a high court judge after tonight's operation, Kobby?" the President demanded.

"None, sir," was the meek response.

"Let's call a break and reconvene here at 10 p.m. then," President Offei ordered.

One of his aides walked in to say Asabea was on the line and that he was about to patch her through on the speakerphone. The TV screens had gone silent since the verdict was announced, even though live pictures of the amphitheatre were still beaming across the broadcast waves.

"Don't patch her through," was the surprisingly firm response.

"Wh-wh-why not?" Vice President Domwine stammered his surprise.

President Offei shrugged. "What else is she going to say? That she needs a high court judge delivered? Or that she is sending our Supreme Court justices back? They kidnapped them. They should find their own way to get them back and try to get through the cordon of soldiers I have stationed around the Aburi area. Let them stew in their own juices wondering what we are up to until they are brought to face my wrath."

And that ended the matter for the Cabinet.

Immediately after the reading of the verdict, the justices were ushered back into the Chief Justice's library and were shortly joined by Efe, Asabea and Dr. Ampem Darko.

"I came here to personally thank your Lordships, and to apologize once again for these frightening inconveniences. The Girls and I are truly grateful for your service and have made plans to transport you all back to the Supreme Court within the hour," Asabea told them sincerely.

"What do you plan to do next?" was the careful question from Justice Wale, the dissenting judge.

"We plan to see you all safely back in Accra, and to have a high court judge run the trial as your Lordships ordered."

"You're going to abduct another judge?" Justice Afolabi queried. "Young lady, when does this all end?"

Asabea looked kindly at the clearly fearful judge and said, "We will never hurt a judge of Ghana's courts. All we seek is justice, and if the verdict in the trial goes our way, the guilty defendant will face justice that will cause men to tremble when they remember it for years to come. But we mean no harm at all on any member of the judiciary."

The judges didn't know what else to say. But when it sunk in finally that they were free to go, each of them hurried back to their rooms to pack up for the return trip.

Which was weird.

Nothing in their rooms belonged to them.

Back inside their living room, the Girls group hugged for a full minute. On camera, all they had said in court was that they were grateful and had taken notice of Duncan King's unhappiness with the ruling. Ansah Premo had asked what was going to happen next in open court, but Efe had responded that that was going to be discussed later, after the judges had been seen back into their library.

But they had more pressing matters to attend to than satisfy the curiosity of Duncan King's lawyer. More pressing matters like this group hug and the sighs and sounds of ecstatic relief. Then, realizing that Owuraku had not been part of the hug, Asabea jumped on him and held him around the neck with her legs wrapped around his middle where he stood. A quiet sob escaped her as she clung to him. And then she laughed like the little girl she was on the inside, grateful for his presence throughout this period.

"How are we getting the justices out of here?" Owuraku wondered out loud when things had quieted down a bit.

"We have a self-driving van that will take them out into Accra," Regina explained when she walked in at that point. "We have a drone that will be stationed on the van and be our eyes on the road."

"What about the high court judge?"

"She is already here," Bubuné said with a smile. "Everyone and everything we need is here with us."

"Fantastic," Owuraku said approvingly. "So, what's next?"

"I need to call the President and let him know I am returning his judges, and that the trial will begin in earnest," Asabea said, reaching for the phone on the table in the middle of the room. One minute later, she hung up the phone and looked at the girls.

"The President has refused to take our call," she announced pensively.

"Did they say why?" Bubuné asked.

"No," Asabea responded, her mind racing.

"If he is refusing to engage then he is about to engage violently," was Owuraku's diagnosis.

"How do you know that?" Dede asked Owuraku.

"I know President Offei," was the unhelpful response. "Remember what I told you earlier that he doesn't give anything away? If he is refusing to take your call, then he either knows you're returning the judges, or he doesn't care because what he has planned for you is bigger and is already in motion."

"But they have no way to hack at us," Regina reminded him, showing green indicators on her laptop screen.

"There are many ways; we only haven't thought about them all," he

INVIOLABLE 110

responded, not unkindly. "But whatever or however they have done it, President Offei is gearing up for an offensive and we'd better be prepared.

"Isn't it weird that all this coincides with the visit of the Opare man?" Nhyira asked in an I-told-you-so voice.

"If it did, would our response be any different?" Owuraku asked.

"Our response wouldn't be," Asabea conceded.

"Then let's get ready."

"I will do a bit of reconnaissance by drone when the judges are on their way," Regina tried to reassure them. "We should be able to know more about what the President plans by then."

"Maybe," Owuraku was skeptical. "But let's work with the assumption that the President now knows where we are."

"If he did, why hasn't he come for his judges?" Aisha asked him.

"What if he just found us?" Owuraku asked her.

"Should that change the situation of the justices?" Oye wanted to know. "If we no longer have the President thinking they are hostages, wouldn't that factor into what kind of action he might want to take?"

"The justices have to leave regardless," Asabea said firmly. "And if Owuraku is right, it won't matter whether they are here or not."

"We can make it matter," Owuraku told her. A plan seemed to be forming in his mind. "Whatever he is planning, the President would like it to be known that he single-handedly rescued the judges. Let's take the wind out of his sail by announcing their release."

Then he paused with a look of confusion on his face.

"Of course, announcing that we no longer have his hostages would empower his Army to come at us with all the violence they are known for," he said. "Do we plan to defend solely by force of side arms, or we have technology to mess them up until the trial is over?"

"We have technology," Asabea responded confidently. "I wasn't counting on their offense until the trial was over, but if it comes to it, we have what it takes to hold them until after the trial – or until Opare comes for us," she finished with a meaningful look at Oye and Nhyira.

"Alright then," Owuraku said with some satisfaction. "My guess would be to prepare to be attacked today."

"We are prepared to be attacked every day," Bubuné informed him with her characteristic, tight smile.

Owuraku acknowledged her confidence but still looked thoughtful.

Asabea said, "Let's see the judges off then, and announce that to the world. And then it will be the Republic's turn to play their hand."

CHAPTER 17
Jubilee House
Tuesday, 19th March; 10 P.M.

THE COMBINED ARMS doctrine among technologically advanced countries referred to the integration and coordination of different military capabilities and assets across multiple branches of a country's military to achieve a synergistic effect on the battlefield. It involved the synchronized and cooperative use of infantry, armour, artillery, aviation, intelligence, logistics, and other supporting elements. This concept recognized that no single military component could achieve success independently. By combining various assets and capabilities, successful militaries aimed to leverage the strengths of each branch to overcome the weaknesses and challenges encountered during military operations.

In this present situation involving rescuing judges of the highest court and neutralizing female terrorists as a combined arms operation, the infantry units would need to be supported by armoured vehicles, artillery fire support, close air support from aircraft, and intelligence gathered from surveillance and reconnaissance assets. This coordinated approach would allow for the suppression of the Girls' defences, provide manoeuvrability of the units involved, protect friendly forces, and exploit opportunities in the operation effectively. In addition, such an operation would require careful planning, coordination, and communication among the various units and assets. The integration of ground forces, air power, intelligence support, and logistical capabilities would allow his battalion to conduct the operation across a range of scenarios, from conventional warfare to counterterrorism.

But this was not the situation facing Colonel Bruce Nartey of the first Infantry Battalion, Ghana Armed Forces. All he had been given were the coordinates to the Fortress and the troops forming his battalion. For artillery, he had a few trucks with a few machine gun nests, and when he asked for air support when he was receiving his operational orders inside the War Room of the Jubilee House, he was laughed out, he and his deputy commanders. If he couldn't apprehend seven female terrorists, he was told, then he needed his uniform removed.

The person who said the last bit was none other than the Commander-in-Chief himself, and all Colonel Nartey could do on the drive from Jubilee House to Aburi-Dumpong in the mountains was to sulk.

Thankfully, he didn't have to do that for long. Major Hanson, a platoon commander on secondment to the judiciary had called him on the request of the Chief of Army Intelligence to brief him on the potential preparedness of the Girls. Some Chief Superintendents of Police on the line had informed him not be fooled by the testimony of anyone if those testimonies were to the effect that these were mere girls in skirt with nothing but soap operas between their ears.

Not long after he had left the Jubilee House, news had reached him that all seven Justices of the Supreme Court had been returned to the government safely. Somehow, the girls had evaded the roadblocks and sentries posted along all major and minor roads leading to and from the Fortress and delivered the judges to the Police. He had reached out to his Generals to inquire if the news of the hostages being released changed anything, and he had been told in unpresidential language that the release of the judges "didn't change shit!"

Personally, he hadn't felt that designating this as a DefCon Three event was appropriate, in which case it should have been the Police CTU spearheading the situation. The idea of sending a whole battalion after just seven girls, whatever they may have done, did not appeal to him, and not because he was chauvinist.

But come on, a thousand troops after seven girls?

The Chief Superintendents of Police had told him to expect an unconventional response to his battalion's invasion of the Fortress, but he couldn't ask him what he meant before he had to cut the call because President Offei was on call-waiting. The President had informed him that he and the entire people of Ghana were counting on his success, and after that warm call, nothing the Police had said mattered in any case. He was Lieutenant Colonel Bruce Nartey, Commander of the 1st Battalion. The girls would find out soon enough what that meant.

Owuraku Ampem Darko stopped his pacing when Regina came to inform him and the Girls that the M-Q9 Reaper they had sent with the judges' conveyance for reconnaissance had returned aerial footages showing hundreds of troops stationed rather indolently around the entire Aburi area, and that columns of armoured vehicles carrying military personnel and artillery were headed their way from Akropong. Owuraku had been pacing because a few hours earlier the trial judge, Mr. Justice Stephen Frimpong, had given fourteen days to the exercise of empanelling a jury for the trial of Duncan King once he had satisfied himself that the bill of indictment that was served on the teenage-raping scum ten years ago still passed legal muster.

The Girls had been unprepared for that turn of events. They had believed it was going to be a straight trial, backed by the fact that the use of juries in criminal trials was not as common in Ghana as in some other jurisdictions. The decision to use a jury or go ahead with a judge-alone trial depended often on the nature of the offense and on the court in which the trial was conducted.

The Girls had seized everyone that Duncan King's counsel had listed in the original trial. The first was Larry King, the defendant's cousin. And then there was Billy Blanks of the fashion show entity who was also Duncan King's friend and a television broadcaster. There were three others including a gynaecologist, a crime scene expert, and the arresting officer. These had all been kept in separate quarters at the Fortress, unknown to Ansah Premo who had smugly informed the trial judge in the opening arguments that evening that no trial could be conducted without his witnesses.

And with the Ghana Army about to knock on their gates, Owuraku was worried that the elaborate process of empanelling jurors was time they did not have on their hands. Not surprisingly, it was Ansah Premo who had argued vehemently in support of a jury trial, but the State Prosecutor and the deputy Attorney-General, who were now forced to work with Efe and Asabea for the prosecution, sided with the judge's first preference for a judge-alone trial. Premo reminded the court that he and his client were the ones who had argued against a jury trial when the Magistrate court had first committed his client to trial at the fast-track High Court, and the prosecution had then smugly insisted on a jury. He had reminded the court that he had been disappointed in that ruling because he had been preparing for that trial as early as one o'clock of that morning.

The process of empanelling a jury in Ghana involved many steps. First the Registrar of the High Court needed to compile a list of potential jurors from the Electoral Commission's voters' register. The list typically included individuals who were eligible to vote and met the requirements for jury service. Then the court issued summonses to the potential jurors, requiring them to appear on a specified date and time for jury service. Then came the vexatious and antagonistic vetting and challenging of jurors by the prosecution, the defence and, of course, the judge, to decide the candidates' suitability for the trial. Both the prosecution and defence could challenge potential jurors based on grounds provided by law, such as bias or lack of impartiality. Only then were the seven-member jury empanelled and sworn in.

How were they to find that list and abduct Ghanaian voters when there was an army at the gates?

When Efe had suggested that they organize the selection process online, Ansah Premo had objected so vehemently that the trial judge had ruled he would take a decision under advisement. The proceedings were then adjourned to tomorrow at 9 a.m.

After Regina had showed them the footages, and the Girls had taken note of all the hardware the Army was coming at them with, Asabea said pensively, "This is what we trained for."

"Kindly forgive me," Owuraku informed her deferentially. "But I don't believe for a minute that you trained to hold a trial, find jurors and hold off a battalion of infantry. No one can train for that."

"We prepared for scenarios far worse than that in Libya," Efe told him confidently.

"At least they are attacking at night," Aisha said with some satisfaction. "Which gives us the advantage of both terrain and cover."

"If Kwaku Opare Addo is with them –" Oye started with meaning, examining her manicured hands.

"– Then we have dibs on his butt," Nhyira finished.

Owuraku gave them a quizzical look but said nothing.

"When do you think the Command column will get here?" Dede asked Regina, looking intently on the screen of the large TV in their living room. She was making some calculations on a tablet.

"By my calculations, at 10 p.m.," Regina told them. "They didn't seem to be in any real hurry."

"That sounds like a midnight attack," Asabea said with a tight smile.

"So predictable," Bubuné said with a little shaking of her head. "None of them will attack unless a Senior Officer appears. Gives us all the advantages of neutralizing a command centre."

"Do you plan to strike preemptively, or you'll wait for their lead?" Owuraku asked, a bit less anxiously after seeing how calm the Girls were taking the news.

Asabea shrugged. "Once they reach the pass it won't matter who takes the first shot," she said confidently.

"Any thoughts about how they found us," he asked Regina.

Regina shrugged. "It doesn't matter now, does it?" she asked helplessly. "They're here now, but I will run some tests to see how."

"You're right, it doesn't matter," Owuraku said to her kindly. "Let's just hope the judge agrees to an online jury selection process. There's no way you're bringing in potential jurors through that," he said, pointing to the many soldiers on the screen.

"Let him decide, and then we'll see," Asabea said thoughtfully.

She looked at her watch.

It read 7 p.m.

"Let's go live at dinner and let them think we know nothing of their attack," she ordered Regina. "And then at the last moment, let's let our audiences know what's happening."

"We will need prolonged eyes in the skies for the Army though," Regina suggested.

"Load a few Reapers and deploy them. If they are attacked, they will drop a few payloads. That should discourage them from stifling our journalistic efforts."

Regina smiled and left their living room to carry out the instructions.

"What are you smiling at?" Bubuné asked Owuraku.

"Command becomes you," he said to Asabea in response.

"You are right about the jury though," Asabea conceded ruefully. "We didn't think of that at all, else we would have had 30 voters waiting in the cellars below."

"But you're sure you can hold the Fortress against a battalion?" He asked her. "While underfunded and just as corrupt as any other government entity, the Ghana Armed Forces have been working to develop and refine their operational effectiveness and the integration of various military capabilities. Can we hold them for shizzle?"

"We'll see before the night is over," Asabea reassured him. "Right now, let's all go have dinner and take what naps we can. We are going to have a rather extended night, and I don't want anyone to miss anything."

The plan had been quite simple, to be honest. Larry and Duncan King had devised it and they had been sure it would work. They had noticed, probably because the Supreme Court justices had demanded it, that none of the Girls carried arms into the more open aspects of their life under abduction. While the justices had been specific about not seeing any guns within a hundred feet of the amphitheatre, the Girls had extended the courtesy to the dining area and corridors of the entire first floor. After the seven justices had left, and during the preliminary motions of the criminal trial this evening, they had noticed again that none of them carried weapons of any kind around this floor, which was where their living quarters were also sequestered.

Ansah Premo was the damp squid of the planning, but he too soon got around to it. He had been particularly displeased when he found out the Girls had intended to carry on with the criminal trial immediately. That they had already seized a high court judge for the exercise made him angry six ways to Sunday, and during the pretrial motions, he had raised so much hell it was a wonder the Girls had not done him some violence right in court. The bitches had argued that they would present whoever Ansah Premo needed as a witness, and Premo had demanded that everyone on his witness list be accessible to him before trial commenced by the judge's decision within fourteen days.

Duncan King had never seen Ansah Premo make that much of a nuisance of himself in any public gathering, so he had thoroughly enjoyed it, and wished it had lasted longer, but the judge had cut to the chase of the matter and ended what was clearly an entertaining spectacle to the watching public, given all the comments and reactions that were pouring in live on social media.

That watching public was the one reason he had supported the plan. Let them know that he and his friends could fight back, and show 'em bitches that they were messing with a god Emcee. It went without thinking, but he thought it anyway, that fully half the people watching the proceedings were on his side. His popularity glass was half full, and that pleased him infinitely.

Dinner this evening was charcoal-grilled steak in creamy mushroom sauce, accompanied by a choice of either buttery mashed potatoes or vegetable fried rice. And all the world knew that steak was eaten by steak knives, and theirs felt particularly sharp for tonight's mission. The dining room had an interior that showcased a tasteful combination of hard wood and rustic floors, creating a harmonious symphony of textures. The rich, earthy tones of the wooden elements lent an air of timelessness to the space, while the weathered appearance of the rustic floors evoked a sense of history and heritage. If he didn't have bloody plans for tonight, Duncan King would have been swept away as he always was at mealtimes by the ambience of walls; walls that were adorned with striking paintings depicting sweeping savannah landscapes, intricate tribal patterns, and vibrant market scenes. The flickering glow of carefully placed antique lanterns cast a gentle, warm light that danced across their wooden tables, imparting an aura of intimacy and conviviality.

Duncan King shook himself out of his thoughts. That bitch from his first days who had quoted Samuel Butler was right, but he was not an animal that was going to be eaten.

He was the eater.

He locked eyes with Larry and Premo when dinner was done. They had agreed to wait until they had had their fill. There was no use going to battle on an empty stomach.

They looked around.

The catering staff were about entering to clear the tables, an all-female staff of four in white aprons and crocs. There were twenty-five people in all in the dining room, maybe more. The only other abductee not present by their reconning was the trial judge who, by Ghanaian custom, could not be seen eating in public. Neither were the supreme court justices found in the dining room when their part of this orchestrated morasses was in motion. Their meals had been delivered to them in their libraries, they had then learnt.

Anyone in the dining room could move as freely about as they wanted, but people tended to congregate among themselves in tight groups. By some unspoken rule, all the abductees occupied the right side of the dining room while the bitches and their aiders and abetters occupied the left side. Exchanges between both sides were brief and surprisingly respectful. The Asabea-bitch sat around a wide table a few feet from the main entrance, dining with all her girls and the young professor, and foolishly unsuspecting.

With the catering staff coming in, this was as good a diversion as they were going to get. With one more visual confirmation, all three of them wiped their mouths with their napkins, rose from their tables taking the napkins balled up in their hands, and headed for the table of their nemeses. It took all of seven steps to close the distance between their tables, approaching at different angles to ensure that at least one of them would be successful.

The more athletic Larry King arrived at the right side of the table first, unveiled his steak knife from the napkin and made a stab with his right hand at the bitch that sat with her back to him. Even while throwing his weight into his arm as he sliced towards the Asabea broad, who sat in the middle of the group, Duncan heard the satisfying scream from Larry's target. But before his hand could complete the arc to Asabea's neck, that prescient professor pushed the Asabea broad out of the way and met his charge with his own arm after rising quickly from where he sat to the left of the bitch. The meddling fool took the stabbing that belonged to the broad in his right biceps. Duncan King hadn't noticed earlier, but the prof did have the upper arm of a regular weightlifter. How he took mental notice of all that while his heart raced with excitement beat him, but having missed his target, he pulled out the knife from the prof's flesh and tried to attack again around the younger man, but he was too slow. The prof punched him heavily on the nose with his other hand and wrestled the knife out of his right hand with the bleeding one. He felt himself about to fall from the punch as had the knife, but one of the bitches pulled him up from his right by the collar and tased him full switch in his neck, her snarly lips a mere inches away from his bleeding nose.

As the electrical charge coursed through his body, time slowed down, and his senses become acutely heightened. He heard Ansah Premo crying out in pain. Before he'd gotten tased he saw Premo's target twist out of the way of his strike with a mere inch to spare and punched him in the jaw so hard that he heard his lawyer's lower mandible snap.

A wave of searing pain then radiated across Duncan King's body like thousands of tiny needles pricking his skin all at once. It was overwhelming enough to engulf his entire consciousness, erasing any other thoughts or sensations, but somehow, the loud crack of Larry King's skull hitting the floor when he fell under the attack of the bitch he was supposed to have stabbed rang in his ears before he too descended into instant nothingness.

CHAPTER 18
The Parallel War Room
Wednesday, 20th March; 8.30 P.M.

THE SENIOR OFFICERS of the CTU and their IGP had had all seven Supreme Court justices brought to the Police Headquarters at 6 p.m. and had extracted from them every information they could concerning their abduction and their forced adjudication. There really wasn't much that the Police didn't already know, but hearing from judges who had personally lived through the experience provided steeped perspectives that could come in handy later.

It seemed to Amadu and the Police that the judges were as much in the dark as they were about the layout of the Fortress. The judges believed there was no more than one floor and a basement, but the district blueprints attested to four floors. The judges did not seem to remember accessing anywhere else other than the amphitheatre, their personal living quarters, including the libraries, and the courtyard. From their windows, all of them attested to seeing mountains and a thick wall. Nothing more. As to the mental condition or psyche of their abductors, Chief Justice Adofiem insisted he had never met more courteous, considerate women.

After about two hours of debriefing, Major Hanson and his platoon escorted the justices to secured locations. The Chief Justice had not seen the need for the precautions, but the IGP had insisted that they needed to be kept under guard for a while.

Not long after the justices had left was when mayhem broke out in the dining room of the Fortress on live television. Everyone in the room stood up to observe what was happening on the screens, and even when the rebellion seemed to have been quelled by the Girls, a lot of questions remained unanswered, foremost of which was why the heck the three men would attempt a coup when it was obvious, even without any display of arms, that the Girls were capable.

"8:30 p.m.," Obuobi kept saying for the duration of the steak knife episode until Atukwei asked him what he meant.

"The Army goes on the attack at 8:30 p.m."

"How do you know?" the IGP demanded. "And it's already 8:30 p.m.," he informed him from looking at his watch.

Obuobi pulled up some satellite imagery and pointed to large columns of troops lined up shortly before the defile of the Fortress on his screens. Also, as if on cue, the Girls started beaming live infrared footage of the impending attack across the televisions.

"There goes their element of surprise," Amadu remarked.

On the television, composite imagery showed soldiers advancing towards the Fortress, and the Girls asking everyone in the dining room to retire to their rooms. A couple of gurneys had come in with armed nurses to pick up Duncan King, Larry King, Ansah Premo and one of the Girls, but no one could tell the gravity of their injuries or which of the Girls had been hurt.

"Not bad to attack during the confusion, to be honest," Atukwei remarked.

"Perhaps," Obuobi responded without certainty. "Confusion and chaos are not exactly good recipes for a hostage situation, to be honest, but with the justices out of the way, I doubt prudence is the goal of this operation."

"The Girls actually plan to telecast the battle?" the IGP demanded of no one when that fact dawned on him. He seemed surprised and stood gawking at the footage coming in of the Army's approach to the Fortress.

"The defile," Amadu was saying with wide eyes as he drew closer to the television screens. "That's like a drawbridge, isn't it?"

"That could only mean one thing," Obuobi caught Amadu's drift and dialed excitedly on the speakerphone.

"What are you doing?" the IGP demanded.

"I am calling Jubilee House," was the determined response.

"What do you want," President Offei asked gruffly, picking on the first ring.

"Sir, you need to abort the attack right now or many men will lose their lives," Obuobi said breathlessly to the President.

"What are you talking about?" the President demanded irritably.

"You have a quarter thousand soldiers gathered on a camouflaged drawbridge," the IGP butted in urgently at that moment, dispensing with the usual butt-kissing protocol of calling him his Excellency. "If the Girls destroy it, as I think they will, no one will survive the two hundred metre fall to the chasm below. Pull the men back!"

"Just who the frack do you think you're talking to?" President Offei shouted angrily on the line and hung up.

Obuobi was never sure whether the call ended first, or that it was the drawbridge that collapsed first, but either way, right on national TV, they saw in clear drone footage a series of sharp detonations that took out what had now been revealed to be a master class in deception. While marked out as a defile on the toposheets, what separated the Fortress from the rest of the land was no pass but a man-made land bridge, covered in rocks and soil to look like land but in essence, a trap constructed of destructible wood, balls and chains. This was probably why the original owners had claimed they could defend it against a battalion.

But there was more. With the drawbridge destroyed, along with more than a quarter of Colonel Nartey's battalion, the Fortress now appeared to sit at the pinnacle of a loan mountain, surrounded by steep, unassailable valleys.

The groans and cries of many men ascended, and it looked like some equipment had caught fire in the surprise fall, perhaps grenade launchers and their contents detonated as they fell. A big fire bellowed from the deep valley below, and the Girls' drones captured the cries of men burning and flames lighting the valleys up in many shades of fiery orange.

"My gosh!" the IGP exclaimed, unable to watch the debacle anymore. He placed his hands on his head and walked away to a window on the far side of the room.

Major Hanson called on the speakerphone.

"Have you seen what's happening?" he demanded when Atukwei picked up.

"We warned you this wasn't going to be a ride in the park, didn't we?" Atukwei shot back. "Can you call the Colonel? He needs to retreat before he loses whatever is left of his men."

"I don't think he'll pick up his phone in this situation, but his command phone can be reached only by three people in a war situation: the President, the Chief of Army Staff and the Chief of Defense Staff in that order."

"The President won't be any help," Amadu told him, his face looking sick from watching the scene on TV. "He cussed at us when we told him to pull back, and this was even before the Girls took out their bridge."

"This is not good," Hanson said on the line.

"Tell us something we don't already know," Atukwei reminded him.

"What do we do?"

"We?" the IGP came in at that point in disgust. "This is all on President Offei and your Generals," he finished angrily. "All of this is on you."

"I-I mean, what can we do?" Major Hanson stammered.

"We wait until the Commander-in-Chief comes to his senses," the IGP responded gravely. "Until then, your best hope is to reach Colonel

Nartey and have him withdraw."

Speed was all Owuraku had thought about when he saw Duncan King pull out a steak knife from inside his napkin from the corner of his eye. He had been about to take one last spoonful of his creamy mushroom sauce at their dining table. He would not have registered anything amiss if the light from the electric lanterns had not glinted off Duncan King's knife the wrong way. And speed was what he had relied on when he'd launched his body into Asabea that had knocked her chair and her neck out of harm's way, to be replaced by his muscular biceps. And the sonofabitch had had the temerity to try and strike at her again. He was lucky all he broke was his nose before Efe had come to neutralize him with a taser.

In the table opposite him, Aisha had taken a knife to her ribs but was pummeling Larry King's face to a bloody potpourri of flesh, spit and teeth until Dede had tased the raping scum's cousin in the neck till he too had dropped to the floor. Ansah Premo hadn't had much luck either, and before long, medics were all over the dining room, seeing first to Aisha and Asabea, before hauling the three men onto gurneys, shackling their feet to the side rail latches before hurrying them into the infirmary.

Regina barged into the room before they could take stock of what had just happened and announced that the Army were almost upon them.

"How did they get past you in Aburi?" Asabea asked her in surprise, while running after Aisha's gurney.

"Half their men were on foot," Regina explained apologetically, "And the Reapers are too loud in mountain echoes to have gotten close enough without their noticing. But they left the bulk of their trucks and tanks behind. We have only seven or so assorted vehicles moving towards the pass."

"Have the dining room and the corridors cleared then," she ordered, "And let's meet in the Press Box in five minutes."

"Are we still live on TV?" Owuraku asked, pushing the gurney as quickly as he could with his one good arm, and ignoring the blood oozing out of his right upper arm.

"We are," Asabea said to him breathlessly, looking at the fast-whirring cameras along the corridor to the infirmary. "Sound has been cut but we are live."

"Good," Owuraku said as he barged into the operating room.

"What's good in particular?"

"We'll have the support of the public when justice is finally done."

"The justice that will be done will be all about the public, Kuuku," Asabea replied confidently.

Three surgeons stripped Aisha of the clothing around her injuries and began to assess her situation. A fourth came to examine Owuraku's arm.

"It needs stitches," she announced and immediately got to work on Owuraku's arm. He winced when the needle first went it.

"Don't be a baby," she scolded him.

Owuraku watched the doctor with a look that made Asabea laugh.

"Will Aisha be alright," he asked the doctor after she was done with him.

"So far, the scans don't show any puncture in her lungs," she said, "And the knife missed her ribs. Any inch above or below the knife point, and I'd have been talking to a corpse."

"I feel alright, though," Aisha told them from where she lay under the surgical lights. "And I'm glad I got my fists into his face," she said with grim satisfaction.

"Where are they?" Owuraku asked Asabea.

"Passed out in another operating room," she said, pulling him to her and leading the way out of the room. "Another team of surgeons are attending to them."

"Alright," he replied, walking with his left arm around Asabea as she led the way. In the corridor to the Press Box, she pushed him gently against the wall and kissed him. She noticed the look of surprise on his face, but that spurred her on, turning what started as a chaste kiss into the irreverent French kind.

"You know this would dent your tough girl reputation if word got out that you kissed?" Owuraku told her with a wink when they stopped to catch their breath.

She smiled at him and said, "I've been meaning to kiss you since I watched you sleeping in your room on campus. Thank you for saving my life." Then she held his hand and led him to the Press Box.

"The Fortress is on lockdown," Bubuné reported as soon as they walked in.

"And I have briefed Justice Frimpong on what has happened, even though he understood much of it from what he saw on his TV," Efe informed the group.

At least seven Reapers were beaming footage of the impending assault into the console of the Press Box, which had standing room for at least twenty people. The Box had technicians working to broadcast the various angles of footage from the cameras inside the Fortress as well as of the troop movements outside.

"The soldiers are now in front of the pass," Regina reported excitedly from her side of the large console."

"Is this where the defense of the Fortress will be organized?" Owuraku asked Asabea.

"For now, yes," she replied. "It is only when they breach the gates that actual combat will begin, but for now, we have a few tricks we can use to hopefully dampen their enthusiasm."

"When you say 'tricks'?" Owuraku asked curiously.

"You'll see in a bit," Aisha said from the doorway of the Press Box. They all turned to stare at her.

"What the heck?" Dede demanded anxiously of one of the surgeons.

The doctor raised her hands helplessly and said, "As soon as we discovered that the knife had missed any vital organs, she got up and left," she said plaintively.

"I am fine," Aisha told them reassuringly. "Besides, I won't miss this for anything," she finished, pointing to all the action about to begin on the screens.

"No," Asabea told her, her face ghostly. "We haven't even had time to process what has happened, but I need you to heal, Aisha."

Then she turned to Dede and said, "Please see Aisha back to the infirmary. Then turning to the surgeon, she said, "Give her whatever you have to so she can rest."

"No one is giving me anything, and that's final," Aisha said, only it didn't sound final when it was apparent her wound dressing was getting soaked with more blood.

"Dr. Modupe!" Asabea said urgently, but Owuraku was already moving, with Dede at his side. He bundled Aisha up in both arms, uncaring about the pain and stiches in his right, and carried her like she weighed nothing back to the infirmary over Aisha's increasingly weaker protestations.

When he returned to the Press Box with Dede, after ensuring that Aisha was appropriately sedated, the Girls were manning what looked like battle stations on the large console.

"What is this?" he demanded curiously.

"These consoles control hydraulic pressure currents to the drawbridge," Bubuné explained. "When we activate them, the entire fifty-foot pass will collapse."

Owuraku gazed at the screens with his eyes wide. The Girls had activated a steel barricade in front of the pass from their side of the dividing chasm, and it was behind that barrier that some several troops stood.

"How many soldiers are on it now?" he asked.

"As far as we can tell, some three hundred," Bubuné advised him. "Any more troops and it will take something more significant to dislodge them."

"If you blow the bridge up any later, you might split troops between the sides," he said. "And desperate soldiers will do anything."

Bubuné looked to Asabea for confirmation.

Asabea nodded her assent but before the Girls could activate whatever they needed to, a series of detonations thundered, vibrating the Fortress in their intensity, and on the screens, the drawbridge came apart in the middle, throwing soldiers and equipment down the abyss.

Asabea was aghast when she said, "*We* didn't do that."

"What do you mean?" Owuraku asked, puzzled.

"When we activate our hydraulics, the bridge swings down, and triggers a net within which the troops would have fallen into. They could have climbed out of it eventually, but *this* is not our doing."

Then, turning to Regina, she ordered, "I need the footages rewound. I need to know exactly what caused that split."

One minute later, more detonations reverberated from deep down the valley.

"What was that?" Efe asked, startled.

"They had a few grenade launchers on the bridge, and several rockets, I think," Bubuné told her. "I expect those exploded in the fall. Look at all that smoke coming in from the valley," she said, pointing to the footage now coming in clearer on the drones' cameras.

Sure enough, blackened smoke was pouring up out of the valley, and with it, the screams of several hundred soldiers. Even in the safety of the Fortress, the smell of burnt bodies hung in the air before the air filters got to work.

Then one of the drones' cameras went dark.

"Snipers," Bubuné hissed. "Release the affected drone's payload," she ordered Regina. "Keep it close enough to sack them but not so close as to hurt them."

Regina typed in a series of commands on her tablet and one of the drones captured the drone whose camera was taken out ascending higher out of reach of the snippers and then suddenly make a series of sorties that dropped grenades around the troops, harrying them from the edge of the open mouth of the pass and burning all the equipment and trucks within the area.

"That accounts for half the battalion now," Bubuné said.

"Pardon?" Owuraku demanded.

"They have lost half their battalion now," she explained sadly. "That leaves another five hundred."

"President Offei isn't going to like it," Owuraku said. "And they have at least two weeks to avenge their troops. This is war."

"Yes, but we didn't start this," Asabea said to him and turned to Regina. "Have you gotten the footage I wanted?"

"Yes, it's on line 4," Regina said.

Fifteen seconds of the footage in question showed a flash of light and smoke emanating from behind the platoons seconds before an RPG or a shell struck the middle of the drawbridge. Smoke engulfed the soldiers on the pass for a second before the bridge split from the impact.

"They fired on their own troops," Owuraku was shocked.

"What I'd like to know," Bubuné said with her eyes widened in surprise at the screen, "is why?"

Amadu and the IGP stood dumfounded directly in front of the screens. They were soon joined by Obuobi who, up until now, had been manning the phones, trying to persuade the President and the defense minister to withdraw the troops. And with the Girls showing they had air superiority, he had hoped to persuade them some more, but all his pleas had fallen on deaf ears.

"This is a disaster," Obuobi said.

"This is war," the IGP said. "And this is what we had been trying to avoid by preaching caution."

"What do you think is going to happen now?" Amadu asked his boss who was turning away from the screens to go find a chair.

"I think it's already happening," Obuobi said with his eyes fixed animatedly on the screens. "They are bringing in the Air Force."

"We have only 14 aircraft in service, and with that, a full nine are not combat ready. Unless the government plans to throw everything it has into the fight, including killing the hostages, this is probably to rescue injured soldiers," the IGP explained.

"This is a disaster," Dr. Obuobi repeated his earlier observation.

"Just for fun," Atukwei asked irritably, "Why is this a disaster from your point of view?"

"The Girls have taken out half the battalion without actually committing to combat," he explained. "If you think about it, they haven't declared war yet. The drawbridge just fell, and if we hadn't shot at their drones, they probably wouldn't have harassed the rear of the retreating troops. Their stance is purely defensive."

"We can see that," Atukwei said with exaggerated patience. "I haven't heard anything about your disaster yet."

"Well," he started and then pulled out one of his maps. "The chasm is a hundred feet long at where the bridge used to be," he pointed out. "That means there is no way to get at them or the hostages except by air. These hostilities have dimmed all peaceful options, and that means the President and the Army will only consider an all-out attack. Eventually, the Girls would have to escape and keeping the hostages is the only way they can do so with a slimmer possibility of not getting killed."

"Unless they planned to die," Atukwei reminded him. "Because even they would need superpowers to escape from the Fortress now that the bridge is down."

"Was the bridge downed completely, or was it lowered in a way that it could be brought back up?" the IGP asked from his chair by the conference table.

"Seems to be destroyed," Amadu responded after squinting at the TV to be sure.

"The Army will feel backed into a corner," Obuobi kept explaining. "And that will mean an all-out attack. There will be no help for the hostages. We need to focus now on the Girls. And find out how they plan to escape."

"How can they escape from this when they have torn down their own escape route?" the IGP asked him. "I thought you were the one who said no one can come at them from behind the cliff?"

"I said only one person could," Obuobi clarified. "If we find out how, we may be able to position ourselves to get the hostages when the Girls try to escape," he concluded.

The IGP chewed on his words for a while. There were too many moving parts to decide what course of action was the best. He knew there was no way the Armed Forces would let his officers in on the action, thanks to President Offei's shortsightedness, but there was not going to be any happy ending without his men.

"Where is he?" he demanded of Obuobi.

"Where is who?" Obuobi asked, puzzled.

"That one man you know who could get to the Girls from behind that cliff."

Obuobi blinked.

"Kwaku Opare Addo will never collaborate with us," he opined flatly. "He has no love for this country in his heart. He'd most probably rather help rescue the Girls if they asked him to."

"Then let's get him to do that," the IGP said in all seriousness. "Let's set him up to rescue the Girls and the hostages and bring them to us."

"I don't follow," Obuobi asked, confused.

"If he is the only one you know who can pull a rescue of this nature off, let's contract him to do just that because no one is coming out of that Fortress alive now that the Army has lost half a thousand men."

Atukwei said with a chuckle, "President Offei won't like it very much if we steal the Girls right from under his Army's nose."

"I don't give two craps about his Girls or his Army," the IGP responded intensely. "My duty lies with those hostages, and if rescuing them requires that we rescue the Girls too, then so be it. Let's give this Opare guy all he needs to succeed, and then we'll see who really has what it takes to resolve this issue."

CHAPTER 19
The Fortress
Thursday, 21st March; 6.30 A.M.

LARRY KING REGAINED consciousness at dawn in excruciating pain. There was a nurse – a doctor actually – who was regulating his medication when he came to, but whatever she was giving him could not quell the throbbing headache fast enough. His neck felt especially stiff and turning it this way or that way served to only magnify his pain. He couldn't move his hands – he had tried that and failed ten times already – and his feet were shackled to his sick bed. If he could move a hand, he would massage the pain out of his neck a little, but the more he thought about the desire, the more tormented he felt until, unable to contain it any longer, he let out a loud scream for help.

The face that bent over his in response was none other than Aisha's, the woman he had tried to murder. The throbbing pain in his head went up a notch.

The woman was also dressed in a patient's garb as he was, but unlike his face, which registered consternation and a sense of dread, hers sported a mischievous twinkle.

"What's with the yelling?" she asked him in the tone assumed by most Ghanaian doctors and nurses in the public sector renowned for treating patients like they do a dish of bacteria.

"My neck hurts badly," Larry heard himself say hoarsely as he looked at Aisha warily.

"That's because I beat the crap out of your neck and smacked your skull on the dining room floor," was the smug response. Then he felt her moving around his bed, but his neck was too stiff to follow her except with his eyes. His beating heart sounded off like a gong following every throb of the pulsating pain in his head and he almost passed out when she bent over his body on the right side.

She tinkered with his straps a bit until he could raise his hand, which reached only as far as the side of his neck before the chain yanked it back a bit. Even that tiny bit of force sent his headache through the roof. Afterwards he was careful not to pull his hand too quickly.

After he had worked on his neck with his fingers, he was able to turn his neck a little bit. He looked at Aisha and asked, "Why are you helping me?"

Aisha grabbed a seat close to his bed and said, "I *will* kill you."

He blinked her into sharp focus. There was no mistaking the

determination in her eyes. But what increased the pain in his head was the calm way she said it. There was no hate, no anger, and no vitriol. Just a beautiful young woman telling her attempted murderer she was going to end his life.

He closed his eyes to pacify the pain a little. When he reopened them, she asked him, "Why did you do it?"

He sighed.

"It seemed appropriate at the time," he said shortly. And then he closed his eyes again. That much effort was sending blows through his brains, causing tears to streak down his face. When he opened his eyes again after what seemed a long time, Aisha was still looking at him.

The truth was he had only seen an opportunity he'd tried to exploit when it had dawned on him that the Girls were lax about carrying their weapons around. It hit him even more now that, other than during their abductions, the Girls weren't really menacing anyone. Perhaps his hatred of helplessness was what had driven him to conceive of a plan to take back some control but the real issue for him was that he had not appreciated being pulled into this whole saga again when everything he had done from day one had been to avoid getting involved. That was what had made him reckless. And he said as much to her.

Aisha looked at him with a look akin to pity, but not much else.

"Where is Duncan King and his lawyer," he asked her with painful effort.

"They are in the next ward," Aisha said without much interest.

"How are you able to walk around after a stabbing?" he asked in surprise.

"You missed my vital organs," she told him. "And I heal fast."

"I'm sorry I did that," he said with meaning.

"Doesn't matter," Aisha told him, not unkindly. "I'm not sorry I burst your head and rearranged your face, though. I'd do it again in a heartbeat."

He smiled weakly and asked, "So what's going to happen to us?"

Aisha shrugged. "We'll patch you up as best we can and prepare you for the trial. You're a key defense witness, according to your lawyer, so I imagine the doctors have been working hard to restore you to as coherent a state as they can. Your friends came to around midnight and are being patched up as much as is possible."

"How bad are they?" Larry asked weakly.

"Duncan King's face isn't pretty anymore, and I don't think Ansah Premo can chew *wele* for a while," was the succinct response.

"Otherwise, they are in much better shape than you are."

"I think you can stop aggravating my patient now," Dr. Ellen Modupe interrupted at that point and gently pushed Aisha away from the ward. Aisha spared just a glance at Larry before leaving, and the injured man inferred from that look that, while kind and courteous, there was no way he was going to get out of this alive if it was left to her.

He sighed deeply and closed his eyes again.

All was quiet on the Army's invasion front, but the Girls and Owuraku hadn't slept a wink. Expecting more from the military, they had stayed awake and alert to respond to whatever the Army planned to throw at them. Bubuné was particularly waspish from her disappointment that nothing had happened through their wake of the night.

"What were you expecting?" Owuraku asked her. "That they'd attack again after losing so many men? Even the dumbest commander can see that continuing an attack after these losses is suicidal."

"I just wanted something decisive to happen so they could leave us alone while the trial continued," she explained. "I don't want to keep looking behind my back. And I don't feel like a firm message has been delivered to them on just how much we mean business."

"Oh, I think the message was delivered alright," Asabea told her. "Look, they are pulling their equipment away from the edge."

"How far can they pull away before we lose visuals?" Owuraku asked Regina.

"We won't lose visuals unless they try to shoot us down," Regina replied. "Beyond these mountains the land plateaus and offers little cover so they have nowhere to hide. It was smart of them to travel at night. We wouldn't have let them get this far if it had been day."

"At some point, they will attack though," Owuraku advised coolly.

"I believe so too," Bubuné agreed. "Which is why I wish it was sooner. We have a trial to run."

"And that trial starts in two hours," Owuraku reminded them. "How are the casualties doing?"

"Aisha went to check up on them at dawn," Dede informed them. "She says the doctors are doing all they can to make them presentable for the trial."

"I suspect they will ask for a continuance," Owuraku complained, looking at Efe.

"We'll try and shut that down," she replied confidently. "Maybe next time we shouldn't beat them up as badly."

"Tell that to Aisha," Bubuné replied offhandedly. Her eyes watched the TV screens shrewdly.

"How's she doing?" Owuraku wanted to know.

"I am swell," Aisha responded from the doorway with a wide grin on her beautiful face. She had just swiped her card and gained admission when Owuraku was asking his question.

"You're a stubborn woman, do you know that?" Asabea said disapprovingly from the middle of the room.

"I know," Aisha replied with a wink.

Asabea shook her head helplessly as all of them gathered around to examine her. She winced a little when Dede hugged her.

"Not too tight," she cautioned her. "My ribs are still a bit tender."

"That's why you should have enjoyed your bedrest," Asabea complained.

"And miss all of today's action? No way!"

"I heard you visited with Duncan King and his friends," Oye asked Aisha with obvious distaste.

"I was trying to see if they were adequately uncomfortable," Aisha replied, laughing lightly. "Larry King was looking the worse for wear, but Dr. Modupe says she will make sure he is fit enough to contribute to the trial."

"What was their plan? To attack us and escape?" Bubuné wondered.

Owuraku turned to her and said in feigned exasperation, "I thought you were never going to ask. All of you have been acting like the assault never happened. Aren't we supposed to at least discuss how we could have missed that in order to prevent a reoccurrence?"

They looked at him, and then looked at each other.

"To be fair, though, it isn't like there's been time," Nhyira came to their collective defense. "We had to handle the Army right after, and it seems we all felt we knew enough about what King and his cronies had tried to do without the necessity of a long discussion."

"What surprised me however was the quality of your reflexes," Bubuné intoned gratefully. "Any slower and I don't know what would have happened to Asabea."

Owuraku blinked. "I didn't raise the subject in hopes of adulation, ladies. I just thought it needed to be discussed so we avoid a repeat."

"It won't happen again, Kuuku," Asabea reassured him. "None of them will come close to anything with which they could harm even a fly."

True to Asabea's words, breakfast at 8.30 that morning was served to Duncan King, Ansah Premo and Larry King in smoothened coconut shell bowls, and the cutlery was made of plastic. Everyone else had silver, and all the Girls carried their weapons and sat in a way that left no doubt in everyone's minds that they were done playing nice. The three attackers clearly had difficulty eating, and after several minutes of groans and moans, Asabea had three nurses attend to them.

When the Court convened in the amphitheatre at ten o'clock, Ansah Premo made a show of his injuries, profusely effecting a lisp and imploring the judge to indefinitely suspend proceedings until he and his clients were in better physical and mental condition.

"Mr. Premo," the Judge responded before Efe or Asabea could rebut his claims, "I have TV in my room as well and know exactly how you came about your injuries. You and your clients should have known better than to attempt a coup. This court is not amused."

"My Lord," Ansah Premo objected, "I would like to inform the Court that the government has begun an offensive to end this hostage situation in a bid to bring these criminals and their accessories to justice," he said, looking in the direction of the Girls. "With guns booming outside these walls, any trial involving my client and his witnesses would fit the description for judicial malpractice and also for trial under duress."

"My Lords," Efe rose at that point. "This issue of duress was raised and overruled by the Supreme Court. What defense counsel seeks to do is to backdoor the same arguments when a higher court has already ruled. As to how military action outside of our walls amount to judicial malpractice beats me, my Lord."

"At the time the Supreme Court ruled, My Lord," Ansah Premo objected again, "guns weren't sounding around us. Last night, our pains were compounded by the sound of artillery and war. This is no condition to subject a trial to," he finished, forgetting to affect his painful lisps the more excited he became.

"If anything at all, my Lord," Efe jumped in, "the sound of artillery inures to the advantage of the defense, and not to us plaintiffs. Each of his witnesses and the accused can answer in the trial confident that no matter what happens, the military power of the state is activated on their behalf and in their favour. How does that inimically affect their defense?"

"But isn't this precisely the reason you wanted his Lordship to order a judge-alone trial?" Premo shot back. "You know that the longer this trial drags, the more likely the Armed Forces would overcome your puny defenses and put you all six feet under the ground. It's that hastiness that generates a trial under duress. The Supreme Court justices never considered the question of duress under artillery fire when they were here. In fact, they didn't even see a gun the entire time they were here. How can opposing counsel claim the situations are the same, my Lord?"

"If your Lordship so rules," Efe responded acutely, "we will happily proceed under a jury trial. We're not worried in the least about the rabble at the gates. I am however compelled to draw this Court's attention to the fact that the deployment of artillery by the Ghana Armed Forces is an indication that the government has little interest in rescuing hostages. If their heavy weaponry had been allowed to function without our taking them out, this Fortress would have been reduced to rubble and all of us with it. That is probably something opposing counsel needs to consider in his quest to unduly prolong proceedings, but that doesn't even matter. The government reserved the right to act like it is doing now but still approved these proceedings when the justices were here. There is no reason to rule otherwise."

"My Lord," Premo rose in exaggerated frustration. "The concept of a trial under duress exists in a situation where a person is compelled to participate in a legal proceeding or trial against their will due to coercion, threats, or other forms of pressure that undermine their ability to make a free and voluntary choice. I am not as concerned for my client because he will hold his own even if the heaven's fall, but any jury we empanel now would provide false decisions from fear of threats of harm to themselves. Guns and artillery will compromise their free will and decision-making."

Justice Frimpong banged his gavel before Efe could think of an appropriate response. The judge looked to the deputy Attorney-General who sat at the prosecutorial side now but had avoided the fray and asked, "What does the Republic make of these arguments?"

Umaru Tanko rose and seemed thoughtful. Efe's last comments about the government not caring about hostages had disturbed him for some reason.

Shaking his head to clear it of the cobweb of confusion bedeviling him he said, "The Republic defers to the wisdom of the Court on this matter, my Lord. We will proceed as your Lordship orders."

With a glance at both sides of the aisle, Justice Stephen Frimpong said, "I rule in favour of a judge-alone trial and set aside the earlier intention of a jury trial because of potential jury intimidation by reason of the abductions, as well as because of the complexity of the case. On the first pillar of potential intimidation, I believe that while jurists such as Supreme Court justices may understand and be unaffected by the abductions as occurred in the earlier proceedings, abducting potential jurors who are not versed in legal discourse could be intimidating to them, and that could affect their ability to make an independent and unbiased decision.

"On the other pillar of complexity, I believe the complex nature of this case would pose challenges to a jury's understanding or application of the law, and I rule against a jury panel to ensure a more accurate interpretation and application of the law. Therefore, we move to trial immediately."

"Thank you, my Lord," Efe said gratefully.

"As the Court wishes," Ansah Premo grudgingly said.

"Is the Republic ready to proceed to trial?" Justice Frimpong demanded of the State Prosecutor and the deputy Attorney-General, both of whom conferred briefly.

Umaru Tanku rose and said, "The Republic stands ready, your Lordship."

Ansah Premo also spoke briefly to Duncan King. All three men sported bandages and masticatory accessories around their heads, jaws and necks.

Eventually, Ansah Premo rose and said, "The defense stands at the ready also, my Lord. We want to get this over and done with quickly as well."

"Very well then," the judge noted. "We are adjourned till ten o'clock tomorrow morning." Then he banged his gavel.

The sound reverberated throughout the Fortress, and there was no mistaking the surprise on the judge's face.

He turned his hand and looked quizzically at the gavel. Then the sound rattled the Fortress again, and they all knew that whatever was happening did not originate from inside the amphitheatre.

Owuraku was already out the door with Efe and Asabea in tow. They had earlier decided that the trio would handle the court proceedings while the others monitored the situation at the battle front. They barged into the Press Box to a frenzied atmosphere.

"What's happening?" Asabea asked.

"They're firing L119s," Bubuné informed them excitedly. "We have activated our shields, and Regina has deployed a couple of birds to try to find the positions."

"L119s," Owuraku repeated the name of the artillery system. "They fire GPS-guided shells."

"Yes, they do," Bubuné responded in a tone that indicated she didn't know why that information was relevant.

"Then we can be sure that they intend to harass us until they can pull enough troops to assault us again. How long can your air defense system withstand a coordinated attack?"

"Not very long," Asabea informed him. "Which is why we must neutralize any threat using the Reapers."

"Do we have enough drones to play war games?"

"Enough to hold them off for a month," Aisha informed him. "So long as they keep only ground artillery fire coming in, we have all the advantages. We will run into trouble when they combine artillery with infantry."

"You don't seem to have considered the Air Force," Owuraku complained.

Asabea laughed at that and said, "Our Armed Forces have a total of eight operational combat jets. No way the Air Force will risk sending them in."

"Alright then," Owuraku said, seeming to relax. "Are we just going to sit around or there is something we can help you with?" he asked Bubuné.

"Right now, aside from our technicians, Regina and Dede are all I need to man our defense. I will let the rest of you know when I need you," she said and quite firmly got rid of the rest of them from the Press Box.

Behind the locked door, Owuraku asked, "What are we supposed to do now?"

Asabea checked her watch. It was only a half-hour past ten o'clock.

"We might as well catch up on sleep," she advised him and the rest of the girls. "We could meet after lunch to discuss testimonies with the State Prosecutor."

"Good idea," Efe supplied.

They mounted the stairs and headed up towards their rooms.

CHAPTER 20
The Akwapim Ranges
Thursday, 21st March; 10.30 A.M.

HE SELECTED HIS four most trusted Rangers for the mission. He himself had earlier on gone to the outdoor shop to buy their clothing and equipment and was watching Justice Frimpong decide the trial motions on the television when Cube, his PA walked into his office with her usual sass. She entered without knocking as usual and sat in the dark grey sofa across from his glossy black desk. She chewed on her lower lip, an indication that she was thinking, and that whatever she would say when she was done was going to be something he wouldn't like.

For an adventure outfit, his office was more tastefully furnished than a bank manager's. He wasn't going to spend twenty-two out of the thirty days in a month running adventures in the Ghanaian jungle to return to the jungle-themed office Cube had suggested when they had rented out the fourth floor of the only storeyed building in the mountain village of Apirede. So, he had spent time removing every trace of adventure in their offices, casting a corporate appearance that was the opposite of the high-powered adrenaline life his company offered to their adventure and extreme sport clientele.

His office was technically known by the moniker FIELD BASE to indicate that he, as the Adventure Leader, worked from there. Field Base moved when he moved to any of his company's outdoor posts in quite the same way any plane hosting the US president became an automatic Air Force One.

He had the backpacks and rescue gear neatly stashed to the right corner of his office as one came in by the sand blasted glass doors. The floor of his office was porcelain tiled in white and dark grey colours, reflecting the amber glow of spotlights from the white ceiling. And he stood up when the TV cut to shells being fired on the Fortress where Owuraku and his women were trying to hold an alleged rapist accountable for years of predation.

"Is this where you're headed?" Cube asked him incredulously. "That's a war zone. I don't want you killed," she finished dramatically.

"We'll be fine," he responded, half-smiling. He noticed that the footage of the attack on the Fortress was the first set of images he had seen of the entire estate since he'd started paying attention to the news concerning the women. He got out of his black swivel chair and walked to a map's cabinet on the right of his desk. He pulled out one and compared the contours to what the drones were showing on the screen. He nodded satisfactorily after a while and asked Cube, "Where are the Rangers?"

"They will be here in a quarter of an hour," she said it with a wrinkled face. "Surely, you're not planning to honour that contract. This is a war zone. My lawyer boyfriend says you can get out of contracts like that by citing force majeure or some crappy French like that."

He just smiled at her. Cube was the only one he could trust with the secret of the mission. Not even the Rangers he was going on the rescue with would know the full story until the last moments. And that story about a boyfriend wasn't true either. Cube was too opinioned and too irritating to keep a boyfriend. Heck, she was just his assistant but even he had had occasion to seriously think about dumping her assertive, annoying Nigerian butt.

But she was good at her job. And she kept him on his toes. And she looked damn good, which helped with wooing corporate clients who didn't expect that an adventure company would have beautiful staff. Only her sassy mouth was the problem, but no one was perfect, so he stuck with her. She stuck with him because she liked him. And that had been her standard refrain. She had on more occasions received better employment offers, but her response was always, "I like my boss."

She never explained beyond that, and he never asked. Loyalty like that deserved big rewards. If only she wasn't fitted with the type of mouth she had, she could run the company and he would retire.

But that mouth.

His phone rang and Cube picked up.

"It's for you," she said after a minute. "Some Chief Superintendent of Police."

"Hello?"

"My name is Chief Superintendent of Police H. Amadu. Am I speaking to Mr. Kwaku Opare Addo?"

"Yes, sir, you are," Opare answered, wondering why anyone would identify themselves by an initial.

"Fantastic," the voice said. "Tell me, have you been following the news these days?"

"Which news in particular?" Opare asked.

"The one about the women who abducted Supreme Court justices."

Opare became suddenly alert and switched the call to his phone's speaker. Then he said, "Yes, I've been following that news." Then he motioned to Cube who was rummaging through the new equipment he had bought to join him but to maintain silence on the call.

"We need your help to rescue the hostages," was the direct request. "And I am making this request on the orders of the Inspector General of Police."

There was a whole minute of silence as Opare digested that. Cube's eyes had already widened in amusement at the odds, but she kept quiet.

"That would otherwise not be a problem," Opare said carefully, "but that Fortress is an active conflict zone now. What guarantees do we have that your Army won't shoot at us if we go in and break out hostages?"

"Why do you say so?" Another voice demanded; a voice accustomed to giving orders.

"Uhm –" Opare begun. "From what I see on TV, your Army has no regard for the safety of the hostages, which is why they are firing shells at the building, targeting the women and their abductees alike. Where is the guarantee that they will wait for us to get the hostages to safety?"

The other line went quiet for a while.

"How come that was your first worry?" the commanding voice demanded. "Why are you worried about the Army, and not about the Girls? They too have guns, you know?"

"This wouldn't be our first extraction," Opare informed the voice matter-of-factly. "But it would be our first with a national Army firing artillery at us. I assume the Army isn't listening to you, which is why you have probably called me."

"No, they aren't," the voice conceded carefully. "But our duty lies in saving as many hostages as we can. We are reliably informed only you can pull that off."

Opare said, "What do you have in mind?"

"Your team could work with my team," the voice said. "You will lead them to getting at the Fortress unseen, and they will take out the Girls and break the hostages out."

Opare mulled it over. Cube was silently mouthing a lot of things about how it would conflict with the contract with the women, and how he couldn't take the Police on their offer, and certainly why he could not work with the Police to 'take out' anyone, and how she was a big fan of the Girls while pulling at him and scribbling unsolicited advice on a piece of paper she had pulled out of his printer's tray.

Opare ignored her and said to the Police, "I can get to the Fortress without anyone noticing, and my team and I can rescue the hostages. I cannot however work with your men."

"Why not?" the voice demanded curtly, clearly only concerned about the part that excluded his policemen.

"Your men would only be in our way," he said without explanation. "After we are done, they could take over from there."

The Police seemed to be chewing his words over.

"We'll call you back," the voice said and hung up.

"What was that about?" Cube bore right into him when the call cut. "Wouldn't it be dangerous if they discovered we were actually planning to rescue the Girls?"

"We could do both," Opare suggested calmly. "There's no way I would have extracted the Girls and left the hostages behind anyway."

"But the hostages would know that you only came to pull out the Girls from an Army that is bent on shooting their butts. Wouldn't the people who work for the government like the deputy Attorney-General be bound by law and by duty to report you to the government?"

"That's where the Police come in. Their contract would give us coverage with the government."

"Bullshit!" Cube's proverbial mouth took over at that point. "Eventually, there will be a conflict. If you take the Girls, you can't hand them over to the Police. And if the Girls insist on keeping their hostages when you break out, you can't hand the hostages over to the Girls. Everyone will think we betrayed them."

Opare looked at her thoughtfully. Eventually he said, "I have made my decision," and was about to walk out of his office when the phone rang again.

"What do you need?" was the curt demand on the line. "This is the IGP."

"I figured," was Opare's response. "Just payment for our services, is all. As well as being present at the rendezvous point when we break your hostages out. We might be operating under intense fire so it's important we make everything work according to plan."

"How much?"

Opare told him.

"That's a lot!" the IGP complained.

"Sorry, sir. It's the economy."

"Payment terms?"

"Full payment before we start. And we'd like to get started before the Army's revenge."

"When do you start?"

"Within 48 hours. We should arrive at the base of their plateau within two weeks. I will text you about our progress every few days so I too may stay abreast of whatever the Army may be up to."

"Do that then," the IGP ordered. The funds will be wired today. Please text your account details."

"Yes, sir," Opare said and then the line died.

"You slut!" Cube told him right to his face. "That's charging double for the same job."

"Watch your mouth," he warned. "Rescuing hostages and extracting criminals are two very different jobs."

"But you're doing them concurrently," she charged.

"Yes, I am," he said and walked out on her.

His Rangers came in, and they convened the briefing in the conference room of his company. He and his team wore their customary uniforms comprising olive green short- or long-sleeved shirts and trousers, and brown hiking boots with black gaiters. Short-brimmed Mao hats completed the bodily outfits, but each Ranger could add on all kinds of survival paraphernalia as they deemed appropriate.

In the conference room, he laid out the map and explained the mission to his boys. These four were the most experienced Rangers he'd worked with. He'd trained them himself since he'd employed them seven years ago and they were accustomed to getting the job done in the most effective ways.

He told them the targets of their rescues and truthfully presented the conundrums of rescuing the abductors and their hostages at the same time, taking the wind out of Cube's mouth.

"It will be dangerous to hack a path since the Army might be able to follow it," Elikem advised. "Perhaps infrared markers?"

"We *will* need a path," Opare disagreed. "We only need to ensure it cannot be seen from a kilometre from any well used roads or tracks. We can freestyle it right to this first mountain and then cut the trail through these three hills to the base of the Fortress," he marked out the contours on the map. "We must assume we will have injured people in our party. It will be too slow and punishing without a well-marked trail."

"Do you think we will be followed once we abseil the cliff?" Wannah asked, also examining the map closely.

"I doubt it," Opare replied. "Chances are, the Army will move to cut off our escape if we get discovered. We can avoid that by leaving our chances open when we arrive a kilometre before the Adawso valley."

"Weapons?" Aaron asked.

"The Police wanted to provide some, but Opare rejected the idea," Cube spoke at that point.

Opare shrugged. "Their weapons might be bugged, and this isn't Tamale. No one will be particularly looking to shoot at us."

"But we'll carry one, at least?" Aaron insisted.

"Your boss is always armed, or you didn't know this?" Cube asked him, almost contemptibly.

All five men turned to look at her.

"What?" she asked with a challenge in her eyes.

They let it pass and began to pack their new backpacks. The bulk of their gear was made up of climbing and abseiling equipment given the two-hundred-foot cliff they needed to assail, but there was camping and outdoor cooking equipment as well, with binoculars, compasses and hammocks. By the time they were done packing, each person's backpack weighed a full half their body weight.

"And we haven't added food and water yet," Kada complained. "I hope the women are nice. It would be painful to go through all this just to rescue some ugly girls."

Cube, who had been helping them pack up their bags rolled her eyes at him. Then she said to Opare, "Perhaps I should join in."

"No!" All five men responded around the table.

"Why the hell not?"

"Your mouth!" was the unanimous response.

The trial of Duncan King started at exactly ten o'clock, and was watched by fifteen million people across Ghana, and by twenty million on the internet. The case had gone viral, and the action instigated by Ghana's military was adding the needed accelerant of intrigue, drama and thrill. Talk show hosts were having a field day running analyses of the proceedings and on the attack of the Ghana Armed Forces. What was surprising to everyone was how calm the courtroom looked on TV composited against booming artillery shells and rockets on the outside. Not a few had commented on the risk to the hostages, but the government and the military high command were enforcing radio silence on their operations. So far, the Fortress stood unfazed by the assault, and the Army's actions were no more than a routine annoyance.

Late last night, the State Prosecutor and the deputy Attorney-General had met with Asabea and Efe for the first time since the abductions. Owuraku had been in attendance because he did not trust public officials and needed to read any diabolic cues that might aid the case of the defendants. While he hadn't believed the trial was necessary to bring

Duncan King to justice, he was fine with the plan of the Girls to maintain the appearance at least of fairness before shooting the son of a bitch. But he had ideas – plans actually – that was going to turn every raping scum's blood to butter by the time he was done with him.

Oh, he had plans.

The meeting had gone surprisingly well. Now that the Supreme Court had ruled that the trial needed to be done, Umaru Tanko had been quite cordial as he and Apaloo went over Asabea's testimony, as well as that of the physician at the medical centre where Owuraku had sent Asabea ten years ago after the assault. Efe had provided what assistance she could, but at that point, everything was literally in the hands of the government's prosecutors.

Umaru Tanko wasted little time making his opening remarks in Court and called Asabea to the witness stand. Asabea recounted her ordeal as calmly as she could, looking every now and then to Owuraku for moral and visual support. By the time she was done, she had exuded credibility as a victim-witness. It was Ansah Premo's time to show the court otherwise.

The defense counsel made a dramatic show of rising in his podium, rearranging his robes on his shoulders, and peering intensely over his glasses at Asabea in the witness box. Asabea was not sure if Ansah Premo thought he had lasers for eyes when he stared at her like that, but she responded with a cool gaze, half-amused by his theatrics. But the renowned lawyer cut right to the chase.

"Why would you follow someone you just met into the washroom of a hotel's private suite?"

Asabea steadied her rising anger at the question as she answered, "I believed him when he said he needed help with his make-up. I was not alone in the living room and did not imagine that he would rape me in a room immediately adjourning the living room while his friends waited. Also, Billy Blanks and the media crew were already waiting and had set up cameras for us in the hotel's foyer for the filming. I had no reason to suspect that all this notwithstanding, Duncan King could find time to rape a person."

"Did you specifically think of all these things at the time you got up and followed him?"

"All young women read the room when confronted with situations involving men in the entertainment industry. So, I considered all the possibilities within that short frame of time and decided, based on the presence of Larry King and everyone else, that I was probably not in any danger. I was wrong about that."

"Did you not follow him because it was a turn-on for you that all his friends had to wait as you – if I may quote my client's statement to the police – 'got you some' while everyone waited?"

"Absolutely not," Asabea fired back. "Up until that day, I had never met him. I didn't follow him because I wanted anything *some*," she finished with obvious distaste.

"How long were you in the washroom with him?" Premo continued as if she hadn't looked at him with all the venom in the world.

"Twenty-three minutes," she responded confidently.

"Are you sure about that?"

"Yes."

"How so?"

"When Duncan King came into the living room to ask for my help, I was texting Owuraku Ampem Darko, my boyfriend at the time about where Abena and I were, and that we had run into Duncan King. I sent the text before dropping my phone into my bag and leaving the room with him. The time difference between that text and when Abena called him after I returned was exactly twenty-three minutes."

Ansah Premo paused a while.

"What was my client wearing?" he asked.

"A purple pair of trousers, a green shirt and a mismatched bowtie. He wore a green undershirt and a wine-coloured Tommy Hilfiger boxer short with a hole under it that exposed a part of his right testicle."

Ansah Premo blinked. And then coughed to clear his throat or buy himself some time to rearrange his line of questioning, no one was sure which.

Eventually, he asked, "Do you stand by your testimony that my client raped you?"

"I stand by my testimony that Duncan King raped me. And he did it twice."

"My client insists that the sex was consensual, and that he wanted just one round, but you insisted that you wanted more."

"I did not consent to sex with Duncan King; I could not have asked him to rape me twice. I begged him to stop hurting me, but he paid no heed."

"But you say the incidence occurred in a washroom adjoining the living room, correct?"

"Yes, that is correct."

"Yet no one heard you."

"Abena Asaa, my cousin, heard the scuffle and when she turned to Larry King with a quizzical look on her face, Billy Blanks rose to increase the volume on the music that was playing. She will testify via camera that the two gentlemen heard the scuffle behind the door. She will also testify that she was stopped from coming to the door to investigate by the same Billy Blanks."

"Did you scream?"

"No, I didn't."

"Why didn't you?"

"I was in shock."

"How do you know you were in shock? Are you a doctor?"

"Objection," Umaru Tanko cut in at that point.

"Sustained," the judge ruled with a stern look at Ansah Premo.

"If you believed that you had been raped, why didn't you seek to hold my client accountable when he was first arraigned?"

"It was too much for me, the pain," Asabea replied sincerely. "I didn't have a problem confronting him in court per se, but when I spoke with prosecutors in the days following the rape, all I kept thinking about was how to carry a gun in my dress that I could use to kill him. And in that frame of mind, I could not be a good prosecution witness."

"You wanted to kill my client?"

"I definitely thought about it."

"So then, if you wanted to kill my client, surely, framing him up for rape after a consensual affair was another way to do it, wasn't it?"

"Objection, wild goose chase."

"Sustained."

Ansah Premo was thoughtful for a while. Then he looked up at Asabea and asked, "You said you had a boyfriend you texted on the day of the incidence."

"That's correct."

"Is he here?" he asked.

"Yes, Dr. Ampem Darko is here," Asabea affirmed and pointed him out in the gallery.

"My Lord," Ansah Premo said.

"The records will reflect that the plaintiff witness pointed out Dr. Ampem Darko in the gallery," Justice Frimpong confirmed. "Please proceed."

"How long had you been dating?"

"Since Achimota School."

Ansah Premo had a quizzical look. "And you guys had never had sex?" he asked disbelievingly.

"No."

"May I ask why?"

"We were saving ourselves for marriage."

"For real?"

"Yes."

"How long were you together before the incident with my client?"

"Two years."

"And he made no uhm – overtures of a sexual nature?"

"Objection, relevance?" Umaru demanded.

"Just confirming the virginity angle of the witness, my Lord," Ansah Premo replied contritely.

"Move along already," the judge warned.

"No further questions, my Lord," Ansah Premo said and abruptly sat down with his hand massaging his temple.

The judge looked at him quizzically and asked, "Are you alright, Counsel?"

"Just a dizziness spell, my Lord, but I am done with the witness."

"Rehabilitation?" the judge asked the deputy Attorney-General.

"None, my Lord," was the response.

"Thank you, Ms. Asabea," the judge said to her. "You may step down now."

Asabea got off the witness stand and made her way towards the prosecution side. Before she could sit, an explosion thundered and seemed about to bring the roof down on their heads. The next one had everyone in the amphitheatre diving for cover under lecterns and desks, including the judge.

Asabea looked up from the floor at Owuraku, who was already on his way towards the Press box. When he arrived Bubuné was frantically searching on her consoles for the offending artillery piece.

"What's going on?" he shouted to be heard above the detonations.

"They are firing mortars at us," Bubuné told him.

Owuraku looked up at the ceiling. It all seemed intact.

"I don't see any damages."

"Our laser shields and air defenses can intercept mortar fire, but we need to neutralize them before they are damaged," Nhyira informed him while she remotely manned her drone, looking for the source of the projectiles.

"Where the hell are they?" Bubuné was asking, querying the screens.

"There," Owuraku pointed to a steilhang on one drone's footage.

"They're firing mortars from there."

"Whose Reaper is that?" Bubuné demanded.

"Mine," Oye answered excitedly.

"Release a payload," Bubuné instructed.

Oye quietly depressed a button on her console. A few seconds later, soldiers dived for cover on the screens when the reconnaissance Reaper deployed a small tactical missile at the artillery unit inside the valley. Two mortar systems were destroyed instantly, but they couldn't tell whether all the soldiers made it away from the mortars in time.

"Good shot!" Nhyira congratulated her twin. "Let's see if there are more of them hiding down there."

"Not yet," Bubuné warned them. "Let's not unduly expose ourselves. Let the birds soar."

"Copy that," Oye replied and took her drone higher and away from the target area.

Owuraku breathed a sigh.

"Are you OK?" Dede asked him. The excitement of battle lit a flame in their eyes.

"I am," Owuraku said with a smile. "You're enjoying yourselves, aren't you?"

"You bet we are."

"Well, don't overdo yourselves," he warned gently and started out.

"How is it going in Court?" Aisha asked after him.

He paused to look at her.

"Aren't you overexerting yourself?" he asked her. She held a joystick over one of the consoles, and with that she performed reconnaissance with a drone over the cliff behind their plateau.

"I am fine," she said with a wide grin. "I'm not missing this for anything."

Owuraku shook his head and headed out. The prosecution would shortly call the attending physician at the medical centre where he had taken Asabea the day of the rape, and he didn't want to miss any part of her testimony. He'd known Ansah Premo was not going to make any headway cross-examining Asabea, but he might put in a lot of effort to discredit the gynecologist.

Owuraku needed to see him try.

INVIOLABLE 148

CHAPTER 21
Jubilee House
Thursday, 21st March, Noon.

THE PAST FEW HOURS had been frantically chewed up placating the Commander-in-Chief of Ghana's Armed Forces, but President Kwame Amponsah Offei would not be placated, and had already fired, rehired and refired the Chief of Army Staff twice over already. And he seemed about to move on to serve the same on the Chief of Defence Staff.

"Three hundred million dollars!" he fumed. "Three hundred million dollars was the budget I approved for military spending this year, and this is what they have had to show for it, this no-show of an operation. I might just as well have sent the Boys' Scout. These guys didn't last twenty-four hours, and Girls – Girls o – have decimated their ranks," he complained, pacing up and down in the War Room and punctuating every other pacing step with swear words.

"Where is Colonel Nartey?" he demanded midstride. "I have asked you to bring him to face my wrath," he said dangerously to his Defence Minister. "Bring him to me, or I will have you removed before this day is over."

"I'm sorry, Mr. President, but we cannot recall a commanding officer in the middle of an active operation," the Defence Minister pleaded cautiously. "That is not a good thing to do."

"It's not like they're doing any good to begin with," he said, pointing angrily to the TV screens. "He has led half his men to their death in a few hours of the operation, and the Girls keep embarrassing us on national TV. This is a disaster! Just look!"

"I am sorry, sir," the Chief of Defence Staff came in apologetically. "The best we can do is send in a Brigadier-General and some reinforcements. If we pull Colonel Nartey out, we will be effectively ending the operation."

"And this Brigadier-General will do what exactly?" President Offei demanded.

"He is here, actually," the Defence Minister informed him.

"Here where?" the President demanded.

"In the waiting room."

"Get him in here!" he ordered.

Within half a minute, Brigadier-General Ghansah was ushered into the War Room, and after offering him a seat, President Offei wasted no time drilling into him about what he thought he could bring into the situation and asked him to prove how he too wouldn't end up being a waste of his time and the opportunity like Colonel Nartey had.

"Sending in the Army was your first mistake, sir," the new arrival informed him with his face firmly set. "And this tirade isn't going to erase that. So, let's first settle down and look at this problem objectively."

President Offei looked like his face was about to explode. Members of his cabinet looked first at him, and then at the calmer Brigadier-General who sat looking at the President like he had been deliberately goading him into this fit and was now looking to see if a desired result would emanate. For a minute the President kept choking on one word after the other until he tired of trying and simply flopped into his chair.

Sensing his boss's difficulties, the Vice President intervened.

"Explain what you mean by our mistake," he asked sternly, keeping one wary eye on the President.

"Civilian hostages, civilian abductors, and an armed civil dispute all have the makings of a Police situation. We had no business sending in our Army. And having done so, we sent them in unprepared. Those Girls took out the home of a public prosecutor, but in none of the briefings did we factor strike drones into our preparations, and worse, we have ignored the fact of hostages and sent in artillery. We have acted foolishly and have paid the price for it. That's the first thing we need to acknowledge."

"Acknowledged," Vice President Domwine said without theatrics. "How do we proceed?"

That took the Brigadier by surprise. As an Officer with extensive experience in military matters, his first order of business was to inform his civilian commanders that they didn't know jack about military matters. He expected opposition to that diagnosis, which is why the Vice President's quick concurrence took the venom out of his sting.

"Carefully," was the response that came into his head. "We need to approach this intelligently and wisely."

"How?" the Vice President insisted, while the President glared at the Brigadier balefully.

"We need to go in quietly," he replied. "Not with artillery and the noise of an Army past its prime, but with the smartness of modern tactical thinking. Pull the Army out, reconnect the lines of communication, cooperate with them as long as your hostages are alive and well until you can find a way to catch them unawares and deal them a justice hand. I am informed the IGP specifically advised such an approach, but it was treated contemptibly by you presumably intelligent lot. Let's revisit that approach and perhaps it might save the day."

Of course, the decision rested with the President, and it seemed all he could do was just look at the Brigadier. When he found his voice eventually, he said, "I am going to hand over all this to you and your commanders," he said with a voice heavy with the promise of retribution if they failed. "I don't even want to know what is going on anymore. But I need all my hostages returned to me alive, and those upstart Girls brought to me to face justice. These are your orders, and you have fourteen days to make it happen. Do I make myself clear?" he asked with a fiery look at the Brigadier in particular.

"Yes, sir," all the uniformed men in the room answered and saluted smartly.

Then the President got up off his chair. Everyone hastily got up as well, as was the respectful custom, but he walked out of the room without another word, leaving them unsure what to do next, and looking to the Vice President for guidance.

"Why are you looking at me?" Vice President Domwine asked the Cabinet with a look of surprise. "Get to work," he ordered as he too took his leave.

Two hours later, all troops were withdrawn from the Aburi mountains. Regina reported the turn of events to Asabea when the Court had gone on an hour's recess because the judge said it would be harder to hold court with all the bombs going off over their heads.

"What do you mean they have left?" Asabea quizzed as soon as she entered the Press box, looking for herself on the screens.

"They have withdrawn to within five kilometres of the Fortress and seem to be grouping in the middle of the Aburi town," Bubuné confirmed.

"That's still not too far off," Owuraku advised.

"Perhaps not," Bubuné agreed. "But there are too many mountains and valleys between us and Aburi that we can safely say we are beyond the reach of their artillery."

"Unless they employ the use of missiles," Owuraku said.

"Yeah," Asabea agreed. "Unless."

"What do you think?" Oye asked the thoughtfully looking Asabea.

"Keep an eye on them," she said. "We need to get back to Court," and then she left hurriedly with Owuraku and Efe.

"What do you think this means?" she asked Owuraku while walking briskly through the corridors to get to the amphitheatre.

"Maybe cooler heads have prevailed in President Offei's government, but that's a dangerous turn," Owuraku replied unhappily.

"What do you mean?" Efe asked him.

"If they're not shooting at us, then they will find another way to get at us. Where we are is no longer a secret. And it's not knowing anymore what they are planning that worries me."

"They can't get at us," Efe reassured him. "Not through the front gate at least."

"As I recall they weren't supposed to have found our location either and here we are," Owuraku told her, not unkindly. "Let's just hope we finish with the trial before they do something major."

They didn't speak again until they arrived in the amphitheatre a few seconds before they had to rise for Justice Frimpong.

She took the stand and swore on the Bible to tell the truth, the whole truth, and nothing but the truth. She would have told the truth at the first phrase. She didn't know why it had to be repeated twice. Unlike the other abductees, she had been invited and had accepted it gladly. She had turned up on her own, met Nhyira at the Aburi Gardens who had secured her car somewhere, and had been driven the rest of the way to the Fortress. It was later that she'd learnt that this was a trial of extremely uncommon circumstances, but she hadn't minded after Asabea had informed her of what they had done and why she wouldn't be going back to work or her family until after it all ended, whatever that meant.

"Can you please state your name and occupation for the Court, and how you came to be involved with the case?" Deputy Attorney-General Umaru Tanko was asking her.

"I am Dr. Mary Densua, a forensic gynaecologist at the Police Hospital in Accra, and was on locum at the Pinecone Medical Centre on the afternoon of the incident," she replied effortlessly.

"And you are the author of this medical report, Exhibit M1, that I hold in my hand?"

"Yes, I am," Dr. Densua responded after a closer look at the report in Tanko's hand.

"Can you read to the hearing of this court the conclusions of your examination of Ms. Asabea?"

"There were abrasions on both labia minora and majora, and hyperemic redness at the external urethral opening as well as at the posterior part of the vaginal opening, with her hymen torn at multiple places, plus pinpoint bleeding areas, with the presence of spermatozoa."

"In layman terms, what were you saying in your report?"

"I was saying that the findings of my examinations were consistent with forcible rape," she replied.

"Objection," Ansah Premo uttered in a voice that expected to be overruled.

"Overruled," the judge announced. "Please proceed."

"And the part about the external urethra," Tanko inquired. "Were you saying that the defendant attempted to penetrate Ms. Asabea from behind?"

"Objection, my Lord. Sodomy was never implied in the charges against my client," Ansah Premo denounced the question.

"My Lord," Umaru Tanko rebutted, "the question before the witness concerns the complainant's testimony that she was forcibly bent over and penetrated from behind, wouldn't you say so, Dr. Densua?"

"Precisely that," Dr. Densua responded. "But the hyperemic redness is the sign that the defendant did not care exactly where he penetrated. He was violently looking for an opening – any opening – and that is partly why the posterior part of her vagina suffered abuse."

"My Lord," Premo began.

"Overruled," the judge replied.

"Would you say, doctor, that the complainant suffered excruciating pain?" Umaru Tanko asked.

"She could barely walk when she presented at the centre," she said, "And I had to administer pain killers and muscle relaxers due to the intensity of her pain."

Tanko let that sink in for a moment.

"One last question," he said. "Whose DNA did the spermatozoa match?"

"They matched Mr. Duncan King's."

"To a medical certainty?"

"Objection. The defendant has already stipulated that he had intercourse with the complainant."

"Then it doesn't hurt to have the expert repeat the fact, does it?" the judge demanded. "Objection overruled."

"The answer is yes, to a medical certainty," Dr. Densua confirmed.

"No further questions, my Lord," Tanko finished.

Then turning to Ansah Premo, he said, "Your witness."

Ansah Premo consulted a sheaf of papers while rising. Then he looked at Duncan King for a second before turning his eyes onto Dr. Densua.

"Before turning up for locum at the Centre, where had you been the twelve hours prior?"

"I'd been at home. It was my day off from work at the Police Hospital."

"Fair enough," Premo said. "And you are one hundred percent positive that the result of your examination supported forcible rape and nothing else?"

"I am one hundred percent sure."

"Doctor, it has been ten years since you authored that report. How can you be very sure that what you believed then is still true today?"

"The report at the time of issuance was a true and fair representation of the examination results. Nothing will change that; not even a hundred years will erase those findings."

"So, you're saying if we examined the complainant today, we'd find the same results?"

Dr. Densua looked at Ansah Premo with a face that questioned his sanity, but Umaru Tanko had already objected, and the judge had sustained the objection.

"Moving on," Ansah Premo recovered, "couldn't all the abrasions have been caused by a dildo, for instance?"

"Objection. Counsel himself has stipulated that his client had intercourse with the complainant."

"Sustained!" the judge grumbled. And then he ordered, "Approach!"

Umaru Tanko, Ansah Premo and Efe approached the bench.

"Are you trying to make a mockery of my courtroom?" Justice Frimpong demanded dangerously of Ansah Premo.

Taken aback, Ansah Premo answered, "My apologies my Lord, but I am in all kinds of physical pain from the assault my body took a few days ago. I am truly not myself, but nothing a week of rest cannot cure, to be honest."

"They decided to stage a coup and engage in violence, my Lord," Efe rebutted. "Unless counsel wants to plead diminished capacity, and there are doctors on hand to gainsay that, I suggest the trial proceeds."

"The State concurs, my Lord," Umaru Tanko also said. "There is no need to drag this trial more than it should. This case is straightforward."

The judge looked inquiringly at Ansah Premo.

"Two hours' rest is all I am asking for, my Lord, so I may clear my head and proceed."

"Alright," the judge granted. "Two hours and a short leash, Counsel."

The two-hour break offered opportunity for lunch in the last remaining half-hour, and Duncan King sat with his lawyer at their table, now far removed from the tables of the bitches because of the stand they had made. He was proud of himself, of course. He had shown the broads that he could take matters into his own hands. If only his jaw wasn't hurting so bad. Chewing was such a painstaking process he wished his food could be administered intravenously.

He finished his lunch with a quarter-hour to spare, a bowl of fufu with his favourite, goat light soup. Then he turned to his lawyer and asked, "What exactly is your problem?"

Sitting around the same table was Larry King who was in such shape he wore a mask to conceal his burst lips and recently fixed broken nose. And next to him was Billy Blanks who apparently had been abducted the same time as Duncan King but had been kept in his cellar the whole time of the trials. He wasn't amused at all and had suggested twice already that they could take on the girls and escape. Larry told him to forget it if he wanted to live. Billy didn't sound convinced, but the trio were too tired and beat up to keep arguing.

"We might have to change our plea," Ansah Premo told them under his breath.

"What?" Duncan King screamed silently. "No way!"

Ansah Premo shrugged. "The victim's testimony was too credible, as was the examining physician's. Everything I have up my sleeve is nothing but legal gymnastics, but ultimately, what is established is that you raped her," he bored into Duncan King's eyes as he said the last part. "You want me to sell to the judge that a nineteen-year-old virgin had consensual sex with you after meeting you for the first time for all of fifteen minutes. Do you yourself believe that cow dung?"

Duncan King was so angry he couldn't find his voice, but Premo was not done yet.

"I will do what I can, but there's no way you walk out of this a free man. Best to consider what other options there are, but I need to take some pain killers before I walk in back there to make a fool of my career on national TV," he finished, got up from the table and walked to the corridor towards the quarter he shared with the two – now, three – men.

"He's right, you know?" Larry King chipped in, wincing from the effort it took to speak. "This is why I'd avoided getting involved right from the beginning. I did not want to contribute, in any way, to your incarceration, and that was what I knew you were going to get in a case like this."

"So, you have believed I was guilty all this while?" Duncan King asked him.

"Guilt is a legal term," Larry King said to him. "But I believed the girl's story then as I do now."

"Then why haven't you said anything until now?" Duncan King asked him in a voice that indicated he felt betrayed.

Larry King shrugged.

"I was protecting you with my silence, but we all heard her screams and her pain."

"Speak for yourself," Billy Blanks came in contemptibly at that point, looking around at the Girls and all the people in the dining room. "I didn't hear crap."

"You did," Larry King told him firmly. And then, turning to Duncan King he warned, "Let your lawyer know it's going to be a bad idea to put me on the stand."

Duncan King's face registered retributive anger.

"But thankfully he wouldn't have to," Larry King said quietly, looking towards the doors where the girls and the other diners were leaving. "You've got Billy to back you up."

Then he too left their table.

Duncan King and Billy Blanks exchanged startled looks before rising and heading towards the Courtroom.

"Forgive my earlier attitude, Dr. Densua," Ansah Premo got right to it when the Court sat down again. "It's been quite a harrowing period," he finished by way of explanation.

Dr. Densua shrugged.

"So, you were saying that you had utmost confidence in the report you authored?"

"That's correct."

"And that nothing could change your mind about its accuracy?"

"Nothing."

"Is this the first such report you have authored?"

"It was my 21st such report. I am usually the one the Police Service calls in when victims of rape and sexual assault report to the Accra Regional Command."

"Are there other examiners like you?"

"There are about seven of us under that Command."

"Would you say you're overworked?"

"I don't understand your question," Dr. Densua told him.

"Seven examiners for sexual assaults in all of Accra can be overwhelmed, can they not?" he clarified.

"The guidelines and protocols for medico-legal examination is routine for those of us working at the Police Hospital, no different from any routine gynaecological procedure, and doesn't take any more time than usual out of a qualified doctor's work."

"So, you're saying you still stand a hundred percent by your report that Ms. Asabea was forcibly raped?"

"A hundred percent."

He paused, letting that sink in, to no effect.

"No further questions, my Lord," he said and sat down abruptly.

"Very well," the judge said, clearly as surprised as everyone else. Then he turned to the witness and said, "Thank you, Doctor. You may step down now."

Owuraku was next on the stand, and he gave the court and the watching Ghanaian public his version of events from the point of view of one who cared deeply about Asabea, and the one to whom it fell to ensuring that Duncan King was not going to get away with what he did. He captivated the court with the story of how he had driven like mad to the hospital in order to ensure that no evidence of what Ansah Premo kept insisting was an alleged crime was going to biodegrade before the doctors had a chance at confirming that the rape had occurred. His testimony lasted some ten minutes but it had everything that needed to be covered from an uninvolved third-party standpoint.

"You don't like my client, the defendant, do you?" Ansah Premo asked him on cross examination.

"Until he did what he did, I had no opinion of him either way."

"You hated him, even, didn't you? Which is why you almost beat him up at the Airport Police Station."

"I was angry at what he had done," Owuraku replied coolly.

"In fact, you sent a couple of blows in his direction," Premo quizzed further.

Owuraku shrugged. "Nothing he didn't deserve if I had, but I didn't."

"And right now, you can't wait to execute him if the verdict goes in your girlfriend's favour, can you?"

"If the Girls wanted to murder him, why go through all this trouble of trials and proceedings? They could just have murdered him at the bar he was abducted at."

"Except that you didn't want to murder him, which has a negative connotation," Ansah Premo told him. "You just wanted justification to do what you all plan to do to my client, didn't you? Which is to kill him regardless of a verdict."

"Objection, relevance?" Umaru came in at that point.

"Your Lordship, I am only trying to show that it is not for any just cause, or even for the criminal allegations against my client that this trial is going on. This trial is happening due only to hate and personal vendetta."

"What personal vendetta?" Owuraku butted in angrily at that point. "Until the criminal defendant did what he did, neither Asabea nor I were interested in anything involving your client."

"When you and she were dating, did you both have sex?" Ansah Premo demanded.

"We did not," Owuraku fired back. "How does that translate into a personal vendetta?"

"You did not like the idea that she was saving herself, not for you as you thought, but for the biggest brand in the entertainment industry, did you?" Premo asked in a cocky and obstreperous voice.

"Objection, my Lord," Umaru boomed from his lectern. "Counsel is desacralizing the allegations, and his insensitivity is offensive."

"I warned you about this, did I not?" Justice Frimpong asked sternly from the bench. And then he turned to Efe, "Do we have a makeshift jail?"

"We do, my Lord," Efe responded. "Defense counsel is actually familiar with it, since that was where he first came to in this Fortress."

"One more inappropriate behaviour, Mr. Premo, and you would buy yourself a jail cell."

"I apologise, your Lordship," Premo responded contritely. "I have had nothing but damaging testimony, and it is either I drop my pants or go on this wild goose chase. I chose the wild goose, and I apologise."

Justice Frimpong looked at him. "Have you informed your client accordingly? This court will not countenance an appeal on the grounds of inadequate counsel."

"I have, my Lord, but he seems content to retain me," he replied tiredly.

"Is that your decision, Mr. King?" the judge asked Duncan King, who seemed startled by the turn of events.

"This is the first time I am hearing of the matter of inadequate representation, my Lord," he settled for the truth. "Counsel only mentioned to me that he felt we needed to change our plea; not change lawyers."

"Would you like to change counsel then, Mr. King?" the judge asked him.

"Could-could I have a minute to confer with him about this, please?" he asked the judge with a lot of uncertainty on his usually arrogant face.

"Take fifteen minutes," Justice Frimpong told them. "In the meantime, Mr. Premo, are you done with the witness?"

"Yes, my Lord," Ansah Premo said in obvious relief.

"Then the witness may step down," Justice Frimpong told Owuraku. "We will take a quarter hour break while defense counsel and his client confer."

CHAPTER 22
The Fortress
Thursday, 21st March; 2PM.

UMARU TANKO SAT around a side room in the amphitheatre with Kwasi Apaloo, the career State Prosecutor at the Attorney-General's Department who seemed almost whole again from his recent indisposition. With them were Owuraku, Asabea and Efe who were assisting the prosecution. It had been ten minutes since the judge had granted the recess, but they were nowhere near finished wondering what they were going to do if Duncan King asked to excuse his counsel. Asabea and Efe were concerned about how difficult that was going to be, now that the Ghana Army was lurking around the Aburi area. Any time they mentioned the Army, Umaru and Apaloo shrugged, indicating that, while they were now content to comply with the Supreme Court decision to immediately bring Duncan King to trial and work with Asabea and her girls to that end, that was the extent of their cooperation. They had a Chinese wall in place for any mention of the military and the government and made no suggestions whatsoever towards any problems that were not directly related to their role as prosecutors.

But Umaru had been thinking deeply of late, eschewing the status quo ante that had seen to his department waiting a decade to prosecute Duncan King. There was no denying that his department would never on their own have resurrected the Republic vs. Duncan King, even if the Girls had asked nicely. And it was that thought that had mellowed him and the State prosecutor. This is why they were giving off their best now.

Not that this was a difficult case. It was a slam dunk, even, and it made him wonder why the previous administration had filed the nolle. Duncan King truly did not stand a chance. He was as guilty as sin, and while he suspected the Girls would not let him walk out of the Fortress without some life-threatening chastisement of sorts, his focus was to seek justice for the Girls and let whatever happened thereafter be none of his business.

So long as all innocent abductees made it out of the Fortress alive.

Umaru Tanko had started out as a prosecutor in the AG's department in Ghana's Savanna Region shortly after graduating law school. Over the next decade he rose to a series of supervisory positions within the department, including chief of criminal litigation, overseeing scores of prosecutors pursuing cases involving violent crime, financial fraud, and public sector corruption. He was known for his succinct and effective courtroom style – so much so that senior attorneys in the department would advise junior prosecutors to watch his trials and take notes. And he had often left defence attorneys bereft of their wits by the quotidian simplicity of his handling of witnesses and his asking of intense questions sotto voce.

No wonder the formidable Ansah Premo, his own colleague from the ruling government, was reeling from the proceedings. Used to the acculturated arrogance of a successful law practice and the wealth acquired corruptly from being at the helm of the presidency, the simplicity of Umaru's prosecuting style was one that he felt was beneath him, and yet was as unassailable as the moon.

But he was about to rest his case. He called Abena Asaa to confirm that she had heard Asabea cry out in pain, and that the sound had carried so clearly that Larry King and Billy Blanks had heard it too, and that Billy Blanks had increased the volume of the music in the living room to mask the cries. This he did, when the court sat again after the recess and Ansah Premo and Duncan King had informed the judge that they were ready to proceed.

Ansah Premo did not bother to cross examine Abena.

"Is defence counsel ready to proceed or would you prefer we retire till the morrow?" Justice Frimpong asked him when the prosecution closed.

"Defence is ready to proceed now, my Lord," Ansah Premo mentioned with more gusto than the situation warranted, "And defence calls Mr. Duncan King to the stand."

The conference between him and his clients had been intense. He had insisted on their changing their plea, but Duncan King had steadfastly refused. Larry King had affected his usual, uninvolved attitude but Billy Blanks had taken Duncan King's side. After the arguments had gotten them nowhere, Premo had demanded to be replaced. There were intense arguments and name callings after he had made that request until Larry had calmed things down by suggesting that he make Duncan King tell his own story. Duncan had been unhappy with that, but Premo had insisted there wasn't anything he could do for him beyond that.

That Duncan King had agreed to take the stand was a surprise to Asabea and to Umaru and the prosecution side. Asabea exchanged a slightly bemused glance with Owuraku who sat in the gallery with his eyebrows raised.

"This should be interesting," Aisha said to Dede in the Press box when the broadcast version hit them upstairs. "I hope his lawyer isn't putting him up on the stand to knowingly lie."

"If his testimony is anything like his statement to the police, the deputy Attorney-General will tear into him," Dede replied.

Duncan King walked up to the stand leaning heavily on an ornate walking stick. He was dressed in a burgundy bowtie on a white top and red blazers atop a blue pair of jeans, a black loafer, and lemon-green socks. Owuraku had never understood why Asabea had had the rapist's wardrobe abducted too. All it did was give the son-of-a-bitch the opportunity to gain a fandom on social media when he should be wearing sack cloth and no shoes.

Duncan King asked if he could swear on all the available religious artifacts on the stand. He accepted to use the cross when he looked up and realised Justice Frimpong was not amused.

Ansah Premo got right down to business after his client had been sworn in.

"You stand accused of raping Ms. Akua Sakyibea Asabea, a charge you have repeatedly denied. Why have you decided to take the stand?"

"I believe that it is important for the judge to hear me say that I did not rape her, and that I maintain the sex was consensual."

"The medical expert and several witnesses have provided testimony to the contrary."

"Ms. Asabea and I will never see eye to eye on what happened that day," Duncan King started, trying, and then failing, to sound contrite and sympathetic. "But while I maintained that I was innocent of the charges, I took cognisance of the effect the brutal media coverage was having on her, and the despicable psychological pressure bloggers and internet trolls were exerting on her on the internet and social media. So, I reached out to her family and settled the matter."

A buzz ran through the courtroom until the judge banged his gavel. Asabea had one eyebrow raised in incredulity when she locked eyes with Owuraku, who smiled in disbelief.

"Shouldn't we be objecting?" Efe asked the deputy Attorney-General.

"Let's see where they intend to go with this," Kwasi Apaloo advised quietly from their side before Umaru could respond. He had a mischievous look in his eyes.

"When you say you settled the matter, what do you mean?" Ansah Premo asked him from his lectern.

"I had my friend Billy Blanks meet up with her family and ask them to name their price to make the case go away," Duncan King replied carefully. "I believe that was when Ms. Asabea wrote to the State Prosecutor to discontinue the case, but the State Prosecutor says he never received such a letter."

"Did you receive such a letter yourself?" Ansah Premo asked.

"Yes."

"Why haven't you tended that in evidence?"

"It is locked up in my safe at home," Duncan King said. "If this was a proper courtroom, I'd have tended it in."

"How much was the settlement amount?"

"Thirty thousand pounds sterling. In cash."

Another buzz rippled through the room.

"Hasn't this gone on long enough?" Efe asked Apaloo with obvious distaste.

"Never interrupt your enemy when he is making a mistake," Apaloo quoted Napoleon quietly.

"No further questions, your Lordship," Premo ended his questioning and indicated to Umaru Tanko that he could have a go at the defendant.

"Generally, Mr. King," Umaru started. "How do you like your sex?"

"Usually boisterously," he answered without hesitation. "I may look old, but I will tell you this: if sex was the Olympics, I'd earn a gold medal for Ghana," he finished with an inappropriate smugness.

Umaru looked briefly at him before asking, "And it is your testimony under oath before this court, contrary to expert medical opinion, that you boisterously had consensual sex with a virgin after meeting her for the very first time?"

Duncan King shifted briefly in the seat before answering, "That is how she said she wanted it."

"If so," Umaru continued, keeping his boiling anger in check, "why pay thirty thousand pounds to settle?"

"I didn't want the public knowledge that she had slept with me to cause her future embarrassment. You know ours is a judgmental society, and as a nineteen-year-old having sexual intercourse on a first date with an older man, I wanted to spare her the stigma by paying her to make the whole brouhaha end. I didn't do it because I was guilty; I did it because I was magnanimous. And I have read a lot about how internet bullying affects young girls' self-esteem."

"Did you read about what forcible rape does to the self-esteem of young girls?"

Duncan King paused a bit, and then he decided to deflect.

"I read a lot, good sir," he said. "Sometimes, while lying next to my woman, fondling, and caressing her to arousal, she assumes I want sex. Often, all I need from her is lubrication so I could use the wetness to turn the pages of a book I might be reading."

Umaru Tanko blinked uncomprehendingly for a minute. It took three gavel bangs for the judge to silence the court.

"Who did you say made the arrangements to settle the matter, as you put it, between you and Ms. Asabea's family?" Umaru asked, trying hard to keep the disgust from showing on his face.

"My friend Billy Blanks over there," Duncan King pointed to Billy.

Umaru turned to point at him too, for the benefit of the court's records, and said, "That man?"

"Yes."

"How did he come up with the idea?"

"He approached me at the peak of the scandalous allegations. After the several court appearances, and what the allegations were doing to my hard-earned brand recognition, he felt we needed to speak with the girl and end the whole matter. I told him I had no way of contacting her after what she had put me through with the allegations. He then somehow reached out to her family – her mum and her dad, who I met at the Gold Coast Hotel a month after the comital hearings."

"You had no way of contacting Ms. Asabea because, up until that time, you and she had never met, correct?"

"That is correct."

"And that is why you did not have her mobile phone number, not so?"

"That's true too. It was just spontaneous sex," he tried to clarify when it occurred to him where the deputy Attorney-General was going with his questions.

"And you often have that kind of sex?"

"Objection!"

"Overruled!"

"Spontaneity is the spice of life," Duncan King answered unabashedly.

"Do go on with how you ended up speaking with Ms. Asabea's family," Umaru demanded.

Duncan King paused, as if to gather his thoughts.

"I remember apologising to her parents for all the unwelcome news and the media rampage, but I insisted that the sex was consensual, only I wanted to make amends for the shame and the dragging into the mud of their family name and the name of their daughter. We started haggling the price down from a hundred thousand pounds. Eventually we settled on thirty thousand. I paid them in cash, had them sign a receipt and a non-disclosure agreement, and saw them off. A week later, I received a copy of a letter signed by Ms. Asabea asking the State Prosecutor to discontinue the case."

"When defence counsel raised the matter before the Supreme Court justices, the State Prosecutor denied ever sighting the letter. The Attorney-General's department denied receipt of any such letter from you or from Ms. Asabea. In the filing of the nolle prosequi, no mention was made in any form that this purported letter was the reason for the nolle prosequi request. The rumours of a letter came two weeks in the media after the nolle had been granted. Is it therefore fair to say, Mr. King, that so far, only you and Mr. Blanks know of any such letter?"

"Mr. Blanks, Ms. Asabea, and her parents, so six people," Duncan King corrected.

"Not even your lawyer saw this purported letter?"

Duncan King looked at Ansah Premo at that point. Premo's face was unreadable, otherwise he too seemed interested in the response.

"It happened so quickly, so I believe that is why he never knew of it," he responded eventually. "Besides, once money had changed hands and a non-disclosure signed, we all believed the case was dead for good. I returned to the UK shortly after and have had no recourse to this issue until now."

"Do you know what the penalty for perjury is?" Umaru asked Duncan King abruptly.

"I am telling you the truth," Duncan King said firmly. "The letter has her parent's handwriting and signature."

"What are their names?"

"Pardon?"

"Asabea's parents," Umaru repeated. "What are their names?"

"They bear the same name as Asabea," he replied as if the answer should have been obvious.

"Both parents cannot be called Akua Sakyibea Asabea," Umaru told him. "If they signed receipts acknowledging payments, and signed an agreement whipped up by Mr. Blanks and you, surely, their full names would have had to have featured, don't you think, Mr. King?"

"Their names were on it, but it's been ten years, so I do not remember."

"What is the complexion of Ms. Asabea's mother?" Umaru

demanded.

"I remember her as a fair-skinned woman."

"Asabea's mother is dark-skinned. She takes after her father," Umaru told him. "If you saw them off from the Gold Coast Regency, what car were they driving?"

"They came in a taxi, so they left in the same taxi."

"Asabea's parents drive a wine-coloured Hyundai Tucson and a white Range Rover. They have never taken a taxi in twenty years. I put it to you that everything you have told this court about the letter and the settlement is false, and you know it to be false."

"Take me to my home, and I will pull out all the evidence for you to see that all I am saying is true. She knows this as well as I do, only she is here lying to the court because she wants to exact a misguided vengeance that will not happen."

"Where is your home, Mr. King?"

"I live at 19 Ringway Crescent, Osu," he responded cautiously.

"Is anyone at home at the moment?"

"No, I live alone."

"My Lord, do I have your permission to bring up his home on the screens?" Umaru asked the judge.

"Objection," Premo shot to his feet. "I fail to see the relevance."

"He claims the document is in his safe. We can check right now to see if indeed they are there."

"How would you have access to his home from here? And how would such an unauthorised intrusion stand legal muster? You are inviting this court to engage in a criminality by trespassing uninvited into Duncan King's home."

"He claims the evidence of a letter and a receipt of payment are in his safe. If he and this court gave permission, I can have a Police detective at his house right now who can enter his bedroom and send us live videos of what is in his safe."

"Do you consent to a search of your home to retrieve the documents you're talking about, Mr. King?" Justice Frimpong asked a now bewildered Duncan King.

"I'm so-so-sorry, my Lord, but I do not consent to having my home searched in my absence."

"Then the objection is sustained, Counsel," the judge ruled with a helpless shake of his shoulders.

"That is alright, your Lordship," Umaru conceded. "No search is necessary because we already know the contents of his safe."

"Objection. Any such content is inadmissible here," Premo retorted angrily.

"Actually, it is, if it is acquired from the defendant's own public activities, and I am happy to show the court this post on the defendant's own social media page. I refer you to the exhibit on the screen – let's call it exhibit RD12."

A photo of Duncan King smoking a cigar was manipulated onto the screen. He sat near a bed in an amber-coloured room, tastefully furnished as a posh hotel room might be. Near the head of the bed was an open safe showing several large wads of foreign currency.

"This is a photo of you, is it not?"

Duncan King looked at his lawyer, but Ansah Premo seemed as confused as he was.

"Yes, that's a photo of me on my page."

"Posted three days before your abduction by Ms. Asabea, not so?"

"I believe so."

The screen zoomed into the safe, and some software ran an analysis of its contents. And right on the screen, condoms, the currencies of six leading western nations, passports, driver's licences in four countries, printed nudes of six Ghanaian celebrities and a substance the software identified as eighty-seven percent cocaine were identified.

"No letter, no receipt, nothing of the sort you have mentioned under oath are present in this photo of your own taking. Tell me, Mr. King, did your lawyer put you up to this stunt?"

"Objection!"

"Withdrawn!" Umaru ruled before the judge could.

"Tell me, Mr. King," he continued, "Are you sure the ones you met were really Ms. Asabea's parents? Because we have here a signed affidavit from both parents testifying to never meeting you."

"Objection, my Lord. This is the first we are hearing of an affidavit from the parents," Ansah Premo interrupted.

"Counsel, the affidavit in question forms part of discovery, marked as RD8," the judge reminded him. "Your objection is overruled."

Premo reached out for the folder on his desk and scanned through the documents, still on his feet and seemingly about to protest. His eyebrows rose in surprise when he found them. He promptly sat down.

Duncan King glanced at Billy Blanks when Umaru demanded he answer his question. Billy seemed more interested in examining the finer details of a piece of artwork hanging by one of the walls.

"Your Lordship, may I please confer for a minute with my lawyer?"

The judge said, "Answer the question first, Mr. King!"

Looking rather forlornly at Asabea, Duncan King said, "I honestly do not know if they were your parents. I might have been deceived."

"Your client's request for recess is now granted," Justice Frimpong told Ansah Premo.

"What the frack, Billy?" Duncan King tore into Billy Blanks the moment they were alone in their shared library in their living quarters. "You set me up, took my money and haven't said a word of truth in this matter until now?"

"It's not what it looks like, OK?" Billy said defensively. "I was set up as well."

"What do you mean you were set up?" Duncan looked ready to tear his friend from limb to limb.

"I reached out to people who said they knew her parents. I trusted them, and when I met the elderly couple, I assumed they were the ones."

"Wait," Ansah Premo ordered them, putting the stamp of his authority on the meeting. "Neither of you actually called Asabea to try to make this go away?"

They looked at each other.

"You mean, not even *you*?" Premo directed his shock at Duncan King, who stood there looking like an angry idiot.

"I reached out through some friends of mine, and the meeting was arranged by a couple of them – media persons, to be honest. I had no idea this was a set up," Billy deflected the blame vehemently.

"I think *you* did the setting up," Larry King told him bluntly from his corner in the library. "You knew Duncan would do anything to not go to jail, so you set him up right from the beginning. Those people were your people, and the money came right back to you. Admit this and let's move on," he advised in his typically practical way.

Duncan King was frothing at the mouth from fury. Such was his rage from this betrayal that he couldn't even find his voice. He limped across the room and clobbered his friend heavily with his walking stick. Billy slumped to the floor, but Duncan would have hit him again had Ansah Premo not intervened. He snatched the walking stick from him while Larry King examined the big welt behind the fallen man's head.

"Weren't you planning to have him testify?" Larry King asked Premo while he turned the unconscious Billy into the recovery position.

"Not anymore," Ansah Premo answered and then turned on the

enraged Duncan King. "Our only recourse is to change our plea and negotiate with the deputy Attorney-General."

Duncan King flopped into a nearby chair and let out a defeated sigh.

"Admitting to this will seriously hurt my brand," he objected eventually. "Let this run its course."

"That is not wise," Larry King told him, rising from the floor where he had been keeping an eye on Billy. "If you confessed, and sought out some kind of plea, the Girls might be moved to reconsider a lesser form of the revenge they seem to have planned to exact on you."

"Let them try," Duncan King said with a gusto that surprised his cousin. "I am not going to go down easily."

"They've got guns, Duncan," Larry reminded him cooly. "That attempt we made in the dining room was as pathetic as any. There is no contest here. Even hand to hand, those girls will beat the crap out of us any day. Own up to your crime and let's see if we can live to see another day," he warned.

"Aha! I knew it. You really believe I raped her, don't you?"

"It doesn't matter what I believe, you idiot!"

"Watch your tongue with me, Cousin," Duncan King warned dangerously.

"Or what?" Larry King taunted angrily. "You'll hit me with your walking stick? I am trying to save your life here. Those Girls did not go through all this to leave you walking out alive. They have made that clear. Murder is what they have in mind, but to kill you appears such a solemn step for them that they needed to show the kind of animal you are to justify your death. This is what all this is about. Plead guilty, apologise for your crimes, promise to make restitution and let's see if that persuades them, and stop being a butthole."

Ansah Premo stayed in the middle between both men, looking from one to the other, determined not to let a second man go limp on the floor but unsure exactly how to manage that if Duncan King came in swinging again. But he need not have worried. Larry was three times fitter than Duncan was, and while the more muscular Billy had been taken unawares, Larry was as alert as a cobra, daring his older cousin to try him if he dared with his eyes.

Duncan saw the challenge but decided against it. He looked at his lawyer and said, "Get me back on the stand."

CHAPTER 23
The Fortress
Thursday, 21st March; 5 P.M.

SUNSET HAD ALWAYS been his favourite part of the day, and this one promised to be no different. Even though he was trapped near the river, he still had much to be grateful for in the amber glow of a near setting sun. Whipped by bruising winds funneled through the valley, the last of the firestorm raged towards him and his few surviving soldiers. Without thinking too much about it, they dove to the bottom of the river until the blaze passed them over. Even buried under water, he felt the heat of the inferno. When it was all over, he and a dozen men took refuge on a strip of rocks along the river and tried to take stock of their situation. Their eyes were seared by the malodorous smoke, and several of his men sported first degree burns, but these were the lucky ones. How many had died would not be known until a full accounting.

Colonel Bruce Nartey of the first Infantry Battalion had been standing with his artillery officers on the drawbridge, sizing up the fortress when the explosions occurred. It was not sound military doctrine for a Senior Officer to be at the fore front of a conflict, and he had been there for no more than a minute, just to assess the pass that the CTU and the Obuobi character had been whining about, but before his last foot could leave the bridge, the bridge had split, and he'd fallen. He did manage to grab one heaving support beam for all of ten seconds before it had given way, and he'd fallen far, far below until he'd hit water. While the section of the river he'd fallen into had not been overly deep, it had been deep enough to break his fall just before the rocky bottom, and even then, his lungs had drained of all air on impact, and it had left him with a concussion that still made his ears ring.

But he was alive, and that was all that mattered. What had appeared to be a deep valley from above was a series of terraced cliffs, and each cliff had a landing of some five or so metres. Many of his troops that had fallen had bounced off a lot of those landings, and that was what had killed them. Those that had quickly realised what was going on had grabbed onto branches and roots to slow their fall, and the luckiest of them had been those, like he, who had fallen straight into the river.

The previous night had been the worst of their experience, when the guns had started going off by themselves, killing the men that had been fortunate to have survived the falls to the first of the landings. The entire night had been spent hearing dying men scream in pain, and there'd been nothing he nor the few men who had gathered by the riverbank near one of the landings at the bottom had been able to do to help. And then, when the fires had come, from grass and dry undergrowth burning in response to the ammunitions and grenades that had exploded before, Colonel Nartey had felt the end had come. The valley had crackled with the ferocity of the fires and thick black smoke from ignited vegetation had filled the chasm and choked many of the men who had found themselves on the upper terraces to death.

He looked up from the rocks by the river and surveyed the steep ravine. They had no equipment to attempt a climb. He clambered over the rocks to see if a side of the river that was hidden from his immediate view could offer any way up to the terrace above. After searching for a dozen minutes, he found a trail gouged out of the rocks above by a trickle of water and called to his men.

Most of his survivors were Privates, but there were three Staff Sergeants as well. He conferred briefly with them and laid out the outline of a plan. If they carefully climbed up one after the other, they might make it to the terrace above them and hopefully find more river- or rain-gouged trails to keep going higher. Once they all agreed, after the confusions had worn off a bit, he asked if anyone had weapons or tools of any kind. Only three pistols and two assault rifles were intact, but their ammunitions were laughably low.

"Let's start climbing; we might find some along the way, hopefully," he tried to reassure the dozen or so survivors.

The climb was painfully slow, and by the time they made it to the landing above them, they were so sore and so out of breath that a discussion to continue was off the table. Besides, it was darker now. The sun had disappeared about a half hour ago. Fumbling around in the blackness of this hostile environment could lead to more deaths, and it was Colonel Nartey's desire to keep all his remaining men alive.

They cleared out some of the embers from the still smoldering terrace and created a safe campsite no more than ten square metres in size and gathered to spend the night. One of the Staff Sergeants had a backpack full of gari, sugar and powdered milk, and Colonel Nartey had had them fill their available canteens with river water before the climb. They prepared gari soakings and tried to get some rest. Colonel Nartey knew none of his men would sleep, but at least they would be refreshed a bit in the morning before they tried to find a way out of the ravine.

One of his men had gone looking with a small torchlight around the makeshift camp and returned with more weapons, more ammo and some ropes. He'd even found a mobile phone and a power bank among an intact backpack. The backpack's owner had died from a fall.

"The bag was still strapped to the body?" he asked the Private.

"Yes, sir."

"What did you do to him?"

"I covered him up with some rocks," the Private replied sombrely.

Colonel Nartey checked the mobile phone and turned it on. It had full battery power but no signal. He turned it off and slipped it into one of his battle dress's pockets, and then went to lean against the side of the terrace they were on and tried to sleep.

A slight drizzle announced the arrival of morning, which was typical weather in the Aburi mountains, and after another meal of soakings, the Colonel and his men attempted to climb up another terrace, but this was more difficult than yesterday's. For starters, there was no river-gouged trail; just highly stacked layers of rocks one could climb over, but the risk of slipping on loose rocks was high, and climbers below were hit by rocks loosened by those above them in the entire attempt. Thankfully, the rocks were no larger than a man's fist, and other than a few cuts and bruises, he and his dozen men made it up three more terraces. From there, they could see the opposing plateau, and could tell that going four more levels up would put them at eye level to the exact same spot they had been standing when the drawbridge was destroyed.

"That means we are just a few levels from where the Fortress stands," one of the Staff Sergeants voiced out that thought excitedly. They all looked up just then to see what the going up would look like, but their hearts sank. They were right under some umbrella of a big mass of rock and under the overhanging edge. The base of this mushroom-shaped cliff was pure igneous, stood about a hundred feet tall and looked unclimbable without equipment.

"Let's split up and see if we can walk around it," he ordered his men. They returned to the same spot within a minute.

"This is the largest part," one of the men announced. "The terrace narrows the farther one walks away from here."

"Same thing the other way," another declared. "Any further and there's a long fall. But there's a metal gate on our side."

"Let me see it," Colonel Nartey ordered and walked with the soldier to the spot. Sure enough, there within the face of the rock was a grating wide enough to accommodate a man and just as high. The landing to the bars was so small that he had to hold on to the grille to avoid falling off the dizzying ledge from his fear of height.

"You think this is some long-forgotten escape hatch from the Fortress?" the Staff Sergeant asked him.

"That would be an amazing turn of events," he said quietly. He looked up at what could pass as the lintel of the opening and his eyes widened. Above that point, hawsers and woven nets of many shapes and sizes flapped quietly in the wind of the drizzle. He wiped his face with his hands and looked again. The hawsers must have been part of the materials that held the drawbridge in place, and the bridge was hooked up to destructible beams only on the approaching side of the pass. On the Fortress side, the beams were permanent, and that was why the ropes were still hanging. If seemed the bridge had been designed to only temporarily be dropped and lifted hydraulically like a trap door.

"Do you think we could climb and grab them?" he asked the Staff Sergeant. He had said earlier that his name was Martin.

Martin shielded his eyes from the drizzle and examined the ropes.

"I think if we climbed a little up using the grille, we might be able to touch it."

"Let's give that a try and see if we can pull the ropes a little further down."

It took some minutes, given the slippery nature of the ledge, and the rain, but Martin was finally able to jump up off the grating and grab one of the bigger hawsers. He almost fell when the ropes gave way briefly, probably because they had not been stretched fully down yet but when they rested, they were fully down to the level of the ledge, and the wooden planks, now hanging vertically, formed a ladder that seemed to reach the other end of the pass on the Fortress's side.

"Good job, Soldier," Colonel Nartey quietly congratulated him before tying the end of the ropes to the grating. Now that he had something more solid to hold on to, he examined the grille in detail.

A tunnel seemed to lead into the rock of the mountain the Fortress was built on, but that disappeared shortly from view because it was dark a few metres from the gate. He passed his hand to the side of it and found a heavy padlock, locked from within. He lifted the lock up a little to see if the light from the outside could let him know what kind it was and deduced that he could probably blast it open with his gun. He'd have to be careful about the ricochet, though, since it was hardened metal and could send the slug back to hurt or kill someone.

Quietly, he released the padlock and advised a retreat. When he and Martin gave the news to the rest of the survivors, the bigger question wasn't so much whether the grating could be breached, but whether they had enough ammunition, weapons and men to take on a clearly prepared team of abductors. Colonel Nartey then remembered he had a mobile phone. He turned it on, smiled that there was signal this time and dialed.

"Major Hanson," the recipient said.

"This is Bruce Nartey, first battalion," he paused to let it sink in.

"Thank God, sir," Major Hanson said excitedly. "We thought we had lost you."

"Not yet," he responded calmly. "I have a few survivors with me as well. Listen, can you have the CTU call me back on this number? We may need their help – and do not inform Command that I am alive just yet until we have spoken to the CTU."

"I am climbing their stairs right now to their parallel war room. We'll call you back in a minute."

Less than a minute later, the call came through.

"Good to know you're alive, Colonel," the IGP himself made the call.

"Feels good to be, to be honest," Colonel Nartey said. "Do you have the blueprints of the Fortress?" he asked straight away.

"Yes, we do," Obuobi came in at that point. "What do you want to know?"

"Well, when we came to, we found ourselves near a river at the bottom of the ravine. We've been climbing up this mountain since last night, and we seem to have arrived at some cave-like entryway with a metal gate, of sorts. I wanted to know where it led to, before my men and I attempt to infiltrate."

"Hang on one minute," Obuobi said and shuffled some papers.

"What condition are you and your men in?" the IGP asked while waiting for Obuobi to do his usual magic.

"We'll live," the Colonel said shortly. "How bad is my battalion?"

"I think you may have lost half of them," the IGP told him sombrely.

"All on that drawbridge?"

"Yes, all on the drawbridge."

"None from drone attacks?"

"They used the drones to harass your troops but they never actually killed anyone."

Colonel Nartey sighed. "If I had listened to your team earlier, this could have been avoided."

"Water under the bridge at the moment," the IGP told him before Obuobi took over.

"That opening is marked as a sluice on the blueprints, and it runs as a long culvert all the way from the basement of the Fortress," he said over the phone. "The grating will not be the only one though; there are three others before you get to the basement. There is nothing else here to guide me on what kind of security system they might have in place, but my guess is that they will not expect anyone to come at them from those depths."

The Colonel chewed on that and then he said, "Thank you."

"What do you plan to do?" the IGP asked him. "And what can we do to help?"

"What is the President planning?" Colonel Nartey asked instead.

"The government plans to send in some attack helicopters tonight," the IGP informed him.

"What about the hostages?"

"The government does not give two craps about the hostages."

"I thought that posture had changed since our routing."

"That happened less than two days ago. Nothing has changed."

"And you think an assault might work?"

"The evidence is to the contrary, but it's really the hostages we are worried about. What are the scenarios where you're concerned? I doubt you have many guns and ammo to make an incursion from below."

"We don't," the Colonel conceded, "And even if we managed to get far, I don't know what we would do with the hostages if we found them. We are on treacherous ledges here under their mountain. If we came rushing with civilians, we might have a lot of fatalities."

"What if we got you some help?" the IGP asked cautiously with a conspiratorial look at the rest of his CTU.

"How can you?" the Colonel asked. "We got here by accident. If you threw people off the cliff they might die."

"We've got some guys coming in from below, but they are technical. We contracted them to assist in hostage rescue. You might team up with them."

The Colonel was thoughtful for a moment.

"Are they cops?"

"No, they are civilians, but with much more jungle knowledge than any of yours and our men."

"Meaning they would not be armed."

"They specifically refused when we offered."

"If their plan was to rescue the hostages and the girls while helicopter gunships were blazing overhead, how were they going to get everyone to safety over these cliffs? It's a miracle we got here to begin with. I can only imagine how hard it would be to run a technical operation of that nature under a missile attack."

"That is why I am seeking to have you both collaborate," the IGP stressed. "They are sure to turn up in almost the same sector as you are now, and if they find a way to you or vice versa, you could team up and save the hostages."

"And perhaps the Girls?" the Colonel asked.

"Yes, and the Girls, if they would accept their help. The order to Opare and his men was to hand them over to us, and that order stands," the IGP said firmly.

"That's understood," Colonel Nartey said wearily. "When will they get here?"

"I believe they're nearby as we speak. After our call, we will reach out to them and have them look for you. Maybe if you all work through those tunnels, you could have a safe place for the hostages before the Fortress is razed to the ground. Then you could come out afterwards when the fireworks die down."

"We will consider all options when we meet your men – what are their names?"

"The leader is Kwaku Opare Addo," the IGP told him. "They wear olive green uniforms, even though they might have variations to blend in with the forest."

"Duly noted," the Colonel said gratefully. "And please keep the information about our survival to yourselves. I don't need our high command knowing that yet."

"You bet," the IGP said with a chuckle. "The government doesn't know about the extraction team either."

About a hundred metres above Colonel Nartey's makeshift camp, Asabea and Owuraku sat on a balcony overlooking the cliff face to discuss the events of the previous day. The time read 6:30 a.m., but there was too much to do to remain in bed. The rest of the girls joined them with champagne. The balcony faced West, and the rising sun from behind the building cast a pretty glow to everything it touched, from the peaks of the mountains closer to their plateau, to the leaves of the trees down the valley below. Owuraku got up to survey more of the view but backtracked quickly when he saw how far it was to the bottom.

"What's wrong?" Asabea asked him curiously.

"Heights make me giddy," he responded.

"And you wanted us to escape over the cliff?" Asabea asked him in amusement.

"Yeah, that was a waste of money, wasn't it?" Nhyira asked as the first to join them on the balcony. "Opare's services will not be needed now that we have sent the army running with their tails in between their legs."

"It's early days yet," Owuraku replied wisely.

Nhyira laughed dryly and sat down on one of several Adirondack chairs on the balcony, each stuffed with leatherettes. It wasn't long before the other girls arrived.

"How are you doing, Aisha?" Owuraku asked her, the last to arrive.

Aisha looked over the glass balustrades at the mountains in the distance and breathed in deeply.

"Never been better," she answered. And then she turned to him and smiled.

Efe led the discussions that followed; the discussion of what to do now that Duncan King had confessed his guilt.

"To be honest, I really wasn't expecting that," Dede announced dryly. "Almost brought a tear to my eyes."

"I think we were all touched, as was the watching public," Efe said sarcastically. "Opinions differ as to what to do to him now. That is currently dithering between letting him off and jailing him for life."

Then, as if on cue, everyone turned to look at Asabea. Since the confession, she'd been noticeably quiet, speaking only to Owuraku in silent tones.

She looked calmly at her team and said, "I think we all know what will happen next."

"Doesn't the confession change anything?" Owuraku asked her carefully, gauging her face as he asked.

Asabea shrugged. "He's lied at every turn since the incident. He even believed that he had paid me off. And holding on to that thought, he'd done nothing but defame me in every media conversation every chance he got. Duncan King is not truly remorseful, and the judgment will be carried out in full."

"Hear, hear!" The rest of the girls raised their champagnes in salute.

"What are we going to do about the hostages?" Oye wanted to know.

"Yeah, with the bridge destroyed, how are we going to let them off this mountain?" Nhyira backed her twin.

"Let the government come for them," Owuraku said with a shrug. "Our task would be to get out of here, and once we are out, we can call the President to send in a chopper."

"I don't know but I kind of feel we shouldn't leave until we have all the hostages out of the Fortress," Bubuné said quietly. "They have really been good to us through everything. We shouldn't leave until they have been rescued first."

"If we leave under fire, it would be impossible to rescue that many people over the cliff," Owuraku said. "Couldn't we find some quiet basement place for them to hole out in until government troops stop their destruction enough to find out they're safe underground?"

"Yeah, we have those cellars down in the basement," Dede agreed. "That might lessen our burdens."

"You really think the Opare person will come for us?" Nhyira asked incredulously. "I'd even forgotten about him."

Owuraku looked at her. "You hadn't really, had you? I bet you spend every waking moment thinking about him."

Oye and Nhyira both scoffed.

Owuraku gave them a knowing smile.

"Is there any other way to get the hostages out of here?" he asked Asabea.

"We could try to restore the drawbridge," Bubuné said thoughtfully. "It could take some days, but we could."

"How so?" Asabea asked. "I thought they destroyed it."

"The hydraulics are intact," Bubuné told her. "The nets and hawsers should be dangling over the gulch."

"And if we don't have beyond today?" Asabea asked, mindful of how Owuraku was thinking.

Bubuné shrugged. "Then we would have to take the hostages along with us. I agree that we cannot leave them behind."

"So, we just wait for the judgment of the court, and then from there, we start packing?" Efe asked.

"Best we start packing now," Owuraku advised coolly. "I have a strong sense that the government will strike today. Let's get ready to bail as soon as the judgment is read."

"But we don't know if your guy will turn up at the foot of the cliff today," Bubuné said with concern.

"Let's do our part," Owuraku advised again. "Best be ready and have to wait, than to be unprepared when he's here."

"Alright then," Asabea decided. "Let's pick only what we need for the extraction and leave everything else. Are the wards ready for judgment?" she asked Dede and Aisha.

"Yes, the wards are," Dede replied happily, and then she looked to

Owuraku. "Are you ready?"

"You bet!" Owuraku responded grimly.

The rope fell seemingly out of nowhere at first, startling Colonel Nartey and his team almost off their ledge. For a minute, he thought it was a hawser that had probably taken its time to drop from all the pulling they had done by the grating, but on close examination, it seemed someone was rappelling off the umbrella edge of the mushroom rock overhead.

True enough, gaited feet showed up on the ledge, followed quickly by a body carrying a fifty-liter backpack. Then a face with sweat glistening on its brow rappelled off and zipped down quickly to the ground. That was when the Colonel realised that he was not the only one with his weapon drawn.

The face of the man was young, but streaks of silver in his short-cropped beard indicated a much older person. Sparing no more than a glance at them, he proceeded to get his equipment out of the way for a second person. The second person glanced only once at them before completing his descent. Their lack of interest in them and in the drawn weapons left him wondering.

"Who are you?" Martin asked the first man, obviously just as rattled as the Colonel was about these silent rappelers.

"I'm Kwaku Opare Addo," the first man said. "And I was asked by the IGP to find you. Now, put away your weapons."

Lowering his pistol, the Colonel demanded, "How did you get up there? Were you already in the Fortress?"

"We hacked a trail from down there to the top," Opare answered, pointing vaguely to the other side of the ravine. "We only had sixty metres of steep rock to climb to arrive at the Fortress."

"And the Girls let you come for us?" Nartey asked incredulously.

"They don't know we are here yet," Opare told him. "As soon as the Police called us, we stopped trying to enter the Fortress and came to find you."

"How do you plan to get the hostages off their hands and off the mountain then?"

"The Police said you had found some caves."

Nartey nodded.

"We are here to see what trail we could cut from the caves to the river. If we are successful, the trail will merge with the one we hacked coming up. It should be possible to get all hostages on that side before

Armageddon rains."

"How do you propose to persuade the Girls to release the hostages?"

"You leave that to us," Opare said to him. "How treacherous is the way you came up?"

"Going to be worse going down."

"But doable all the same?"

"Yes."

"Good," Opare said and took off his backpack. "There are supplies in here – food, medicines, drinks. You eat and get your strengths back. My Ranger and I will abseil to widen the trail and connect it to ours on the other side of the river. We shouldn't be gone too long."

"What is abseil?" Martin asked Opare.

"Rappelling."

"Why are you calling it abseiling then?"

"British English. Rappelling is American English. Ghana speaks British," Opare said, seeming anxious to start descending again.

"We couldn't access the other side of the river. There was a rock too steep to connect, and the mosses there were slippery," the Colonel informed him. "How do you propose getting around that?"

Opare shrugged. "That's why we are here," he said simply and began to abseil off their landing.

They were gone for four long hours, and the taut ropes were the only evidence that the adventure guides had been there to begin with. Nartey was surprised at how silently the two worked. Military strategy always involved an awful lot of noise – what their training calls shock and awe – but the work of these two jungle enthusiasts revealed to him another world of strategy, and the irony wasn't lost on him that for all the military posturing and government activities that had enabled these abductions to take on an outsized role in national security discussions over the past weeks, a bunch of obscure adventure experts had breached the Fortress without anyone's detection.

The ropes began to shake, indicating activity. He looked off their landing to discover the two men climbing up the rocks but in a diagonal way, creating footings in the rocks with devices they held in their hands. When they arrived at the top, they stashed their gear in the now empty backpack that had contained all the food and drinks.

"You didn't leave us any," the other Ranger, a taller man in dread locks complained when he took the backpack off Martin and peered inside.

Martin stood there looking sheepish.

"If the hostages walk backwards in the more treacherous parts, they should be able to make it safely," Opare announced to the Colonel. "We have made footholds in the promontory so it should be easier to go over those parts. Once you're over the rocks, our trail starts right off, and will lead you to the Adawso township where the CTU will be waiting."

"What about the hostages? How would you get them to us?" Col. Nartey asked.

"We will find a way through the caves to the grating over there," Opare said. "It will be our first order of business. If we get into trouble when the Air Force strikes, we will come down quickly to get you so you may deal with them. But all things being equal, that will not be necessary. Do you have a radio we could reach you on?"

"We lost all our radio guys," the Colonel said sadly.

"I am sorry for your loss," Opare said and handed a handset to the Colonel.

"It's already set to our channels," he told him. "All you have to do is to turn it on within a couple of hours when we expect to have announced our presence to the Girls."

"What do we do if things go south?" the Colonel asked carefully.

"If the Air Force attacks before we get up there, use the resulting disturbances to break the locks," he advised. "The Girls and their surveillance sensors will not be able to distinguish between the rockets from above and the noise from below. However bad things get up there, we will get the hostages down to you."

"Good," Nartey said simply. "And thank you."

Opare smiled. Then he and Wannah, his partner, pulled up their ropes from below and pooled them at the base of the towering rock from which they had abseiled. Then they both attached French and foot prussiks and started the arduous work of ascending the ropes. It took them half an hour to climb over the overhang and out of the view of Colonel Nartey's men.

It was when the ropes were pulled completely off the ground and out of sight another hour later that it occurred to the Colonel that they had arrived at the Fortress.

"Best get ready," he said simply to his men.

CHAPTER 24
The Fortress
Friday, 22nd March; 9 A.M.

"WE HAVE MULTIPLE sensors going off since five this morning," Regina reported. "And our drones have detected a lot of movement from the Aburi Girls Senior High School football field."

"What do you think that means?" Asabea asked the nerd.

"Movement of troops, arrival of choppers, and movement of a lot of drones," Regina responded. "I didn't think the Air Force had that much equipment."

"Ours don't," Owuraku mentioned gravely. "But we have an American military base here in Ghana. I believe they might have loaned us some equipment."

"I thought that was a myth," Bubuné asked him.

"The government likes to encourage that notion because of how bad a dent the truth makes on our pan African and non-neo-colonialism agenda, but we have had an American FOB for seven years now," Owuraku said. "Does that change our defense preparedness?"

Bubuné chewed thoughtfully for a minute on a lower lip.

"We can hold off as long as possible, but that depends on what projectiles they use," she said eventually. "If they hit us with a barrage of rockets and missiles, we won't be able to do much except respond with our drones and launchers; there is no way we will outlast American hardware. Our safest bet would be if they came in with choppers and wingmen. So long as they set foot here, we will have the advantages."

"So, our worst case would be to hunker down and let drones do the fighting?" Asabea asked.

"Our worst case will be to leave before the first missiles strike," Bubuné replied bleakly. "I am sorry, but I did not consider outside help to the Ghana Armed Forces in our equations. And even if we did, we could not have been able to acquire more equipment than we did without raising serious eyebrows."

"I understand," Asabea told her reassuringly. "I just needed to know what we were dealing with."

"Do we have any estimates of when they might strike?" Owuraku asked Bubuné.

"At this rate of activity," Regina answered for Bubuné, "perhaps by noon at the earliest."

"We have a noonday deadline then," Asabea said gravely. "The judge will pass judgment at ten. Let's get the wards ready for Duncan King and Billy Blanks and get things moving very quickly. Oye and Nhyira, I need you both to come up with a plan for securing and protecting the hostages because the government does not care much about them.

"Owuraku, Efe and I will man the Courtroom to ensure the criminals do not plan a repeat of the dining room jamboree. The rest of you need to keep an eye on what the military is doing so we are not taken by surprise.

"Three things need to happen no matter what, and in this order: Duncan King needs what's coming to him, so that is priority number one. The hostages, and their safety, is number two. And our escape or defense is number three. Are we all on the same page?"

They all were.

And the next hour was spent frenetically getting equipment and gear in place for what was shaping up to be the fight for their very lives.

Duncan King did not take it kindly at all to being restrained for the final phase of this bizarre trial, but the twins held him roughly against the wall and slapped on the shackles on his wrists and ankles. They did the same to Billy Blanks, whose attempt to resist using his ginormous muscular build was scuttled when Nhyira aimed her pistol at him. And then they both were led out, with Larry and Ansah Premo in front, and the twins bringing the rear. It had been decided the previous night to leave Ansah Premo alone, and to treat him as a hostage.

The decision to do the same to Larry King had been a hard one. Aisha and Owuraku had contended that Larry was as much a willful participant in the crime as was Billy Blanks, but the others thought he was more of an unwilling loyalist. Asabea had then decided that Larry would be handcuffed and restrained to watch his friends suffer, but he himself would be spared any personal injury in the execution of judgment. And this was why, although shackled at the wrist, Larry King had been spared the indignity of the ankle shackles.

Judge Emmanuel Frimpong did not waste time.

"In the matter of the Republic vs. Duncan King on the charge of rape in the first degree, this Court finds the defendant, Duncan King guilty on the evidence of the prosecution, as well as on his own plea, and while I take note of his plea for leniency, it is this Court's determination that the callousness of the crime and the absolute lack of remorse in the defendant's demeanour and public utterances since then, requires the imposition of the maximum sentence allowed under Section 97 and 98 of the Criminal Offences Act of 1960. The defendant, Duncan King, is hereby sentenced to twenty-five years' imprisonment in hard labour in a maximum-security prison."

Then the judge peered over his glasses at Duncan King and asked him, "Does the defendant wish to say any last words?"

Duncan King looked quietly at the judge and said with all the disdain he could muster, "Fuck you!"

"My Lord," Ansah Premo rose apologetically. "My client did not mean to say that," he said with a murderous side eye at Duncan King.

The judge smiled wanly and banged his gavel.

"This court is adjourned."

Ansah Premo walked quickly to the prosecution side and asked Asabea, "Now that you have gotten what you want, what are you going to do next?"

"We have to get you and everyone else but these three people to safety," Asabea answered seriously, pointing at Duncan, Larry and Billy. "The government is about to conduct a bombing operation against us, and they consider the innocent members among you, our abductees, as collateral damage. That is the first order of business."

"Are you going to use us as human shields?" Umaru Tanko asked her.

"We will never do that to innocent people," she told him honestly. "We have tunnels and bomb-proof basements. You can hide in them until the military concludes their campaign."

"What about you?" the judge, who had been led by Efe to where they were all standing asked.

"We know how to take care of ourselves, Your Lordship," Asabea assured him respectfully. "All that matters is for nothing to happen to you."

"What about those three?" Ansah Premo asked curiously.

"Those three are another matter," Owuraku informed him.

"You'll kill them?" Ansah Premo asked with a sickened expression.

"No more and no less than they deserve, Counsel," Owuraku told him coolly. "I believe you need to run to your quarters and take what you need to shelter in place against a bombing campaign. Time is of the essence now."

With a few glances at the trio of shackled men, the court emptied out, leaving only Owuraku with the three men. Shortly after, gurneys arrived to cart the three to the ward.

"What is this?" Larry King demanded when the gurneys were wheeled in by the attending nurses.

"No talking," Owuraku warned, pulling out his side arm for effect.

Wordlessly, the three men were conveyed to the cell that Duncan King had first been imprisoned in when he was brought into the Fortress. But the cell was no longer what it used to be. It had been converted into a modern ward, complete with heart monitors, metal beds, IV lines and such gizmos as to make any public hospital ward green with envy.

Duncan King was moved roughly by the surgically masked nurses from his gurney into the central bed in the new ward with Owuraku's help, and his shackles were secured in a manner to keep him sitting upright. He could move, but not enough to fall off the bed.

Billy was subjected to the same treatment. Larry King, on the other hand, was not stripped but was shackled to a metal seat that had been drilled into the concrete floor. His legs were free, but his cuff restraints were connected to the chair somewhat. He could not escape unless he broke out of his chair.

"What is this?" Larry King demanded again. "Are you planning to poison us?"

Owuraku ignored him and got to work getting some other equipment ready. When the lights came on, the three men realised they were camera equipment. Owuraku spoke into a mouthpiece and adjusted the lights on the instructions of whoever was on the other end.

"What the hell is this?" Duncan King demanded angrily. Of course, he knew lights, cameras and action when he saw one, but not like this. Why did the public need to see him strapped like a common criminal?

But Owuraku was not done. He brought in a masked person who first stripped both men of all their clothing using sheers, and then inserted an IV line into both Duncan's and Billy's arms. Both tried to resist but the shackles made that ineffective.

"What are you *doing*?" Duncan King demanded desperately, almost tearfully. "Are you trying to kill me? The judge said imprisonment!"

"And you said to fuck him," Owuraku retorted coolly. "I don't know what fucks you've got to give now."

"Don't do this!" Larry King pleaded frantically from his chair, looking from both Duncan to Billy, and to Owuraku. "Listen, let's talk about this!"

Then Asabea walked in. At the sight of her, Duncan King began to wrestle with his restraints. "I will kill you, bitch!" he screamed. "I will kill you and fuck you bloody for this!"

"Language," Asabea said admonishingly. "Is this any way to present yourself to the livestream?"

Duncan shut up after that and tried to keep a composed façade.

"That's much better," Asabea said, patting his arm approvingly. She wore a pair of surgical gloves from a gloves box to a side of Duncan King's bed, grabbed an apron and proceeded to insert a miniscule IV line into the deep dorsal vein, the prominent vein that ran along the shaft of their penises. She ignored the startled responses from her patients and held the near-microscopic needles in place with bits of surgical tape until they were positioned to her liking, and then she kept both penises upright with a thread she tied from an overhanging spool. She then calmly took off her surgical apparel, sat on a stool in the middle of the two beds and spoke while the cameras whirred.

"There is a 2008 movie, Untraceable," she began, looking quietly at Duncan King and Billy Blanks. The masked doctor came in at that point to set up the doses for the IV feeds and quietly left.

"It's a movie about a particularly sadistic criminal who arises on the internet," she continued. "This tech-savvy killer posts live feeds of his crimes on his website, and the more hits the site gets, the faster the victim dies. Have either of you seen that movie?" she asked, looking from Duncan to Billy.

Both men glared at her.

"What about you?" she asked Larry King, who had his mouth open and his eyes wide as the implications of her words struck him.

Asabea smiled wanly at him and said, "I was planning the same fate for you, Larry, but Aisha pled your case. Somehow, your chat with her in the other ward softened her stance towards you. She said you were sorry for your role in this, and that you were simply in the wrong place at the wrong time."

She paused to let him reflect a little bit.

"I still think your silence helped the perpetrator, and you deserve the same fate as these two, but Owuraku sided with Aisha, and here we are. But you will watch your two best friends die, Larry, and there's not a thing you can do to help their screams. A good comeuppance for what you did, wouldn't you say? You heard my cries, but you did nothing."

Larry King just looked at her.

Continuing, Asabea said, "I hope you two have said your final prayers, because the hell you both are going to has no air conditioning. Now, we have prepared some special cocktails. The first, the clear one, is harmless." Then she turned on the lines on both their arms and there was no visible effect on both men other than the fears on their faces.

"The problem occurs when I turn the other lines on," she explained and turned on just a drop of the purple line. Duncan King was the first to scream. He arched his back, and the veins on his neck and head pulsated prominently as his face turned a shade of green. Billy's screams were even louder and more guttural, contorting his muscles into a veritable mass of undiluted pain as he began to thrash around spasmodically on the bed.

After what seemed to the dumbfounded Larry King like a long time, but was no more than ten seconds, the contortions stopped and both men fell back breathlessly unto the beds.

"The thing is," Asabea kept explaining like nothing dramatic had just happened, "while the cocktail plays the role of enhanced neurotoxic and haemotoxic venoms, it does something entirely different to their genitals."

"What?" Duncan King declaimed from his bed.

"It keeps your family jewel engorged; a side effect of the blood pressure brought on by the cocktail," she explained nonchalantly. "When you die, though, the sudden drop in pressure has an inverse effect. Your genitalia will explode."

It was hard to describe the look on the faces of the three men in the ward, a cross between disgust, rage and fear.

"So, you went through all this self-righteous set of events just to end up as a murderer?" Larry King accused her sadly when he found his voice. "Stop this right now, Asabea. This is not you."

"You misunderstand me, Larry; not that you know me, but you misunderstand," Asabea told him with a small shake of her head. "*I* am not the one going to kill your friends. The women of this country are the ones who are going to decide their fate."

Larry King looked at her uncomprehendingly.

"The story I was telling you about the movie," she explained. "We are livestreaming Duncan King's execution. Only women are allowed to vote, and if they vote 'Yes', every hundred votes allow drops of the deadly cocktail into their veins. All that is needed to literally cook Duncan King alive is a million votes. Let's see how that goes on the internet."

As if on cue, eighteen women, only seven of whom had no surgical masks on, walked into the ward to stand around Duncan King and Billy Blanks, singing a song of shame for them.

Having recovered from all his earlier shocks, Duncan could clearly see what was going on. He was already fully aware that every person working in the Fortress was a woman. He had long calculated what his odds would have been to bed some of them had the circumstances been different, and the odds in his twisted mind had been steeply in his favour.

But now they all just stood there, staring at him. It was the most uncomfortable thing he'd ever experienced: eighteen pairs of hot women eyes staring at him and his guilty-of-rape penis in judgment.

Summoning what strength he could, Duncan King pulled his arms together to try to break through the restraints, but the effort ended in tears glistening in his eyes and nothing more.

The girls looked at him with pity when their song ended, and then they filed as sombrely out as they had come, as if they had just finished conducting his funeral.

The first projectiles struck at 10.30 a.m. Owuraku and Asabea were on the balcony reviewing their next set of actions after overseeing the livestreaming of Duncan King's execution when a Sikorsky Hawk, an upper variant of the US Air Force's famous Black Hawk helicopter, banked into view from the valley below. Two missiles flew towards the balcony, and they barely had time to hit the floor before the missiles flew past them and on through the open balcony doors before reducing the entire opposite wall of the third floor to rubble.

The ear-shattering explosion did indescribable things to their brain, but Owuraku mechanically pulled Asabea off the floor and staggered as quickly as he could with her towards the stairs leading to the lower floors. By the time they made it to the Press Box on the first floor, six more had struck, and the third floor was no more.

Barging groggily into the box, Owuraku asked, shouting to be heard above all the noise, "What is the status of the hostages?"

"They are secured in the basements now," Efe reported. "Oye gave them the keys to all the gratings and has instructed them to keep moving until they arrive inside the outermost cave, where they are to wait until they are rescued."

"Very good," Owuraku said. "Is everyone else in place?"

"I don't know," Efe said with eyes quite wide. "Bubuné is in charge of battles."

"Where is she?"

"She went up to activate the missile launchers," Aisha pipped in.

INVIOLABLE 188

"They are on the roof of the third floor."

"But why?"

"I think the automatic sensors got damaged in the strike. She's gone to activate the manual override so we could man it from here."

"The third floor is no more," Owuraku said worriedly. "You stay here and get the drones in the air now. I'll try and track her down." Then he pulled on a bullet proof vest and helmet and fled the Box, running back up the stairs.

"Where is Regina?" Asabea asked when the ringing in her ears subsided enough for her to hear herself speak.

"I am here," Regina spoke from one of the consoles. "They have drone jammers in place so it's difficult to get them out of their hangars."

"Launch the ones near the river!" Asabea ordered.

"We were saving those for later; for emergencies," Dede reminded her.

"This is an emergency," Asabea told her. "If we don't do that, we won't be able to break through with anything."

"Right away," Regina concurred and launched ten drones from the abyss. The drones flew rapidly above the Fortress, and beamed footages into the Press Box as well as to twenty million households.

On the internet, and already seeing the attack happening in real time, many of Ghana's young women logged on quickly to hangduncanking.org to cast their votes and carry out the death sentence of a prolific rapist.

Inside the Fortress, two of the Reapers broke off swiftly towards the Hawk and let fly a couple of RPGs before the pilot could comprehend what was happening.

"Good strike!" Asabea exclaimed when the helicopter was hit. "Now, give me eyes on Owuraku and Bubuné," she ordered.

On the top of the roof, which was still intact after the strikes, Owuraku was helping Bubuné turn on electric power to a portable missile defense launcher on the roof.

"Turn the drones to the left," Asabea ordered but Regina was already doing that. Another Hawk came into view, but this time, it wasn't the drones that did it. Owuraku and Bubuné turned the launcher towards the chopper and let fly a volley of projectiles. The Hawk banked sharply out of the way and disappeared over the pass towards Aburi.

Shortly after, Owuraku and Bubuné turned up at the Box to cries of relief from everyone.

"What's your SitRep?" Owuraku asked Asabea when she was relieved of her command by Bubuné.

"Right now, the hostages are on their way towards the caves, led by the deputy Attorney-General. They will be safe."

"Good, good," he said. "Do we all have to stay here in the Box?" he asked her.

Asabea turned to Bubuné with a silent query.

"I only need six people in here to man the drones and the launcher," she said. "Where do you need everyone else to be?"

"We need to guard the hallways and stairs in case they drop paratroopers," Owuraku advised. "The launcher and drones will not last as long as we might want."

"I can fly the main drones out now so they don't get jammed in their hangars anymore," Bubuné agreed. "But keep to the main columns and stay away from doors and windows. Don't forget to wear your masks on your way out. And carry the HKs!"

Owuraku, Asabea, Oye, Nhyira and Dede were barely out in the first hallway of the first floor when another missile struck the Fortress and sent them careening to the floor.

"They have struck the launcher," Bubuné announced to them over the radio. "We are deploying drone counter measures now."

"What does she mean by that?" Owuraku demanded from where he took shelter on the floor behind a pillar.

"She is sending ten drones out to fish out the Hawks."

"Have her scan a wider area," Owuraku advised. "These ones came at us from the valley. Don't we have sensors there?"

"It was too steep to install sensors, and we weren't really expecting to be attacked from below," Asabea explained.

"There are ten choppers coming at us, and at least fourteen drones," Bubuné announced rapidly over the radio. "You guys should just forget the upper floors and join us down here. "We are about to be destroyed."

Asabea and Owuraku exchanged startled glances.

"Our drones can't shoot theirs down?" Asabea asked over her mouthpiece.

"We can't take on both drones and choppers," Bubuné told them. "And we have already deployed the standby drones, so we are all exposed now. Please get down here and don't be heroes just yet."

Wordlessly, Owuraku and the girls retreated as fast as they could to the Box and watched the aerial battles play out on the screens.

"We need to cut their access to the internet," Obuobi spoke horror-struck when the number of votes supporting death to Duncan King exceeded a hundred thousand on the execution website within minutes of going live. Thankfully, the execution was no longer being televised. The broadcast systems must have been taken out when the Air Force first struck. On the screens, there were already a million visitors and counting, and the two suffering men were thrashing around grotesquely in their beds. Duncan King was already frothing at the mouth, and all Larry King could do was to struggle uselessly against his restraints.

"I think we lost the power to do so earlier," the IGP reminded him as he also watched, sick to his stomach.

"We can't just let two men get murdered live on the internet," Obuobi complained. "Do something!"

"Maybe if we put out a warning that we will find and prosecute anyone who voted on the site, it might discourage people from doing so," Major Hanson suggested without much confidence.

"Women, not just anyone," the IGP offered unhelpfully. Everyone kept saying unhelpful things because there was nothing they could do if the government and the NCA itself could not shut down the site.

Then the phone rang.

It was Colonel Nartey.

"We have the hostages now," he announced. His voice had a strange note of satisfaction.

"Perfect," the IGP replied. "Let me bring in the Chief Superintendents," he said and initiated the conference call.

"We are in position," Amadu announced as soon as the connection was made.

"Colonel Nartey has the hostages," the IGP informed him.

"Fantastic!" Amadu crowed. "How did the Rangers manage that?"

"The hostages turned up through a basement and an adjourning tunnel. We have not sighted the Rangers," Col. Nartey told him.

"Then how did the hostages escape?"

"They said the Girls gave them the keys."

"Just like that?" the IGP asked suspiciously.

"Yes. The deputy Attorney-General said so."

"Well, then get them all out of there before the fireworks starts," the IGP ordered. "I assume they are all in good health?"

"They all are," Col. Nartey confirmed. "Only the State Prosecutor and the President's lawyer seem to have some difficulty walking, but the Rangers created a trail that is wide enough to have some of my men carry them."

"Great," Amadu said at the end of the other line. "Atukwei and I have found the trail from the Adawso side. We will hurry along so we can help your men with carrying the injured.

"Have the Air Force started engaging the Girls?" Atukwei asked.

"The girls took out one of the Hawks," the Colonel reported, "But we can still hear fighting going on above us. We need to leave now," he said and abruptly cut the call.

CHAPTER 25
Jubilee House
Friday, 22nd March; 11 A.M.

FOR MORE THAN twenty years, both the Government of Ghana and the Government of the United States had benefited from downplaying the size and scope of the U.S. Military footprint in Ghana and in Africa. AFRICOM, the US Military's Africa Command posture on the continent consisted of no fewer than twenty outposts. The government of President Offei chose to shroud the fact in mystery and outright denial to avoid accusations of neo-colonial abetment with a world power and prevent angry pan-African and anticolonial protests. The U.S Military, on the other hand, liked to describe its base in Ghana as miniature and non-enduring, with minimal permanent troops and drones dedicated only to performing critical missions necessary to quickly respond to emergencies.

A whopping quarter of a million US dollars was underwritten to support the so-called miniature base. Ghana was chosen particularly because Ghanaian society was burdened by few, if any, of the political sensitivities that the United States military confronts at its other locations in West Africa and in the Sahel region. So far, the bulk of the base's operations had been dedicated to counterterrorism and antipiracy in the Sahel and the South Atlantic Ocean respectively.

This was the first – and President Offei hoped with all his heart – the only time US Base equipment and personnel had been used against targets on Ghanaian soil. And the news that one Hawk and four Reapers had been downed by the girls was giving him palpitations of the pissed-off kind. The last thing he needed was for some nosy journalist to discover this and blow up his government's cover.

Which was why he had wanted the operation to bring the Girls to justice done at night. But the defense attachés at the U.S Embassy waxed on and on about striking while the iron was hot. And now they were the ones bearing the heat.

"The third floor is clear now of missile defense," one pilot's sitrep came in live. "Tango Zulu Niner is go to clear the second floor."

"How did they get their hands on an air defense system?" President Offei demanded of his Chief of Defense Staff. "There is such a massive security overhaul I'll be conducting after this is over, y'all just watch," he warned gravely.

Vice President Domwine looked at his boss and asked, "Have we given any thought to the hostages? If those pilots and drones are clearing floors, shouldn't we give some thought to being careful we don't kill innocent abductees?"

This was not the first time the Veep had raised the subject of the hostages, and every time he did, President Offei and his Army Chiefs seemed inclined to ignore the subject.

"Second floor cleared now," the sitrep announced.

Without waiting another second, Vice President Domwine grabbed the microphone and demanded, "Do you have eyes on the hostages?"

President Offei grabbed the device right back, turned it off and demanded angrily, "What do you think you're doing?"

"What hostages?" the Strike Force Commander, an American, demanded over the satellite communications system. "No one said anything about hostages."

Glaring balefully at his deputy, President Offei responded, "Targets might present some of their own kind as hostages. Please treat everyone in the Fortress as hostile."

"Are you sure?" the Commander demanded. "We need to abort if there are civilians involved. Can your CDS say under penalty of a court martial that there are no civies involved?"

"Yes, he can," President Offei spoke firmly. "My government and I bear full responsibility for any fallout from this operation."

The Strike Force Commander's silence after that put the Cabinet on edge for a minute. Eventually, he said, "Sir, there will be serious consequences if there are civies involved. Please acknowledge."

"Acknowledged," President Offei said.

"Copy that. Eagles are cleared to take out the first floor."

The look President Offei directed at Vice President Domwine could have melted stone, except the Veep was no child to be intimidated by a scowl.

"Are we seriously treating your own lawyer, the deputy Attorney-General, a State Prosecutor, a High Court judge and several other abductees as collateral damage?" he demanded in disgust.

"We discussed this!" President Offei berated him. "It was to either go all out or nothing. I have lost soldiers and much, much more to these Girls, and I'm not letting anything stand in my way. This is exactly what we discussed," he shouted.

"We never agreed to killing innocent abductees in the process, Mr. President. None of us agreed to any such foolishness," the Veep retorted in the same tone of voice as the President. Then he looked around at the members of the Cabinet and his bottom jaw dropped.

"You all are in on this?" he demanded in surprise.

"It's the only way to end the madness," the CDS said apologetically. "If there was any other way, we'd have done it."

"And the window of opportunity to ask for the help of AFRICOM was a narrow one. It was either this way, or we lose more soldiers and men," the Chief of Army Staff added.

President Offei turned to his deputy and said, "If you do not have a stomach for this, I suggest you leave," he said meanly.

Vice President Domwine spared only one surprised glance at the President before he said to him, "This situation calls for pragmatism, not desperate skullduggery. You have just lied to a powerful ally. All the Girls need to do is to leak videos of innocent hostages cowering in some dark room as you and the US Air Force fire missiles at them. We can't even shut down the live stream of the murder of a convicted rapist; how do we think letting the US Air Force shoot at the Girls and their abductees will not make it to public light? How can you all be so remarkably dense? I don't think I want to be part of this."

He then packed up his stuff, which consisted of a single digital notebook and an electronic pen and walked out of the War Room.

"Anyone else wants to follow him?" the President demanded, looking with calculated fury at each of his Cabinet in turns.

No one else left.

Then he turned in his chair to follow the secured feed of the bombing of the Fortress by the US Air Force on Ghanaian soil.

"How many drones have we lost?" Asabea asked Bubuné in consternation as missile after missile was dropped on the Fortress by more Hawks and Reapers than they believed the US government could have afforded to give Ghana.

"All of them," Regina answered wistfully. "We took out twelve of theirs though," she added, as if that was any consolation.

"Probably why they're trying to raze the Fortress to the ground," Owuraku shouted to be heard above the explosions rocking their ground floor shelter, a cavernous dome built of reinforced concrete that extended deep into the rock of the mountain itself. It had been untenable to maintain their position in the Press Box after their drones had been shot down by the more powerful drones operated by the assisting Air Force. It was a miracle none of all nineteen of them had been injured in the mad dash down the stairs when a powerful air-to-surface missile cratered that floor. Now, the debris from the upper floors had settled to form a mask of concrete all around the ground floor, rendering that floor insuperable to any more missiles.

"How long until they drop paratroopers?" Nhyira shouted from her vantage point behind a column. After they'd escaped the attack on the first floor, Bubuné had ordered them into some kind of arrow formation around the columns on the ground floor. Owuraku was the tip of the arrow, and the corona was stacked closely by Asabea, Aisha and Bubuné herself. Dede and the twins were lined up behind them as the shaft, and Efe and the rest of the medical, technological and catering staff huddled as far into the cavern as they could.

"I think they will ensure this floor is cleared first before they attempt to land troops," Owuraku replied. Then, looking far behind him, he saw the corridor that led to Duncan King's execution cell.

"Can anyone get at us from behind?" he asked carefully.

"No one can," Bubuné answered shortly. "Only the abductees."

"I hope you're right," he answered nervously. Then he steeled himself behind his column as missile after missile was rained down, blowing out all that was left of windows and doors, but otherwise having no effect. They were safe from the air strikes, and the Strike Force seemed to feel the same way, because the detonations stopped.

"Now what?" Oye demanded of no one in particular.

"We wait to fight," was Bubuné's calm response. She aimed her weapon when a thick slab of concrete hunkered to a side of the beams above them, exposing an opening that must have been shorn off the top concrete of the first-floor decking in the earlier attacks. The opening narrowly revealed the courtyard, and as far as she and Owuraku could tell, it was the only place troops could get at them from.

They looked at each other and repositioned themselves among the concrete debris littering their dome.

They had all the advantages at this point.

Unless the Air Force could land tanks from the air.

Then they heard the rotors of a couple of Hawks close by.

Owuraku exchanged a startled look with Bubuné.

"They're dropping troops on top of us," Bubuné shouted above the deafening noise.

"What can we do?" Asabea asked her, looking up at the ceiling as if she thought she could see through reinforced concrete.

Owuraku chewed thoughtfully on a lower lip. They could hear

bootsteps above them.

"I think all we can do is to wait to light them up when they appear at the courtyard," he told Asabea. "There's not much they can do to us from up there."

"Ouch!" Aisha screamed from her position behind the column, with her hand massaging her temple.

"What's wrong?" Asabea asked in consternation.

"My head aches."

"The beginnings of a serious concussion," Owuraku informed them. "If we survive this, we are going to need an awful lot of brain therapy."

"What can we do?" Nhyira asked, also massaging her temple as well. "It feels like there's a drummer hitting gongs in my head."

"Let's just hope they don't come in throwing grenades," Owuraku shouted the unhelpful suggestion, before he and Bubuné fired off a couple of shots, taking out three men that had jumped onto the courtyard from the broken slabs.

"And so it begins," Asabea told them, also aiming her weapon at the courtyard.

Having lost three paratroopers, there was silence outside except for the whirring rotors of the Hawks.

"Grenade!" Owuraku shouted and made a run for the back of the cavern, with all the girls in pursuit. They made it safely out of range before the detonation, and the subsequent explosion of three more.

Now, they were at a disadvantage. Having lost the vantage point of that opening, there was no telling who or what was going to pour out into the cavern to engage them.

"Let's maintain our positions," Bubuné ordered, even while removed from that opening. "It's not large enough for that many people to crawl through unless they bring in a bulldozer."

Sure enough, three soldiers rolled into the cavern with guns firing indiscriminately. Owuraku, Asabea and Bubuné each squeezed their triggers once, and that ended all the indiscriminate shooting.

"When we have time," Bubuné said to Owuraku, "You will have to explain to me how you came by your familiarity with guns and fighting strategy."

Owuraku shrugged and shot at a few more soldiers that had followed the lead of the first three.

"Video games," he said simply, and popped another entrant.

A flurry of grenades was thrown through the opening, again to no effect other than the deafening explosions and the attendant risk of the concussions.

"What's the plan now?" Aisha asked wearily from behind her column. The explosions were messing her head up, and she wasn't sure she could take them any longer.

"There's no plan, except to hold out as long as we can," Bubuné informed her. "This is our last line of defense, and we never counted on the drones bailing out on us."

"It was good thinking to escape from the Press Box though," Owuraku commended her. "We'd have been trapped."

"I think we already are," Nhyira told them seconds before a robotic car tumbled over the jumbled concrete of the opening and righted itself on the floor, before its sensors begun calibrating in search of human heat signatures. A second robot joined the first, and both began fanning out mechanical arms to hurl grenades down the cavern.

Bubuné wasted little time. She laid on the floor and fired off a shot at the first robot, denotating its payload before the robot could hurl the grenade. Owuraku followed her example and decapitated the second robot. Then six miniature drones buzzed into the cavern through the opening like angry hornets, followed quickly by six men spewing gunfire.

"We need all hands!" Bubuné ordered, pushing the switch on her AR-15 Semi and letting loose volleys at both the drones and the men. Asabea and Dede at the back shifted positions and downed three of the drones while Owuraku and Bubuné exchanged fire with the men. Aisha, Efe and Nhyira aimed and quickly took out the other three drones. It was all over as quickly as it had begun.

"That was close!" Efe said in obvious relief.

"We need to retreat though," Owuraku shouted to Bubuné and Asabea. "If another grenade goes off here, we're toast."

"I agree," Bubuné said. "But if we retreat down the pipes, we are toast all the same. The pipe leads to the valley, and I am not sure the landing there is big enough for our party. Besides, even a blind soldier can follow it and find us if we abandon this position now. We'll be killed like rats in a fire."

"Is that where we sent the hostages?" Owuraku asked.

"Yes," Bubuné told him. "It would get awfully crowded down there."

"Let's retreat at least to the back a bit," Owuraku told her. "It gives us more room to shoot down drones and robots before they can land a grenade or missile."

There was some quiet after they rearranged themselves to the back of the cavern.

"They are taking their time now because they can tell we are trapped," Regina informed them.

"How can you tell?" Owuraku asked from his position.

Regina pointed to a device that covered the palm of her hand. "I can hear what they're saying above us – at least what those close to the courtyard are saying."

"Are you connected to ground sensors?" Owuraku asked her over the loud sounds.

"Yes," Regina replied.

"Can you tell sounds from each other? Over the noise of the choppers?"

"Not really, except for new sounds."

"What do you mean?"

"I can hear the choppers, and boots running or walking. After a while, I can hear only new sounds that weren't there before the choppers and boots, but only at the time when those sounds are made. Afterwards the new soundwaves go under the dominant chopper rotors. For example, I just heard a gate open – and the sound of a few pairs of booted feet."

"Have you always been listening? I mean, before the incursion of the Air Force?"

"We had the drones then, so I didn't need to," Regina said to him. "But once we lost all our eyes, I had to activate our ears – there are feet running towards the opening," she warned Bubuné.

"How many?" Bubuné demanded, crouching low behind her column.

"Does it matter?" Owuraku demanded, also squatting behind his column.

Bubuné shrugged and aimed, but these soldiers were different. They carried bulletproof shields when they tumbled quickly over the opening and seemed infinitely more disciplined. As soon as they had hit the floor, and on the quick orders of one of them, the men interlocked their shields and immediately begun to advance. The bullets from Owuraku's and Bubuné's weapons ricocheted ineffectively off the shields from thirty metres away.

"We can't hit them with these," Oye told Bubuné.

"I can see that," Bubuné shouted back as she crouched behind her column to reload.

"Then why are you reloading?" Nhyira demanded.

"Do I have something else to do?" Bubuné shot back.

"We have grenades," Owuraku suggested quickly.

"Is that wise?" Asabea asked, eyeing the approaching men nervously.

"We risk bringing down the roof and all the other floors' debris on us with these closed-space explosions."

While they seemed unsure what to do, seven drones entered through the opening as well and fired at their positions, forcing Owuraku and Bubuné, who had been planning to keep firing at the approaching soldiers, to duck fully behind their columns. Also, no longer having to keep their shields interlocked because they were no longer being fired at, the advancing soldiers began to fire their weapons as well, complicating things for Owuraku and the Girls.

"Let's do the grenades!" Bubuné decided with barely a glance at Asabea. "It's that or death."

Both flung their grenades in wide arcs at the advancing soldiers and sheltered in place, blocking their ears from the anticipated blast.

It took everything they had to maintain their sanity after the detonation, and Owuraku, the first to recover from the ear-shattering explosion watched from around the column to see what had become of the soldiers. None of them had survived, of course. And the drones had also been destroyed in the blast.

"Enough of that," a deep voice spoke sternly from behind the cavern.

Owuraku and all the Girls turned towards the voice, which sounded so surreal with their ears only now retreating from the shock of the detonations, that they each thought they might have imagined the speaker, but this was no battle madness. Three men in olive green fatigues stood at the narrower entrance to the pipes, watching them all.

"Who are you?" Oye demanded, leveling her weapon.

"We are your rescuers," the voice said matter-of-factly. "Were you expecting someone else?"

"Opare?" Owuraku asked in surprise. "Gosh, I had forgotten all about you!"

"I wish I could say the same about you," Opare said to him blandly. "Tell your Girls to point their guns in any direction other than my face, and let's get out of here."

"You want to extract us through the cave?" Oye demanded disbelievingly. "We might get trapped in there!"

"Have you seen the size of the troops out there?" Opare asked irritably. "It feels like all of the Ghana Armed Forces want pieces off your butts."

"How did you know about the caves? Did you see the abductees?" This from Nhyira.

"Is all this really necessary?" Opare asked them in exasperation.

"How do we know you're not on the side of the Army? What if you're leading us into a trap?" Oye got back at him again.

Opare looked once at his Rangers and back at Owuraku and the Girls. And then, quite practically, he and his men turned around and headed to the caves where they had just come in from.

The Girls exchanged startled glances among themselves and with Owuraku, who just shrugged, took one look behind him to see if any more drones or soldiers were coming in through the opening, and then made a quick dash after Opare and his men.

Asabea followed next, and eventually, even the trying twins were following. When they passed by Duncan King's ward, Asabea asked, "What's the status of the execution?"

Regina consulted her pad and said, "Just a hundred thousand votes to go and he is dead."

They walked on, following the silent Rangers until they arrived ten minutes later at the open grating.

"Where are the hostages?" Asabea asked Opare in surprise. Where the hostages should have been were only two more Rangers.

"There was a squad of soldiers that survived the fall from your bridge," Opare explained while calmly tying a knot with a sling. "I had them move the hostages. They must be with the CTU now."

"Wait, what?" Bubuné demanded.

But Opare had moved on off the subject. He turned to Wannah, his deputy and said, "See them to the other rock. I'll join you all shortly." Then, turning to Owuraku, he asked, "May I have a couple of your grenades?"

"What the hell for?" Nhyira asked suspiciously, but Owuraku had already handed three of the miniature avocados over to Opare.

"Won't you need a gun?" Owuraku asked helpfully.

"I don't plan to kill anyone," Opare said shortly and disappeared back into the pipe they had just come out from.

"Let's get moving," Wannah, the tall dreadlocked Ranger ordered shortly and then stepped over the open mouth of the grating by holding on to the butterfly knot Opare had attached to the overhanging bar of the grating's frame. Then he swung down and stepped lightly over the intervening space to the small landing.

"It's your turn," one other Ranger said to Asabea. "Just do as he did."

Gingerly, Asabea followed suit until she was pleasantly surprised that the landing widened appreciably before it started to descend to the ravine below. She sat down to catch her breath on dreadlock's instruction when the sound of an explosion thundered deep in the caves.

"What's happening?" Bubuné asked nervously.

"That's Opare," the third Ranger responded as if that was explanation enough, peering into the pipe that led into the caves when he spoke.

"I hope he doesn't get too excited," Oye said sourly. "There's no need to blow the top off this mountain."

Kada – the second Ranger – looked inquiringly at her with a half-amused expression but said nothing.

It took a quarter of an hour to get everyone but Dede to trust the rope for the short traverse to the landing. Kada went ahead of her to show her how safe it all was, but Dede just froze.

"What's kept you?" Opare asked Kada when he returned to the mouth of the outlet. The look of fright in Dede's eyes – she virtually jumped out of her own skin at the startling sound of his voice – told him all he needed to know.

"Unfortunately, there's no time," he told her and untied the sling to her surprise. Then he looped the rope with the butterfly knots around one of the bars of the open grating, tied another end of the rope into a waist harness he was wearing, and then grabbed Dede by the waist.

"Hold on tight," he said, before jumping off the opening with Dede screaming her lungs out. They swung out in a wide arc and landed right next to Asabea on the wider landing.

As soon as Dede could stand unaided from being rubber kneed from her fright, Opare left her and went to help his Rangers release the ropes.

"We don't need ropes to descend the rest of the way," he informed Owuraku and Asabea when he returned. "And we need to move fast."

"Because of the soldiers above?" Asabea asked calmly.

"They can't see much of us from up there," Opare said while finding his footing for the descent from off the edge of the landing. "And I bought us some time by blocking off the passage. Now, let's go."

Because his tone tolerated no objections, they made good progress to the bottom of this first terrace and saw another flight of holes running diagonally opposite the terrace they'd just come down from. But Opare led them the other way to another narrower ledge and started to tie a series of knots to a set of devices he seemed to have had anchored into the face of the rock by drill bolts of sorts.

"What are we doing?" Dede asked nervously. She'd had trouble coming down those foot or handholds, she couldn't tell which they were, and had shivered the entire way, only doing it because Owuraku had been right underneath her, encouraging her down the ledge. But folks were crazy if they thought she was going to jump off a ledge, rope or no rope.

Rather than answer her question, Opare finished his set up and handed helmets, harnesses and gloves over to them from the large backpack he wore.

"Put these on," he instructed shortly.

"Put what on?" Dede demanded fearfully. "I'm not doing whatever you think you're going to try to make me do," she finished flatly.

Opare jerked one of the ropes forcefully to test its resistance and threw the other end down. The rope disappeared over the ledge.

"How far does it go?" Asabea asked while rubbing Dede's back gently.

"About thirty metres," Opare shrugged.

"Doesn't sound that far," Asabea tried to reassure Dede.

"How long is that in feet?" Dede asked him suspiciously.

"A hundred feet."

Dede turned instantly pale and jumped back farther away from the ledge. "I'm not doing it!" she cried.

Owuraku exchanged a perplexed look with Asabea, and then turned to Opare and asked, "Is there another way?"

"There isn't," Opare told him. "This ledge has overhanging cover; it will shield our abseils from those overhead drones."

"I don't think she can do it," Bubuné said. "Can't we take our chances and go down the other terrace – the one with those footholds we just left behind?"

"The drones aren't the only thing we are worried about," Wannah informed her.

"Before we attempted to climb the cliff off your plateau, we cut a trail from Adawso to the terrace we just avoided so we could help the CTU of the Police Service extract the hostages," Opare picked up from where Wannah left off. "Those men and the commander of the battalion you threw off your bridge are shepherding them to Adawso as we speak. If we left by way of the same trail, we risk running into them."

Asabea looked carefully at Opare and said, "Do you want to run that by me again?"

Opare looked calmly back at her and asked, "Which part do you need the rerun for?"

"The part about helping the Police, of course," Nhyira cut in self-righteously at that point.

"I'm happy to explain the finer details, but I doubt a war zone is the place for it. We need to leave now," Opare said firmly.

"If the Police are nearby, how would abseiling off this cliff help us?" Bubuné asked. "Wouldn't they just shoot our butts off in midair?"

"They can't shoot at us from this side," Wannah told her. "But that depends largely on how fast we get off this terrace. Besides, there is a steep rock separating this side of the ravine from the next. We are avoiding a lot of unpleasantness." And then he strapped himself in and jumped off the ledge until he disappeared down the ravine.

"I am not doing that," Dede repeated tearfully with a snuffle.

"Why not?" Kada asked while he too strapped into his karabiners for the drop.

"I am afraid of heights," Dede whimpered.

"What did heights ever do to you?" Kada asked before he disappeared over the ledge.

"Couldn't they at least have waited to talk us through this?" Owuraku asked in perplexity.

"That's up to Aaron and me," Opare said. Then he and the other Ranger walked right to the edge of the precipice and connected another rope to the series of slings they had had anchored to the rock, and then both pulled out another set of ropes out of their backpacks.

"You need to put on your harnesses now," Opare instructed.

"We don't know how," Aisha said, looking with confusion at the device she held in one gloved hand.

"You just wear it – like a boxer shorts."

She looked at Opare uncomprehendingly.

"Or a G-string," Aaron said, half-impatiently and then he walked over to show her.

"The rest of you do the same, and let's get off this rock," Opare ordered.

"What are we going to do about Dede?" Asabea asked him worriedly.

"You leave her to me," Opare told her.

"You're not pulling that spiderman crap on me again," Dede warned him seriously.

"Who's first?" Opare asked like he hadn't heard Dede.

"What about our weapons?" Oye asked.

"You can abseil with them. And with your backpacks too. Just strap them out of the way of the ropes."

Bubuné and Asabea went first, after Opare and Aaron had given them a crash course in feeding their ropes on abseil. All they really had to do was lean back and trust gravity to do the rest.

The most difficult part was the ledge, because it cut away into nothingness, and both girls found themselves screaming at the abruptness of their fall. But once they got over the ledge, it wasn't so bad, and Asabea found that she was beginning to enjoy it, laughing out loud like a schoolgirl before Wannah abruptly cut short the thrill by shushing them.

"I hope you don't plan to announce what we are doing to every soldier a hundred kilometres in each direction," he berated her sourly.

It took about a half hour to get everyone else down, and by the time it was over, Wannah looked like a thunderclap from all the noise they made.

"It's as if you don't remember that you're in a war zone, with people looking to kill you all dead," he grumbled.

Opare and Dede were the last to abseil. Only Aaron knew what persuasive skills Opare had had to employ to get Dede to finally agree to be harnessed. The frightened woman had clutched Opare so tight she had almost suffocated him midway. And now at the bottom, she wouldn't let go, not trusting him when he said it was all over now.

She quieted down and opened her eyes when she heard the familiar voices of Asabea and the other girls and broke into fresh howls of weeping until Wannah shut her up rather unceremoniously.

"We need to leave now," Opare said wearily, as soon as he and his Rangers had stowed all their gear back into their backpacks. Then he pulled out a machete from the back of his backpack and started down a rocky opening in the thick underbrush.

CHAPTER 26
The Fortress
Friday, 22nd March; 2 P.M.

COLONEL BRUCE NARTEY sat on the edges of a gutter along the Aburi road to Adawso and tried to rest his back from the tedious hike with the abductees. Things would have taken a turn for the worse if the CTU personnel – numbering fifty police officers – had not turned up when they did along the difficult trail. His men had not been in the best of shape to be shepherding abductees after surviving their own ordeal, especially when they had taken turns to carry the still-injured Kwasi Apaloo, the State Prosecutor.

The trail had been brutal, and it had been shrouded in what had turned out to be an impossibly dense forest. To have cut a trail through this stretch of land, he and the Chief Superintendents agreed, must have been a masterpiece of Opare's experience. As they had ventured beyond the moss-covered rocks of the river where the Rangers had left them, they had found themselves surrounded by towering trees, their colossal trunks reaching as far as the sky itself. The air had been thick with the heady scent of moss and damp earth, and the former abductees, wearing all kinds of office and court shoes, had kept tripping and falling over roots and stumps, and sometimes over their own shoelaces.

The most serious challenges had arisen with the rivers – fast-moving torrents that had cut through the undergrowth with a relentless fury coming down from the Aburi mountains. He and his soldiers had had to fish not a few of the former abductees out of the river. Rocks covered in slick moss had presented the most unstable bridges, and the water's cold grip had tested even the resolve of the CTU Officers who had not gone through any of the ordeal he and his soldiers had. Each crossing had been a heart-pounding test of balance and nerve and sitting here on the hard asphalt of a rural road, he still couldn't believe they had survived the walk. Those Rangers had made it seem easy when they had described the trail, before they had left them to rescue some three other people they said the Girls had failed to release.

After he had rested for a while, he got off the road and went in search of Amadu and Atukwei. He found them in the front seats of their Police trucks, looking even worse than he and his men did.

"What's next?" he asked them.

Amadu respectfully got off the seat at the driver's side to meet the Colonel and said, "The IGP has dispatched a Police bus that should be here any minute to convey the hostages and your men to Accra."

Nartey looked around at the former abductees. They sat around doing their best to look like martyrs, not so much from their captivity because snippets of conversations he had heard on their way to this road had let him know they had been treated like royals, but from what one of them had described as a killer-hike.

"Why didn't the Master-Guide come with us?" he asked the two senior Police officers.

"You mean Kwaku Opare Addo?" Atukwei asked tiredly.

Nartey nodded.

"He said they needed to get Duncan King and his friends from in there as well," Atukwei said while stifling a yawn. "Frankly, I don't much care for those three."

"Spoken like a true Police Officer," Amadu teased.

"I heard him say that also," Nartey said thoughtfully, referring to Opare's excuse to get back into the Fortress. "But I thought their responsibility would have been more towards these people – at least two Rangers could have accompanied us on that hike. Didn't it seem weird to you that all five were more interested in the welfare of a convicted rapist than they were in the wellbeing of these people?"

Amadu and Atukwei looked at him.

"What are you suggesting, Colonel?" Amadu asked eventually.

"I am not impugning anything untoward to those boys, you understand?" he said carefully. "My men and I would probably be dead if they hadn't found us when they did, but it occurs to me, with all the bombing the Air Force was doing when we were leaving, that only those men could possibly extricate the Girls from the shelling up there."

"You think that Opare only used rescuing Duncan King as an excuse to attempt to pull the Girls out?" Amadu asked whimsically.

"It's a possibility, isn't it?" Nartey asked him. "Many people do sympathize with the Girls, don't they?"

"Not Opare," Atukwei insisted. "Have you met the guy? He doesn't give two craps about this country. Unless he was forced into it by the Girls and their weapons, and if so, we can wait to nab them as soon as they break out of there."

"If my theory is right, I don't believe Opare would bring them out here. If anything, he would cut a new trail."

"A new trail in this jungle? Tonight?" Atukwei scoffed. "Did you see the size of the forest?"

"Perhaps not," Nartey agreed ruefully. Even he shuddered at the thought.

"But let's still say I am right, and that those men are going in to really get the Girls out," he continued. "What would you recommend we do about it?"

The two Police officers thought about it.

"There is no way I am going back into that dark forest," Amadu flatly announced. "There has to be another way."

"We don't have to be the ones to do it," Nartey suggested. "We can send in fresh bodies, perhaps a mixture of infantry and counterterror."

"Smart," Atukwei conceded and reached for his phone.

"Let's not tell the IGP or my Command yet," Nartey advised carefully.

Amadu stared at him.

"What's your game, Colonel?" Atukwei asked suspiciously.

"What do you mean?" Nartey asked mildly.

"It seems to mean a lot to you not to report to your higher-ups," Amadu accused him. "It's like you have a bone to pick with your superiors, and while I can understand that, given your circumstances, we do not have that same problem with our bosses. Either you tell us what you're up to with all the subterfuge or you'll have to speak with the IGP yourself," Amadu finished coolly.

Nartey looked a bit crestfallen at the accusation, but he seemed to brush it off when he said, "You were the only ones to warn me that things were not as they seemed about the Girls. If I had heeded your advice, neither I nor my men would have been standing on that drawbridge when it blew up. While the Girls were obviously well-prepared, even for an Army, things would have been manageable if we had taken the notion that this was better a police hostage situation than a military operation. If we show that the situation was saved because of a regard for a better, more thoughtful way of doing things, perhaps we might just have begun a process to save the Ghana Armed Forces from its brawn over brains doctrine. If not, they will credit the old ways with their success and that will sicken me more than I can ever let it be known."

"But all this is President Offei's doing," Amadu informed him.

"It is the duty of our Generals and Service Chiefs to talk any president out of doing stupid things," Nartey said forcefully.

"Our IGP did that, and we were all thrown out of the War Room," Atukwei said. "I don't think your Generals would have had better luck crossing President Offei on this. It's all politics for him; nothing more."

"We are on our own then," Nartey concurred. "And I suspect this is why you and the IGP sent Opare and his men instead of your own officers or any of Major Hanson's men."

Amadu shrugged. "Everyone said Opare was the best. After the President sacked us from the War Room, we couldn't get involved anymore without risking our jobs, so we had to find neutral assistance."

"We are absolutely on the same page then," Nartey conceded. "How do we proceed?"

"Let's call Opare and ask him," Atukwei said.

"Ask him if he plans to rescue the Girls?" Nartey asked in surprise. "I'd be surprised if he admitted as much. He would know it would be treasonous to aid and abet."

"I see this differently, too," Amadu admitted. "The Girls could force Opare to get them out of there instead, like Atukwei said. There's no way he will work for the Girls voluntarily. He's too legally savvy to want to get entangled in that sort of thing."

"His line is off either way," Atukwei announced, pocketing his mobile phone.

"And I lost range with his radio almost as soon as we crossed that winding river the first time," Nartey added. "Still doesn't mean I'm wrong he went for the Girls."

"The only way to find out for sure is to get men into the forest," Atukwei admitted thoughtfully.

"You really want to get back inside there?" Amadu asked Atukwei with a shudder.

"If it helps us get the Girls and save Opare, why not?" Atukwei said it with a grin.

Atukwei looked at Nartey. He too had an impish grin.

"You both are nuts," Amadu declared, just before the bus the IGP had sent came rolling in.

It took no more than ten minutes or so to get all the hostages onto the bus. A catering company had been contracted to provide hot meals, and medics also appeared with an ambulance and an emergency truck full of warm blankets and changes of clothing.

Major Hanson and his deputy jumped out of the emergency truck as soon as it stopped, grinning widely at the two Chief Superintendents until they saw Colonel Nartey. They saluted smartly at attention until he freed them. The awe on their faces was telling, but Nartey warned them not to breathe a word that he and some of the men had survived. They understood, of course, and stood aside as another bus carrying his platoon parked by the truck and disgorged his troops. The troops marched smartly and formed several ranks and files along the road in front of the Colonel until everyone faced the right direction. They were soon joined by the fifty counterterror officers on the opposite side of the road, also in perfect order.

It was time for the issuance of their orders, but Nartey and the two Chief Superintendents saw to the departure of the hostages first, ordering the drivers to move in convoy to the Police Headquarters, where the IGP and the Police Command would see to their wellbeing and keep them out of the eye of the public until later.

It was when the convoy of buses, vans, and trucks had left, leaving only two buses to convey the counterterror and infantry units that were left did Nartey turn his attention to the troops.

"We are all aware that the Air Force and its partners are currently bombing the Fortress and trying to reduce the mountain upon which it sits," he began. "But we all know that no military action is complete without the involvement of the Army – and our friends in the Police."

"Ahoya!" was the thunderous affirmation.

"We suspect that the air strikes have failed, and that the Girls that have ended the lives of almost five hundred of our brothers in arms may have escaped into the jungle. Our job is to find them, wherever they may be hiding, and bring them to face our justice," he let that sink in.

"We want them alive," he cautioned. "And I need everyone alert because these are the smartest Girls this country has ever seen. We underestimate them at our own risk. I have done that once already; I will not do that again. So, keep your eyes open, and your mouths shut, and bring in all your years of jungle warfare training to bear on this night. Am I clear?"

"Ahoya!"

"Good. You have fifteen minutes to load up and deploy!"

"Ahoya!"

There was no trail at all, but a moss-covered route gouged out by a dried-out tributary of the nearby river during the last rains, and it was as rough as it was steep, and several times during their escape, the Girls believed with all their heart that Opare and his team of Rangers did not know where they were going. But the Master-Guide kept walking, and the Ranger with the dreads brought up the rear and looked disapprovingly at anyone that loitered too far behind the rest of the group. After a long time of shimmying down large rocks and boulders and tumbling off an especially long terrace of riverine rocks, Dede laid flat on her tummy and refused to budge. Cries of exhaustion racked her body, causing the Girls to look none too happy at Opare, and especially at Wannah.

The look the Ranger gave them had not a care in the world traced upon it.

Opare looked up nervously at the sky. Then he tried to encourage Dede to get up and said, "There's an overhang a few metres down this rock that we can rest under."

"I am not going anywhere," Dede refused, sniffling.

"If we don't get away from this exposure, any drone up there will find us, and all that we have done so far will be for nothing," he advised her calmly.

Dede looked up at him through her tears and got off the ground.

"If you promise to hold me, I'll be fine," she told him meekly.

"I promise," Opare told her sombrely and led the way around another boulder to a jagged ledge overlooking a terrace of high mahogany trees. No sunlight filtered through the thick branches and leaves above them when they spent the next half-hour negotiating what turned out to be a difficult descent into the entrance to a cave framed by the intricate roots of the towering mahogany whose branches they had seen from the terraces above.

"This penchant of yours to understate difficulties is beginning to rub off the wrong way," Nhyira warned Opare at the entrance.

As soon as she stepped into the cave, Asabea's senses were immediately overwhelmed by the pungent smell of bat guano. It wasn't long before she could hear the cacophonous chatter of the bats, and it made her skin crawl. Opare turned on a flashlight, and hundreds of them hung from the cave's ceiling in the light's wake, their tiny, delicate forms suspended upside-down with baleful, yellow eyes that seemed to protest the interruption of their daytime nap. Some hung solitarily while others clustered together, forming dark, shifting masses that reflected their curiosity as they observed their human visitors.

"Is this your idea of a rest stop?" Oye asked Opare distastefully. He was clearing the section of the stony floor with a booted foot and dropped his heavy backpack.

"It's the best I can manage under the circumstances," Opare told her coolly.

"How long do we have to stay here?" Nhyira asked with a shudder.

"We'll leave after we've had a bit of lunch."

"You want to eat in this smell?" Asabea asked him.

"I'd eat anywhere drones cannot shoot at me," he replied and began to rummage through a second backpack handed over to him by Aaron. As he did so, a rumbling sound tore through the air and the cave shook with it. The startled bats flew out, frightening Asabea and her Girls out of their skins. Most of them fell to the ground to avoid the agitated chiropters flying into their faces. Another explosion caused rocks to fall off from the roof of the cave, forcing Opare to abandon his search for lunch, strap on his backpacks and instruct everyone to the cave's mouth.

"What is happening?" Asabea demanded nervously. They now stood at the projection of the cave entrance, where debris were falling from way up above them to the valley below. "Are they throwing concrete slabs at us?"

Opare glanced once up the terraces above and barked, "We need to leave now!"

"And go where?" Asabea asked anxiously. "We might get crushed by all these falling rocks."

"We will get crushed by the cave if we don't leave this landing now," Opare said and grabbed Dede by the hand. Then he started off by sliding down the thick shallow roots of the mahogany with Dede screaming fearfully down behind him.

They all got to the bottom of the valley without injury; the roots that hung down from the caves formed some kind of arboreal slide, and now that they were safe at the bottom, they looked up to discover that was the only way they could have gotten off the cave's ledge, emergency or not.

"This penchant to keep information to yourself is beginning to rub off the wrong way," Oye said sourly to Opare. "You could have told us this was a vegetative slide, and we would have been fine. We jumped off thinking we were going to fall to our deaths."

Opare shrugged and started off on another river-gouged trail.

"Aren't we going to be allowed to catch our breath?" Asabea asked breathlessly.

"The rocks above us are unstable because of all the bombing up there," Opare told her with a glance behind him. "If we don't move where falling debris won't find us, we might be buried before nightfall."

With just one glance at the upheavals above, everyone followed the Master-Guide without hesitation as he led them deeper and deeper into the highly forested valley. Eventually, the rocky paths gave way to earthy game trails that became increasingly mossy and muddy the farther away from the mountains and into the valley they walked, and this continued for more than an hour until the disappearing sunset made it unsafe to keep blundering into the dark forest.

When Opare called the stop next to the river whose sound they had been hearing for well over their entire walk from the cave, there were exaggerated sighs and grunts from the Girls as they flopped onto the grassy bank of the river. Opare and his Rangers shook their heads at all the drama and began to set up tents. By the time they were done, the forest had turned pitch black.

Asabea turned on a flashlight she removed off the scope of her weapon.

"I wouldn't advise that," Opare said to her calmly. Then he turned on a device that activated barely translucent objects all around the tents, bathing their campsite in quite some beautiful hues.

"These are enough to see by," Opare explained, "But your flashlights will reveal our location to any thermal drones three hundred metres above us."

"Thermal drones don't need flashlights to find us," Regina said to him.

Opare pointed to another light filter installed above them with a thick camouflaging net of leaves, dirt and earth that formed a large tent canopy. He and his Rangers had launched the cover above the campsite when they were setting up while Owuraku and the Girls were mopping about on the ground in the exaggerated martyrdom of their exhaustion.

"Smart," Regina said. "So which tent is which? I really need to sleep," she complained wearily.

"We have to eat first," Opare told her, and then he turned to the others. "We have enough tents for us all, but folks need to pair up and share. Drop all your weapons and equipment into your tents and go wash up in the river. Afterwards come to the tent marked with the little yellow ribbon for your suppers."

"Won't we fall into the river in this darkness?" Owuraku asked.

"We have marked the shallow parts," Opare said. "The blue trail is for men and the orange for women."

Owuraku and Asabea repaired to the blue trail to have their baths together since the Rangers seemed to have already had theirs. Translucent lights marked the path until they arrived at the river no more than twenty metres from the camp. Like Opare had said, there was a buoyant red ribbon marking the edge of the shallower part of the river. Both stripped to their underwear and took their baths without talking much. They returned to find that supper was hot and ready, and consisted of chicken light soup and boiled rice and yams. No one needed urging to eat all they could until nothing remained.

Afterwards, Opare had them wash the dishes, and then he ordered a meeting in the command tent for debriefing. The night air suddenly ruptured with the sound of further bombing, and it sent Owuraku and the Girls falling to the ground under the camping tables. They looked wildly around for their weapons.

"It's just the echoes," Opare said kindly when they got off the ground.

"Shouldn't they have bombed themselves out by now?" Bubuné asked, looking chagrined about her reaction to the false alarm in the faint light of the camp.

"They're probably assuming you are hiding out in the basement," Opare said. "I imagine they won't rest until the entire building is razed enough to see your bodies in the subterranean floors."

"They could just walk into the cavern now and find out for themselves," Bubuné complained. "Why hurt the mountain?"

"I blocked off passage to the pipes, remember?" Opare asked her.

"How did you manage that without getting yourself hurt?" Owuraku asked him.

"I threw the grenades into the cellar just before the opening to the pipes," he explained. "It brought that part of the ceiling down."

Asabea exchanged a look with Owuraku and said to Opare, "Duncan King was in that cell. You just might have quickened his death."

Opare's eyebrows shot up when he asked, "What do you mean 'quickened his death'?"

"You haven't been watching the news?"

"We've done nothing over the past days except cut trails and prepare back-up extraction plans while your friends up there kept up their attacks, so no, we haven't been watching any news," Opare told her with a flash of anger in his eyes. "What do you mean by Duncan King's death?"

Owuraku and the Girls exchanged deliberate glances. Eventually, it fell to Asabea to bring the Master-Guide up to speed.

"The Court found Duncan King guilty of rape," she begun. "And we meted out judgment in a cell inside the basement."

Opare blinked.

"When you say 'judgment'?"

"By lethal injection," she simplified.

"Then it presupposes he was dead before I brought that roof down, does it not?" Opare demanded.

"We set up the injection to an internet timer controlled by voting women, so his demise would be slow and painful," Asabea explained without feeling.

"That's satanic, wouldn't you say?" He denounced her with disgust on his face. "It wasn't enough for you to just kill him?"

Asabea looked at the Master-Guide and replied, "It wasn't enough."

Then another series of explosions thundered, and the valley was lit for a minute by the light of a giant fireball.

Owuraku and the Girls looked towards the mountains nervously, but Opare didn't even seem to flinch as he kept his eyes locked on Asabea.

"We are already accomplices to all kinds of felonies and crimes by extracting you, but I never thought we would be accomplices to a sadistic execution. This is gross," he said.

"Yes, we know," Asabea said. "Except, given the same set of circumstances and resources, we'd do it again."

Opare turned to Owuraku enquiringly.

"She's right," Owuraku said coolly. "We'd do it all over again."

The next explosion sent sparks flying, and a while later, some unseen debris hit their canopies but caused no damage to their campsite. Opare and his Rangers donned infrared googles and announced that the debris were nothing more than fist-sized pieces of concrete and wood.

"Don't you think bigger sized materials might hit us when we sleep?" Bubuné inquired.

"We are three kilometres away from the mountain," Opare told her. "Only light debris will reach us."

Once things quieted down a bit on the bombing front, Owuraku, Asabea and Bubuné recounted all that had happened in the Fortress to Opare and his Rangers, beginning from when Opare had left. The other girls were happy to just listen, having been well warmed by the meal they'd just had.

"I think I know how the Police found the location of the Fortress," Opare said carefully when they were done telling the stories.

"How?" Regina and Owuraku asked in unison. Owuraku looked particularly interested.

"Trilateration by satellite," Opare said. "Before I came over to meet your twins at the Gardens, I had gone hiking in the Klowem Hills and had my GPS watch on. When I returned home I found I had mapped the journey. Of course, I knew the way after the first trip, so the mapping itself was irrelevant. Except that it proved useful to our trail-cutting and extraction manifests later. I think that if the CTU had hacked you from beyond the War Room, then my watch helped them zone in their search if it beeped in response to the satellite queries when I was there. But that means you weren't paying attention to your nodes."

"I ran a lot of scans," Regina said defensively, looking once at Owuraku.

"You didn't know what to scan for. Trilateration acts on mimicry," Opare explained.

"And you would know that how?" Regina asked in surprise.

Opare shrugged. "I am a Navigator. I know how satellites work."

"How did you get involved with the Police then?" Nhyira demanded.

"Shortly before my team and I left Field Base to start the trail to the back of your plateau, the Inspector General of Police called," Opare told them. "He had heard we were experts at hostile extraction, and he needed us to extract the hostages from the Fortress. They sent us coordinates and all, which was what got us wondering how they may have acquired it. I stacked the coordinates along the metadata of my GPS watch, and they were a perfect match. The Police request was to do it quietly because they didn't want word getting out that they had sent in rescuers on the blind side of the President and his Cabinet."

"The government didn't care about the abductees," Asabea said.

"It didn't," Opare affirmed. "But the CTU did."

"Did they pay you?" Aisha asked.

"What if they did?" Opare asked back, not unkindly.

"That would be a conflict, wouldn't it?"

"Which is why we are using a route different from the one we created when we handed the hostages over to the Police," Aaron mentioned the obvious.

"If we had come out of the Fortress at the same time as the abductees, we would have walked right into the arms of the Army," Efe accused.

"Aha," Asabea said quickly, as if she had just remembered something important. "What was that you said about the Army when I asked you near the grating?"

"We couldn't come for you from the base of the cliff as we initially wanted because of all the drone activity," Opare answered. "We realised this when we got to Bat Cave, and it was there that the IGP called to say a Colonel Nartey, the Commander of the Battalion you decimated on your drawbridge survived. We then figured there might be some terraces we could assail on that side of your mountain. That's how we found him and a dozen or so of his soldiers. We had already cut a trail to that side but had diverted it because we were aiming for the cliff base then.

"When we found them, they were mostly unarmed and hungry. We'd already been grappling with the dilemma of how to hand over the hostages to the Police without putting you at risk, as well as the dilemma of not letting the Police know the hostages were not the only targets of our extraction. The Colonel was our way out of that predicament. He was the one who found the grating and was wondering what he could do with only a pistol and minimal ammunition. When we informed him we could free the hostages, it gave him purpose to lead them out."

The twins tried to find fault with Opare but couldn't seem to work up any real indignation after his explanation.

"Your plan would have failed if we had refused to set the abductees free, you know?" Aisha complained.

"You were not going to harm the hostages," Opare told her confidently. "Otherwise we would have insisted. And it was good we found you when we did, wasn't it?"

"We would have been fine in a minute or two," Oye said with more haughtiness than the discussion warranted.

Wannah scoffed. "The way we saw it," he told her with a knowing look, "you didn't have a minute or two."

Bubuné, looking thoughtful, asked Opare, "What happens next?"

"The Air Force may have found out by now that you have made it out of the Fortress," Opare said, looking up and cocking his ear to one side at the uptick in chopper and drone activity above them. "They must be hunting for you with their heatseeking technologies, which is why we have anti-thermal equipment installed to fool them. During the day we'll be fine walking in this jungle, but we must always hide at night."

"What about the soldiers and counterterror Police you warned us about?" Bubuné inquired.

"That risk was only for while we were abseiling," Opare reassured her. "There is an impenetrable jungle between their trail and this camp."

"So we shouldn't expect to be murdered in our sleep tonight?" Nhyira asked, looking suspiciously at Opare.

"What really is your problem?" Opare asked her, half-amused.

Nhyira looked long at him before answering, "I honestly don't know; I just don't trust you."

"My Rangers will take turns guarding the camp," Opare told her. "Whether you trust us enough to sleep or not is not our problem," he told her succinctly.

CHAPTER 27
Jubilee House
Friday, 22nd March; 5 P.M.

DUNCAN KING'S FINAL moments were hard to watch, even for those who voted to kill him. Vote by painstaking vote, one million Ghanaian women took the decision to slowly but punitively end the life of a prolific rapist, live and in HD. This was what Asabea had referred to as death by a million cuts and his execution was witnessed by over a hundred million viewers on the internet.

When voting began, the first hundred thousand votes activated the cocktail of medication that sealed Duncan King's and Billy Blank's fates. It started by targeting their central nervous system, interfering with the transmission of nerve signals in their bodies. By blocking the communication between the nerve cells and muscles, a long, drawn-out muscle weakness and paralysis ensued, and Billy Blanks suffered the most because he was of muscular build. He was also the first to die.

By the next three hundred thousand votes, respiratory distress had begun to be observed in both men, and Duncan King's breathing became wheezy. He looked like he could go into complete respiratory failure any minute, but something in the cocktail prevented that from happening until his blood pressure dropped, causing intense circulatory shock. By the time it was over when the one million votes threshold had been crossed, bodily tissue damage had resulted from the severe pain, swelling, and tissue necrosis in every part of his body. His skin finally began to flake, he came apart while his body convulsed, and froth flew from his mouth.

All that was left of him was his erect penis which exploded when he died. The pressure from the neurotoxic execution had no other way to escape than to cause penile tissue blast in the end.

The livestreaming ended when an explosion took out the basement cell. Viewers could not tell if Larry King survived the blast, but if he did not, many believed he deserved it for enabling his cousin's predatory lifestyle.

Unlike on the internet, President Offei's War Room did not fall silent when the execution ended. Footage and sounds of the missile and bomb attacks on the Fortress continued to be beamed by the Strike Force as they worked to reduce the Fortress to ruins. The loss of twenty-five paratroopers had been communicated to the Cabinet, and the saving grace for President Offei was that only Ghanaian troops had participated in the ground assault. The US Air Force pilots had ejected before their Hawks were downed, avoiding all kinds of unpleasantness for both governments. Ghanaian lives on the other hand could be swept under the carpet and the silence of their families could be paid for in Cedis.

President Offei was incensed when, after retiring to his residential suite in the Jubilee House, the CDS came by to inform him that only three bodies had been recovered from the decimation of the Fortress, and that none of the bodies belonged to any of the Girls.

"You mean to tell me that they somehow escaped?" he tore into his Chief of Defence Staff.

"The evidence suggests so, Mr. President," the CDS replied contritely.

"Then all we have done up till now has been unprofitable," he lamented angrily. "What about the hostages?"

"No sign of them also."

"Have the Fortress searched brick by brick until you find them," he ordered. "In fact, take the whole damn mountain apart stone by stone if you must. I want those Girls delivered to me dead or alive, you got that?"

"Yes sir!" The CDS agreed and hastily left the President's office.

In the corridor leading away from the residential suites the Chief of Army Staff was waiting for him.

"He wants the whole mountain removed stone by stone," he responded to his colleague's silent enquiry as they walked briskly down the corridor back to the War Room.

"How does he propose we do that?" the Army Chief asked. "With the Fortress destroyed, AFRICOM isn't going to hang around much longer for rescue and search operations."

"The Strike Force Commander says they will only assist for the next twenty-four hours because they also need to find their two missing pilots," the CDS said. "That gives us a day to hope that they find the Girls and the hostages as well."

"Now he is interested in the hostages?"

"I am as shocked as you are."

"What if they don't find the Girls and the hostages?"

"All hell will break loose."

"Why don't we send a search party into the surrounding jungle," the Army Chief asked.

"When I asked him yesterday, he almost bit my head off. He said something about not losing more men on a wild goose chase."

The Army Chief gave one look around and pulled the CDS into an embrasure along the corridor, and then he said sternly, "It's time to take full control of the operations, Major-General. Having these politicians decide everything isn't looking good for us, and people are beginning to talk about accountability for the loss of Colonel Nartey's battalion."

"What do you want me to do?" the CDS demanded helplessly. "Our Commander-in-Chief insists on directing every move himself and deciding every action. If we cross him, our heads will roll."

"If we all agree on what to do next, whether the President likes it or not will not matter. We have our operational processes. Let's cut out these political bastards and do what our Armed Forces do best."

"Which is?"

"The complete running of this operation in line with C2 principles," the Army Chief said meaningfully. "These slapdash methods are not the modus operandi of our Armed Forces, and you know it. Is it any wonder they have failed at every turn?"

The CDS knew what his Army Chief was talking about. C2 was a military abbreviation of Command and Control, a fundamental concept that referred to the exercise of authority and direction in the planning and execution of military operations. It encompassed a range of performances, routines, procedures, and arrangements that enabled military commanders to make informed decisions, issue orders, and ensure the effective implementation of those orders. The primary goals of C2 doctrine were to achieve unity of effort, enable decision making, exercise leadership, communicate, monitor and assess, adapt to information technology and protect information and communications. Now that he thought about it, he could see how its non-application had brought Ghana's Armed Forces to its knees.

"I fear it might be too late now," he eventually told the Army Chief and began walking again towards the War Room.

"It's never too late, General," the Army Chief said wisely.

The CDS stopped abruptly at that and asked, "At this stage of the operations, how exactly will C2 help us?"

The Army Chief was ready with his answer.

"We have our own men with the Strike Force. About a hundred of them. Let AFRICOM drop them into the jungle near the Fortress and have them comb every inch of that forest until they find the Girls and the hostages."

The CDS looked at him for a minute. "How would I explain that to President Offei."

The Army Chief gave him a withering look. Eventually he said, "I was hoping we wouldn't tell him, but if you absolutely must, you can tell him we are trying to locate the missing pilots."

"You want me to lie to the President?"

"I would never ask you to do that," the Army Chief said wearily, looking directly into the CDS's eyes. "But if you tell him that we are hunting down the Girls you would be compromising C2, and the rules are clear that any General who does that is unfit to lead."

"But he is the President," the CDS complained.

"And Colonel Nartey is dead," the Army Chief said bluntly. "The politicians don't care about the consequences of their foolish politicking, but we are soldiers. Our duty is to our men and women in uniform, not to the fools who command us because they lied to gullible civilians and got voted into democratic power. Democracy ended when President Offei ordered us into the fray. Let's be soldiers, for frock's sake."

"Can I at least inform the Defence Minister?" the CDS asked plaintively.

"It's your call, General," the Army Chief said and resumed walking. "Just understand there will be consequences if C2 is compromised."

"Are you threatening me?" he asked the Army Chief without breaking stride.

"We've lost a thousand troops, General. That's enough threat on its own without the Service Chiefs and I adding to it," the Army Chief deflected effortlessly, just before aides opened the glass doors to the War Room and saluted.

At the parallel War Room of the Police Headquarters, the top brass of the Service, numbering eighteen men and women, all of whom were of the rank of Commissioner of Police except for five that were deputy Commissioners, were gathered to follow the operations of the CTU live on the screens in the room and to advise accordingly, having all already met with the hostages in their coded location and deciding that they were all too excited about the search to retire to their homes.

At the head of the Police Management Board was the IGP, of course, whose removal from the War Room at the Jubilee House had rubbed off everyone on the Police Board the wrong way. And now, having secretly known of the IGP's plan to rescue the hostages, they hadn't wanted to go home while history was being made – the history that it was the Police, and not the Army or the President, that had rescued hostages and abductees in a situation of national proportions.

They followed with keen interest as their CTU and a handful of tag-along soldiers and a Colonel that was apparently believed to be dead but shared in the Police's plan to keep a lid on the operation traversed the dark forest of Adawso in search of a team of Rangers and the Girls. Chief Superintendents Atukwei and Amadu – and Colonel Nartey – reported that the grating at the end of the tunnel that the hostages had earlier been rescued through, while still visible, was beyond reach. The Fortress and the mountain had been so pummeled by the Strike Force that only the grating hung loosely on the side of the mountain. So much debris had collected at the base of the grating's terrace that even the foot and handholds that the Master-Guide had dug for the Colonel and his men – and the hostages – had disappeared.

"Two things then," the Colonel said over the satellite-encrypted mouthpiece to the IGP. The CTU Officers had come to this operation with some cool toys. They had night vision goggles, which enabled them to see better through the dark woods, and these satellite phones that had receivers tagged on their belts and blue toothed mouthpieces.

"The Strike Force already did a sweep of the destroyed Fortress using high-powered thermals," the IGP chipped in before Colonel Nartey could get to his two points. "They have three dead civilians and some twenty or so dead soldiers; no Girls."

Colonel Nartey was quiet for a minute before saying, "Then there is only one thing: the Rangers rescued the Girls and extracted them another way."

As the implication of that struck him, the IGP asked, "You think they had time to cut two sets of trails? Amadu told us the jungle is thicker than the Amazon."

"I don't think they need trails to extract anyone. Those men I met were extremely resourceful."

"Then they could be anywhere in that jungle," the IGP said. "What are you going to do?"

Then the IGP had a call on his mobile phone. After speaking for a short moment, he said to the Colonel, "Your Military High Command has decided to pull a C2 on the operation. How would you like us to proceed?"

"What's a C2?" Atukwei asked in his mouthpiece.

"Do they have Officers to pull that off?" Colonel Nartey asked, seemingly surprised.

"Major Hanson says they plan to drop all the boots they have up at the Fortress into the valley to search for the Girls," the IGP said. "Those paratroopers will have a CO, wouldn't they?"

"It would either be a Major or a Colonel."

"Do you see the advantages here?" the IGP demanded carefully. His tone indicated that he needed Colonel Nartey to grasp his meaning.

The Colonel did with a tight smile and said, "That doesn't work for us at all."

"No, it doesn't," the IGP said and asked Amadu, "Do you really believe that Opare planned to rescue the Girls at the same time we asked him to extract the hostages?"

Amadu seemed thoughtful before he replied, "I don't quite believe he deliberately deceived us. He might have been forced to extract them in exchange for the hostages, or something. I just don't buy the double agent theory."

"Which still makes him an accessory, does it not?" the Director-General for the Criminal Investigative Department, one of the Commissioners of Police asked.

"We may have to think carefully outside the legal box when it comes to Kwaku Opare Addo," Atukwei warned. "Even if the Girls had contracted his help, and he still agreed to help us, then he might have been dealing with an ethical conundrum, especially if he did not know at the time that the Girls were abductors wanted by every law enforcement agency in Ghana. You need to remember that many people supported the Girls enough to kill a rapist for them."

"But how could he not know?" the CID DG asked disbelievingly. "It's been all over the news."

"The man I met doesn't give two craps about the news," Colonel Nartey said thoughtfully. Then he shook his head. "They hadn't even given a damn that we were armed and pointing weapons at them when they found us. They seemed uncaring of all things that did not involve the jungle. But whatever their dilemma, I am glad that they agreed to rescue the hostages. My remaining troops and I would not have made it without them – and the hostages too, since it was clear that the Girls had not given thought to what to do with them if things went south."

"You all need to get out of there, though," the IGP suggested.

"Yes, and No," Colonel Nartey advised calmly. "Under C2 rules, we may work with the boots being thrown down towards a mutual end, and neither of us would have to reveal to the others how we ended up here."

"But what if Opare has taken the Girls out of the jungle already?" Atukwei asked, now that he understood what Command and Control entailed. "It might first be hard to explain to the Air Force what we are doing here, and second, it might be harder to explain who Opare is and

INVIOLABLE 224

why we are looking for him."

"Which is why you need to get out of there now," the IGP insisted, consulting a clock on the wall and one of Obuobi's maps. "Opare runs an adventure and rescue company. He'll eventually have to return to it. We can calmly wait for him at the end of his extraction and then get him to sing, but if we get found out by the Air Force, we will be the ones singing, and I doubt President Offei would like our song."

Even after the call with the IGP had ended, Colonel Nartey didn't seem to think so well of the idea of quitting, so Amadu had to get him to see the point.

"In all of this country, Opare was the only one we found with the skills to extract the hostages," he explained. "And yourself can testify to his skill with the trails. Now imagine looking for someone like that in this jungle. What are the chances that he would allow himself and his clients to be discovered? Heck, even with a wide trail, we had some trouble trusting we were on track to meet you. The Air Force can search all they want, and they will neither find him nor the Girls. It's better to just let them do all the work beating around this non-proverbial bush. In fact, I have a mind for us to do whatever we can to enable Opare and the Girls to evade capture. And then we can meet them wherever the end will be, and take our Girls for a well-earned glory, don't you agree?"

Nartey mulled that over until the beginnings of a smile began to play on his well-chiseled military face.

"I just didn't want this trek again into the jungle to go to waste, but your ideas are superior to mine," he conceded.

As they started to retrace their steps on the Rangers' trail, another call came through from the parallel War Room, this time from Dr. Moses Obuobi.

"Remember the GPS device that trilaterated the Fortress?" he asked Amadu and Atukwei.

"Vaguely," Atukwei said, making a face. "What of it?"

"A device with the same digital signature is about half a kilometre from the Aburi-Adawso Road," Obuobi told him. "If your theory that the Rangers have the Girls holds, then I can track them from here, and you don't need to do anything but wait until it stops moving."

"What if the device goes off – due to low battery or something?" Atukwei asked.

"I'll reconnect to it anytime it comes back on," Obuobi said confidently. "I have six satellites homed in on that device."

The Chief Superintendents mulled that over for a minute. Amadu asked, "When did that device first ping its location?"

"A week ago, when I tried to back-hack the Girls from the War Room."

"Can you track that device's movements from that point until today?"

"I can't, not without access to the device's data over the period, but I can trace it because it is accessing the same satellites I am. Why do you ask?"

"I just wanted to know at what point the Girls might have contracted Opare."

"Why is that important?" the IGP came in at that point.

"The sequence of contact is important to guess what their next steps will be," Atukwei explained. "If the plan is to get the Girls out of the country, we can't wait for some device to stop before we act. That might be too late. We need to actively pursue that device and overtake it where we can. If it ends up inside the Togolese Republic, for instance, there'll be nothing much we can do to apprehend them."

Atukwei's logic caused the troops to pause their night hike as the top brass chewed it over. While they waited, they could hear rotors noisily whirring overhead as the Strike Force's activities on the other side of the mountain reechoed throughout the valley. There was no mistaking that the Girls' actions had upturned the nation's security processes and procedures. And it looked like there was more to come.

"We need to stay with the signal that Dr. Obuobi is tracking," the IGP informed them when he came back on the line. "We can't afford to have them leave the national jurisdiction, and that is a viable risk now that we are aware of the possibility. I am having one of our operational vans meet you at the rendezvous point with supplies and a fresh team of troops borrowed from Major Hanson, as well as counterterror operatives from Koforidua. And because this might take you all through some jungle terrain, I'm having Police choppers hang around the Adawso area for any eventualities. Dr. Obuobi will stay online to guide you on the track. We want you no more than half a kilometre behind them so you can move in when it becomes apparent the border is their goal. We also have men moving in to secure all of Opare's islands. Let's bring this operation to a quick closure, and we'll remain here to guide you as best we can."

CHAPTER 28
Akwapim Highlands
Tuesday, 26th March; 5 A.M.

THEY TREKKED NORTHEAST for three nights. They hiked the entire day after the first night, stopping only to eat quick meals. And then that night as well, because Opare had changed his mind about the thermal searches and said they might run into nosy farmers if they hiked within the day. Farmers were these days armed with all kinds of mobile phones and might report to the Police, he'd said.

If their day journey from the first campsite had been tough, it had been nothing compared to the night hike that followed that day's first forty-kilometre trek. Asabea had never had to pay as much attention to the metric system as she had that night, and while she had enjoyed the pleasure that came from Google maps blurting how many more kilometres she had to go to arrive at her urban destinations, that knowledge in the forests and mountains were pure torture covering those distances on foot. She and her Girls were sporting cuts, scrapes and bruises from non-existing trails full of thorns and vegetative weaponry.

Just last night, they had painstakingly crawled twelve kilometers on their bellies, reminiscent of rats navigating a maze. The thorny branches above knee level were so densely armed with spikes that the Rangers estimated it would take an entire day just to clear two kilometers. In a moment of frustration, Efe rose to her full height in a small clearing, only to narrowly avoid an eye injury from a particularly vicious bush. From that point on, they all adhered strictly to the Rangers' instructions.

The towering trees, which had initially seemed welcoming amidst the thicket of thorns, now cast eerie shadows in the darkness, amplifying the Girls' unease. Rustling leaves and the occasional hoots of unseen nocturnal creatures added to their apprehension. Despite their headlamps cutting feeble paths through the darkness, they struggled to discern the twisted roots and slippery rocks underfoot. These hazards made each step precarious, leading nearly everyone, except the Rangers, to stumble repeatedly throughout the journey.

One of the nights had been rainy, and no matter how much they had tried, Opare had not budged from not waiting out the storm to plunge them into what they had feared would be their watery graves. The temperature had dropped so drastically Aisha had believed her chattering teeth could be heard all the way back at the Fortress, now some hundred kilometres behind them. The least said about how the weight of their backpacks and weapons felt on their backs the better, and the uncertainty of what kind of forestry lied ahead had contributed to a physically and mentally draining experience. At some point, when Wannah, the Ranger with the dreads had asked Dede who had been lagging whether she wanted to go back to the Fortress, Dede had replied tearfully, "If I knew this was what the extraction was going to be like, I'd much rather have stayed."

They arrived on a grassy plateau overlooking Lake Volta a few minutes after midnight, having been freed from the foreboding humidity of the mountain forests into an even more challenging terrain full of steep descents, rocky outcrops, and fast-flowing streams. Each step had been a battle against fatigue, and the endless descent had made them yearn shockingly for those parts when they had had to go on their bellies.

The lacustrine beach the descent ended at before dawn was a welcoming flat land. Owuraku and the Girls flopped onto the sandy beach and refused to get up even when Opare warned that a storm might hit before morning. Feeling sorry for them, the Rangers had pitched all the tents by themselves.

Asabea and Owuraku were inside their large sleeping bag when the storm came. Owuraku snored through it while she listened to the storm rage outside and flap the loose accessories of their tents in the wind. She was too tired to sleep. When she opened her eyes from what sleep came several hours later, the storm had passed, and Owuraku wasn't inside. The sunshine that followed in the storm's wake made the tent too warm to remain inside so she dressed and stepped out to a clear blue sky and a wavy blue lake, as well as to the unmistakable smell of a good breakfast.

The beach they were on was sandy and yellow, and it sloped into the water. It was right at the water's edge that her Girls and the Rangers sat eating a breakfast of boiled rice and spicy goat sauce.

Owuraku's head bobbed up out of the water next to them. He had been swimming.

"Good morning," she greeted.

"Good afternoon, actually," Efe replied, looking at her watch. "It's noon now."

"Really?" Asabea asked and looked back at her tent. It should have been too warm for her to have slept till noon. Then she saw that the Rangers had set up the tents under vast trees that had sheltered her from most of the sun's heat.

"So, this is lunch?" she asked when she turned back from the tents.

"Yes," Bubuné said and dished out a bowl for her. Asabea grabbed a camping stool and sat around a table made of tarpaulin stretched taut by several large tent pins.

"Who cooked," she asked after the first spoonful.

"The boys did," Bubuné told her. "None of us woke up in time."

"And can you blame us?" she asked with a slight wink.

After lunch, the Girls joined Owuraku in the water to cool off. Only the Rangers seemed preoccupied a few metres from their encampment with their satellite phone, but Asabea was too tired to wonder what was so important that swimming had to wait. She ached everywhere, and even the cool swim felt painful to her body. She said as much to Efe, who laughed and said, "Even talking hurts."

After cavorting in the water for a while, the sun dipped behind some thick clouds, and it became bearable to come out of the water. But their state of lassitude increased for the rest of the day until sunset when Opare came around with his Rangers and called for a briefing. Even that took a half hour before all the weary nineteen people from the Fortress gathered around the tarp.

"Dare I ask how you all are doing?" Opare asked gravely.

"Best to move the conversation along," Oye replied honestly with a tired wave of her hand.

Opare smiled wanly and got straight down to business by pulling a map out of a sheath and spreading it over the tarp.

"This is where we are," he pointed to a mark of a beach on the map. "And these are our twin islands – Survival and Discovery," he pointed to a couple of what appeared to be smudges on the map. "They will be your new homes for the foreseeable future, and they are the land masses you see in the middle of the lake," he pointed them out in the distance.

"How far are they?" Bubuné asked, tiredly shielding her eyes from the glare of the late afternoon sun on the restless lake.

"Seven kilometres out."

"You know what," Nhyira said to him, also tiredly. "I'd pay you ten thousand cedis to never say 'kilometres' ever again."

Opare bowed mockingly.

"How do we get there?" Asabea asked him.

"We have a Landing Craft that will come for us when I give the signal, but we can't head to them just yet. Cube called on the sat phone to say the Police CTU has scores of men hanging around our facilities and offices. It's safe to assume they might stake out our islands as well at some point."

"The same people you gave our abductees to?" Bubuné asked, trying to sound more alert than she felt.

"Yes."

"I'm not sure how I feel about your act as a double agent," Asabea said plaintively to him from where she sat next to Owuraku.

"So long as both contracts had the aim of keeping you and the innocent hostages safe, we had no real ethical dilemma," Opare told her.

"Abductees," Efe supplied.

"What?" Opare asked, puzzled.

"They were abductees; they were never hostages."

"You seriously believe there is a distinction?" Opare asked her.

"We would never have harmed them," Owuraku explained.

"It wouldn't have mattered if we hadn't gotten to them in time," Opare said seriously to him. "And it would have mattered even less if we hadn't gotten to you in time, too."

They fell silent.

"The CTU did not ask us to arrest you or anything because we refused to carry arms. There isn't so much they can guess about our arrangement. Cube says they believe we stole the hostages from under your noses, but that you may have forced us to extract you as well, which is why they are running surveillance on all our sites."

"What happens next then?" Aaron asked Owuraku and the Girls after that. "What's your plan now?"

The Girls exchanged glances and then looked at Owuraku.

"They had no plans beyond the Fortress," he said simply. "Bringing you guys in was my plan."

"Who's 'they'?" Wannah demanded.

"I wasn't in on the operation until later," Owuraku explained. "I was the one who suggested they contact you as back up. The Girls planned to fight till the end."

"That would have been suicidal," Aaron said, surprised. "And nothing you have done so far is any indication of that kind of stupidity."

Asabea looked at him with a frown and asked, "Are you all this brutally direct all the time?"

Aaron shrugged. "The jungle doesn't offer us the opportunity to mask our feelings," he replied.

"We didn't care, so long as we had Duncan King," Bubuné answered his question.

"And how is that working out for you?" Kada demanded critically. "You've murdered him, and you didn't die in the Fortress. Now, every able-bodied Policeman in this country is looking for you – and us. You must be proud."

"Pride had nothing to do with it," Bubuné responded in a stern voice. "It was all about justice."

"And all nineteen of you planned to die in that Fortress?"

Bubuné shrugged. "You can take a poll and see."

"You're all nuts, you know?" Aaron diagnosed them with feeling.

While the bantering was going on, Opare seemed to be in deep thought. Asabea looked at him and asked, "What's going to happen next?"

"Why are you asking him?" Wannah asked with a scoff. "You are the ones who took on a whole country just for the opportunity to murder a rapist. Why don't you give us a plan?"

Asabea looked intently from Wannah to Opare and asked, "You disapprove of me?"

Opare looked back at her, seemingly a little irritated to have been pulled out of his thoughts. Eventually, he asked, "Does it matter what I think?"

"It does to us all," Oye piped in.

Opare's eyebrows shot up, and then he said, "You and your colour copy have hated my guts from the moment you met me. How can you care about what I think?" Opare demanded of the twins.

"We were wrong to distrust you," Nhyira admitted to him but in a weirdly challenging tone. "And don't call me a colour copy."

"And the change of heart is sponsored by what exactly?"

"The extraction," Bubuné came in at that point in a subdued but firm voice. "I know we complained every step of the way, but it beggars belief that you got us safely out to here without the detection or interruption of law enforcement. Also, I didn't think all of us would have made it, especially with Dede's intractable fear of heights."

Opare looked kindly at Dede, and then at the rest with an inscrutable expression. "What do you want from us?" He asked.

"Keep us safe until we can figure out what to do," Aisha told him on everyone's behalf.

"You're the ones with guns," Opare reminded her. "But how long are we talking about?"

"For as long as it takes," Asabea told him. "Like Owuraku said, we didn't take surviving the Fortress into consideration. And now that we have, we don't know what to do with our lives."

"It occurs to me that you could leave the country," Wannah offered promptly.

"They will almost certainly be found and brought back to face justice," Opare answered him. "Our francophone neighbours don't tolerate cross-border fugitives." And then he turned to Asabea and asked, "What's in this for us?"

"You want more money?" Asabea asked in surprise.

"You have no money," Opare rebutted firmly. "If you planned to die in the Fortress I don't imagine you have money stashed anywhere."

"That's correct," Efe answered.

"Our freedom means more to us than cash, even though it is a good medium to exchange our inconvenience for, but if we help you, we will be the subject of intense law enforcement interest. I hate that kind of attention. I need to know what is in it for us if we decided to help you. What would we gain?"

"You could marry us," Oye suggested without a care in her tone. "You know, share us among yourselves since we can't go anywhere."

Opare gave her a withering look.

It was a tough question, and one that had Owuraku and the Girls looking at each other with not much to say immediately. They knew the Master-Guide was right. They had become liabilities of the highest order. If they got found the charge sheet would be kilometres long. Whoever harboured them would suffer the same fate, and the idea of concealing them indefinitely was impossible. But from what they had gotten to understand from Owuraku, and by what they had themselves observed when the Rangers had led them through the Ghanaian jungle, exhibiting such intimate knowledge of how to avoid capture, only Opare could pull of hiding them indefinitely.

"Our need is our plea," Owuraku told Opare simply when no one else could speak up. "And we need to be hidden from everyone that is looking to jail or kill us."

Opare looked at the academic and said, "You held Duncan King accountable for his crime; why shouldn't you be?"

"Because it was our duty to hold him accountable," Asabea said in an unapologetically firm voice. "This had to be done, Opare. Do you know how many women in Ghana Duncan King assaulted?"

Opare shook his head in the negative.

"A thousand four hundred and fifteen!" Asabea said and stormed off to her tent.

Opare's face darkened after her.

"How is that even possible?" He asked Owuraku.

"But it is," Aisha interjected. "Duncan King had a Book of Sex that he kept in his safe. In it, he had details of all the women he had slept with since he turned twelve."

"Gross," Opare said with distaste, "But not illegal."

"He describes every encounter in his book," Dede supplied. "And particularly details those he forced or raped. The more the resistance, he wrote, the more the pleasure, and of that number of those he wrote that resisted, our interviews with more than eighty-seven percent of them was forcible."

Opare blinked. "You are making the numbers up," he challenged.

"We aren't," Asabea came out of her tent at that point and threw a book onto the tarp, on top of Opare's maps.

"This is Duncan King's Book of Sex," Asabea told him, pointing. "It's like an accountant's ledger. You will find the names of his victims, their age, colour of skin, and where he first met them. A majority are women who worked for him in entertainment and fashion – secretaries, other firm's secretaries and personal assistants, and a disproportionate majority are beauty queen contestants; a whole ninety percent of those we interviewed."

"But there always is only one beauty queen a year, isn't it?" Opare asked skeptically.

"Some years had five – because there were several pageants – but he not only targeted the winners, he targeted across the application spectrum and had more success with those who didn't make the various cuts. Not even university hall beauty queen-wannabes were spared."

"Surely, you jest," Opare asked in surprise.

"There's the evidence," Owuraku told him, pointing also at the book.

Opare flipped through the pages, and he had not read more than two before revulsion began to taint his handsome face.

"He raped women who were in their periods because he thought they were only using it as an excuse to not give him what he wanted?" Opare asked out loud while reading one of the annotations in disgust. "'And when I found out that they were, I couldn't stop because blood is still a good lubricant'," Opare quoted and threw the book back on the tarp.

"You haven't seen the worst of it," Bubuné told him with an intensity born of hate. "You just scratched the surface with that one."

"How did you come by it?" Aaron asked, looking at the book like it was a snake.

"I worked for him as a house cleaner some years ago and got raped," Aisha told him. "I fought him so hard I broke his lip, but he still had me.

Afterwards, he brought out the book and read me the list, while I was crying and bleeding, of the better women he had had, and how I wasn't his type, but that he only needed a domestic vagina for starters before he found the woman he really wanted to be with that day."

"And that's when you stole the book?" Opare asked.

"Oh, we knew the book existed," Asabea explained. "No one knows more how vain he is than we do, and we took it the day we drugged him from Osu."

Opare's mouth opened for an instant as the thought occurred to him.

"You are all his victims?" he asked incredulously.

"We are," Oye told him with eyes as hard as flint.

"And we got sworn affidavits from all the women named in that book – at least those we could track. Some are no longer in the country, and some could just not be traced. Our aim was to find all of them and have them cut Duncan King up piece by piece, but when that proved difficult at the planning phase, we found an internet solution to the problem," Asabea continued.

"So, putting it all together summarily," Efe said to Opare with meaning, "That motherfucker deserved to die – in Samuel L. Jackson's voice."

It would have been funny if not for how serious the allegations were, and for a whole minute Opare and his Rangers could not find anything to say that would be appropriate.

"I don't think it's possible to hide nineteen people," Wannah seemed deep in thought, clearly disturbed by what he had heard.

"Unless they were fine with never seeing anyone – ever again," Opare added thoughtfully as if the Girls and Owuraku were not sitting right there. "And by that I mean not another soul but us."

Wannah looked at his boss and added, "Even at that, sparingly."

"We won't even be seeing you?" Dede asked Opare with something close to fear. "Where will you be hiding us?"

"On our twin islands," Opare told her, half-inattentively. "But this discussion is premature. I need to get back to the IGP and try to talk him out of pursuing you."

"You can do that?" Owuraku asked in surprise.

Opare shrugged. "I have to report back to them eventually," he said. "I don't know what I am going to say yet, but I need to show my face and take whatever happens after that from there. I wish I knew what the news was saying though."

"I can help with that," Regina offered. "I'll have our digital systems up in half an hour."

"I hope it'll be untraceable?" Aaron asked carefully.

"It's satellite powered," Regina explained with a glance at Owuraku before heading towards the tent she shared with her assistant. "It's as secured as your own satellite phones."

"Don't you want to think about what you'll say to the IGP and the Police CTU when you meet them?" Asabea asked Opare worriedly.

"What do you care?" Wannah asked curiously from his seat in a hammock right next to the central tarp. "From what I understand about what you have done, you Girls were ready to die. What do you care if you get caught eventually?"

"I didn't care much about living when this started," she confessed to Wannah. Then she rubbed her hands together shyly and held Opare's gaze. "But I am pregnant, and now, living free and not getting caught or killed is all I've been thinking about since we left that cave of bats."

Then she turned the full force of her gaze on Owuraku and refused to look anywhere else. Not even the surprise questions from Bubuné, or the celebratory screams from Oye and Nhyira, or even the congratulatory pats on her back from Aisha and Dede could move her gaze until the realization appeared on Owuraku's face that the exchanges of affection and the closeness with which they had passed some of the more anxious nights during the trial and the assault of the army had borne fruit. Only when the almost imperceptible smile of acknowledgement and acceptance of fatherhood splayed across Owuraku's handsome features did she shyly look away.

But the rest of the escapees had questions that could not remain unanswered for long.

"How did that happen?" Efe asked.

"Through the usual way," she replied with a very mortified glance at Owuraku. "You really had to ask?"

"Are you sure? It hasn't been a month since Owuraku joined us at the Fortress," Aisha asked with mischievous glee.

"I have a twenty-one-day cycle," she crowed, covering her face with her hands as she said it.

"But Owuraku is a virgin," Bubuné protested slyly. "Did you assault him?"

"I did no such thing," Asabea replied. "It just – happened."

"When did it happen? I hope it wasn't during the night the military was bombing us?" Nhyira said with a half-hearted petulance. "That kind of buffing in a moment of war is a bad precedent."

"Would you all just stop?" Asabea complained shyly. "You're embarrassing us."

On and on it went, and the campsite that had since morning looked like a serious, almost-military establishment suddenly turned domestic with discussions about baby showers and godmothers and guesses as to the baby's sex. Wannah and the rest of the Rangers brought them the evening's foodstuffs to peel and cut for dinner's preparations and the chatter continued throughout the early evening. Even Regina got sidetracked after returning from her tent with her tablet until the 6 p.m. news bulletin reminder beeped.

The news that Regina accessed on her tablet on the hour started with an address from President Offei. After dispensing with his signature greetings, which elicited steups of derision from a populace disappointed in his government's economic incompetence, he announced that it was he who had authorised the military operation against the women who had abducted the country's Supreme Court judges and killed innocent abductees. He detailed his command to military leaders to leave no stone unturned to track the Girls, and having done so, to dole out the justice that had been rained on them and on their hideout. He declared that all the Girls and a certain Dr. Darko had been killed because they had refused to surrender. He bemoaned the participation of the public, calling supporters of the Girls deranged, and indicated that he had ordered the Cybercrime Unit of the Police Service to track down, arrest, and prosecute everyone that had voted online in support of the murder of the three gentlemen. After denouncing the nation's slide to moral corruption and thanking his service chiefs for bringing closure to a difficult one month, he declared the operation over.

When the news anchor took over, signaling the end of the President's speech, Owuraku looked across the tarp at Opare and said, "If we are declared dead, then the hunt for us is over, isn't it?"

"I don't think so," Opare said, darkly musing the President's speech over in his mind.

"Then what does that mean?"

"It means the President is an idiot, he doesn't fully know what he is talking about, and the CTU is operating above his radar."

"If the President is saying things contrary to what his IGP knows, doesn't that mean you're giving the CTU more credit than they deserve?" Bubuné asked.

"The CTU is the finest fighting force of the Ghana Police, and its most intelligent unit," Opare explained. "If I am right, and they are operating beyond the President's knowledge, then you can bet that *their* search is not over."

"You're saying they will countermand the President's declaration as lies and parade us publicly if they found us?" Bubuné asked disbelievingly.

"I imagine that would be embarrassing for the President," Aaron said with a chuckle.

"The current IGP is a professional Police Officer and not as prone to political gimmickry like the IGPs before him," Opare said. "He would do what was right even if it meant losing his job."

"As far as we are concerned, the hunt for us will continue?" Asabea asked worriedly with a hand on the upper side of her belly.

"Yes."

"What do you plan to do?"

"I plan to get to the IGP for a discussion."

"He might arrest you on sight."

"He doesn't know I have you."

"Then what will the discussion be about?"

"I'll ask him to call off the manhunt for you."

"Then he *will* arrest you on sight."

"We don't know that. He'll be in a pickle himself after the President's speech, and I think I might have a solution he won't refuse."

"Care to share the solution?"

"I haven't cooked it fully yet."

"Do you realise our whole lives are hanging by a thread, and that thread is you?"

Opare smiled tolerantly when he said to her, "Your whole lives have hung by a thread since you took on the government, and none of that has been because of me."

CHAPTER 29
Police HQ, Accra
Wednesday, 27th March, Noon.

VICE PRESIDENT ERASMUS Domwine's motorcade lacked the technological advancement of President Offei's armoured entourage. Which wasn't surprising: his job was to play second fiddle to an Executive President in whom and in whom alone resided all true political power in Ghana. While the role carried substantial responsibility and importance to the country's democratic governance system – he was head, after all, of Ghana's Police Service Board as well as of most of the Boards of all the country's internal security agencies – that was only in name and on paper. The reality was that the General Secretary of the Party had more power than the Vice President.

That power had switched only once, when a president died while in office. The Vice President that succeeded him, once he had tasted real presidential power, had treated his deputy with the same disdain and contempt. And it wasn't difficult to see why.

Most vice-presidential candidates came from lesser tribes and regions, and often from minority religions as well, with the sole purpose of winning over those tribes and religion adherents who typically might not vote for a leader from a dominant tribe due to precolonial grievances.

Things should really have been different with him and President Offei, though. Not only had he brought the minor tribes to bear on their election, he had brought his intellect as an economic guru to the party ticket. Most of the country's intellectuals had had no love for President Offei until his expositions of the previous government's economic incompetence had rallied intellectuals to the party's cause. Unfortunately, becoming vice President had revealed to him that it was politics, not economics, that decided the allocation of scarce national resources.

His motorcade arrived at the HQ of the Police Service, and the aide opening the door of his armoured limo pulled him out of his thoughts. He got out of the car and wasted no time going up the stairs of what he already knew was a parallel War Room. He had had his motorcade silenced before he was driven into the sprawling Police HQ, so he wasn't surprised at all by the flustered surprises of the top brass of the Police Service. They were tripping over themselves and their chairs to stand at attention and perform the usual honours when he bulldozed his presence into the room and grabbed the nearest chair.

He spared one glance around the room, and indicated with his hands that everyone could sit. Then he turned to the IGP and demanded, "Give me all the *real* news there is about the judges and hostages."

Through all the stammering and coughing and flustered reporting, the IGP and his top officers briefed him on all that they had done since the Girls blew up the bridge in Aburi. Dr. Domwine sat quietly through the telling, occasionally nodding his head in understanding, but never once betraying his emotions about what the Police – his Police – had been doing behind his boss's back. When they were done, he mulled a lot of things over while the men sat on tenterhooks waiting for the inevitable axe to fall.

"Great job!" he said admiringly, breaking the long spell of uncomfortable silence. "This is good patriotic work!"

The Police Officers were so skeptical that their sighs of relief were tinged with suspicion.

Dr. Domwine laughed easily and said, "I'm not telling President Offei what you have done because it's brilliant and, sadly, he hasn't the mind to appreciate it. We will have a fight on our hands if we produce the Girls against his declaration. The only saving grace is that he made no mention of the hostages, but the abductees will talk eventually, and all we need to unravel Offei's lies is one nosy journalist."

"What do you suggest we do, sir?" the IGP asked carefully.

Dr. Domwine scratched at his short beard for a minute and asked, "Are we confident we can apprehend the Girls?"

"We were, until about four days ago when the GPS device we were tracking went offline. We have every facility ran by the adventure company under twenty-four-hour surveillance, but our fear isn't that they will turn up in any of those facilities. If they do, we won't be bothered so long as we know where they are and can fetch them after we cure the President of his current behaviour. Our fear is that they might be heading towards one of our external borders. We don't know how to instruct the Immigration Service to be on the lookout for people the President has declared dead."

Dr. Domwine frowned as he chewed on that for a minute.

"President Offei has always been rash and unthinking," he said darkly. "But the way I see it, we have to set ourselves directly against him for the right thing to prevail, and I don't mind that fight in the least."

Then he turned to one of his aides and ordered, "Call the Inspector General of Immigration and tell him to maintain vigilance at all our borders for the Girls, and to maintain same until I order otherwise."

Before the aide could run out to carry his order, Obuobi barged into the War Room from an adjourning room where he had been working on reconnecting with Opare's GPS watch.

"The GPS device is back on line," he announced with excitement, "and it's right here at the Police HQ."

Obuobi held one of his devices, and it showed a blue dot approaching closely to the War Room. He looked strangely at the door and asked, "Whoever is coming, will your security detail let them through?" he asked the Vice President.

"If he states his business properly, yes," Vice President Domwine replied.

A soldier poked his head through the mahogany doors of the room just then and whispered to another soldier inside. That soldier then announced to the aide that a Kwaku Opare Addo was requesting urgent audience with the IGP.

"Let him in," the IGP ordered in unison with the Vice President, and Opare was ushered into the room, flanked by Aaron. Both men blinked when they saw the Vice President.

Opare greeted the IGP formally and nodded respectfully at the Vice President. And then he waited, looking pointedly at the IGP from the end of the long conference room table until he was offered a seat. As soon as he and Aaron had sat, Chief Superintendents Atukwei and Amadu, Colonel Nartey and Major Hanson barged excitedly into the room.

"Why are you here?" Vice President Domwine asked Opare.

Opare looked inquisitorially at the IGP.

"His Excellency has been fully briefed and is aware of everything you have done," the IGP informed him with the tone one addressed a person in trouble with.

Opare glanced once around the room and noticed Obuobi and his gadgets.

"I assume you were the one who tried to hack my GPS," he accused him noncommittally.

"And a merry good chase you've led me," Obuobi replied with grudging respect. "At what point did you detect I might be onto you?"

"Before the extraction," Opare replied. "But I felt your tag-along was benign until later on."

"Let's not get sidetracked," Vice President Domwine said with a scowl in Obuobi's direction.

Obuobi looked a tad apologetic.

INVIOLABLE 240

"What can we do for you?" the Vice President demanded again.

Opare said to him, "I have eighteen women and a gentleman in my possession who are wanted possibly for every imaginable crime in Ghana's criminal code. And I am here to negotiate a deal that does not require me to give them up."

One needed to understand public service in Ghana to describe the looks the top brass of Ghana's Police Service directed at Opare. There were scoffs and growls and glares – the type born of never-challenged authority – that promised all kinds of unpleasantness, tinged no doubt with the incredulity directed at the sheer balls Opare must possess to make such a demand.

The IGP was the first to find his voice.

"Where are the Girls?" he demanded.

"In a safe place, for now," Opare replied.

"That was not our deal."

"I understand, and that's why I am here."

"You know there's no way we can agree to your demand."

"I thought you might feel that way, but what have you got to lose? Your Commander-in-Chief has already declared them dead. You know what the consequences will be if you countermanded him."

The IGP exchanged a startled glance with the Vice President, who had kept his eyes focused on the younger man this far in the conversation.

"Never mind what the President said," he told Opare. "Your job was to deliver the young women to us. It's none of your business what we do with them."

"Actually, my job was to rescue the hostages, Mr. Vice President," Opare told him respectfully. "Extracting and handing the Girls over was not part of our deal."

"But now that you have them, you are obliged to hand them over," Vice President Domwine said reasonably. "This is an urgent matter of national security. And you risk being prosecuted for obstruction, you know?"

Opare stared calmly back at the Vice President as if he was giving the threat some serious consideration. And then he said, "Honestly, I don't give two hoots about the Girls per se."

No one at the table or in the room believed him, but he went on.

"I am only here on a matter of efficiency," he explained. "You have a no-good President whose love of political expediency is almost pathologically imbecilic. He jumps the gun and declares the Girls dead.

If I surrender the Girls, and you do the right thing by telling him they didn't die in the Fortress, he will refuse to go back to the Ghanaian people to admit he was wrong."

"You don't know that," the Vice President told him plaintively.

"Oh, I do," Opare objected. "And I suspect you do too, because doing so means that his Police and counterterror chiefs – and his Vice President – are showing they're smarter than he is. President Offei will have the Girls and Ampem Darko shot on sight or murdered on the way to any court in this country. Because the last thing he wants is another public display of his incompetence. And I am here speaking to twenty presumably intelligent people who know exactly what I'm talking about. Your jobs will be on the line, and perhaps your lives as well. Why not just let sleeping dogs lie? Sentence the Girls to life imprisonment with me, and I promise they will be dead to you. Any other option, and theirs will not be the only lives in danger."

The IGP said, "Your theory is extreme, and this is not the movies. No one can hurt anyone in this room, and when we show the President we have the Girls, he will happily walk back his words. Finding them would be a more glorious ending for him than declaring them dead."

Opare said, "I don't think you really believe that, sir. Especially after President Offei already murdered half a thousand troops."

The Vice President's eyes narrowed. "What do you mean?"

"He ordered the artillery units to fire on Colonel Nartey on the drawbridge. I believe he was counting on a national outrage from their deaths."

Colonel Nartey leaned forward and said, "I'm sorry, what?"

Opare said, "Review the drone footages the Girls telecasted that day, and you will find that nothing was fired from their drones at the time you were on the bridge. Your men were killed by your own artillery."

The IGP glanced once at Obuobi and said quietly to the Vice President, "It was the footages that convinced us President Offei cared less about the hostages than he did about how this made him look. That was why we intervened."

Vice President Domwine shook his head and said, "Even if this were true, the Girls are the cause of all this. His proposal to let them get away with it is preposterous."

"I'd like to interrogate that story a little bit more, though," Colonel Nartey said with eyes as hard as ice. "You're telling me that I lost men because the President wanted a more compelling justification to wipe out the Girls?"

"Not just the Girls; the judges and other hostages too," Opare told him. "And I don't believe he will stop at anything to cover his butt. Which is why I believe everyone in this room will be at risk when he finds the truth about the Girls."

"Isn't this story of yours cooked up by the Girls because they don't want us to find them and hurt them the way they deserve?" Major Hanson asked incredulously.

"Major, do you get the impression that President Offei gives a hoot that the judges are alive?" Opare asked him seriously. "Has he granted them any audience since their return?"

Major Hanson seemed less sure of himself as he mulled it over.

"If this is some kind of a show you're putting up to defend the government, I think you're overdoing it," Opare said what his mind saw clearly to the Vice President. "But if you genuinely believe that what I am saying is the truth, then let me spell it out well: I will hand over the Girls only when I have your assurances that they will receive a fair trial untainted by the murderous wishes and actions of your President. Since you cannot guarantee that, how about I keep them until you decide if your own lives are worth the price of telling President Offei that you have undermined his worst impulses since he kicked you out of his Cabinet?"

"We have resources to keep the Girls hidden until we get to the bottom of your accusations," Vice President Domwine told him. "It's non-negotiable that you turn in the Girls. We have heard you and will take what necessary steps we can to handle the President."

"I'm sorry, sir, but maybe I haven't made myself clear," Opare told him seriously. "The Girls aren't going anywhere or bothering anyone until you clean up the mess that is your President. I don't care if you believe me enough to save your own lives, but I'm not giving them up until such a time as is safe."

Vice President Domwine blinked and glanced once at the aide to his right. At once, his aide approached Opare threateningly, quite self-assured that a couple of slaps might dissipate the Master-Guide's belligerence. The two soldiers at the entrance approached Opare from behind as well.

What followed next unfolded in a blur, but when the chaos subsided, Aaron and Opare were in possession of the sidearms belonging to the aide and the soldiers. They held the weapons steady, aimed at the three individuals who now stood with their hands raised in surrender. The Vice President's other aides and three Secret Service agents from the adjacent room where Obuobi had been working rushed in, armed and ready to assist the beleaguered trio. Colonel Nartey and the two Chief Superintendents quickly intervened, defusing the tension by asking everyone to 'calm the frack down'.

"You'll regret this," the Vice President threatened Opare when he and Aaron had handed over the guns to the Chief Superintendents.

"I am not new to living with regrets, your Excellency," Opare replied without disrespect, "but I'm not your enemy. I am only trying to save your lives, and the lives of my chargés the same way I saved your hostages. I need you to respect that, at least, whatever happens from here on."

"How did you do that?" Colonel Nartey asked Opare when he and Aaron resumed their seats. "How did you seize their weapons so fast?"

"We may not carry weapons, Colonel, but we are never defenseless," Opare replied with a look at the Vice President. "Now, how do you want to proceed, sir?"

"Perhaps you can answer some questions first," the IGP said with a respectful inclination of his head towards the Vice President. "At what point did you turn?"

"Actually, the Girls contracted us first," Aaron explained. "We were on our way to extract when your call came through."

"But you met with them earlier, didn't you?" Obuobi asked Opare. "Your GPS device helped my systems with a satellite ping."

"That is correct," Opare answered. "I was unaware I hadn't turned it off from a hike before I met the Girls at the Fortress."

"So the Girls had planned to escape?" Amadu asked carefully, with a glance at Obuobi.

"They had planned to fight to the end," Opare disagreed. "It was Ampem Darko that amended their suicide plans and called us."

"Did you have to cut a new trail?" Atukwei asked suddenly.

"No, we played it by ear. There was no time to do that with the Air Force blasting at the Fortress, and with you on the other side of the jungle."

"Did you know we were following you?" Obuobi asked.

"I knew you were tracking me at some point, and that was when I turned the GPS off. But I had no fears that you could follow us physically. Your men aren't cut out for jungle survival."

"We train for jungle survival at Achiase and Bondassi," Colonel Nartey quickly came to the defense of the Ghana Army.

"For all of three months," Opare told him coolly. "Afterwards you return to your bases, get fat and forget what it was like. You're soldiers because you have uniforms and guns. At what point did you stop following us, though? We could hear you around the grating after the Air Force stopped bombing the Fortress. Then it got dark, and we couldn't hear you anymore."

"We thought we could follow you from the Adawso Road, but we lost the GPS connection once we left the forest."

"How long did it take you to get to your destination?" Obuobi asked.

"Oh no," Opare laughed easily. "You're not going to trick me into revealing where the Girls are."

"Then let's explore your theory concerning what President Offei would do if he got wind that the Girls were alive," Vice President Domwine said to him. "You sound quite sure that his response would be murderous."

"You weren't at the Fortress like we were, your Excellency," Opare told him. "The Strike Force attacked in a scorched-earth fashion. They cared little for anything else except to clear out the building and kill everyone in it. And if Colonel Nartey and your counterterror officers had been sighted, they would have killed you too," Opare told him bluntly.

"The operation was not to recover people at all," Aaron added. "If the Girls had planned to keep the abductees as bargaining chips, they and the hostages would all have died, and we suspect you know this already because Colonel Nartey was there."

"We'll leave you to ponder over what President Offei would do to you if he discovers that you have thwarted all his efforts to erase the Girls and the hostages from living memory," Opare picked up from Aaron. "In the day that you can show the hostages were as important to him as they were to the IGP, we would hand the Girls over. Until then, they will stay with us. At least, you know who they are with, and that should be good enough for now. If the President makes you pay, the Girls would be protected. If he doesn't, I'd hand them over. But I'd need more than just words and the intractable scowl of your aides as assurances."

After a half-hour of arguments, a consensus was reached, backed especially by Colonel Nartey, Major Hanson and the two Commanders of the Counterterror and VIP Protection Police. Opare and his men would maintain custody of the Girls while the Vice President and the IGP investigated the allegations surrounding the death of Colonel Nartey's men, as well as test the impulse of the President towards news of the Girls. Under the negotiations, Opare was forced to reveal the current location of the Girls, but when he did, he reminded them that the Girls had carried half their arsenal along from the Fortress, to discourage any belligerence on the part of the Vice President.

"What did I do to you to incur your hate?" The Vice President demanded when Opare had cast that aspersion.

"Your government was willing to kill hostages to save face," he replied calmly. "I have no love for people who only think of public relations instead of pragmatism in moments of crises, and PR is all President Offei ever thinks about."

CHAPTER 30
Jubilee House
Wednesday, 27th March; 6 P.M.

THE NEWS STRUCK the seat of government like a thunderclap. Radio Foxx, the capital's leading frequency modulation operator dedicated an entire hour to exploring deep-throated source allegations that President Offei's government had had no intention of saving the life of the hostages. The evening news also accused the President of recklessly endangering the lives of troops and officers of the Ghanaian Army just to build a false pretext for the vicious assault on the Fortress. The newscasters revealed the involvement of foreign forces on the blind side of Parliament, and the absolute disregard for the lives of the hostages during the assault.

The radio station played sound bites to prove that dying soldiers knew they had been fired on by their own artillery, and the screams of soldiers falling to their demise appalled the nation. They had experts identify the sounds of drones and compared those to nothing the Ghana Air Force had. Then there were interviews of local farmers and hunters from Aburi and Adawso saying they had seen scores of police officers and soldiers rescuing hostages from the deep forest under missile fire from their own colleague soldiers.

President Kwame Amponsah Offei needed to be charged with the murder of innocent soldiers, the news concluded, and his whole handling of the hostage situation bordered on criminal behaviour just so he could cover his butt.

The response of President Offei's government to the damning allegations was swift. National Intelligence Bureau operatives ransacked the radio station minutes after the news broadcast and arrested, on charges of false reporting and treason, anyone they could lay hands on inside the sprawling studio complex at North Ridge in the centre of Accra. They manhandled the reporters and newscasters and would have done worst if Atukwei and Amadu had not arrived at the station with a hundred counterterror Policemen. The IGP himself was with them, and his presence prevented a tense standoff between the Police and the NIB from assuming a dangerous magnitude. Atukwei broke the jaw of one of the Agents when he and Amadu had tried to restrain them from messing up with the journalists and their leader had not taken kindly to the assault at all. If the Inspector-General had not been present – and that was also because he had preeminence over all intelligence agencies in the country except Military Intelligence – there would have been a showdown.

When things quieted down with the departure of the NIB, the IGP walked up to his men and said, "You couldn't stay out of trouble, could you?"

"They started it," Atukwei said defensively with a wide grin.

The IGP shook his head and said, "Seems Opare was right. I didn't expect that President Offei would visit this much violence on a radio station."

"Planting the story was a smart move," Amadu approved. "Now let's wait to see what he does next."

"Don't get distracted," the IGP warned him, looking angrily at the scene of destruction the NIB Agents had. "TV123 will carry the television version at 9 p.m. You better move it over there before the NIB goes attacking, and this time, I want more than broken jaws."

"Yes, sir," Atukwei said with an even wider grin.

The incident was repeated at the studios of TV123, but this time, Atukwei and Amadu prevented the Bureau from entering the premises of the station to begin with. When some of the agents screamed jurisdiction and attempted to push the counterterror officers aside, Amadu was the one that clubbed him at the back of the head with his AK47's butt. The Agents responded with violence of their own that was quickly suppressed by Atukwei who came to the gate with a hundred fists swinging. The NIB withdrew as fast as they could with a dozen injured men before the IGP arrived at this scene too, and there was no mistaken the pleasure on his face.

When these incidents were reported to the Cabinet of President Offei at the Jubilee House, there was a fight among the members as to who's duty it was to inform the President. But President Offei had already heard and seen the news, and the intensity of his anger when he barged into the War Room was plainly evident on his face.

"What the hell is all this that I'm hearing?" he demanded before he was half seated at the head of his Cabinet. He looked around and seemed to be taking attendance with his eyes.

"The involvement of AFRICOM has been leaked to the Press," the Chief of Defence Staff responded meekly.

President Offei gave him a withering look. "Not that you moron," he chided. "What is this I hear that you sent soldiers and police officers who were seen rescuing the hostages?"

The CDS gave the Army Chief a nervously brief look, but the President caught it and raised his eyes inquiringly.

The Army Chief shrugged and said to the President, "We decided to initiate a military protocol to reduce the fatalities among our men. Locals might have seen us and assumed we were rescuing hostages, but we were looking for our soldiers and the two missing AFRICOM pilots, nothing more."

"Who fracking gave you permission to enter an operational area on my blind side?" President Offei demanded angrily.

The Army Chief seemed momentarily angered by the question, and a strange resolve passed over his countenance.

"Do I have your permission to speak freely, sir?" he demanded, rising from his seat, but he didn't wait for it.

"Army protocol is clear that we never stop looking for those lost in combat. Our duty has always been to find, recover, and identify servicemen and women who remain unaccounted for from all conflicts and operations. This assumes more significance when the loss of troops is as tragic as half a battalion in one incident. The answer to your question, sir, is that Army protocol was enough. We did not need your fracking permission."

President Offei cocked his head to one side and watched the angry Brigadier-General take his seat with an ominously amused expression.

"You forget your place, don't you?" he warned the Army Chief.

"You can fire me if you choose, Mr. President," the Army Chief retorted. "But don't you talk to me about permissions and military doctrine. We did what we had to do for our men, and while we are at it, those pilots would not have been found in time otherwise."

The Cabinet looked between President Offei and the Chief of Army Staff, expecting the latter to be sacked when President Offei opened his mouth, but the sound of a dozen boots marching into the War Room drowned out what the President said in response.

Barreling through the swinging doors of the War Room was Colonel Nartey, flanked by the deputy Attorney-General, Umaru Tanko, and the Inspectors-General of Police and Immigration, and several other high-ranking officers.

"We apologise for the intrusion, sir," the IGP announced, "But the message we received sounded urgent, and here we are."

The President stared at him and asked in surly surprise. "What message? I thought I warned you to stay out of my way."

Then Vice President Domwine walked into the room as well and said, while pulling out a chair at his customary place at the right hand of the President, "The message was from me."

President Offei looked at him with ill-concealed contempt. "What are you doing here?" he demanded.

"Have you seen Colonel Nartey?" the Vice President asked the President.

"I thought you all said he was dead?" President Offei asked his equally surprised CDS, suddenly seeming to wonder himself what a supposedly dead Colonel was doing in his War Room.

"We thought the same as well," Dr. Domwine said. "Until we found the captain of the artillery unit you ordered to shoot at the troops."

President Offei looked at his deputy with a dangerous glint in his eye. "What are you talking about?"

"You ordered the killing of the soldiers on the bridge because you had a twisted belief that it was only by the death of our troops that support for a complete destruction of the Girls could be generated among the Ghanaian populace," Dr. Domwine told him. "Do you deny this?"

"I deny it!" President Offei vehemently said.

"Deny all you want," Dr. Domwine retorted. "But this is a Cabinet meeting. Confess to us now, or we will cause Parliament to impeach you for these crimes. Not only did you cause the death of half a battalion, you attacked media houses and put innocent hostages including your deputy Attorney-General and a High Court judge in physical and mental danger."

"These are serious allegations, sir," the deputy Attorney-General warned.

President Offei looked around with what would have been a red face if he hadn't been black. No one among his Cabinet found him guiltless.

Turning to Colonel Nartey, he asked, "Tell me what happened on the bridge."

Looking surprised, Nartey asked, "I don't see how that's relevant to the question of the deputy Attorney-General."

"Let me be the judge of that," the President retorted with a snort of derision in the direction of Umaru Tanko. "And his useless threats notwithstanding, I am still President, and as Commander-In-Chief, I demand a full accounting for what happened on the bridge."

"Let us do you one better, then, sir," the IGP said, calling Obuobi into the room. "We'll lead video evidence so there can be no doubts."

President Offei looked sourly at him and at the nerdy academic but did not interrupt when Obuobi plugged his devices into the main console.

"Like everyone else that saw the broadcast on the night of the operation, we at Police HQ believed it was the Girls that had blown up our troops." He manipulated drone images and some footage of the drawbridge collapsing.

"And we believed it until these images were beamed by AFRICOM's own drones to the Pentagon in Arlington, Virginia."

On the screens, three images were placed side by side showing the moment of impact of three missiles on the drawbridge. Three things became immediately apparent. The first was that the missiles came from behind the troops, where the 66th Artillery Regiment was stationed, and not from the Fortress. Secondly, the missiles were aimed directly at the troops and not necessarily at the bridge itself, which explained the large number of fatalities. And finally, the missiles were engraved with Indian manufacturer details. Ghana imports a full two-thirds of its ammunition and artillery needs from the government of India.

But images were not all Obuobi projected. He showed footage from one of the Girls' drones showing Colonel Nartey and his troops standing on the drawbridge with their eyes looking upwards at the drone, and the instant when artillery fire erupted from one of three mortar units behind the infantry line. Less than a second later, the drone covering Colonel Nartey zoomed in to him and his men falling down with the destroyed bridge, many of them in pieces of human anatomy. This also explained why the drawbridge's lowering hawsers were intact near the grating above the Fortress's sluice pipes.

"This proves nothing of my involvement in the soldiers' deaths," President Offei said after Obuobi's screen went dark.

"It does because we have a record of your call with the Gunner," the IGP informed him and had Obuobi play a conversation in which President Offei was instructing the young artillery officer, his nephew, to shoot at the troops on the bridge. His nephew disagreed until he threatened him with a court martial and worse if he failed to carry out his orders.

The President still appeared intransigent.

"You know what," the Vice President said in resignation, "I'll give you one minute to own up to your crimes. If not, we will pass a vote of no confidence in you and inform Parliament accordingly."

"Watch your tongue with me, Dr. Domwine," the President growled at him. "None of you has any power over me. You are shifting the attention of Ghanaians from the evil those Girls have done. Do you seriously think Ghanaian voters care about how I got the job done?"

"You got nothing done, Mr. President," Colonel Nartey shot back. "It was the Counterterror Police and Major Hanson's troops that rescued the justices and the hostages. They succeeded while you all sat here scratching your butts."

"But you didn't get the Girls," the President taunted. "The Girls are dead because of me."

"Do you have proof?" the IGP asked him with a wan smile. "Have you seen their corpses?"

"I won't even respond to that," President Offei said in disdain and then looked at each of his Cabinet members in turns. Up until now, not one of them had been disloyal.

"If I called a vote," he asked with a residual trace of surliness, "how many of you would vote that I resign?"

All hands went up quickly in the room. Even the unqualified Obuobi and Chief Superintendents voted to resign.

Looking disappointed, President Offei asked, "What protections do I get if I do so?"

This time, it was Ansah Premo, his lawyer, who answered. He had reported earlier for work but the President had shown no interest in meeting him. He hadn't even acknowledged his presence at Cabinet until now.

"The State will not press murder charges against you, and Vice President Domwine will grant you immunity from prosecution with the endorsement of the Supreme Court."

"Speak for yourself," Colonel Nartey spoke scathingly to what he considered as a ridiculous protection for a murderer. "I demand justice for the men that he has killed. Any immunity that denies them justice is a travesty."

"There will be a bigger travesty if he remains President and has to go through impeachment, where the party's majority might vote to acquit him. This is the best we can hope for," Ansah Premo told him sadly.

Colonel Nartey looked at him quizzically. "Whose side are you on?"

"Sadly, I am both his lawyer and a victim of his stupidity as a hostage who was rescued from the barrage of rockets he launched at the Fortress. I must do my duty by him."

"Hey, I haven't said I'm agreeing to your proposals," President Offei butted in arrogantly. "I am only asking what protections I get if I were to consider it."

"Then consider this," the deputy Attorney-General said to him seriously. "Your crimes will be revealed to the public, after which we will leave it to an angry Ghanaian population to force Parliament to impeach you. If you are susceptible to the shifting sentiments of the populace enough to kill for, then so are they. Eventually, once impeached, nothing in our laws will bar me from prosecuting you to the full extent of the law. So, you decide, sir."

President Offei rose to his full four-and-a-half-foot stature and said, "I will take your offers under advisement."

Then he stormed out of the War Room.

Many of his appointees breathed heavy sighs of relief after the President's departure, causing Colonel Nartey to turn his angry eyes on them.

"You all need to resign as well," he said. "Apart from the IGP, you showed the worst spinelessness I have seen in governments since 1992. Shame on all of you."

The Army Chief said, with a glance at the CDS, "Not all of us were cowardly, but you're right. We should have done more."

"What happens next?" This, from Patricia, the Attorney-General.

"I meant what I said," the IGP told her, rising. "The nation must know what has happened. After that, everything else will fall into place."

"That question you asked about the Girls – does that mean they are still alive?"

They turned towards the doors to see that President Offei had returned to ask that question.

"What does it matter? They're dead to you," the Vice President shot back at him. "And you have a minute until all hell breaks loose."

"It's too late now," the IGP said at his watch. "It's just a few seconds to 10 p.m."

"Then stop the press," President Offei said. "I will announce my resignation on the condition of complete immunity for my actions."

The Cabinet stared at him, wondering if he was serious, but Colonel Nartey wasn't going to be bullyragged.

"Like the IGP said, it's a little too late for that now," he said. Rising from his chair, he took the remote control and tuned into the evening news on one of the television stations, and sure enough, the murder of the troops by President Offei was all over the headlines. Some of the Cabinet members tuned into other stations on some of the other televisions in the room as well and the news was the same everywhere, with footages depicting how the attack went down superimposed over the audio of the President's call with the artillery commander.

The blood drained from the President's face as even more footages showed the gruesome deaths of the soldiers, amid a blazing inferno and screaming from beneath the erstwhile bridge. Even the battle-hardened Generals couldn't help but look away. The media were too angry to care about not showing videos of the dead and dying after having heard what the NIB had done to their colleagues at Foxx, and by the time the bulletins were over, an army of protestors had arrived at the gates of the Jubilee House demanding the resignation and prosecution of the entire government of President Offei.

CHAPTER 31
Police HQ, Accra
Thursday, 28th March; 6 A.M.

IT HAD NEVER HAPPENED before. A midnight protest was as unheard of in Ghana as a snowstorm. But such was the anger and spontaneity of the Ghanaian people that many could not wait for daybreak to register their disgust with the President and his government. And that turn of events had pissed off President Offei no end. He had refused to resign, of course, and had dismissed the entire Cabinet after the media blitz. Only executives of the ruling party had huddled together in the War Room afterwards to plan a strategy out of the predicament.

The Police Command arrived back at the parallel War Room with Vice President Domwine and half of the Cabinet to prepare the Articles of Impeachment to present to Parliament. That job fell to the politicians, while the IGP coordinated with the FPU – the Formed Police Unit – to contain the protests and to still protect the seat of government.

Opare and Aaron were still waiting inside the room when the functionaries arrived, and at the sight of him, it was apparent that he had been all but forgotten.

"Interesting night, correct?" he asked the IGP in an almost annoying understatement. "Even better, do I get to keep my Girls or not?"

"Who is this?" the CDS demanded when they had grabbed seats around the glass table. More chairs had to be brought in for the rest of them.

"These are the men whom we hired to extract the hostages – and the Girls," Amadu announced before the IGP could finish drinking his coffee to answer.

"Then where are the Girls?" the deputy Attorney-General quizzed.

"He is asking to keep them – at least until all this blows over," Vice President Domwine announced sardonically.

"That doesn't sound unreasonable," the Army Chief said, thoughtfully chewing on a lip. "As a matter of fact, it's a brilliant idea. If President Offei gets wind of their whereabout, he might have them killed, and then he would turn the full force of his defense on our inability to show he tried to have the hostages murdered. He blames the Girls squarely for this mess."

"Are we providing any protection for any of the hostages?" the finance minister demanded with a look of concern but Major Hanson, Amadu and Atukwei were already heading towards the door.

"You seriously think the President wants to add the murder of the hostages to his crimes?" the Immigration Chief asked in surprise.

"If you knew half of what we have seen, you might be inclined to believe even our very lives were in danger," the IGP told him.

"Exactly how did we get here?" the Interior Minister asked in perplexity.

"You got here because you overindulged the President."

The room turned to look at Opare. Their raised eyebrows did the questioning.

Opare looked back at them and shrugged, "The way I see it, the President was heavily affronted by the abduction of the justices of the Supreme Court. He became unhinged the longer the trial dragged on because the optics looked bad for him in an election year. But the Girls trying Duncan King and keeping the hostages after the release of the justices was the last straw for him. You contributed to it by not letting him know trying to hurt hostages wasn't going to wash. In his mind, they were no more than collateral damage. He took matters into his own hands and now here we are. Unfortunately, rather than have the whole case be about what the Girls had done, it is now more about what he has done."

"That's the more reason we wouldn't let you keep the Girls," the Vice President said. "We need them to prove to the country that we had a better way to resolve the problem without killing our own soldiers and innocent hostages."

"I agree with you in the proof part," Opare said, rising from his chair. "But I disagree with you on the keeping part. At least you know they are with me. And these ministers and functionaries are witnesses to what I am about to say. I will have the Girls do a video – with a newspaper or timestamp or whatever the heck will prove they are alive and well and have them post on their channels. In the day this blows over and a trial is demanded, I will present them at trial to answer for their crimes. This is as good a deal as you're going to get, and I suggest that you take it. If you insist on taking the Girls immediately, then I'm afraid you and whatever soldiers you send after us will have to bleed for the opportunity. Either way, we are leaving. The IGP has our number and knows how to find me."

He waited a full minute for the Vice President to make up his mind, but when neither he nor the other important people in the room seemed sure about what to do, he and Aaron bowed respectfully and walked out of the parallel War Room unhindered.

Dr. Mary Densua, the forensic gynaecologist at the Police Hospital in Accra who had been the star expert in Duncan King's murder trial at the Fortress had just finished examining her last rape victim of the day when she got called on her mobile phone that she needed to move her car. Another specialist needed to drive out of the overparked lot of the Police hospital, and her BMW was blocking his way.

Usually, she would have said something caustic to the guard, but she had an interview at a TV Station concerning what being a hostage of the Girls had been like. They wanted her perspective as a hostage, so she threw her stuff into her handbag and got the hell out of the consulting room before they sent another patient her way.

She looked in the direction of her car when she made it to the parking lot and stopped for a second. The lot wasn't as busy as she'd thought it would be. And her car wasn't blocking anyone either. The car park of the Police hospital was nothing but a field strewn with tar and chippings, and the corner of the field where she'd parked coming in this morning had thickly trunked trees with long branches that provided the shade she needed for her car from the usually hot sun. Over the past twelve months alone, she'd changed her leather covers twice.

Which is why she preferred to park there.

She looked suspiciously around and saw no one. She dialed the number of the guard that had called her and got no answer. She approached her car with a heightened sense of caution, looking around to see if anyone was watching her. Her plan was to quickly get into her car, activate the air conditioning and the door locks and look around to see who was playing pranks on her.

The man jumped off one of the branches of the nearest tree just when she'd opened her car door and shoved her hard enough to send her ungraciously across the driver's seat into the passenger seat, her head missing the window of that door by inches. She looked fearfully at her attacker and saw the gun he whipped out of a waist holster. She didn't wait to find much else out because she knew her car. She opened the passenger door and rolled off the seat and onto the hard ground, her surgeon's coat flying every which way. She quickly got off the ground and would have made a mad dash for the more open side of the car park when another man in dark clothing grabbed her around the waist, pulled her to himself and fired a gun.

It took a full minute for her to realise that the attacker in her car had been shot. Then she turned to look at the man holding her and the smoking gun.

"I'm Chief Superintendent H. Amadu with the Counterterror Police," he announced, looking over at her car to be sure the lone gunman was dead.

"We expected that hit men would come after you and the other hostages," He explained. "I was sent by the IGP to keep you safe. Seems I got here just in time."

All Dr. Densua could do was blink.

By noon, the hostages had been retrieved from their work and residences and handed over to the Witness Protection Unit of the Police Service. Vice President Domwine sat quietly inside the parallel War Room with what the media had termed the Run-away Cabinet. They had stayed abreast with the hostage retrieval process, and it had cost the lives of four yet-to-be-identified killers and one Police officer. No attempt had yet been made on the lives of the hostages that were government appointees, and the Police Headquarters itself was on high alert, as was Central Command of the Ghana Armed Forces. Now, President Offei had made no overt moves yet, and Parliament had accepted the Articles of Impeachment and was getting it ran through the House's procedures. The Chief Justice, being the third in line from the Presidency, had also been brought to the parallel War Room and briefed on the situation so far.

"Much as I hate to admit it," Dr. Domwine said quietly, "That Opare character was right. What I don't get is why the President has suddenly turned so dangerous. This is too straightforward an issue for him to be murdering soldiers and putting marksmen on the backs of hostages. What are we missing? These developments do not make sense."

"What are you thinking, sir?" the Chief of Military Intelligence asked.

Vice President Domwine looked pensive for a minute.

"I'm trying to construct the sequence of events in my mind again," he said. "First, the judges get abducted while he and I are on the ground on our butts. Then the Girls reach out and issue their ultimatums. The trial starts while we do our best to find our judges. Eventually, the judges are returned to us, and then Duncan King's trial starts. That's when he deploys the Army and all hell breaks loose."

"Up until he deploys the Army," the IGP chipped in, "everything was played by the book. But his intolerance and anger began to show more after Colonel Nartey was issued his commands, and he was not civil to any of us afterwards. We were his first anger-management casualties."

"What happened between when the judges were returned and the Army was deployed to cause such a seismic shift in his behaviour?" The finance minister asked.

"I think I have the answer," Obuobi came around from his cubicle behind the parallel War Room.

"The answer for President Offei's behaviour?" the IGP inquired.

"Fifteen years ago, he was accused of rape by Efe Plange, the woman who was Asabea's lawyer at the trial."

"Really?" a dozen voices demanded.

"Those allegations got dropped for lack of proper evidence at the English courts, but he couldn't practice as a lawyer for a while. The case was high-profile and no law firm would have him. Efe Plange was the daughter of the Ghanaian High Commissioner to the United Kingdom at the time, and there were talks that the High Commissioner had put a price on his head in the back alleys of East London. Four years later, years he spent paupering all over London, he came to Ghana and changed his name. His name before then was Harry Amponsah King. It's possible what the Girls did, and the role of Efe Plange in particular, got him to a point where anything was on the table so long as she stopped breathing."

Vice President Domwine blinked at the academic.

"You have a weird turn of mind, Prof," he said. "If President Offei used to be called Harry King, then his actions would be influenced more by his relationship with Duncan King than they would be by an antiquated rape allegation, even by one of the Girls."

Obuobi's eyes widened.

"Forgive me, but I was so focused on the Girls I failed to see the more glaring fact," he apologised. "Did he show any indication that he had an affinity with Duncan King during the events?"

"He did not, to be honest," Dr. Domwine said thoughtfully, scratching at his short beard. "If anything, he seemed more concerned about Ansah Premo."

"Are we alleging that President Offei is related to Duncan King?" the Chief of Defence Staff asked disbelievingly.

Obuobi slid quickly into the chair that was his at the other end of the table and got to work on his computers. The Run-away Cabinet watched his screens as the computer responded to his query and searched the government databases of several countries.

"Bingo!" Obuobi said with the slur that comes from talking around the lollipop stuck in his mouth. "They are direct cousins and lived together in London in the same house at the time of the allegations. President Offei's father, Hubert King, is the senior brother of Duncan King's father, Humphrey King."

"And nothing of these allegations came to light within the party for us to interrogate during the primaries?" the Vice President asked.

Obuobi scoffed at that until he caught the Vice President's disapproving look and said, "Political party primaries are not the place to find skeletons, your Excellency. Only money talks at those rallies, and President Offei had a lot of it four years ago."

"It's time for the media to draw the connection then," the IGP said without a hint of emotion. "Let's bring this business to a close."

The process to impeach a sitting president follows a specific set of constitutional procedures set out in Article 69 of Ghana's 1992 Constitution. The grounds for impeachment typically involve serious misconduct, violation of the constitution, or other high crimes, a circuitous procedure that until now had never been invoked. By nine o'clock, the Motion for Impeachment had already garnered the support of more than the one-third parliamentary membership threshold needed to proceed. And the speed to dispatch with the procedure was fueled by Parliament's fear that not acting decisively could force members of the Ghana Armed Forces to carry out their threat to oust the President through a coup and then dissolve Parliament itself, and that had already happened thrice before in Ghana's political history – in 1966, 1972, and 1981.

Now that the motion had passed, the Speaker of Parliament set up a committee to investigate the allegations against the President. The committee would gather evidence, conduct hearings, and assess whether there were sufficient grounds for impeachment. Amadu, Atukwei and the head of the CID were in charge of facilitating witnesses and assisting Parliament with its investigative work. Amadu had just returned to the parallel War Room from informing the Chief Justice, who had been required to return to the Supreme Court at dawn under heavy Police protection to receive the judicial copies of the Articles of Impeachment. By constitutional instrument, he would chair a tribunal with four of the most senior Justices of the Supreme Court to inquire, in camera, whether or not there was a prima facie case for the removal of the President after

Parliament was done with its investigations.

Atukwei had delivered the President's copy to the President and had reported that the President had complained that it was the Girls, and not he, who should be held accountable for the death of the soldiers, and that he would prove that for the world to see.

When he said so, Vice President Domwine asked, "What do we have so far on the Girls and their Rescuer?"

"We can trust Opare," the IGP told him. "We know where his business is, and he isn't going anywhere. If the Girls leave the jurisdiction, it's his butt we'd be hauling to jail."

"We are not tracking him or anything?" Umaru Tanko asked Obuobi disapprovingly.

"No, we are not," Obuobi responded absently, looking more frequently at one of his screens. "But we can find him when we need to. I wouldn't worry about Opare, to be honest. I'd worry about what President Offei intends to do now that he is about to be impeached. There's a lot of cryptic conversation going on between the Jubilee House and a particular office in Ouagadougou. I've been trying to crack it all night, but I'm not making headway with these equipment."

"You're eavesdropping on Jubilee House?" the Minister of the Interior asked with discomfort.

"We are always eavesdropping on Jubilee House," the IGP said unashamedly, like he couldn't believe the Interior Minister would ask a question like that.

"Yeah, but I don't recall a Professor Obuobi on any clearance list."

"These are special times, sir," Obuobi said noncommittally. Then he turned to the Vice President, "You think you can get me into SIGINT at the Bureau, sir? This is some advanced stuff, but if we can't break it, we might be dealing with the President from a blind spot."

"I can get you in there," Vice President Domwine assured him. "But what should I say is my reason to get you into Signal Intelligence when the National Security Minister asks?"

"That President Offei is seeking to contract Wagner."

Dr. Domwine stared.

"The mercenaries?" the information minister asked in surprise.

"They are the only ones we know in Burkina Faso with equipment I can't immediately hack," Obuobi explained. "And if the President is desperate, I need to know what he will do between now and when he gets removed. I need to move fast, too."

The Vice President made one call, and in two minutes, Dr. Obuobi was racing out of the parallel War Room like his weird hair was on fire.

"You think he's going to contract the Wagner Group to remain in power after his impeachment?" the Attorney-General asked. "How does he think our American and European security partners are going to feel about that?"

"We'll find out when Dr. Obuobi gets to SIGINT," the IGP responded wisely. Signals Intelligence, commonly known as SIGINT, is a branch of Ghana's National Security apparatus that performs intelligence-gathering through the interception and collection of information from electronic signals.

"Tell me," Umaru Tanko asked. He seemed bothered about it for a while. "Is he a professor or a doctor?"

The IGP chuckled. "In the US, he is Prof. Obuobi, but in Ghana and under the English system we inherited, he isn't a professor yet. It can get quite confusing for us but he doesn't seem to mind what we call him. Sometimes I just call him Moses."

CHAPTER 32
Lake Volta
Thursday, 28th March; 4 P.M.

LAKE VOLTA HAS over a thousand lacustrine islands, and Opare knew them all. His favourites were close enough to be reached by boat from the Akosombo hydroelectric power station, and they were close enough to shore to access supplies and fuel, and to receive his company's adventure customers. Both islands were also on the grid, meaning the Police knew about them and would consider them first if they tried to find the Girls. His team had sought to persuade him to hide the Girls in one of the more obscure islands deep in the interior of the Voltain basin, but he had rejected the idea, instead opting to hide in plain view. When the Girls informed him they had caches of weapons and ammunitions that could be delivered to make any island impregnable to the military, that had convinced his doubtful team, and the decision to inhabit and hold the twin islands – Survival and Discovery – was firmed up.

From the beach where the Girls and the rest of his team had been waiting, one of his larger boats first came to haul all their gear and equipment across the eight-kilometre expanse of the lake to Survival Island. A second boat came for them while the first was half-way to the island and the one-hour journey across the choppy water of the lake was over quite quicker than the fearful Dede thought it would be.

Increasing rainfall due to climate change had caused water levels to rise in the lake, held back by the Akosombo Dam. Where there once was sandy beach all around the island was water right to the tree line. Opare had already had a floating dock constructed as a result of the beach deluge, and it was to this that the boats docked, offloading their equipment and hauling them up a three-hundred-foot-long incline to the top of the island. The island existed as a peak of a mountain that had been too high to be swallowed up by the rising water when the Akosombo Dam was built in 1965, and the rocky land had withstood the waves of Lake Volta right up to this time.

Many birds called the island home, but it was too hot in the day to see them. And if she were half as smart, Asabea felt she too would have had no business hauling tonnes of equipment up the island in the stifling heat.

Opare had explained that Survival Island was one of the hottest spots on the lake due to the humidity brought on by the evaporating surface water, which then got trapped under the thick canopies of the heavily wooded island. He did explain it in geographic and climatological terms but she – and probably most of the Girls – had been too uncomfortable in the humidity to listen. Before they'd left the other beach, Opare had had Bubuné call in to their support units via the sat phone and had had the rest of their equipment and ammo delivered on the reception shore, and all that load needed to be hauled up to the top of the island. Opare ran her and the Girls like he was a drill sergeant, refusing to let anyone rest until everything was packed in neat stacks in storage bunkers built under the trees near the middle of the island.

It was only when everything was put in their proper place that Opare called for a rest. The Girls gave exaggerated sighs of exhaustion as they flopped heavily onto tables and benches built under a thick clump of trees near the island's centre. The island itself was rocky, but with enough top soil to support this many trees, and at the very centre of it was the campsite, built on elevated wooden platforms with tented structures on top to both minimize the environmental impact and offer a sense of elevation, allowing them all to relish the panoramic views of the lake, with its boisterous waters extending in all directions. The benches and tables were part of a communal area for dining, socializing, and campfire activities. The space was canopied by a lot of coconut trees, and the seating arrangements were quite open and comfortable. In the middle of this space was the bonfire pit for evening gatherings, storytelling, and stargazing.

Aaron and Kada brought coconut, which Owuraku and the Girls drank and ate ravenously to the amusement of the Rangers. After the refreshing drinks and the fruit, a couple of women came into the area with serving platters of braised rice, jollof rice, and fried yams accompanying several kinds of Ghanaian soups and sauces. Not much was said over the course of one hour as they tucked into the meal. Even the exhaustion was forgotten, to be remembered only if Opare and his Rangers came up with more chores in the immediately foreseeable future.

By the time dinner was done, and the tables cleared of all food residue because Opare had warned there would be an army ant invasion if food particles were left on the ground, it was already well past dark. The Girls retired to the eastern side of the island to take their baths while the males went west. The island had no electricity; but Opare had solar powered batteries on hand to charge phones, torchlights and their laptops. And it was around these power stations that they gathered before 9 p.m. to follow the evening news and to discuss Opare's trip with Aaron to Accra.

Opare and Aaron left little out of their report, but Owuraku and the Girls were left at the end of the telling feeling that there was a catch that would spring sooner or later, but Opare just shrugged it off.

"No way!" Asabea said. "They're just happy to have you hold us until they decide what to do with us?"

"Oh, they will come around to that eventually," Aaron assured her, "but they've got bigger fish to fry at the moment."

"And how long will that take?" Bubuné asked worriedly. "After the President is impeached?"

"Yeah," Aaron answered. "Because if they tried to haul you in now, President Offei might have you all killed."

"He did try to have us all killed," Owuraku reminded him. "What I still don't get is how you convinced them that finishing the job he started is bad for the Vice President, bad for the Police and bad for the country."

"That's because he had to murder half a battalion to try and justify the attempted killing of innocent hostages. That was his mistake. In hindsight, even he would admit that was a sick line to cross," Kada tried to explain.

"We get that," Bubuné said. "But why would Vice President Domwine let us off the hook? I mean, all of this is our fault. If we hadn't gone abducting and all, President Offei wouldn't have had soldiers killed. It all comes back to us. Why let us be for now? And it doesn't look like they have that much of an upper hand against Opare in any negotiation. You practically threatened to shoot up his own guards to prove that he wasn't as powerful as he thought he was, no?"

"You're right, it was easier than it should have been," Opare said quietly from his perch atop one of the tables, scratching thoughtfully in the light of the small fire at his short beard.

"What do you mean?" Dede asked in a startled voice.

"I expected they would march me out of their War Room with a platoon tasked with the job of torturing the truth of your whereabouts out of me and hauling you before a firing squad. While it wasn't exactly easy to persuade them, I really didn't think they'd let me keep you."

"Keeping my resentment of your allusion to us as a prized possession at bay," Oye said to him, "why did you march in to see the government if you didn't think they'd give you what you wanted?"

Opare shrugged. "It was the only way to gauge what was possible and what was not. As it turned out, once the murder of the soldiers came to light, your sins paled in comparison."

Nhyira made a face. "What are you, a priest?" she asked gruffly.

Opare continued with only a brief glance at the annoying twin, "As it stands, we must wait for the impeachment process to be completed, but I have this sense of – I don't know what to call it – dread? I just have this strong feeling that President Offei will attempt to have the very last word on what you have gotten him to do."

"We didn't get him to do anything," Bubuné protested.

"Did you think he was going to take your abduction of judges without a fight?"

"No, but we didn't ask him to murder his own soldiers. He was welcome any day to attempt to murder us, but killing hostages and soldiers was all on him, not on us."

"Agreed," Opare said tiredly. "Just how much weaponry and ammunition do we have?"

"Enough to stop a battalion – a platoon actually," Regina said and corrected. "Losing the drones was such a bummer."

"Perhaps it's for the better," Opare mumbled.

"What do you mean?" Asabea asked.

"Drones will draw attention to the island," he replied. "Best to do this the old-fashioned way if President Offei pulls in a surprise. We must keep watch and pay attention to who – or what – comes close to the island."

"Do you recommend closing the adventures here?" Aaron asked.

Opare thought about that for a minute.

"No," he said eventually. "Let's maintain normalcy in our operations. It will help to mask what we are doing here."

"But your clients might recognise us, won't they?" Owuraku enquired.

"Not if you remain in the underground bunkers when they're here," Wannah informed him.

"Underground bunk – you have underground bunkers?" Asabea asked in surprise.

"The top bunker you kept your ammunitions in have secret stairs that go thirty feet deep," Aaron said. "We'll show you in the morning."

"Please show us now," Dede insisted. "If the President comes attacking tonight –"

"– we'd have to repel the attack without hiding," Opare supplied. "It can wait till morning."

Dede seemed crestfallen for a minute. Then her eyes widened, and she asked, "Why on earth would you have a secret bunker on an island? Is there more to you than this adventure and jungle façade?"

Opare looked innocently at her and said, "Let's catch all the sleep we can. Tomorrow, we'll show you the island in its entirety, and plan how to keep you all truly off the radar."

It took three whole days to get the hang of living on the island. Nights were cool and almost cold because of falling dew from condensation, but days were brutally hot, and for all the wave action driven by wind on the lake, not much made it up to the high rise of the island. The few breezes that did were blocked by the trees that grew so close together they formed a wall the wind could not penetrate. Trips down to the beach and dips into the cool water of the lake were quite common among the Girls until Opare warned that their alternating cooling and heating adventures would cause their skins to peel the same way lizards shed their skin. That imagery kept them confined to the shadows under the trees, given how women feel about anything that would mar their presumably immaculate skins.

Those three days were also spent exploring the network of tunnels under the island. Some of them were big enough to drive a tank into, and crisscrossed the island in ways that meant they would be a subterranean nightmare for any invading force, allowing defenders to move around the island undetected, and destroying portions to trap invaders and make their lives miserable and short. The tunnels were constructed of concrete pipes, ensuring their structural integrity, and were ventilated by steel pipes pushed out into the topsoil and strapped to trees that concealed them from the unobservant eye because they had so much foliage around them.

"Did you say why you have these tunnels and bunkers?" Owuraku asked Opare over lunch the third day. He and his team had been particularly less talkative about their rationale for building tunnels.

"I didn't," Opare replied shortly.

"Oh, stop that!" Bubuné demanded waspishly. "You had these built in case you needed to hold off against an invading army. That much is obvious. What I don't understand is why you thought you needed protection from an invading army."

"That's what we are not telling," Wannah told her. "Just let it drop."

"But you'll let us use them if the Army comes knocking?" Aisha asked with her mouth full of tuna from the garden eggs sauce she was eating with boiled plantains.

"Yes, we would," Opare answered. "Which is why we must distribute all your weapons and ammo into the bottom sentries and stock according to the plan I shared two days ago."

Asabea looked thoughtful.

"Three days ago, you didn't seem interested in taking on the Army if they came hunting," she accused him.

"If they came asking nicely, there would be no need for a fight," he emphasized. "I am not having anyone's blood spilt on my island."

"If they came asking nicely, you'd hand us over to them for a trial, you said," Asabea said. "But there is nothing in our plans that included surrendering to the Police or the government. Why can't they just leave us alone knowing they'd be bleeding profusely if they came after us?"

"That would have been possible if we were inclined to go off-radar with you, but we've got a business to run and, unlike you, we prefer to live without a price on our heads," Aaron told her. "That's why we went to see the IGP. To take the heat off by letting him know we have you, and he trusted us enough to call off the dogs. We must keep our side of the bargain."

"Unless they lost interest," Opare added quietly.

Nhyira looked at him.

"You're going to make me ask, aren't you?" she said to him.

"What?" Opare asked, not understanding.

"You know," she said with a trace of irritation, "I think you speak in mysterious tones because you know it infuriates people."

"I don't know what you're talking about."

Oye sighed exaggeratedly also and asked, "What do you mean by 'unless they lost interest'?"

Opare glanced at Nhyira before responding, "Currently, they are focused on impeaching the President. This typically takes about a month, though realistically, it could drag on for three months given the lack of urgency in our country. President Offei is aware that you are alive, but he cannot publicly acknowledge that. Doing so would be detrimental to him legally because it would highlight his involvement in the deaths of the soldiers while you survived. The Vice President and the Inspector General of Police have built their case around the President's alleged murder of soldiers and his supposed attempt to have the hostages killed. For now, neither the President nor the rest of the government sees any benefit in revealing that you survived the attack. Your whereabouts are currently inconsequential to the case because you represent the Vice President's leverage over the President. If the President were to pursue you, it would be seen as a significant move that could nullify his portrayal of you as villains. Our strategy, if we manage to survive, is to make them lose interest in you."

"And if we don't survive?" Asabea asked carefully.

"Then we go down in a blaze of glory," Aaron answered. "The Vice President did think you'd be at risk if they brought you in for a trial. He knows what might happen if you got murdered. Much as they hate it, your cause has a lot of support among Ghanaians."

"The President is unhinged then," Efe supplied diffidently.

"He has been since you attacked his government," Opare told her. "Which is why I get the sense that we haven't heard the last from him."

"What do you want us to do?" Bubuné, ever the strategist, asked.

"Spread weapons at the designated points in the tunnels, and let's beef up our surveillance," Opare suggested. "I'll bring in my other Rangers tomorrow morning to assist, if we survive this night also. But we need your Stinger antiaircraft and Javelin missiles spread at the five corners of the island at the sentry points. We'll take turns watching in pairs, and I recommend three-hour shifts so watchers can remain alert."

"Are we positive the government doesn't know where we are?" Bubuné asked Opare.

"We are positive about the Vice President, but the President is another matter. He wants you all dead, and if it's the last thing he does before he goes down, he'll rest easy."

"And all this was revealed at the meeting with the IGP and Vice President?" Owuraku wanted to know.

"Essentially, yes."

"Might he use the Strike Force again?" Regina asked in a weak voice. "I haven't recovered from the loss of all our drones."

"I really can't say," Opare said. "All I know is we'd better get ready for anything."

CHAPTER 33
Survival Island
Friday, 29th March; 4 A.M.

NHYIRA HAD PAIRED up with Opare for the midnight shift on the western side of the island, and both had thick blankets draped over their heads as they sat on stools on a sentry platform at the same level as the trees. They had just relieved Asabea and Owuraku on that side who had both looked at them with knowing smiles when they'd climbed up the ladder to the post. Survival Island was pentagonal in shape, and their post faced the direction of the Akosombo Dam. They could see the lights from the hydroelectric town over the mountains thirteen kilometres away. The mountains formed the gorge that had enabled the construction of the gargantuan dam, and Opare preferred to stand guard facing the town, where he knew any government action was likely to emanate from.

Nhyira scanned the lake with her infrared binoculars. Other than a few local fishing boats, all was quiet on the lake. She reported that to Opare, who relayed that to Oye and Aaron on the northern side, Kada and Aisha on the eastern side, Bubuné and Wannah on the southern side, and Regina and Elikem on the south-eastern side. Then he took the binoculars from Nhyira when she was done and scanned the night sky.

"You're looking at the stars?" Nhyira asked him from a corner of the rectangular platform, hemmed in by wooden balustrades. The usual belligerence was absent in her voice.

"I'm trying to see if there are drones flying overhead."

"We'd hear drones," she told him matter-of-factly.

"Perhaps," he responded skeptically.

Nhyira looked at Opare when he sat down on one of the stools, a plain, dependable man, certainly older than he looked, wrapped in a blanket over his Ranger's uniform and at home in the wilderness setting of the island. His eyes did not seem dulled at all by the short, three-hour sleep he'd gotten from taking the first shift with Efe from 10 p.m. until 1 a.m. His alert eyes continued to scan the lake and the tree tops. His other Rangers' call up had been moved forward, and five new Rangers manned the missile mini silos, as they called them, from the ground below, to take out any drones or UAVs the government might throw at them.

Nhyira could not tell at what point the pacifist Rangers had switched from disinterest in weaponry to manning weapons systems. Opare himself carried two side arms on belt holsters and another one on a thigh holster. Strapped to his back, its muzzle sticking out from behind his head was a Heckler & Koch G28, a sniper rifle. Now that she thought about it, they hadn't asked to be taught how to use the rifles, and somehow, the Girls and Owuraku had not thought to question whether they knew how to use them.

That thought disturbed her, for some reason, and it brought to mind all her earlier discomforts with Opare since she'd led his pick-up from the Aburi gardens weeks ago. Even the newly arrived Rangers had taken to handling the Romanian Gepards as if that was something they did on a daily basis. She had so many questions, except she and her twin seemed to be the only ones asking them.

Well, here was her chance.

"How are we going to pass the rest of the night?" she asked quietly, in the tone of a person making small talk. But when Opare's eye brows shot up inquiringly, she remembered she had a perpetually husky voice that most men considered sexy. She started a little bit and said, "Not like that."

"Not like what?" Opare asked, slightly puzzled. Nhyira could tell, even under the light of the full moon, that his face did not associate any sensuality with her request.

"Never mind," she said eventually. "But are we just going to sit around doing nothing while we wait for something to happen? Talk to me."

Opare shrugged indifferently. "What do you want to talk about?"

"That's not at all how to hit it off with a woman, you know? Women like men who take charge, not men who ask, 'what do you want to talk about'," she reprimanded him lightly.

Opare smiled tolerantly when he said, "I don't mind the silence, to be honest."

That was not at all the response Nhyira was expecting, and her quick mind began to find his nonchalance a bit irritating. With some accuracy, it could be said that she found everything Opare said or did a bit irritating, only she couldn't explain why. She frowned as she chewed on that thought for a while.

Opare sighed and asked, "I take it that wasn't a good response to your question either."

"Why do you say that?" she asked him.

"Doesn't seem to take much to offend you, I've noticed, and I see your frown at my answer."

"I frown when I'm thinking."

"You've been frowning since I met you."

"I've been thinking since you met me."

"You don't seem to think much when I'm not close by," Opare quipped.

Nhyira looked at him in the light of the moon. The intervening space between them was no more than ten feet so she could see his face clearly, even shrouded on either side by the blanket, and he seemed genuinely interested in her answer.

"I honestly, don't know why," she answered truthfully. "At first, I thought it was because I did not trust you, but I sense it isn't that because you've proven yourself trustworthy."

Opare had no response to that.

"The thing is," Nhyira told him thoughtfully, "I kind of enjoy being angry at you."

Opare's eyebrows shot up.

She shrugged. "I'm true to my feelings."

"Feelings you share with Oye," he said wisely.

"That can't be helped, I guess. Only, she's a bit more objective than I am, and she thinks you're a little OK."

"I'm happy to hear that, at least," Opare said dryly.

Nhyira chuckled. "She thinks I'm in love with you."

Opare said, "Ha!"

Nhyira looked at him with her customary frown.

"Don't overthink my response," Opare said conciliatorily. "I'm only saying that would be a weird way of showing it."

"And whose fault would that be?" she asked, feigning complaint. "There appears more to you than you let on."

"And that makes me untrustworthy?" Opare queried. "You had guns and threats when I first met you."

"Then tell me who you are."

"You already know who I am."

"How do you know about guns and tactics and military hardware?"

"What?"

"None of you has asked us to teach you how to operate our guns. When we were down the shaft at the Fortress, you refused to handle a gun like it was a snake. But here you are, holstering three handguns and swinging a submachine gun. Where did you get your training in arms from if you're nothing but adventure Rangers?"

Opare looked a little amused but his face turned serious for a second before he fell on his back onto the floor boards of the post and signaled Nhyira to do the same. With his binoculars, he scanned the early dawn sky and found the object of his query.

"There's a reconnaissance drone overhead," he announced over his mouthpiece and read the sighting coordinates from the binoculars to the rest of the team. "Radio silence is imposed until it passes," he ordered. "But keep your eyes on it, and break radio silence if hostile maneuvers are observed."

There was a tense minute as the drone loitered over the island on the western side before hovering directly over the middle. And then it banked sharply away to Discovery Island to do the same. After five minutes, it returned to Survival Island to do a thorough reconnaissance.

"That should be enough, shouldn't it?" Bubuné demanded quietly over the radio. "If we allow it to loiter too long, it might gather information we don't want revealed. We need to shoot it down."

"Now that you have broken radio silence, we need to," Opare said crisply over the radio. Keeping radio silence would not have alerted the drone to electromagnetic activity, but now that someone had spoken over the radio, destroying the drone was the better defense strategy. He ordered his Rangers manning the south-eastern post to fire on the UAV.

It was over in a flash of fire and smoke. The shoulder-fired Stinger missile took out the spying drone in a matter of a second and sent what was left of it spiraling to the ground on the island.

"Stay put, everyone," Opare ordered. "And stay off the radio unless you detect another UAV."

"You don't want us to examine the drone?" Nhyira asked Opare directly.

"We will," Opare reassured her, while continuing to scan the sky. "There might be a backup drone behind this one. Recce drones move in pairs."

"And you the expedition guide will know this how?" Nhyira queried.

Opare did not answer because Aaron came onto the radio, announcing that a second UAV had appeared over the lake on the northern side.

"Prepare to neutralize," he instructed.

The drone came purposefully over the island seeking the exact point where the first had gone down and was also shot down by the team near Aaron's location. Regina moved in quickly with some of the Rangers to collect the debris and move them into the bunker and down to the tunnels. That exercise took an hour while the rest of the team scanned the lake and the sky to warn of any other incoming craft. By the time all seemed quiet again, it was almost 8 a.m., and time for breakfast. Another team of twos were manning the sentries when Nhyira and Opare sat down under the cover of the coconut trees for breakfast.

"Can we continue our conversation?" Nhyira asked Opare when she sat down next to him with a bowl of spicy yam pudding.

"Have you ever heard of SERE?" he asked her before dipping his spoon in his bowl for a bite of the hot meal.

"No, I haven't," Nhyira said after a short frown.

"It stands for Survival, Evasion, Resistance and Escape."

Nhyira thought about it for a while and then asked, "What is that?"

"It's an intensive global training course on how to stay alive behind enemy lines, and involves survival courses, outdoor education programmes and military simulations. Every Ranger or Master Guide is a certified SERE graduate. There's nothing about survival we do not know, and weapons handling are the least of our skills."

"Wow," was all Nhyira could think to say.

"Your mistrust of me was based on how you expected a hostage to behave. I did nothing of the usual, and that's what made you uncomfortable. I was not like any other abductee. You read that as a threat, and that's why you've been mean to me ever since."

"That's not the only reason she's been mean to you," Oye butted in from around the table when she plopped unceremoniously onto the bench beside her sister.

Opare raised his eyebrows inquisitorially.

"Have you told him, or should I?" Oye asked her sister.

"Let's see if he's smart enough to discover it," Nhyira replied with a slight twinkle in her eyes.

"Sometimes the smartest ones are the dense ones," Oye lamented. "I can bet this fool here will detect bees mating a kilometre away in the air but can't tell when a woman next to him is in love. I suspect it has to do with the whole Ranger training process. The curriculum needs to be overturned and rewritten. No education can be complete without a course on romance and copulatory buffing."

"Isn't that too many big words for a simple breakfast?" Asabea joined in at the table with Owuraku in tow.

"I could have said the same thing," Opare said with an amused look.

Bubuné also joined shortly with Aaron, and a quick debriefing ensued when Regina returned to the dining area to report her preliminary findings about the drones.

"They are Shahed-107s but with Russian components, and not the American Switchblades I was expecting," Regina reported.

"Where were they launched from?" Owuraku asked.

"From Accra, near Hanger 14 at the Kotoka International Airport."

"How's the hangar important?" Bubuné asked Regina.

"It's the presidential hangar," Opare supplied, before putting the last spoonful of his breakfast into his mouth and dialing a number on his sat phone.

"And you would know that how?" Asabea asked him, surprised.

Opare exchanged a quick look with Nhyira who smiled knowingly and said, "Opare knows everything."

Asabea seemed even more puzzled. "I thought you didn't like him," she complained.

"People change," was Nhyira's cryptic response.

Opare spoke into the phone for a short while and hung up. Then he turned to Asabea and said, "President Offei has contracted Wagner to hunt us down. Those were their drones."

"He can both work with the Americans and Russians?" Owuraku asked in bewilderment.

"Apparently so," Opare told him, rising to go and relieve the others so they too could come for their breakfast. "The Russians won't know this but the Americans will. Either way, we'd better prepare. President Offei wants you all dead for shizzle, my nizzles."

"How did you find this out in less than a minute on a phone call?" Bubuné demanded.

"That was Dr. Obuobi and Chief Superintendent Amadu I spoke with," Opare announced. "A minute was enough time."

"What do we do?" Oye asked worriedly.

"We need to eat first," Opare instructed. "Then we'll know what to do."

"We have enough confirmation now, sir," Dr. Obuobi was informing the Vice President in the parallel War Room with the run-away Cabinet. "Opare has confirmed that the Girls shot down two Iranian-made drones with Russian components at dawn."

"And you say the conversations you intercepted at SIGINT were between President Offei and the Wagner Group in Burkina Faso?"

"Precisely, sir."

Vice President Domwine turned to the Defence Minister and said,

"You have to inform our American allies of this development. As well as the African Union Ambassador."

"What do you expect them to do, sir?" the IGP enquired.

"It will be up to them," Dr. Domwine replied. "I think the Americans have done all they can for us, even though the information coming to light of their being used is making AFRICOM uncomfortable. As for the AU, it's one more evidence of how Russia is meddling in African matters."

Amadu, who sat next to Obuobi seemed thoughtful when he asked, "Wagner is a problem for the AU, correct?"

"Yes," the Vice President replied.

"And for the Americans too," the Defence Minister said.

"Do we know where they shot down the drones?" Amadu asked.

Obuobi's eyes widened at the question and his nimble fingers began to work his keyboards for a minute before he answered triumphantly, "Survival Island, where Opare's company runs their adventures."

"Are you sure?" the IGP demanded.

"I just accessed the Civil Aviation database," Obuobi said with confidence. "Two Shahed-107s left the presidential hanger for Akosombo after midnight and have been scouring the Lake Volta area. Both were downed several minutes apart on the larger of the Twin Islands."

Vice President Domwine smiled. "To think they were hiding in plain sight. Did we think to search the islands?" he asked the IGP.

"We did in the beginning," the IGP said. "We didn't think Opare would take them there when he knew he was the target of a manhunt."

"He's a smart man, I think we all concur," Amadu came to the IGP's defense. "But I see opportunities here as well. Now we know where the Girls are, and we know what President Offei plans to do to them. While his impeachment trial proceeds, doesn't this offer us a unique opportunity to put Ghana on the map?"

The Cabinet looked seriously at the Policeman.

"Do we know if Wagner troops are in-country?" Dr. Domwine asked the Defence Minister.

"There are a lot of troop arrivals at KIA now, but we thought they were Americans," the Minister said, reaching for his mobile phone. In one minute, he confirmed that a Russian Antonov An-12 transport plane had disgorged troops at Hanger 14 at the Kotoka International Airport inbound from Ouagadougou."

"Who authorized their arrival?"

"The Commander-in-Chief," was the Defence Minister's response.

"Is that legal? While he is under Articles of Impeachment?" Amadu asked in perplexity.

"He is innocent until impeached," Dr. Domwine said unhappily. "What can we do?" he asked the Defence Minister.

"We could go to the aid of the Girls."

When he felt everyone's censorious stare after speaking ahead of the Defence Minister, Atukwei continued, "It's the only way to get Ghana on the map as the African country that took on the Wagner Group. It will cement our standing with our ally, the US, and circumvent President Offei's schemes. There's no other way."

Vice President Domwine looked perplexed when he said to the Defence Minister, "Do you agree with him?"

The Defence Minister looked once at Atukwei and then at a very expectant Colonel Nartey and said, "He's right, your Excellency. A fight with the Russians is the only way out of the current situation. We cannot overtly challenge President Offei while he remains President."

"Nothing in the Constitution gives us power to stop a President under Articles of Impeachment? Even if he was doing something inherently evil?" Vice President Domwine demanded in surprise at the Attorney-General.

"Our constitution is sadly a presidential one, your Excellency," the Attorney-General responded sadly. "He has all the power until his removal."

"But the law allows us to instigate civil disobedience, and I believe that is what the IGP has been doing since his ouster from Cabinet," Umaru Tanko advised.

"It would be an uncivil disobedience if we deploy troops to take Wagner on," the Attorney-General pointed out.

"That's why it will be the counterterror Police," Amadu mentioned.

"And their friends in the military, who will be wearing civil Police uniforms," Colonel Nartey suggested seriously.

"When do we deploy?" the IGP asked, moving the conversation along before the skeptical Vice President had the chance to scuttle the plan.

Obuobi pulled out a map and said, "You could go by land to Asikuma and then access the Twin Islands reception through this dirt road here," he pointed it out. "You'll need the Marine Police's help, though."

"They'll be ready," the IGP said confidently. "How long do you think until Wagner hits the island?"

"By midnight, at least," the Defence Minister said.

"Let's get moving then," the IGP said with a cursory glance at the Vice President.

"We need to inform Opare," Obuobi said.

"I'd rather we didn't," Atukwei advised coolly. "He and the Girls have said they have all they need to fight a battalion."

"And the only way to safely reveal our presence is when Wagner is too engaged in the fight to worry about a hidden Police force," the IGP said. "Wait until SIGINT and Signals of the Ghana Army announce Wagner has committed all its forces before you attack. You could have them surrounded before they know it."

Obuobi said, "I don't think the Girls will survive if you wait too long."

"But Opare would," Amadu announced, to looks of surprise from across the table. "He'll keep his chargés safe to the last minute."

"You're going to wait for me ask how?" Vice President Domwine asked him irritably.

"He used to be a civilian instructor to the CTU before I took over from the last Commander," Atukwei said shortly, as if that explained everything.

With a sigh, the Vice President said, "Let's get moving then. Keep a zero-casualty rate on this operation, and I want updates every hour, understood?"

"Yes sir," the uniformed officers saluted and disappeared from the parallel War Room.

CHAPTER 34
Survival Island
Saturday, 30th March; 11 P.M.

THE CONSTRUCTION OF the port at Akosombo was initiated upon the discovery that Lake Volta provided favourable conditions for inland navigation. This development aimed to alleviate the strain on Ghana's road transport system and provide a more cost-effective and competitive route between the northern and southern regions of the country. Under President Offei's administration, a commendable initiative was the expansion of rail lines from coastal ports to the Akosombo inland port. This strategic move aimed to facilitate regional balance and foster resource development by unlocking the agricultural and industrial potential of Ghana's economically disadvantaged northern regions. Of course, a full half of the 21-billion-dollar project would end up in the pockets of politicians and their side chicks, and one such side chick, the PA to the Chief Engineer of the Akosombo Port, was counting some kickback money late into the night when her boss called her to demand she step out and oversee some transfer of goods from a freight train onto the dock.

"Transfer of goods at almost midnight?" she wondered to herself. "What kind of goods was the Volta River Authority transporting by lake at this ungodly hour?"

She stepped out of her first floor counting room and looked out over the railing at the dock. The cranes were hauling teams of cargo carts onto the dock. Light from more than a hundred torches bounced around out of the cars but a bullet found the back of her neck before she could count how many armed men the train had brought.

Over the past decade Wagner operatives had been providing security to African leaders seeking to stay illegally in power, as well as boots on the ground to fight rebels and extremist groups alongside underequipped national armies. Operatives had been accused of widespread torture, mass killings and rape in Mali, Burkina Faso and in Niger where they operated south of the Sahara. Wagner's ambitions in Africa had been the talk of many speculators; that they were able to deploy very quickly under the invitation of President Offei spoke to one aspect of their ambitions – ready guns for hire. With 1,645 Wagner personnel in Mali alone, the Ghanaian president had no difficulty securing the services of a hundred or so operatives to do what his own Army could not do. Even when his closest advisers had asked him to call off the operation, President Offei had been too frightened to contemplate withdrawing his request because of Wagner's iron-fisted methods.

In spite of its fearsome reputation and brutal tactics, neither the Russian military nor Wagner itself had been able to escape infiltration by the American intelligence establishment, and this is how Atukwei, Amadu, Colonel Nartey, Major Hanson and a hundred other counterterror officers could follow the movement of twenty-five speedboats and a dozen drones from the Akosombo Port to Survival Island. They were no more than four kilometres away from the island on the opposing shore and could hit the island in a minute once Wagner was engaged by Opare and the Girls.

"I still wish we had given Opare some advance warning," Obuobi, who was manning the communication side of the counteroperation on behalf of SIGINT said from behind a camouflaged booth full of computers and consoles in the thick of the Anum jungle – the general name for the biodiversity surrounding the islands' side of Lake Volta.

"That call we had was enough warning," Amadu said quietly, his alert eyes measuring how long it would take Wagner to reach the island on Obuobi's consoles.

"We might lose some of the Girls," Obuobi said worriedly.

"It's a war, my friend," Colonel Nartey, standing quite comfortably near the booth and donning a Police vest, said with his eyes also on the tracking screen Atukwei held in a hand. "And it would look weird in this story if one or two of the Girls didn't die in this their quest."

Obuobi gave the Colonel one peculiar look but said nothing more.

Asabea stood watch with Opare and Owuraku on the southern platform when the first speedboats came into the view of their infrared binoculars.

"How many can you count?" Owuraku asked Opare.

"Twenty speedboats – wait, twenty-five. There are several lagging behind."

"How many in each?" Asabea asked. Her eyes could not do a proper count of bodies in each boat over the dark, boisterous lake.

"Twelve in each," Opare answered.

"That's three hundred mercenaries," Asabea did the math. "Just to recap, our best chance is to blow them all out of the water, right?"

"Let's blow as many of them out as we can," Opare said to her, and to the mouthpiece hanging near his lip. "But they have a drone cover of eight," he announced. "We need eyes in the sky."

"I'm on it!" Regina announced in the earpiece. She had salvaged what she could of the first two drones and had managed to reengineer one of them to fly with parts from the other. Buzzing like an oversize mosquito, the reconfigured drone lifted off the middle of the island, hovered for a bit, then raced toward the fast-approaching boats. With a pair of virtual reality goggles strapped around her head, Regina used joysticks to steer the craft and its payload of about a kilogramme of explosives towards the mercenaries.

Now that they were sure Wagner was attacking from the south, Opare moved his Rangers and most of the Girls to the south side, leaving no more than four – Dede, Efe, and two armed medics – to watch their northern and eastern flanks. He stood on the outpost with Owuraku and watched the drone approach the Wagner operatives in their binoculars. Opare was curious about how Wagner would react to their loitering munition.

When the drone arrived above the first couple of boats unimpeded, Opare said to Regina over the radio mouthpiece, "Can you drop the payload without harming the drone?"

"I think so," Regina said back. "They don't seem to have noticed us above the combined noise of their outboard motors."

"They will, after you bomb them," Owuraku added quietly.

"If there's a chance to save the drone, let's," Opare said wisely.

The drone dropped its payload, and three boats were taken out with devastating accuracy. A fourth boat had a hard time navigating the ripples that followed the missile explosion, eventually dunking its occupants into the dark waves of the lake. The other boats swung out in a wide arc to avoid the epicenter, and it was the signal Aaron and his team of shoulder-firing rockets needed to target the remaining boats.

"Can I get a sitrep on the drones?" Bubuné inquired in the earpieces.

"They are almost overhead," Regina reported as she tried to bring back her drone to reload. She didn't understand why her drone had not been attacked yet.

"What can we do with one drone against eight?" Asabea asked from the designated frontline, a copse of trees that lined the southern beach of the island. Wagner's boats were no more than a quarter-hour's distance from the island now, and two of them were struck by Aaron's and Kada's RPGs. Twenty more still bore down on them in bouncing sprays of speeding deadliness.

"We must first take out the kamikaze one," Opare said of the drones. "We could try and shoot the rest with the Javelins.

Barely were the words out of his mouth than one of the Wagner drones swooped down on the roof of their outpost. With surprising alacrity, Opare grabbed the startled Owuraku by the belt and jumped off the landing backwards towards the leaves of the trees beneath them. Not even the painful landing prepared them for the shock waves that the exploding drone generated, and on the ground, all they could do was lie down and wait for the painful ringing in their ears to subside.

"Are you all alright?" Asabea demanded worriedly in their earpieces, which accentuated the ear-shattering din so much that Opare pulled the device out of his ears just to keep his temporary insanity in check. Some branches had slowed down their fall, but it didn't feel like that at all in his bones where he had made impact with the brushy undergrowth.

Owuraku was on the ground, bleeding from behind an ear. His left ear had caught a prickly vine on the fall from the watch platform and bore a deep cut from the helix to the lobule. How Opare saw all that in spite of the pain in his head beat him, but he pulled out his first aid kit from his mini backpack and got out a wad of cotton wool. Owuraku was too locked up in the throes of his headache to notice his own ear was bleeding. Opare balled the wool and pressed it against the professor's ear. Then he pulled him off the ground with both their heads ringing and pointed to the frontline.

In spite of all that head throbbing, Owuraku understood Opare's exaggerated gestures, held the cotton wool in place with his left hand, and staggered after the Master-Guide towards the forested shore. All around them were explosions, and Owuraku hoped Asabea was alright as they ran towards the shore where they guessed Wagner's forces might have already attempted to beach.

Sure enough, the Rangers and the Girls were firing incessantly at the boats. Even in the dark, bodies could be seen bobbing up and down with the waves. The carnage on the lake would have been complete if the drones hadn't been harassing the defenders, and Opare was surprised no one had been seriously hurt so far. He ordered his Rangers to keep firing at the boats while he and Aaron made it their immediate purpose to neutralize the drones.

It took three Stingers and four missiles to do the work of downing the drones, and two of them released incendiary gases that lit up a part of the forest with fire near the frontline when they exploded. The searing heat swept over the defenders near the shore, and there would have been all kinds of degrees of burns if Opare hadn't shouted for those closest to the fires to jump into the lake from their elevated shore.

While six of the defenders were jumping to their escape in the water, Bubuné and Aaron were firing RPGs at the almost beached mercenaries who had started to fire back at them on the island. They eliminated four more boats in the process.

"We need to cover the jumpers," Opare warned Asabea, who had been out of the range of the inferno that had temporarily swept over the lowest parts of the defense line. "If any of them beach, they will spot and shoot at them," he said as he raised his pistol and fired off several shots with practiced accuracy, dropping five bodies out of one of the approaching boats. With those deaths, the remaining boats – numbering twelve now – swung out of the way of all the artillery aimed at them towards the northern shore of the island.

"The jumpers will be safe at least," Bubuné said and tore after Opare, Aaron and Kada, who, once they saw the rest of the boats swing away from the southern shore, had begun to race along the island's trails to prevent their landing.

"Who's in the water?" Asabea demanded of the team below her on the frontline.

"All of us, I think," Owuraku shouted up from below where small waves were washing the shore. "I am here with Aisha, Efe, Nhyira, Oye and Elikem. We are coming up now."

"Is everyone alright?"

Owuraku hesitated for a second before saying, "Nhyira lost some of her long hair, Aisha lost her hijab to the flames, and Oye has a little burn on her left hand; otherwise, we are all alright. Where is Opare?"

"He is running to the northern beach with Bubuné and most of his Rangers."

"We need to join him then," Owuraku said panting. He and his motley crew of jumpers were now running up the island to the centre. "Our best chance is to prevent them from beaching no matter what."

Opare's strategy was not to relinquish their current momentum to the mercenaries, else they would find themselves outmanned and outgunned. Russian warfare doctrine centred on amassing enough operatives or soldiers to storm a defense line and overwhelm the defenders, and true to form, over three dozen mercenaries were racing towards the trees when Opare, Bubuné and the rest of the Rangers joined Dede and Efe on the northern side. Efe and Dede were already firing at a wave of mercenaries who were screaming and shooting even before they beached. The other waves were cut down in horrifying fusillades from Opare and his newly arrived team.

Out of one of the nine remaining boats still some half-kilometre out on the lake, four more drones took to the air, banked sharply out of the range of the defenders' sniper weapons and fired the incendiary weapons again at the island.

"Aim for higher ground, everyone," Opare warned sharply.

"What about the plan to prevent them from stepping foot?" Bubuné demanded.

"Did you see the fire those things burned from the south end? We have to abandon that plan now!" Opare shouted to be heard above the explosions as he fled up to the top of the island. "Stay in the trees but keep going higher."

"What about everyone else that isn't here?" Bubuné demanded.

"Ask them to race towards the bunkers," Opare replied breathlessly. "So long as we remain out of sight of those drones, we'll be fine for the moment. We need to stop firing so we do not give our positions away until the last moment when we can see them."

"We still need eyes on the beaches, though," Wannah warned in the earpieces. "I think the boats have landed north and north-east now."

"Can we do anything with our drone?" Asabea's voice demanded.

"We are about to find out," Regina said determinedly in the earpieces. Her drone quickly went airborne and was just as quickly shot down in a flurry of shells that lit up some of the trees and forced Regina and her small team of nerds into the cover of the other trees.

"We need missiles near the bunkers!" Vernal screamed into his mouthpiece.

"We are coming with them," Kada responded from where he and a couple of Rangers were hauling the portable weapons through the trees.

"Do we know where all the mercenaries are at the moment?" Asabea asked when she caught up to Opare and Owuraku at a point above the first tree lines designated as Defense Line Two, a line that was the shoulder of the island's contour. Those trees were higher than the trees of the first line and provided the advantage of exposing anyone below that line but concealing the defenders above it.

"I have stationed Rangers who have eyes on all the twelve trails coming up," Wannah announced when he arrived at the eastern side of the line. Anyone that pops up out of the trees from below will be dead before they know it."

Gunfire abruptly erupted from the eastern line. Owuraku and Opare opened fire from the northern line in response and took out four mercenaries in short order.

"Report ranges of sight," Opare ordered.

"One hundred and eighty degrees on the eastern side," one of the Rangers announced in the earpieces. "All clear."

"One hundred and eighty on the southern side," reported another. "All clear, except floating mercenaries."

"About ninety degrees on the north-eastern side," Aaron announced from his new position. "A boat full of mercenaries has been taken out."

"We have mercenaries approaching cautiously on the northside," Opare informed them. "I need total radio silence until I say otherwise. Use your heads from here onwards," and then he switched off the entire comms control from his device.

Now came the waiting game.

There were now a total of thirty-three people defending the island. Asabea's team from the Fortress remained a solid nineteen people and, together with the arrival of new Rangers, Opare had augmented the team with his fourteen. Most of the defense plans had been drawn by Bubuné the previous night, but Opare had reminded her of what Mike Tyson had once said.

"Everyone has a plan until they get punched in the mouth."

Asabea looked carefully through her weapon's scope at her designated watch at Line Two. She was on the ground, camouflaged against a rock and the undergrowth. Owuraku laid to her right, and the silent Opare was on her left, covering the ninety degrees of clear sight they had from their position to the beach. Not far from Opare was Nhyira who, in the confusion that had followed the second wave of drone attacks, had found her way to Opare's side.

It seemed the mercenaries had learnt a few lessons from the earlier chastisement and were no longer obvious targets on the trails or under the trees. Only their drones kept scouring overhead, trying to pierce the density of the canopy to land a strike.

She looked over at Opare when she sensed a certain restlessness from his position. He had turned onto his back and seemed to be taking aim at one of the drones. He seemed to change his mind at the last minute as a thought occurred to him. He signaled silently with his hand and pointed to a nearby tree. Then he quickly slung his sniper rifle behind him and scurried up the tree over a look of protest from Nhyira.

During their training in Libya, Asabea had discovered that the majority of military and counterterror snipers were known as marksmen, capable of shooting people at around three hundred metres. Then there were scout snipers who could take out a man two kilometres away. Those were experts, because to do that, they needed to account for wind speed and direction, temperature and barometric pressure before slightly depressing their triggers. As far as she could tell – and the look of disbelief that had crossed Nhyira's face at Opare taking aim through the tree's branches let her know she wasn't alone – Opare was no sniper. Also, pulling the trigger would come at a cost. The drones may have trouble reading thermal heat signatures of people in the intense humidity of Survival Island, but no drone can mistake the heat signature from a fired weapon. That kind of exposure required that the reward of the kill needed to outweigh the risk.

Before she could signal her disagreement to Opare, she heard the shot. And almost instantly, one of the drones buzzed towards their position.

They had been found out.

She got up as hastily as she could – Owuraku and Nhyira did the same – and was about to race out of there when she saw Opare catch the drone with his hands from his perch in the tree. Then he flipped the vehicle over and disabled it. He let it drop into Nhyira's hands and indicated with hand signals to convey it to Regina.

Nhyira nodded her understanding and disappeared. Opare repeated his attacks and downed another drone. Shouting, in what Asabea assumed to be Russian, could be heard not too far from the beach after the third drone was lost to Wagner's troops.

"How are you doing that?" Asabea whispered to him up his tree.

"I'm killing their drone operators," Opare whispered back.

"You can do that?" This was Nhyira, who had returned from the bunker where Regina and her nerds were working on the drones.

Opare shrugged and gave one last sweep of the beach with his scope. It seemed the operatives had found a good reason to stay concealed on the ground. He was about to get down off his tree and resume his watch on the ground when he heard them. He gazed at the lake from his perch and verified the phenomenon from his binoculars. A swarm of drones were flying in from the south – a hundred or more, as far as he could count. He jumped off the tree, turned on everyone's radio and said as calmly as he could muster, "We have a hundred drones coming at us."

"What do we do?" Asabea asked worriedly. "How long until they hit us?"

"Three minutes tops," Opare answered calmly, and then told Owuraku, "Get yourself and the Girls into the bunkers now!"

"What do you plan to do?" Bubuné asked on the earpieces, sounding as worried as Asabea.

"If those drones attack, it means the troops down there do not intend to come up until it's over," Opare answered. "It makes the beach the safest place to be. The Rangers and I will take the fight to them while the drones are attacking. By the time it's over, there shouldn't be a mercenary on the shore alive."

"Do we know how many there are?" Nhyira demanded.

"Probably sixty to eighty men, but it doesn't matter. Get into the bunkers now!"

"We are on our way to the northside then," Wannah announced.

"I'm going with you," everyone heard Bubuné tell Wannah on the radio, packing her weapons and getting up after him, whom she had been watching the eastern side with.

"And I'm staying with you as well," Nhyira told Opare.

"Those suckers are about to swamp us," Opare warned her, not unkindly. "You've already seen what one kamikaze drone can do. Get into the bunkers and stay there. We'll be fine."

"I'm as good a fighter as Bubuné," she complained.

"I know you are, but this is for the best. Those things will breathe more fire than we can risk."

Nhyira seemed unsure until Asabea gravely insisted they needed to listen to the Master-Guide.

Wordlessly, she walked over to him, moved her weapons out of the way, threw her arms around his neck and kissed him seriously on the lips. Then she pivoted on her feet and disappeared into the trees towards the bunkers.

CHAPTER 35
Survival Island
Sunday, 31st March; 2 A. M.

MAYBE THE IDEA was to incinerate the island and turn all its trees into charcoal. Perhaps it was to flay the defenders alive and give them a taste of Russian barbarism and brutality. The more plausible excuse was that three hundred Wagner mercenaries had been killed by a little more than a tenth of that number in Rangers and Girls, and someone needed to pay for that inexplicable imbalance. Burning Survival Island would provide a coda to a week of political chicanery for President Offei.

Incendiary weapons, among the cruelest munitions used in contemporary armed conflict, produced heat and fire through the chemical reaction of flammable substances, especially napalm and phosphorous, and caused excruciating burns. Survivors of an initial attack often experienced organ failure, lowered resistance to disease, lifelong disability, muscle weakness, and psychological trauma, and the first reaction to the use of incendiary munitions was that the air itself became so hot that any lungs that breathed in the sublime residues suffered immediate inflammation. This was why Opare had ordered the defenders in the immediate vicinity of the first use of the munitions to go below the point of explosion and towards the water, where they had found relief and protection from the weapon's wake.

But the shelling this time was indiscriminate, and evergreen trees turned instantly to char wood from the onslaught of the drones. It was a good idea to have believed that Wagner might not attack their own operatives at the beach. He and his Rangers had caught them by surprise when they went after them. The operatives believed he and the Girls would be too busy trying to hide from the drones to brave an assault. Now that they had killed all of them, the drone operators, most likely observing and attacking from the port at Akosombo, would not know that there were no Wagner survivors until the black smoke and fires from the attacks subsided. After that, nothing would stop them from attacking and destroying the island with a literal, scorched-earth abandon.

"What do we do now?" Wannah asked Opare while looking worriedly at the fire bearing slowly but surely towards them from the top of the island. "Do you think the bunkers can withstand this inferno?"

Opare looked up worriedly as well.

"We've never had to test them with incendiary munitions, so I can't really tell. But the only way to stop this is to take out the drones."

"And how do you propose we do that?" Aaron asked half-sarcastically. "We dare not leave this beach, and if the drones circle back to check up on their comrades, we are barbecue."

Opare thought pensively for a while. He seemed less and less sure the longer he thought. Radio communications had not worked since the attack.

"Can a couple of you try to get to the south end?" he eventually asked. "I need to know if they're going to send in any more mercenaries. What we do next depends on that information."

"I'll go," Aaron volunteered. "I'll take Dennis with me so he could run back with the information you need."

"Thank you," Opare said simply.

The wait was a nervous one. For one, the blazing inferno was not letting up from above, as more and more drones exploded across the island, causing Opare and Bubuné to worry about the rest of the team holing down in the bunkers. With the water level in the lake at its highest ever, Aaron and Dennis would have a harder time covering the five hundred metre distance between the north end and the south end over slippery rocks. Accessing the south end by the trails would expose them to phosphoric flames, and the impact of a lot of the drones had caved some parts of the tunnels in on the south side. By the beach, at least, they could dive into the lake to minimize their exposure if they got fired upon.

Half an hour later, Dennis was back with grim news.

"There's another twelve boats or so coming at us from Akosombo," he reported. "Aaron thinks they could get to us in about half an hour."

Opare looked relatively hopeful.

"That's twice as much time as we need to get to the south end from here so we have to split," he assessed. "Half of us can try to hold them off while the other half tries to pull the Girls to the northeastern beach before they cook in the bunkers."

"I don't think that's a good idea," Bubuné advised. "We trained for scenarios such as this. Let's each do what we must, trusting that the others would do what they must to stay alive. Let's focus on the new threat instead."

Opare nodded and asked, "I assume we have run completely out of Javelin missiles?"

"We have only five left," Kada replied.

"And there are fifteen of us here if I include Aaron. I need four Rangers on the southeastern side, and three Rangers with me here. The rest of you will go to Aaron and take the fight to the mercenaries. If any avoid you as they did earlier, those of us here can finish them off. I suspect some may swing towards the eastern side to escape the southern fires, and that's when I need some of you there. Leave us two shells with one stinger here. We'll need to take out any drone-laden boats that will attempt to add on more fire."

An electric jolt of lightening flashed across the sky just then, no doubt brought on by the sudden heat engulfing the island and pushing thermals towards the atmosphere.

"Good luck, team," Opare said before he dismissed them towards their positions. He took his three Rangers up the contours of the island as close to the fires as he safely could and assembled one of the Javelin systems.

"Let's take out a couple of drones and see if the other drones might come to investigate," he said. "I'm uncomfortable with having to take on enemies on the water and in the air at the same time."

After a few minutes, one of the drones loitered above a nearby tree with its mounted camera facing south, presenting the opportunity that Opare had been hoping for. Wordlessly, his team fired on the drone.

"Reload and prepare to fire again," he calmly advised Stephen, the Ranger manning the system. A quarter of a minute later, another drone buzzed angrily into view, its camera facing the triangulated source of the Javelin shell. It, too, received the same treatment as the first.

"Now they know we are still alive," Opare said quietly. "Get your rifles ready. I believe a third drone might come around to verify."

On the southern end of the island, Aaron and Bubuné watched the approach of the boats in their night-vision binoculars while five other Rangers hauled themselves up the trees that were not yet affected by the fire destroying the island. Dawn still seemed a far distance off, but the moon shone bright over the now-quiet lake, giving a silvery tinge to everything they saw, except inside the binoculars.

"How close do you intend to let them get to the island before we welcome them?" Bubuné inquired, measuring that it would be a couple more minutes before the mercenaries hit the beach.

"Close enough to see the look on their faces," Aaron said with meaning.

"They'll shoot back at that range, you know?" Bubuné warned.

"I'd be disappointed if they didn't," Aaron replied, just before thunder struck loudly over the island and ushered in a sudden downpour. They both were drenched, even under the thick cloister of trees at the beach within seconds, and Bubuné directed one hell of a surprised look at Aaron.

"The fires," Aaron said by way of explanation, with water dripping from the end of his nose. "It might help us pick the mercenaries off one by one even at this distance, don't you think?"

"I agree," Bubuné answered with a look upwards from under the trees they were shivering under now. "But the rains will help the drones to easier detect our body heat signatures," she worried.

"One trouble at a time, my friend," Aaron cautioned. "You yourself said it. Let each take care of their shit, and everyone else's shit would be taken care of."

Bubuné looked at him. "I said no such 'shit'," she protested.

Aaron looked back at her.

"Or shit to that effect," he corrected carelessly. "Here they come."

There were twelve boats in columns of three less than a kilometre away over a lake that had suddenly turned boisterous from the flash flood. The waves forced the boats to slow down. Before Aaron could give the order to start firing, a large Reaper hovered suddenly above them with its guns and camera trained on the approaching boats. With his eyes opened in the rain with surprise, Aaron looked at Bubuné and his Rangers and put his fingers to his lips, demanding total quiet. They looked up at the drone, whose rotors were whirring the vehicle steady before bursts of missiles streaked from its large body towards the approaching boats.

Ten more drones assembled side by side near the first one, and in ten minutes, not even the angry waves of the lake could conceal the bloody aftermath of the Reapers' strikes. When it was plain that no mercenaries had survived, the drones buzzed off towards the mostly punctured and sinking boats as if to ascertain that none were alive, before dashing back to the top of the island where the rain had put out any remaining fires.

"What the frack is going on?" Aaron asked no one in particular.

"It can't be Regina," Bubuné mused in the still-angry downpour. "All our drones were destroyed at the Fortress."

Aaron looked across the lake one more time, as if to ascertain that all the boats had really been taken out, and then he ordered, "Then let's get up there and find out what's going on."

After kissing Opare – and on the lips of all places – Nhyira refused to think about why she'd done that. Instead, she focused on the task at hand and led Owuraku and Asabea up the trails to the top of the island where the main entrance to the bunkers was. The rest of the Girls were already assembled around a couple of the drones that Regina had managed to shoot down with theirs.

One of the fallen drones emitted a shrill whistle, and before they comprehended what that meant, six drones buzzed overhead and rained incendiary munitions on them that sparked blazes of fire. If it hadn't been for the thick trees surrounding the opening to the bunker, their stories would have differed. Even then, Aisha and Efe received shrapnel in their left arms from grenade blasts hurled by some of the drones. Even after Owuraku had manhandled them into the bunker opening and closed the steel hatch over their heads, the concussions had them walking along the tunnel's walls like drunken people.

But in a few minutes, the cool, earthy feel of the tunnel gave way to oven-heated humidity, and when Owuraku accessed what looked like a periscope on one side of the tunnel walls, all he could see was phosphorous streaks emitting from shells that ignited the air and created the infernos.

"You think the tunnels will withstand the heat?" Asabea asked him with concern. She was already sweating profusely.

"I don't know, but Opare mentioned there were six emergency exits. Let's find them and prepare to leave if it gets any hotter than this."

Nhyira turned to him and said, "It already is hotter than it should be."

She walked down further into the tunnel and found walkways extending in six directions. Each one felt relatively cooler than the chamber they were presently standing in.

"I think I've found one of the escapes," she announced.

"Where does it go?" Aisha asked, holding the injured arm that one of the medics had treated and disinfected. Sweat was pouring off her face and made her extremely uncomfortable.

"We'll know when we split," Asabea said, already walking towards the nearest one to escape the heat that was swirling around the chamber. The others did the same for the other four.

All the exits led downwards to the trees marking the end of the beaches from the northeastern to the southwestern corners. They ended at steel doors camouflaged by boulders and rocks on the outside, as well as by shrubs and some bushes. Nhyira held her door open inward with a rock to let in as much cool air from the beach as possible before she dashed back to the chamber. She could not re-enter because the heat had turned the chamber into a furnace. She raced back to her opening to find that the other Girls had congregated by her northeastern beach, looking on nervously as the tree line on that side so far held against the fires bearing down on them from the top of the island.

"Do you think Opare, Bubuné and the others will survive this?" she asked in a weak voice as the trees above the fifty-metre contour crackled and spat sparks in reaction to the searing heat generated by the incendiary munitions being relentlessly rained down by the drones.

"It's Opare's Island," Oye remarked. "If anyone can survive this, it would be him."

It wasn't long afterwards before Nhyira realised that they were trapped at the beach. Whipped by infernal winds, the firestorm had raged its way northeast toward her and the others and now formed a horseshoe with the trees on the northern side that hadn't yet caught fire.

Kada and one other Ranger came tumbling out of the tunnel exit on the east side until he too saw the fire from the northeast side. He knew there was only one place to go – toward the water. He guided the Girls and Owuraku to scramble over knee-high rocks to the actual beach of the island on this side and took refuge on the tiny strip of rocky beach by the water.

"Where's everyone else?" Nhyira asked Kada, shouting to be heard above the noise of the attacking drones.

"I don't know," Kada replied. "Opare asked us to keep an eye on the reception near the eastern side, and that's what we were doing until the fire got to us. We escaped it by jumping into a caved-in tunnel and here we are."

Asabea asked curiously, "Why did he ask you to keep an eye on the reception?"

"You'll have to ask him when you see him," Kada replied, and tried to look around the trees and vegetation spread over the water's edge to see if he could still see the reception from here.

The fire roared through the rest of the trees that had hitherto been untouched and unleashed a choking wall of thick smoke down towards them. The oven-like heat pushed them farther down to the water's edge until they had to drop their weapons at the edge, sit tight in the water itself, sometimes submerging themselves under the gentler waves on that side to cool themselves down. Even then, the hot embers left Nhyira's sleeveless arms with some burns. Her eyes were seared by smoke, but she was more worried about Opare and the rest of the Rangers.

"Are those boats approaching?" Owuraku inquired, pointing a surprised finger across the lake to the opposite shore where Opare's company had their reception.

"Seems so," Kada responded, his face registering wary interest as he gazed thoughtfully at the boats – numbering ten in all – that were approaching the island in an awful hurry.

"Let's get ready to fight," Nhyira said grimly as she got out of the water and reached for her weapons. She wished she could warn Opare and Bubuné, but the fires seemed to have extinguished all radio signals.

Then a drone buzzed overhead and prepared to release the incendiary bombs.

Without thinking, Kada and Nhyira opened fire and shot at the Shahed. The drone banked quickly out of the way when the first bullets grazed one of its propellers, righted itself over the water and was about to release its weapons when a bigger, fixed wing Reaper emerged high above it in the air and shot it down into the lake. The Shahed exploded on the surface, and its munitions were doused by the suddenly rambunctious waves. That incident was the precursor to a sudden downpour that shifted the surprise of her and her team from the fight of the drones to the weather. And by the time they started shivering from the deluge, one of the boats was upon them.

"Should we start firing?" Dede demanded.

"I think these are friends," Kada answered carefully.

Asabea looked at him in amazement.

"You mean Opare had friends waiting all this while at the reception who were content to do nothing while we literally got roasted?"

"I don't know the answer to that," Kada told her quietly. "I only know these aren't Wagner."

"Are you all alright?" A man armed to the teeth asked kindly from one of the boats. He was dressed in the dark garb of the counterterror police, and was joined by another boat, while the rest headed out to the other sides of the island.

"We will be if you tell us who you are," Asabea asked him cautiously.

"I am Colonel Bruce Nartey," the man told her. "I was commander of the battalion you decimated at the Fortress."

"Oh crap," was all Owuraku could say.

Dawn had begun to colour the eastern sky rosy when Opare, the Colonel, Major Hanson and Chief Superintendents Atukwei and Amadu stood in the centre of Survival Island to assess the damage wrought by Wagner's drones. The once beautiful island, a lush sanctuary teeming with life, now stood blackened and desolate looking under the light of the rising sun. The centre, pockmarked by craters and broken rocks, was a testament to the savagery of the assault, and the air was thick with the acrid scent of smoke, comingled with the earthy aroma of charred wood. What was once a vibrant tapestry of greenery now resembled a bleak landscape of destruction. The remnants of the island's trees stood as solemn sentinels, their gnarled branches reaching out like pleading hands to the heavens. The once-thick canopy that blanketed the island was now reduced to twisted skeletons, their blackened limbs reaching upwards in a futile attempt to escape the inferno that had consumed them. The birds, from yellow-crowned gonoleks to snowy-crowned robin chats, starlings, yellow-billed kites and the water thick-knees that called the island home now circled overhead, their frantic calls a desperate protest against the destruction.

At the shore, the Counterterror Police were bagging three hundred and ninety dead Wagner operatives. Ten were missing, taken away by the current and the waves. They would be found a few days later by the fishermen who worked the lake in villages dotted along the shores.

Opare and the Commanders were joined at the centre by Asabea and her Girls, together with the Rangers and Owuraku. There was nowhere to sit.

Not anymore.

Fortunately, the bunker had camping stools and tables stored that escaped the furnace of the tunnel's chamber, and the Rangers brought them out and formed a seating area amid cold ashes and withered leaves. Opare's estimation was that everything would grow back, perhaps after a year or two.

Nature always won in the end.

The introductions were done quickly. Obuobi had been brought in by some of the boats when they returned to pick up the body bags, and he recorded the debriefing.

After the stories were swapped, Colonel Nartey asked Opare what he intended to do with the Girls now that his island had been destroyed.

"I thought that was the reason you had come," Opare asked in surprise.

"No," Colonel Nartey and Major Hanson replied simultaneously.

"We came to back you up," Amadu explained, looking around with a grave face. "And a good thing we did, too."

"But it took you long enough, didn't you?" Opare asked plaintively.

Amadu shrugged. "You all seemed alright to me – until we saw the other contingents coming in while the fire was spreading."

"But you've been here since dusk," Opare protested. "If you were our back up, why did you wait until almost dawn?"

"How do you know when we got here?" Obuobi asked in surprise.

Opare shrugged. "It's my island," he said. "I know everything and everyone that approaches within a five hundred metre radius. If your plan was to help us, you took your sweet time to get to us."

"Don't get snippy with us," Colonel Nartey told him firmly. "We didn't know how many mercenaries they were going to bring, and we were here to actually prevent an encirclement. You got them bogged down on your southern to northern flanks, so we knew you were fine until the drones got here, and even so, we figured we needed to wait it out a bit to see if those were all the aerial resources Wagner was going to commit."

Opare didn't look convinced.

"Besides," Major Hanson chipped in, "you were the ones that kept saying your Girls could hold the island against a battalion. Perhaps this was the test of your unfounded arrogance. You may have gotten lucky in the Fortress, but this is how war is waged. How do you like it now?"

That last question got Asabea looking seriously at the Major.

"You let them cook us because you think we deserved it?"

"No," Major Hanson replied truthfully. "We let them cook you because you needed to feel what half a thousand troops felt when they got pushed into a burning abyss."

"We had nothing to do with that," Bubuné declaimed. "I thought Opare had made that already clear to you."

"We know that," Major Hanson replied conciliatorily. "Still, you had to have a taste. You may not have directly killed those troops, but your actions are the cause, and their deaths were the effect."

"Then why are you here to help all the same?" Owuraku asked him.

"Because President Offei's brinkmanship, and his sybaritic nihilism is pissing us all off," Atukwei came in verbosely at that point.

"And we did make a deal that you could keep the Girls until further notice. The IGP is a man of his word," Amadu explained further.

"Therefore," Colonel Nartey said for the Commanders, "what you need to say to us is 'thank you'".

"And you're all quite welcome," Major Hanson finished.

Opare looked quietly at the Commanders for a minute and simply shook his head.

Amadu looked at the destruction around them and asked, "Where are you going to go after this?"

Opare glanced at Asabea and Owuraku and said, "Discovery Island has the same facilities and conveniences as this island, so we will remove there and try to nurse this one back to health from there."

"Splendid," Colonel Nartey replied, rising from his camping chair seat. "We have the start of an impeachment proceeding to get to tomorrow and have a lot to unpack to our superiors before that. Y'all stay safe until we get back to you."

And with that, the Counterterror Operatives left Survival Island.

"What are we going to do now?" Asabea asked Opare.

"Breakfast," Opare replied, as if that was the only logical thing to do. Nhyira looked at him.

"Where are you going to find breakfast? Everything is burnt."

"How much of the tunnels did you explore?"

"We didn't explore. We just looked for the safest exits."

"Probably a good idea that you did, but the main chamber has a trap door underneath, and that's where we have food, water, drinks and supplies stashed."

"And then?" Asabea demanded.

"And then what?" Opare asked mildly.

"What happens after breakfast?"

"We shut down the bunkers and head out to Discovery Island."

"Where the Police can find us at will."

"After today, the Police will always find us. That was the deal. We aren't going anywhere that they won't know about, and if that hasn't sunk in already, it aught to. Without them, we might all have died."

"I'm grateful that they helped. I'm just not comfortable that they can get at us on short notice. That worries me."

"First, let's eat. And then, we can worry."

CHAPTER 36
Parliament House, Accra
Monday, 22nd April; 8 A.M.

THE SUPREME COURT, by the Notice for Removal signed by two-thirds of Members of Parliament, which was twice more than was required by the 1992 Constitution, and on the request submitted to it by the Speaker of Parliament, had constituted itself into a tribunal of five to consider the Notice of Removal, attached to which were the Articles of Impeachment, identified in the Constitution as statements in writing setting out in detail the facts, supported by the necessary documents, on which it was claimed that the conduct of the President be investigated for the purposes of his removal from office.

The impeachment trial of President Amponsah Offei resembled a criminal proceeding in many ways: There were evidence and witnesses presented for and against the President, a chance for cross-examination, and, ultimately, a decision on his fate by the five most senior justices in the legal adjudication business, including the Chief Justice.

The trial focused on allegations brought by several of President Offei's own appointees to the Committees of the Interior and Defence in Parliament, including the Attorney-General and Minister of Justice, the Defence Minister, and the Inspector General of Police. The Articles accused the President of acting in willful violation of the Oath of Allegiance and the Presidential Oath set out in the Second Schedule to the Constitution; and to have conducted himself in a manner inimical to the security of the State.

The tribunal initially met in closed sessions, even though all decisions, including rulings to objections raised by lawyers of both sides, as well as rulings to what evidences were allowed and which were not, were made public. If the Constitution had not specifically demanded in camera trial for the President's removal, the Chief Justice would have allowed a public broadcast of the proceedings.

This invited a challenge in constitutional court, where the Ghana Journalists Association contended that those portions of the constitution were inconsistent with the provisions of other parts of the constitution. For example, the same Article 69 of the Constitution, while demanding the secret tribunal also demanded that the removal vote in Parliament be held in public. What was the sense, they contended, to be opaque about the trial that might end in the removal only to turn around and demand transparency about the resultant coup de grâce?

The trial lasted three months and was inundated with twelve constitutional challenges. The most contentious one resulted in a limited Supreme Court ruling that, while under trial, and given the gravity of the criminal charges, President Offei could not continue to exercise his powers as President until the final verdict. Vice President Domwine was handed the reins of government in the interim to prevent abuse of power by the President during the period.

President Offei went to great lengths to show that it was the Girls, and not him, that had been the cause of all the crimes he stood accused of, and that everything he had done had been to protect the nation. He presented his accusers as enemies of the State, and as people that had taken the Girls' side. He went further to try and have the Chief Justice recused on grounds that, having himself being an abductee of the Girls, he might have suffered reverse psychological sympathies towards them. That motion was soundly rejected by the tribunal, and later on by an appeal argued before the full Supreme Court panel.

The prosecution, on their part, presented the tribunal and the rest of the country with irrefutable evidence of all President Offei had done to put the country's troops in harm's way, to bribe his way towards creating that harm, and to invite mercenaries and foreign troops into the country without parliamentary approval, including turning foreign troops and mercenaries against Ghanaian citizens on Ghanaian soil.

At the heart of the charges was his relationship with Duncan King. The prosecution proved by DNA that the President's relationship with the convicted rapist, and a sexual assault allegation history with one of the Girls had made him angry and determined to make the Girls suffer at whatever cost to his own troops and government.

There was never a dull moment in court, and the trial also saw to 189 motions of law, the most motions in any trial in Ghana. More than fifty thousand pages of testimony, documents, evidences and affidavits were filed, and the nation stayed glued to television sets the entire time.

In their closing arguments, President Offei's lawyers mentioned that his methods, however much the prosecutors hated them, got results.

"As we stand here today, Asabea and her gang of criminals are no more," the lead Counsel said. "Never again will anyone hold our justices and the justice system hostage because they will remember what befell the last band of criminals who attempted that. Yes, we lost troops and lost a few men as a result, but the prosecution disrespects their sacrifice by attempting to punish the one man who actually did something, while the military and police were at their wits' ends. No wonder they are here making those Girls out as heroines. President Offei took an oath to the people of Ghana, and he discharged that oath faithfully."

It took the tribunal three days to submit the verdict, being its findings, to the Speaker of Parliament. The Speaker announced the verdict to a jubilant House the next day, which immediately moved a resolution to remove the President. The resolution unanimously carried, and one hour later, Vice President Dr. Erasmus Domwine was sworn in as President of the Republic to carry out the nine-month remainder of President Offei's term.

The first meeting President Domwine held after leaving Parliament House as President was with the run-away Cabinet in the Black Star Office – the name of the office of the President at the Jubilee House. The government was essentially bankrupt, and this was discovered in the three months that the trial of Mr. Offei was underway. It was discovered that he had paid Wagner a billion US dollars to take out the Girls, running the economy fully aground with that singular expenditure. The new government would demand the money back from the Russian government in exchange for four hundred Wagner bodies.

"Exactly how broke are we?" the Defence Minister asked the deputy Finance Minister. His boss, the substantive Minister, had also been barred from holding himself as such while the tribunal was in session because he'd been found in deep cahoots with Mr. Offei.

"Well," the young deputy Minister said. "We will have to turn to the International Monetary Fund for an 18th bailout."

"How much are we going to ask for?" President Domwine asked worriedly.

"3 billion dollars, at least."

"Surely, that would have to be our last ever application for a bailout," the Defence Minister said.

"That would rest heavily on a wing and a prayer, unfortunately."

The discussions had lasted deep into the night about how to fix the extensive damage done to the Ghanaian economy in the few weeks following Mr. Offei's sacking of his then-Cabinet and the commencement of his impeachment trial.

"How could this much damage be done in a mere month?" President Domwine asked in surprise.

"He bent every resource he could marshal towards destroying those Girls," the deputy Finance Minister said gravely. "Essentially, he let those Girls bring this nation to its knees – literally."

The meeting with the IGP, scheduled for ten o'clock in the evening, started at midnight. Present were the Commanders of the Ghana Armed Forces and the highest-ranking Police Commanders. On the table was one item – what to do about the Girls now that Mr. Offei was no longer President.

"Why did we not rebut Offei's assertion that he had killed the Girls?" President Domwine asked the Attorney-General, who had had to stay on for the meeting.

Patricia Quayson looked once at the IGP before she said, "A rebuttal would have required proof, and at that time, Mr. Offei was still fully President. Bringing in the Girls would have been dangerous, and the IGP reminded me there was a deal that needed to be honoured before we could haul them in – a deal with Mr. Kwaku Opare Addo."

"You still insist we leave them alone?" the President demanded hawkishly of the IGP.

"The entire country believes the Girls are dead," he responded. "If we can keep it that way, let's."

"Where would be the accountability then?" President Domwine demanded.

"If I may," Amadu asked diffidently. "What would be their punishment if they were found guilty of kidnapping and murder? Life imprisonment, right?"

"Multiple counts, but yes," Patricia replied. "For the murder of Duncan King, Larry King, and Billy Blanks."

"Why don't we just lock them up on Discovery Island for life?" Amadu suggested.

"How would we enforce that?" the President questioned.

"Ankle monitors, wrist monitors, chip implants – the list goes on," Obuobi supplied at the tail end of the presidential table. "If we made it a matter of national security, we could get the Supreme Court to endorse it, and this matter would disappear once and for all."

"Wouldn't we be giving too much power to this Opare character?" the President complained. "I don't like that he's had us by the balls the entire time."

"I believe it is the Girls that have had us by the balls," Atukwei chipped in. "Opare kept his side of the bargain to us, and his side to them. He is nothing but an innocent go-between. And, thanks to

Wagner, the Girls no longer have the firepower to withstand even a squad of soldiers if this comes to light one day and we are required to bring them in. I say let's tag them and leave them on that island. We can trust Opare to keep them there. If they disappear, no one can track them better than Opare himself."

There was a little back and forth, and the decision eventually went in the IGP's favour. The President asked the Attorney-General to draft the necessary papers and begin the process to engage the Supreme Court on the matter.

"And if the justices breathe one word of doubt about this," he warned, "I want you to pull the plug and haul them all in, you feel me?"

"Yes, sir," Patricia responded.

An aide walked in and whispered into the President's ears. He looked up at the IGP and asked, "You put him up to this?"

"Pu-put who up to what?" he stammered.

"Let him in!" the President ordered the aide shortly.

Shortly after, Opare walked in with Aaron in tow.

"What can I do for you, and how did you manage to get into the Jubilee House without prior appointment?"

"I brought you the list, sir," Opare said calmly and handed a file over to the President.

"What is this?" the President demanded before opening the file.

"This is the list of everyone that I have on my island from the Fortress," Opare told him. "Names, IDs, and tracking information on all nineteen people. So far, you have only known the seven Girls. Now, you have all the people, aiders, abettors – everyone that pulled the whole justice operation off. This is a good faith gesture."

President Domwine looked at the list and then back up at Opare and said, "You are seriously trying to get me to trust that the best place for the Girls is not inside a prison but with you, aren't you?"

Opare did not answer.

"Especially now that I won't have to bleed to get them," the President added with a tight smile before locking eyes with Opare.

Opare held the President's gaze. He was unflinching, but he did not convey any challenge or disrespect to him or his high office.

On his part, the President felt that the young man who held his gaze could be an ally, a friend. Already, he and his cohort of adventure enthusiasts had taken on the much-feared Wagner Group and prevailed. It was probably best if he didn't piss such a person off to begin with.

The President rose up to his full seven-foot height and extended his hand to Opare. Without missing a beat, Opare reached forward for the President's hand and shook it firmly.

Then, turning to a smiling Attorney-General, the President said, "See to it that the justices grant our request – in fact, make them."

At the car park of the presidential palace, the Commanders that had been present at the Black Star Office gathered for one last word with Opare. Word had spread among the Armed Forces about the Battle of Survival Island, no doubt embellished to the point of legendary, and some of the Commanders wanted to meet him in person.

"You didn't say how you got into the Jubilee House," Major Hanson inquired.

"I have friends at Public Affairs," he replied.

"It's a good thing you came around," the IGP said approvingly.

"I know how difficult politicians can be, even when it's a win-win situation. And I also needed to thank you for the support during the attack. We honestly would not have survived it."

"We know that," Colonel Nartey said to him, patting him gently on the back. "It was the least we could do for saving me back there at the Fortress."

"And I am seriously glad that the Girls had a taste of a real battle," Major Hanson said slyly. "It was good to see their arrogance diminish with the flames – I am sorry about the island, though."

Opare laughed easily and shook his hand as well.

"I wish you all the best," the IGP congratulated him. "We'll be seeing you once the Court draws up the relevant papers."

"Yes sir," he answered. "And thank you."

Opare and Aaron drove out of the parking lot in their Jeep Wrangler, which bore the mud marks of their outdoor adventure business. Cube had been waiting for them while they'd gone in to see the President, unhappy to have been excluded from the discussions.

"So, what's next?" she asked, half-sourly.

"We go back to business as usual," Aaron answered for Opare. "This nightmare is over."

"I didn't think you thought it was a nightmare," Cube told them. "And you've got eighteen Girls to take care of now. I think the real nightmare just began."

CHAPTER 37
Discovery Island
Monday, 7th May; 7 A.M.

IF THERE WAS one thing Asabea could change about living life on a riverine island, it would be to banish every woodland dove in a 2-kilometre radius of the lake. The generally grey to dusty brown birds had distinct calls that she would do a lot to have changed. Morning, noon and dusk, all that stuck out, even above the often-boisterous waves of the lake was the mourning cry: *ooh-ooh, who-who-who-who; ooh-ooh, who-who-who-who.*

She was so fed up with it that when Owuraku told her she sometimes mimicked the tune in her sleep, she vowed she'd stop listening to the birds. But their call was as common to the island as a cockcrow to an African village, and while there were more than thirty species of birds on the island with thirty different call sounds, none stuck out or irritated her more than the ooh-ooh, who-who-who-who that rang out every minute.

But today promised to be another lovely day, and she wasn't going to let any bird mess it up. She had taken on Duncan King and his goons and gotten away with it. Of course, the island could technically be called a prison, but compared to an actual prison, especially the Ghanaian kind, this was paradise – if one took out the ooh-ooh, who-who-who-whos.

Gosh, she hated those birds!

Discovery Island was only half as big as Survival Island but it had the same contours. Also, while Survival Island had massive top soil to sustain large trees, Discovery had so many rocks and boulders that getting to the top was like scrambling up a mountain. It was also closer to a shore than Survival was to its shores, and that shore had a range of mountains behind which was a wilderness of thorns.

The transfer expedition from Survival to Discovery was by the two boats that had conveyed them to Survival Island their very first time. Before the fight with Wagner's troops, Opare had had the presence of mind to move the boats far away to escape destruction.

They had started building a city. Opare and his Rangers had hauled in sand, chippings and quarry dust over the lake last week and had brought in architectural plans to build an island city. The notion of building a city with their own hands had so appealed to Asabea and Owuraku that they had insisted against hiring artisans unless they were crucially needed. They had dug the foundations throughout the week of a twelve-storey apartment complex, designed to be powered by wind and solar, and to be entirely independent of the rest of the country.

A Girls' Republic!

Opare and his Rangers hated the name and had shut the idea down before the Girls could get too excited about it, but this was going to be an independent Republic of Girls, a monument to Girl power and all that women could achieve, especially if they made demands with smiles while waving a few guns.

In the meantime, they sheltered in tents as they had when Opare had first extracted them from the Fortress. The monsoon season had just begun so it was not unusual to be sweating one hour digging a foundation trench with spades and mattocks, only to be dashing under a rainstorm to shelter in the tents the next hour.

Asabea's pregnancy was more visible now, as was Owuraku's penchant to dote on his pregnant wife. Opare had found a priest from a village not too far on the opposing shore to officiate their marriage. All the Girls had been bridesmaids and all the Rangers groomsmen. Opare had not been excited about the idea because he said God could not bless a marriage that had already been consummated in fornication, but the priest had said there was a fee that could motivate him to pray on the couple's behalf and make everything OK.

Two Thousand Cedis later, the beautiful sunshine on a cloudy wedding day was the signal of forgiveness they had prayed for, and the party that night had bonfires and a great deal of happiness that even the skeptical Opare could not help but smile about.

"Looks like you won't be getting any action while dating until you marry that jungle boy," Efe warned Nhyira playfully later that evening after they had carried Owuraku and Asabea over the broom at their tent door and warned them to add another baby to the inventory before daybreak.

Nhyira's eyes sought and immediately found Opare among his Rangers by the firepit. She could always find him no matter where he was. They seemed to be laughing over a joke he had shared. The Rangers' devotion to their Master-Guide was deeper even than the Girls' devotion to one another, and no matter how much they had tried, they couldn't penetrate the bond that existed among them.

It wasn't like they felt jealous or anything about it, but they had had to do so much together as Girls to pull their Girls Justice off that they had missed what it was like to work with boys. While there was no deliberate attempt on the part of Opare and his men to exclude them from their fellowship, there were just some things that were for men only.

"I'll have him whenever I want," Nhyira replied quietly, and then added, "He's mine, actually. He just doesn't know it yet."

"I heard you kissed him right in the middle of the bombing on Survival Island," Oye teased.

"He's lucky that was all I did," Nhyira replied with a wicked look in her eyes.

"Did he come back to you for an encore?"

"He's acted like it never happened, but I know he thinks about it every waking moment. No one gets over my kisses."

"I think we should each decide who they want before this gets any further," Bubuné declared, half-jokingly. "I've got dibs on Aaron."

"You're calling dibs on a human male?" Efe asked, pretending to be outraged. "That's so gynarchic."

"Let them sue me. We are an island, and I'm the resident Sherriff," Bubuné said.

"I like Wannah," Oye said slyly. "I find his dreads attractive, and he has that virile musk about him."

"And y'all keep your hot eyes off my Kada," Aisha warned with a giggle.

"I had plans for Kada," Efe protested jocularly. "But no worries, I'll settle for Kayleb and that Ranger with the stutter – Rey, I think his name is. I think he's cute, too."

"Save some for the rest of us, you sluts," Dede said with a laugh.

"It's our island," Efe said with a shrug. "We can engage in all the polyandry we want."

"What's that Cube character's story, though?" Bubuné wondered out loud. "She's like Opare's shadow. She's always on his tail."

"She's his assistant," Nhyira replied. "And the design brains in their business outfit, I found."

"She's hot," Efe reminded her.

"I know," Nhyira said, shrugging. "She can watch when I start making him eat out of my love palm."

"So, you'll let his assistant story stand?" Dede asked.

Nhyira looked at her amused friends and said, "When all is said and done, that Master-Guide will be Mr. Nhyira."

The Girls laughed.

"We sound like boys now," Dede said with a wrinkled face. "Boys staking out the girls they'd want to sleep with."

"Maybe to complete the outfit, we could rape a few tonight and see how they feel about it in the morning," Efe wondered slyly.

"You all disgust me," Dede said half-petulantly.

"Is it because you originally wanted Opare?" Oye looked at her seriously. "He did take good care of you during the escape."

Dede looked at Nhyira and said, "But Nhyira has kissed him, so he is no longer the virgin I was saving for myself."

They all laughed at that so loud that the Rangers turned to look at them. That made them laugh out loud more.

"Did you seriously want him, though?" Nhyira asked Dede.

Dede made a face like she was thinking about it.

"I kind of did," she admitted ruefully.

Nhyira turned to look at her seriously. "That man is mine."

"I'm not disputing that," she said back to Nhyira with a twinkle in her eyes.

Nhyira looked back at Opare in the distance.

"Alright, we can share him," she said magnanimously. "You can have him on any day that starts with a No."

This time, their laughter was enough to bring Owuraku and Asabea out of their tents.

"Hey," Bubuné told the couple, "Get back inside and give us another baby, we said."

"All your talking and laughter woke us up," Asabea told her. "And Opare could be married, you know?"

"We don't care," Dede and Nhyira said in unison.

Then they laughed.

Looking for more thrillers by JayJay D. Segbefia?
Discover your next read at https://jaysegbefia.com
Interact with JayJay here
for all the latest news, giveaways
and more.

JayJay D. Segbefia, born in May 1982, is the author of the Executive Hallucination, and is West Africa's leading outdoor adventure operative. He runs a lacustrine, mountaineering and outdoor adventure guiding company in his home country Ghana. He is a Mandela Washington Fellow and trained as a journalist at the Ghana Institute of Journalism.

JayJay is an entrepreneur as well and acquired his business management education from non-degree Fellowships run by Dartmouth College and Ohio University, both in the United States under the USG's Young African Leaders Initiative and holds a MSc. in International Business from the University of Ghana Business School.

He writes novels like this as a hobby.

Continue reading to
Enjoy an Excerpt from
EXECUTIVE HALLUCINATION
by JayJay D. Segbefia,
on sale since 2019.

PROLOGUE

Accra. The black automated gate slid open when the dark government car entered the Platinum section of the Regimanuel Gray Estates. A dozen armed men saluted smartly when the vehicle rolled to a stop before the kerb at 17. The right passenger door opened, and the Bureaucrat stepped out before the driver could get out and do the honours. He quickly entered the house.

Inside, a fat man in dark grey suit walked restlessly about in a small living room. He stopped midstride when he heard the door open. The Bureaucrat was ushered in. He held a large manila envelope in one hand.

The fat man approached the visitor and stretched a hand for the envelope. There was no mistaking the relief on his fat face at the sight of it. Another hand reached casually inside his jacket.

Too casual, the Bureaucrat thought. He'd been watching the fat man.

As he was turning the envelope over, the Bureaucrat flicked his wrist to the right and swept his hand and the envelope out of the reach of the fat man's hand. He then deftly grabbed the fat man's sleeve, pulled him to himself and delivered two blows to his chest with his free hand. He finished by jarring his knee into the man's groin.

The fat man doubled over, clutched his groin and groaned noisily. A gun slid out of his jacket onto the carpeted floor.

The Bureaucrat grabbed the gun from the floor and emptied the cylinder. Then he backed the fat man menacingly into a sofa, grabbed a dining room chair and sat opposite him. Slapping the envelope gently in his palm, he demanded, "What's this?"

Sneering, the fat man replied, "You'd be dead if I told you."

The Bureaucrat shrugged.

"You were going to kill me, anyway, weren't you?"

The fat man winced and shifted his weight.

"Victor," the Bureaucrat asked calmly, "I'd like to know why?"

The fat man remained mute.

Big mistake.

He found himself lifted off the sofa – big bulk and all – and slammed heavily onto the Persian of the floor. There, he felt more than saw the knife slip to his fat throat. Blood began to drip onto the floor from the small incision.

"Don't kill me," he cried. "I'll tell you what you need to-to know," he stammered.

"Wrong," the Bureaucrat replied calmly. "You'll tell me *everything* there is to know. I'd start from why you reached for your weapon."

"In *this* position?" the fat man begged, suddenly experiencing a bout of claustrophobia.

"Besides," he further urged, "I don't know *anything!*"

"You'll stay where you are, and don't even think about calling for your guards, or lying. Either way, you'd be dead by the time they get here. Now, start talking."

The fat man shifted his bulk, shuddered with the knowledge that blood was dripping from his throat wound to the floor, and began.

"The envelope contains top secret documentation issued by the BNI. I have been ordered to neuter anyone who's come into contact with them – the secretary who typed them, the courier agent who delivered the envelope to your office, your receptionist, and the driver that just brought you in – everyone who's perceived to have seen or so much as brushed by the envelope."

The Bureaucrat pressed the knife deeper into the fat man's flesh at that. He quietly observed, as if talking to himself, looking off at a point on the far wall, "The BNI wouldn't have the balls to do that. You are a bureau of national incompetents, after all. That kind of order can only come from the Castle."

Then he looked down and said to the fat man, "You're lying to me, Victor, and I don't like that. Here's the deal. You'll lose a body part every time you lie to me. Now, how about your right ear?"

The pain as the Bureaucrat cut off the fat man's ear was almost paralysing. His scream would have been heard all over the Estates if the Bureaucrat hadn't instantaneously stuffed a balled handkerchief into his mouth.

The fat man tried, in the passion of his pain, to push the Bureaucrat off him. At the same time, he stretched his hand as far as he could towards a red button under the sofa. If he could touch it, it would trigger an alarm. He was rewarded with a sharp kick to his right hip for his efforts and the button stayed smugly beyond his reach.

Sniveling, the fat man took out the handkerchief and laid still, holding the side of his head and trying fruitlessly to stanch the flow of blood with it. Then, when the Bureaucrat advanced on his throat again with the knife, he lashed out a foot which connected solidly with the Bureaucrat's knee and sent him crashing over into a glass table set to a side of the small living room.

Desperately, he jumped up and raced towards the door, but the Bureaucrat was swifter. Limping diagonally, he effectively cut off the fat man's escape.

Angered and frustrated, the fat man threw a punch meant for the Bureaucrat's neck, then quickly changed his mind midway when the Bureaucrat thrust his hands upwards to ward off the blow and sent it to his ribs instead. The Bureaucrat doubled over to the floor, clutching his side, unable to breathe.

The fat man gained the entrance, crashed the door open and shouted with all his might for the agents.

Still reeling from the force of the blow, the Bureaucrat staggered to his feet and limped round the living room, seeking an escape point, knowing the guards would be on him any second.

The window!

He raced for one of three glass windows facing north. The window overlooked manicured lawns and a flower garden. Fortunately, there were no bars. He returned to pick up the envelope from where it had fallen on the floor when he crashed into the dining table, studying the room with his quick eyes in the process. He saw a plastic mat in front of the kitchen door and picked it up. Then he raced back to the door and turned the lock seconds before heavy footsteps signaled the arrival of the fat man's guards.

Taking a deep breath, he ran towards the choicest window and jumped, turning in mid-air so his feet would collide with the glass. He broke through and tucked his knees under his body as he fell.

He landed noisily on the turf below in a shower of broken glass and rolled over the grass rather painfully. He was getting too old for this kind of thing, he mused. He got unto his feet and ran into a copse of trees behind the house.

The house was surrounded by a medium wall topped with electric cables. The wall was, however, his only means of escape. The guards would shoot to kill. Already, he could hear half a dozen of them running round the house, shouting and pointing to where he'd broken through the window. Only a matter of seconds remained until they pinpointed his exact location. He climbed up a tall sapling and threw the mat over the electric fence.

The first shot took a chunk off his right shoulder. He ducked quickly out of the way of the second, which took off the limb of the young tree inches from his head.

In spite of the excruciating pain in his shoulder, he refused to touch his arm. The shooters had found his tree. If he didn't move soon, it would be a matter of time before more accurate bullets flew.

Move!

He leapt off the tree, grateful for the help of the springing action of the recoiling branch. In mid-air, he somersaulted over the fence and gripped the mat both for balance and as a springboard over to the ground on the other side.

Inside, the fat man was gyrating in anger. "Get me the envelope you idiots," he barked, "Else I'll personally supervise your execution in the barracks! Hurry! He mustn't get away!"

The Bureaucrat had reached Apricot Avenue, the street behind this section of the Estates and was running due north. Taxis were rare in this affluent part of Accra so his sole alternative was to scale the Estate's border wall. His driver would have already been killed. There was no point wishing for his car.

The wall was a concrete barrier some eighteen feet high. It would get him on one side of the Spintex Road. It would also put him in plain view of the BNI agents. They had gained the street he'd just come out from but he had no choice.

The wall!

It, too, had an electric fence.

"Damn!" he swore softly. He'd had no time to keep the mat.

He turned quickly around and saw the first couple of agents round the corner of Orange Street. He was cornered and he knew it. That's when his error hit him. He should have kept Victor's gun.

He was hit in the left thigh.

He screamed and run crouching for cover behind a thickly trunked tree by the street, poking his head out to observe the approaching agents, his mind racing in spite of the pain.

The two agents were soon joined by five others and they were taking their time because there seemed nowhere else he could run to. Apricot Avenue was teeming with agents too and the next – Sugarcane Link – led to the secured entrance. He would be caught in a crossfire if he raced for that area.

If only a car would come by.

They kept firing at him but the tree shielded him.

Then a sound.

A car!

A taxi. It was approaching from the left at the corner where Orange Street met with Sugarcane Link. Between him and the taxi, if he could stop it that is, was a hundred metres of open space; a space any amateur shooter would find ample enough to finish him off in. Still, he thought it wouldn't hurt to try. He'd be dead either way. Better to die running.

Breathing in sharply, more from what he was about to do than from the pain in his thigh and shoulder, he limped quickly towards the approaching taxi as a couple more bullets found their mark in his right upper arm. There was no stopping however, for the taxi was just a few meters away.

The next shot took him full in the chest but he flung himself directly onto the bonnet of the approaching taxi.

The taxi driver realized instantly what was afoot and took the quick decision not to get involved. He braked and shifted rapidly into reverse gear.

Good thinking, the Bureaucrat thought gratefully. He held on to one of the windshield wipers with his good arm. His injured arm held the envelope.

The fat man's guards were now in hot pursuit of the taxi. Their weapons were held out as extensions of their arms. They fired indiscriminately at the cab and shouted for the driver to stop. He refused to, until he had reversed into another street where he could safely shift into forward gear. When he did so, his unusual passenger was rammed sidelong into the windscreen. At the same time, a couple of bullets disintegrated the passenger side of his window. One slug knocked off his sunglasses, missing his nose by a hair's breadth.

Sparing only a glance at the guards, he sped off, his unwitting passenger rolling precariously against his windscreen all the way to the intersection that led to the secured entrance. Then he stopped, quickly got out of his taxi and pushed the wounded man off his bonnet.

The Bureaucrat fell heavily onto the kerb, groaning in pain as rivulets of blood coursed erratically down his chest and arms.

"Please," he pleaded mournfully. "Help me."

The taxi driver gained his seat and shifted into gear as more shots rang out from behind. Half a dozen or so agents were running furiously towards his cab. They couldn't yet see that their bloodied victim was lying down on the kerb.

The cab driver could not explain what made him stop, but he knew he couldn't leave him there like that. There was something about the dying man's eyes when he begged that was haunting. He applied his brakes, reversed and got himself out onto the kerb. The guards were now a mere three hundred metres away.

Miraculously, none of the bullets hit them as he bundled the Bureaucrat up in his arms and hurriedly placed him in the back seat.

With tires screeching and burning, he sped off, wondering how he was going to avoid the usual delay at the secured entrance. The guards at that area were notoriously slow at releasing the steel-and-concrete ramp. There was also the possibility that the exit guards would lock the ramp as a result of the sound of gunfire.

The driver was dismayed as he rounded the corner and saw his fears materialize. Three armed guards stood right in the middle of the street, barring his way. Even if he ran them through, there would still be the upturned ramp to contend with. He began to slow down and instinctively worked up a string of colourful invectives and curses from each and every *kenkey* house in the *Ga Mashie* area. After one particularly vile curse, the gods must have been goaded into action because a vehicle that had just gained admittance was entering through the opposite lane. While the ramp was coming up again behind the entering vehicle, the cab driver floored his accelerator and veered sharply into that lane.

The taxi narrowly missed running the guards over and literally flew over the ramp, almost ramming into an oncoming SUV. The taxi driver veered sharply to the right, let fly a string of vile oaths, and fought with his wheel and his brakes intermittently.

Once fully out, he raced for the Spintex highway and turned left towards the Tetteh Quarshie Interchange as if the devil himself was on to him.

The driver finally pulled into the Accra Mall off the interchange, after having determined that no one had followed him from the Estates. He turned his attention to his passenger whose profuse bleeding was bloodying his backseat.

The Bureaucrat knew it was over, but there was one more thing he had to do. He opened his mouth to speak, but no words came out, only blood.

The driver got out and opened the door.

"There's a clinic in there someplace," he said, indicating the mall. "I have a friend-nurse who can patch you up quick. Let's get you inside, and don't you die on me, *onu*?"

There was no time!

The Bureaucrat shook his head and, in spite of the throbbing dizziness that told him the end was near, he made a sign for a pen. The driver understood, but his expression indicated he didn't quite see the relevance. In any case, he swept his hands under the Bureaucrat and attempted to lift him up out of the car, but the wounded man shook his head vigorously in the negative, making a more exaggerated gesture for a pen, pencil or whatever the heck he could write with.

Alarmed, the driver obliged him, handing over a pen that had been stuck to his breast pocket.

Focus!

He was on fire. Every fibre in him screamed for the release of death, but his mind wouldn't let go.

Focus! Don't drift!

Gripping the pen more firmly, he turned the envelope over. It was almost entirely soiled with his blood. He found a dry spot and began to write.

He died after a few feeble attempts.

He only wrote one line.

It was a name.

ALEXANDER J. CATTRALL.